AMY INSPIRED

Amy
Inspired

BETHANY PIERCE

BETHANYHOUSE
Minneapolis, Minnesota

Published by Bethany House Publishers
11400 Hampshire Avenue South
Bloomington, Minnesota 55438

Bethany House Publishers is a division of
Baker Publishing Group, Grand Rapids, Michigan.

Printed in the United States of America

Library of Congress Cataloging-in-Publication Data

Pierce, Bethany, 1983–
    Amy inspired / Bethany Pierce.
        p.   cm.
    ISBN 978-0-7642-0850-8 (pbk.)
    1. Authors—Fiction. 2. Authorship—Fiction. 3. Women college teachers—Fiction.
4. Adultery—Fiction. I. Title.
    PS3616.I346A83   2010
    813'.6—dc22

                                                                    2010016347

For my grandmother,
who taught me the art of optimistic thinking.

PROLOGUE

"Find something you love to do," my father told me, "and you'll never work a day in your life." Optimistic advice from a man who spent fifteen years selling insurance, a job he detested for fourteen. Eventually, my father did follow his passions, out of insurance and into the arms of a local attorney who loved him, presumably better than my mother, and made six figures.

If my parents had anything in common, it was the shared belief that life was good. When Anne Frank's *Diary of a Young Girl* left me in a rage, my mother recommended that I read something nice; it was best not to think about things I couldn't change. She believed in marriage, despite her divorce. She had no pain in childbirth.

In our home, glasses were half full; when God shut doors He opened windows; and you could be anything you wanted to be when you grew up, even—and especially—the president of the United States.

Mostly I wanted to be an astronaut. I studied constellations and memorized planet names and orbits. I hung upside down from the school monkey bars to practice zero gravity and studded my ceiling with glow-in-the-dark stars. Grandma's new refrigerator, a black shiny monolith with blinking green and red lights, functioned as Ship's Main Computer. Alone in the kitchen, I'd push the flat plastic buttons, whispering, "Red alert!" and "Fire torpedoes when ready!"

"You all right, Sugarpie?" Grandma would ask when she spied me in conversation with the ice dispenser. She later voiced her concerns to my mother: "You'd better get that girl's teeth checked. All she wants to do is eat ice."

Mom had heard worse. Only a week before I'd subsisted five days on little more than freezer pops and baby food to train my stomach for an all-liquid diet. "Moon food," Mom called it, pureeing peas into paste for my dinner. "Moon?" I asked. I had my sights on Mars.

When I was informed we couldn't afford Space Camp, I realized it was best to have a few backups. A girl has to keep her options open.

⁓

My top ten careers in descending order of importance, as outlined at age ten:

1. *Astronaut*
2. *Pilot*
3. *Stewardess*
4. *Showboat singer*
5. *Prima donna in manner of Mariah Carey*
6. *Forensic scientist*
7. *Olympic gold-medalist figure skater*
8. *Wedding cake baker*
9. *Bank teller*
10. *Famous novelist*

I spent my childhood rehearsing to be an adult, tripping over legs that grew faster than my ambition, testing my abilities with scientific objectivity.

I got motion sick on the merry-go-round, which eliminated astronaut for good, taking pilot, stewardess, and Olympic figure skater (all that twirling) with it.

I had a nice voice but was never properly recognized as a budding talent. Though I campaigned diligently for the part of the Virgin Mary in the Christmas pageant, Mrs. Blythe, the children's church director, favored piety over talent and lacked the imagination to accept a redhead as Mary. She refused to give me the solo three years running, discouraging my chances of parochial celebrity and, by extension, obliterating any hopes of international acclaim.

I got a *C* in chemistry, the only letter other than *A* I'd ever received on a report card. I decided I hated science.

What talent I had in reading recipes could not surpass my pleasure in reading fiction. Lost in a *Baby-Sitters Super-Special* when I should have been watching the butter I was warming in the microwave, I melted my mother's favorite Tupperware bowl instead. The microwave was replaced, my kitchen privileges were suspended, and I never earned that coveted Girl Scout cooking badge.

At fourteen I received my first checkbook. Consequently, banking lost its appeal.

By the age of fifteen I had eliminated every career possibility but one.

For better or for worse, the love of writing stuck.

part 1

1

That he showed up to our first date wearing a pink-collared shirt and that he looked prettier in pink than I did should have told me everything I needed to know about Adam Palmer had I been paying attention.

"I just think if you consider all the factors at play here, it seems time we consider where exactly we're going with this relationship," he said now, less than three months later.

Outside the window to our left, students spilled onto campus, flooding the sidewalks. It was the turn of the hour: Adam had a class to teach in ten minutes. I realized he'd timed our break-up to allow himself quick escape.

"It's just that I need more time for my work right now, and I can't give you the time you deserve. I can't give you what you want."

Adam always bought me lunch at the cafeteria, where we both had faculty discounts. I flattened my meatloaf with the butt of my spork. The sporks were new on campus, part of the ongoing save-the-earth incentive: SPOONS + FORKS = HALF THE WASTE!!! The Committee for Earth Health used twelve thousand fliers to educate the student body on the importance of hybrid flatware.

"And I know you have your convictions: I respect that. You have to see that I respect that," he was saying. "I've tried to see the world through your eyes." Here, I assumed he referenced the Saturday afternoon he'd agreed to volunteer with me at the church soup kitchen, from which he walked away eager to transcribe a conversation he'd had with a homeless veteran. "You can't make this stuff up!" he'd declared, eyes bright with fresh inspiration.

"I've tried to walk in your shoes," he said. "But you haven't done the same for me. I need to be with a woman who can look up to me for my convictions, my beliefs."

I frowned. "You don't have beliefs. You're an atheist."

"I believe in nothing. I need you to respect that."

I set the spork spinning on the table. "I respect you for that."

"You resent me for it."

"So what is it I want exactly?"

He watched my little operation with annoyance. "What do you mean?"

"You just said you couldn't give me what I wanted. I'm curious: What is it that you think I so desperately want?"

He thought a moment. "I'm not ready to settle, Amy."

Had he meant settle or settle down? He could have left the *down* out on accident. But he was a writer. He chose his words carefully.

"I'm not ready to settle down either," I protested.

He gave me a patronizing smile. "You were born settled."

I stared at him, surprised: I hadn't thought him capable of hurting me.

"It's no specific desire," he went on uncharacteristically flustered, trying to revise or at least mitigate the severity of his last statement. "It's all desires. Cumulatively. The things you want and the things I want for our work, our future. They don't add up." He snatched the spork from my hand. "Will you *stop* that."

The people at the table behind us turned to see what was going on. I blushed to my scalp. It wasn't a good look for me.

"I've been feeling it, too," I said with resignation.

In fact, I'd meant to initiate this conversation a month ago, but vanity had fueled my procrastination. The novelty of dating Adam had worn off within the first three weeks, but for the two months that followed he'd been a nice accessory, something to wear on my arm at faculty mixers and gallery receptions. A first-time novelist still riding the critical praise of his debut work, *Home Is Where the Heart Lies*, he had a magnetism at social gatherings, an air of importance that transferred to me when we were in public.

He cupped my hand in his. "I hope we'll remain amicable? There's a poetry reading tomorrow. Maybe we could go together?"

I pulled my hands away and clasped them between my legs, drawing my knees together as if to keep my fingers warm. "Actually, no. Everett asked me to go."

"If you ever want to talk—if you ever need a second opinion for one of your stories. I still think 'The Other Day' has a lot of potential. It's just that one scene that needs trimmed . . . Well. Just call me."

"You know," I said as he gathered his things. "For a novelist that was a rather clichéd break-up."

"I have to go."

I nodded. He squeezed my hand, a last apologetic gesture, and rushed for the door.

We'd met in the English Department library. I had been trying to noiselessly rip scraps of notebook paper to mark noteworthy pages in *The Scribner Anthology of Contemporary Short Fiction*. He'd walked over and handed me a small stack of bookmarks he had pulled from his briefcase. "Thought you might need these," he'd whispered. The bookmarks were for his novel. Each featured a photograph of his smiling face.

∽

At age twenty-nine, my own idealism beginning to fray around the edges, I kept faith in my mother's sanguine outlook on life: It was still reflex to call home when I toed the edge of failure.

"Hi honey, how are you?" Her voice came tinny and distant through my old office phone. "I can't talk long. The Baldwins are on their way over, and my curlers are going cold. We're going to Applebee's to spend those gift cards Uncle Lynn gave us for Easter."

I had called with the intention of announcing the break-up with Adam, but at near-thirty you can't just come out with that kind of news without warning. As preface I complained about grading. Scoring seventy-four college essays four times a semester had begun to seem impossible—and this was only paper two of the term.

"I'm so exhausted."

"I know," she said. "It's too much."

I stared out the window at the overcast November day. Behind me, my office mate Everett typed furiously, reaching blindly every five minutes for the mug of twenty-five-cent office coffee he kept at his elbow. The coffee cup sat next to a second nearly identical mug filled with tacks and paper clips. I was waiting for him to grab the wrong cup.

The English Department offices occupied the fourth floor of the Humanities Building, a gray stone structure that commanded the highest hill on campus. Our window overlooked a courtyard lined in summer with tulips that leaned toward the sun. The tulips had long since died, and overnight the ivy that grew along the building's facade had shriveled around the windows, clinging in gnarled ropes. Central campus sprawled to the left, and across the lawn sidewalks clustered in crisscrossing pentagons made their way downhill toward the Fray and Fuhler Art Buildings, twin cement complexes as modern as the Humanities Building was old.

"Am I insane to be doing this?" I asked.

"Maybe you should get some help," Mom replied without answering my question. "Why don't you have Zoë grade some?"

"Zoë's never graded an essay in her life. Besides, this is college composition, not algebra—everything's subjective. I can't just outsource grading."

"I don't think it's such a terrible idea. You need to delegate. No one would know."

I remembered how in the seventh grade when I couldn't seem to stretch my report on President Lincoln from five pages to the required seven, she advised I enlarge the font and narrow the margins.

"Those kids don't read your comments anyway," she was saying. "You know they just throw the papers in the garbage as soon as they see their grade."

"I appreciate the vote of confidence, Mom."

Everett was gathering his things. With his arms full of loose-leaf papers, he waved briefly at me. I nodded my good-bye.

"Did you take a look at that guest list?" Mom asked, transitioning without warning into her latest favorite topic of discussion: my younger brother's impending nuptials. *Nuptials.* The word sounded overtly sensual. Too similar to nude. Navel. Nubile.

"Marie didn't put the McCormicks on there."

I tapped the string of the window blind against the glass. "Alice and Jenny? They were my friends, not Brian's. Why would he want them at his wedding?"

"Alice was over all the time when you kids were little. She was such a nice girl. I used to hope Brian and her would get together."

"They were ten," I replied. "Who's officiating?"

"Pastor Patrick. Brian and Marie meet him once a month for premarital counseling. They have to meet on weekdays, which are so hard for Brian with his schedule, but weekends just won't work for Pastor Patrick. He has his sermon to prepare and then Saturdays he bowls with some guys from town. They're a real rough bunch— smoke like chimneys, but the pastor says it's his ministry—something about 'in the world but not of it.' "

Mom was a devoted member of the First Fundamentalist Church of God. She considered ties on Sunday tantamount to Scripture reading. At thirty-two, their new minister, Patrick Peterson, was the third youngest member of the congregation, and he'd been creating no end of turmoil since arriving. ("You should hear the songs we're singing in church now," Mom reported. "We have a guitar player and a drummist. It's all very modern.")

"So they're sticking with Mr. Peterson?"

"Call him Pastor Patrick, honey. He prefers it."

With a sigh I turned back to the window. Waves of cold emanated from the glass. On the benches below, a young girl in a red coat slapped her male companion on the arm, laughing. He pretended to be hurt before sweeping her up in his arms.

"I'm just glad they're sticking to an all-American wedding. I was worried a while there that they would want some weird Indian religion, but really her parents are very normal."

The couple in the courtyard began to kiss.

"I have to go, Mom."

"Don't worry about the papers. You'll get them done. You always do. Tell Zoë hi for me."

I promised I would and sent love to my brother. Hanging up, I pressed my forehead against the windowpane and closed my eyes, letting the cold numb my thoughts. I started back when the window-pane shuddered. A moment later a second rock pelted the glass. Peering down cautiously, I saw Everett standing on the sidewalk below, waving his arms frantically.

I unhinged the lock and shoved the ancient window up. "What?" I called.

A dozen students crossing the sidewalks below looked up in surprise.

"My briefcase—I left it!" he shouted.

I found the briefcase on the floor, leaning on the trash can. It was stained and studded with pins: *No Blood for Oil* and *Too Many Freaks Not Enough Circuses*.

"I'll bring it down," I called.

"No time!" He waved wildly, indicating I should throw it. His hands looked jittery even from four flights up. This was not unusual; Everett lived in a perpetual state of panic.

I gave the bag my best pitch. Midway through the air, the top latch sprang open. A dozen papers flew into the air and snapped in the wind like parachutes. They made their way floating to the ground.

I leaned out the window. "Sorry!"

Everett scrambled to gather the papers one by one, wiping them clean on his pant leg. Without a second glance up, he ran down the sidewalk. He had the awkward gait of a man not used to sitting in office chairs all day, more caffeine than blood in his veins: the run of kids who don't get picked for softball teams.

I slouched in my chair, tapped the bobblehead Garfield with my pencil, and watched its mute smile nod up and down. A form letter lay on the scattered essays cluttering my desk. I picked it up, reread:

Dear Author,

Thank you for sending us your manuscript. After careful consideration we have decided that we will not be able to publish it.

Although we would like to send an individual response to everything, and particularly to those who request comment, the small size of our staff prevents us from doing so.

Sincerely,
THE EDITORS

The rejection was a week old, but I had yet to file it away. It had come with a coupon for a subscription to the magazine. I balled up the coupon and threw it at the wastebasket, missing by a foot.

I took the to-do pad Mom had given me for Christmas, a stack of carefully lined paper with the heading *To Do Today* typed cheerfully in blue. Beneath *buy milk, fruit, lunch stuff; organize student exemplary files*; and *finish grading 11:00 essays*, I wrote *new batch of submissions—mail Monday*.

I also tabulated the rejections in my blue binder. There were two columns: submissions on the left, rejections on the right. Finding *Exatrope* magazine, I recorded the date *November 7* opposite the date I'd mailed the story, placing a red check mark in the margin beside the magazine's name for good measure.

Tapping my pencil along the titles, I counted the number of magazines that had sent this particular story back. I did this every time I received a rejection.

Twenty-seven. For *one* story.

When I quit my job at Millbury's (the twenty-sixth best elementary school social studies textbook publishing house in the country) to pursue a life of writing, I had specific visions of my new life: Between scribbling works of literary genius I would attend art galleries and work in soup kitchens, walking busily from one matter of importance to another, curls billowing in the wind à la Carrie Bradshaw. I had not imagined pulling all-nighters grading student essays with thesis statements like "*In the Age before the Depression, America reeked benefits at the expense of the countries poor.*"

Dejectedly I gathered my things. I found the empty, flattened Cheetos bag stored in my pencil drawer. Everett and I had been passing it back and forth since May. At his desk I examined the photographs of his dog Karenina. The purebred Shih Tzu was the one thing Everett loved more than books. There were piles of books crowding his desk, leaning skyscrapers of his private world. I slid the Cheetos bag into page 341 of *The Brothers Karamazov* and clamped the novel shut.

⁙

Home was less than half an hour by foot, but it was too cold for a walk. I took the cement steps down the steep hill adjacent to the

Humanities Building to catch the purple bus line. From my seat in the back I watched the campus pass by outside the window.

Copenhagen, population 4,569, was hidden in the cornfields of Ohio just seventy miles from Columbus. When I told my brother I was moving to Copenhagen he thought I meant Denmark. Copenhagen was not the only town guilty of borrowing its name. Ohio was full of them. There was London, Ohio, and Oxford, Ohio; there was Dresden, Sparta, Manchester, and Lebanon. It was as if many Ohio cities, like many Ohio residents, wanted to be somewhere else.

The bus followed campus two blocks before turning right toward downtown. Main Street had all the romantic essentials: cobblestone streets, window shops with candy cane-striped awnings, and gas stations that still chimed to alert the station manager of new customers. The locals lived peacefully, if not a little resentfully, beside the crowd of students that kept their town afloat on the expensive appetites of well-groomed consumers. When school was in session, the noise and color of youth obliterated any semblance of normal small-town life. The first week of class the students wiped the Wal-Mart shelves clean; college kids ran all shop cash registers; all downtown waitresses were younger than twenty-two; and frat boys outnumbered mothers at the grocery store on a Friday afternoon. We lived on a private planet populated entirely by the barely post-pubescent who plotted their dreams carefully on the black and white lines of academic Day Planners.

My housemate, Zoë, and I maintained a quiet bubble of existence amidst the general chaos. We lived above Kathryn Wilson, head of special collections at the university's main library. She drove a golf cart instead of a car. For fun, she went to the local public library to read newspapers. Zoë and I rented the apartment above her garage, a building set back on the opposite end of her lawn. Some said that her son had killed himself in the room where Zoë slept, that she hadn't stepped inside the apartment since for memory of his death. We chose to disregard this theory.

The apartment was cozy with hardwood floors, built-in white bookshelves, and a kitchen so narrow it took considerable maneuvering for both of us to make breakfast in the morning. Kathryn's property was situated one block from Main Street. It was a ten-minute walk to the coffee shop where Zoë worked, a fifteen-minute walk to the first edge of campus. Best of all, the roof of the adjoining shed constituted a porch off of our breakfast nook. From our vantage point on the roof we observed the comings and goings of college life. We watched packs of girls in high heels and low-cut blouses tripping their way home from weekend bar hops. We watched the numbered 5K runners pacing uniformly by like schools of fish. It was a little like having a private parade every day.

"There's always so much going on!" my mother would exclaim. "It's like living in The City, all these people all the time, and all of them so well dressed—even the young men." And she would swell with pride and declare it was all so "fashionable," her highest praise. She'd spent most of her professional life as a teacher, and still she thought I had a very glamorous job. No matter how many times I told her my title was Visiting Faculty or Adjunct, she insisted to everyone at church that I was a university professor: professor sounded better.

My mother had a peculiar way with language. She called her ob/gyn a "genealogist" and thought a filibuster was a dust vacuum. My obsession with words evaded her. She considered language a common tool with which to get common things done, and she rather liked it when people laughed at her way of mixing things up.

I was never so amiable. As a child I struggled with my S's and found bizarre ways to mix up my consonants. My mother's friends loved my unintelligible blabber. They would ask me what I was doing in school or what I learned in Sunday school, and I would unwittingly prattle away. When I finally understood that they did this to amuse themselves, I clammed up.

I spent the first grade in speech therapy. Outside of speech class I refused to talk. Silently, I listened to my father as he explained he wasn't going to be sleeping at home anymore. Silently, I listened to my mother weeping into her pillow every night for the first year after he left. And silently, I entertained my baby brother with Tinkertoys and Matchbox cars while she showered or cooked or mowed the lawn.

When free of the obligation to watch Brian, I preferred books to playmates. I spent recess sitting on the detention wall reading Nancy Drew mysteries and *Anne of Green Gables*. I kept a journal of vocabulary words to learn and quotes to memorize.

By the third grade my lisp was gone, the familiarity of my father's presence leaving with it. The books stayed.

⸙

Zoë hollered for me the moment she heard the back door open.

"Amy? Is that you? Come here!"

"Hold on," I said, throwing my bag to the floor and gratefully shaking off my winter coat.

"Amy!" Zoë yelled.

"*Coming*."

She stood on tiptoe in the kitchen, patting her hand blindly among the vast array of spices in the top cupboard. Her blond hair was pulled into two short pigtails, uneven and coarse as broom bristles. She was wearing the same red-checkered apron she used when she painted furniture. When cooking, she preferred to wear aprons stained with a worker's toil. It was her way of reclaiming the traditional symbol of the domesticated woman.

At the sight of me, she gave up her search for the elusive spice. "I have news!" She sang, pivoting her hips back and forth in a little two-step dance.

"What is this?" I asked, lifting the lid off the skillet.

"Curry with potatoes and tofu," she answered. "Sit down."

"Can I try it?"

"No, sit."

Placing her hands on my hips, she led me toward the table.

"Okay." Obediently, I sat. "What's the big news?"

She stood in front of me, hands behind her back. "Guess."

"You got a raise."

"No."

"Your parents are coming to visit."

"No."

"Youuu . . . are getting married."

"Um, no." She rolled her eyes.

I found this response annoying considering the uncensored schoolgirl manner in which she'd gone on lately about her boyfriend's many admirable attributes. She'd told me twice in the last week that she and Michael were "getting serious."

"You're leaving The Brewery."

"I love my job and you know it. You're not even trying."

"I give up."

She pulled a magazine from behind her back and held it forward happily.

"You bought an *UrbanStyle* magazine," I stated, confused.

"I'm going to be *in* the *UrbanStyle* magazine," she announced.

"You're what?"

"They bought my essay."

I let this sink in. "Zoë, that's amazing."

"I know!" She squeezed her eyes shut and did a giddy hop. "I sent in that article—the one about career women in academia. They loved it, but said it wasn't quite right for their reader base, so, whatever . . . that was that. But then they wrote me this week and said they had an opening in the March publication for general women's interest and would I be interested in submitting another essay for the issue." She flipped through the magazine, stretching its spine open to show me the spread where she would be featured. "It'll be for this column—four pages with illustrations and everything."

remote control once, and that was to hold her novel open while she ate.

"I have one vice." I poked at the potatoes with my fork. "I'm going to enjoy it."

I noticed Michael noticing Zoë's legs. Her legs were beautiful, the product of rigorous work. She trained for a marathon every year, circling the indoor track when the weather prevented her from running on campus. She'd met Michael at the gym. He'd introduced himself, but Zoë had been the one to suggest dinner.

Before meeting Michael, Zoë went through men faster than she went through clothes. When they started dating, I'd assumed he was a fling, a diversion from the emotional exhaustion of seeing her mother through the latest round of cancer treatments. But the months passed, Fay stabilized, and Michael stayed. His inability to speak more than five minutes on any subject of substance wasn't half as annoying as the fact that some primordial urge left me inexplicably tempted to flirt with him every time he came over.

He sat on the coffee table so that his back blocked my view of the television. I nudged him with my foot. He batted it away.

"We'll be back late," Zoë said.

"Adiós," Michael added with a two-finger salute.

In the shower I stared at my thighs with a routine and vague disapproval. Facing the mirror, I twisted my wet hair into a bun at the nape of my neck, debating a haircut. I worried I was growing a mustache.

All my life I'd mocked commercials for wrinkle reducers and hair dye, believing that if I remained optimistic and ate more vegetables than chocolates, I would age gracefully and one day wake up a well-dressed, fit woman of composure and grace. Studying my reflection, I knew I wasn't miraculously going to be anything at thirty that I hadn't struggled to become in my twenties. In other words, I was off to a very bad start.

2

When I gave up my predictable nine-to-five job to study writing, people were, by and large, bewildered.

"Oh, like for newspapers and such?"

"I didn't know people still studied that." (As if English were a dead language.)

"Can you make a living?"

And my personal favorite, "I was never any good at calligraphy," from my mother's best friend, Sandy Baldwin, who thought I was going to graduate school to perfect my cursive.

The acclimation to graduate school wasn't so much an adjustment as a kind of coming home. I loved the busyness of campus life, the undercurrent of ambition that kept the libraries afloat. At the university, students and professors alike were either having a party or doing work. Both were taken very seriously.

Leaving a good job for graduate school was the single most courageous thing I'd ever done, and for the first six weeks I lived in a state of barely suppressed hysteria of excitement and anxiety. Once school was under way, my route through campus fixed, and my circle of friends established, I lived a small life, anchored to my apartment by cycling deadlines and stacks of assigned novels. I wrote more or less regularly. I read constantly, while walking, eating, bathing. It was a happiness second only to the blissful memory of childhood summers spent home before my father left.

It was the longest and shortest two years of my life. I emerged from my thesis defense bleary, relieved, and clueless. All but three of the writers from my class left town after graduation. The rest fled to bigger, brighter lights. I wished them well, saw them off to Chicago, New York, Pittsburgh. Where did they get the energy? I was too physically exhausted to move and too emotionally spent to consider another career change. Two months before defending my thesis, I accepted a teaching position at the university. As a part-time teacher I was paid by the class, which meant no summer salary and no health benefits. It was not a terrible job, but sometimes in class, halfway through a lesson, I'd wake up from what felt like a suspended dream and become suddenly very aware of the twenty young faces staring back at me, waiting. During one such spell of wakefulness, I laughed so hard at the absurdity of the situation I couldn't collect myself and had to dismiss class twenty minutes early.

I'd left a stable career to pursue my dream. One master's degree and $10,000 later, I was back pushing paper. Only at a much smaller desk.

Zoë was my saving grace. We met while working the Thanksgiving food pantry at a small local church. It was my first semester of teaching. I'd been a more or less faithful member of Copenhagen Baptist since arriving in town, drawn to the little church by its charismatic leader, Pastor Maddock, a minister whose dual degrees in theology and literature colored his sermons with a writer's love of metaphor and subtlety.

Zoë had lived in Copenhagen longer than I had, but had been systematically trying out every church within a fifty-mile radius since arriving. With her petite figure and colorful wardrobe, she could have passed for a high school student; I was shocked to find out that she had just graduated from the university. The church secretary used our shared love of writing to introduce us. Within ten minutes we were fighting about C. S. Lewis.

"Overrated," she claimed.

"You're kidding," I said. "He takes spiritual concepts hackneyed out of all originality and makes them new again. You have to at least give him credit as a storyteller—what about the Narnia books?"

"Overrated," she repeated. "You ask any Christian writer who their favorite author is, and I'll bet they'll say C. S. Lewis. He'll at least be in the top five."

"He's popular because he's good," I countered.

"He's got bandwagon appeal. He's Christian trendy—like girls with nose rings." When she crossed her arms, her plastic glitter bracelets jingled.

She made a point, she explained, of remaining indifferent to anything praised by the popular vote. This philosophy applied to movies. She hadn't seen five of the recent blockbuster films *because* they were blockbusters.

I reverted back to C. S. Lewis. "So what if no one you knew liked him. What if everyone thought he was a joke. Then would you list him as one of your top five?"

"Maybe. But that doesn't matter because I don't think he's good."

"Everyone's entitled to their opinion," I said. I made no effort to conceal my annoyance.

A week later, while driving home from work, I saw Zoë winding around town perilously on an old-school banana-seat bike. It was below zero, the wind bullying the snow into huge drifts that covered the roads and clogged the sidewalks. She had three canvas bags full of groceries hanging from her handlebars. They caught like sails in the wind. She swayed dangerously in one direction, then the other.

Hearing my car approach, she maneuvered shakily to the curb. I pulled up beside her, lowering my window.

"You want a ride?" I asked.

She was wrapped in scarves and wore a beanie cap with earflaps. Her freckled cheeks were bright red from the cold.

"Where will I put my bike?"

"That's my place." I gestured up the block. "If you leave it there, I'll take you the rest of the way home."

She studied the road ahead, glanced back over her shoulder. "All right," she said. "It is kind of freezing."

I drove slowly so she could walk her bike in the trail left by my tire tracks. We chained the bike up to a tree behind my apartment and climbed back into the car, shaking the mounds of snow from our wet shoes.

"Which way?" I asked.

She stopped rubbing her chapped hands together long enough to point mutely to the right.

"Did you ride all the way up from Kroger?" I asked, eyeing the grocery bags at her feet.

She nodded. "It wasn't bad there, but I thought I was going to die taking that hill back up."

"Don't you have a car?"

"I don't believe in them," she stated.

"How can you not believe in cars?"

"They are noxious, air-polluting machines of death."

"Machine of death seems a bit harsh."

"Have you ever *been* on I-75? Have you ever gone to the junk-yard to see the mash of metal that snapped your friend's leg clean through? Besides, I don't need a car."

"But what if you move?"

"I'm going back to the city eventually," she explained. "You need a car more here than you do in the city."

"What if you need to leave town?"

"I hitch rides."

"So you believe in other people's cars, just not yours," I said.

"Let it rest on *their* consciences," she replied.

She lived in a cramped studio apartment decorated with tie-dyed wall hangings and pots of overgrown Pothos vines. Clothes hung from the futon, the desk, the lamp. I couldn't see the floor.

Before leaving, I wrote down my number. "Next time you need a ride, just call."

"Do you always have paper with you?" she asked, nodding at the three-inch ringed notebook I'd pulled out of my purse.

"I always have something nearby," I replied. "In case I need to write something down."

"I do the same thing." Excitedly, she showed me the folded piece of blank paper tucked in her back pocket. "Just in case."

She thought I kept the paper to write down story ideas. I had meant writing to-do lists.

"Remember," I said on the way out the door. "Call anytime. I mean it."

Despite my insistence, I hadn't anticipated she would actually take me up on the offer. I quickly learned that Zoë is good at accepting invitations. From then on, she never hesitated to ask me for a ride to the English office (she liked to print her manuscripts at my expense) or a pit stop at the grocery. That winter we spent the better part of the post-Christmas blues at each other's places reading through stacks of novels and drinking black coffee from her French press.

It was her idea that we combine rent. I hadn't considered having a roommate, but my teaching salary did not stretch so far as I would have liked. I worried about losing my privacy, but my doubts were no match for her logic: It was ridiculous to keep separate places considering we had become inseparable.

When I renewed my lease in April, she moved in.

⁓

As housemates we got along well enough, for all intents and purposes. Zoë agreed to put my DVDs back in alphabetical order after viewing and to clean out the hair from the shower drain so long as I stopped using plastic bags at the grocery store and promised to wash the carcinogenic toxins off our fruits and vegetables. I updated her on all the eighties flicks she'd missed growing up with parents who discouraged the watching of television. In exchange, she taught me how to cook without refined sugar or meat (or "animal flesh" as she liked to call it).

She attended Copenhagen Baptist with me when she had Sundays off work. Afterward I listened passively to her diatribes against the Americanization of the Christian Church. Occasionally, she got her panties in a twist over one or another of the Baptists' faults and transferred to the Methodist church on Hyde and Locust. I never worried. Eventually the Methodists would offend her too, and she'd come back to us.

I didn't mind her bitterness with the church or her vegetarianism or her moods—all of which were frequently inconvenient. Ironically, the very thing I thought would make us most compatible was the one and only thing I resented her for: her writing. Zoë was prolific. Where it took me hours to produce single paragraphs of decent merit, she could kick out ten, twenty pages a night without getting up from her chair.

Nothing life threw at her could ruin her routine. She'd spent years on the edge of losing her mother, whose battle with metastatic breast cancer was epic. In fact, it had been a while since anyone considered it a battle. It was more a strategically won détente: Every few months Fay Walker went back to the front line and, against all odds, secured another cease-fire. This constant proximity to death had given Zoë a talent for living on the edge of terror. Anxiety only drove her back to the laptop, where typing calmed her worried thoughts. She was disciplined. Every morning before leaving the house she ran her five miles, ate her organic oatmeal with soy milk, and wrote her two-page minimum.

When I asked her where she discovered such a daily wealth of ideas, she said things came to her best when she was running. I had only ever used the word *marathon* to describe the five hours I spent on the couch watching *Lost* DVDs.

Zoë was unembarrassed about her work and preferred reading manuscripts aloud to me when they were finished. Her stuff was entertaining and articulate, though rarely as polished as I insisted it would be if revised. But she hated second drafts and rarely managed a third. The writing was good, that was all she wanted, and, above all, it was unfailingly *constant*. She didn't believe in writer's block: There was no excuse not to type.

Things Zoë believes in:	*Things Zoë doesn't believe in:*
Jesus	Writer's block
Global warming	Third drafts
Recycling	Cars
Cycling	Cable television
Ghosts	Standardized testing
Vitamin supplements	Christian romance novels
Birthdays	Door-to-door evangelism
Marriage	Trickle-down economics

Where Zoë believed in product, I believed in process. This meant she maintained a weekly page quota while I preferred lying in dandelion fields fishing stories out of blue skies.

This was exactly how I described our differences to Adam.

"That's style," he replied. "I asked you about your respective writing philosophies."

"I'm not interested in philosophies of writing. I just want to write."

"You're going to use that line when you're interviewing for future teaching positions?"

"I'm not going to teach forever. This is temporary." I waved my hand at the library to indicate all of academia—its faculty boards, its failing copy machines, its endless grading.

"Temporary until what? Your big book advance?"

He winked. I scowled.

"You know, I did the math," he said. "I spent two years on my novel. Let's assume it was a full-time job and let's assume a full-time employee is due compensation for forty hours of work each week. If you divide my royalties into a standard wage it comes to a little less than forty cents an hour. You need a job, Amy. And this is as good as it gets."

I told him I didn't care to borrow from his disillusionment. He told me that was fine, I would soon be given enough of my own. It was the first time I'd realized maybe I didn't care so much for his company. That I was tired of growing tired of men and that something was wrong with me if I couldn't stand to be with one for more than four months at a time.

Hoping for clues, I forced myself to remember every man I'd ever loved, a line of boys parading back to elementary school where I'd first felt that nauseating swell of hope and anxiety every time Bryan Holmes walked into the classroom. Holmes was the James Dean of the sixth grade and the notorious nemesis of Mrs. Mallarmy, meanest teacher in Rosewood Elementary. He wore pants on his hips, greased his hair with Vaseline, and sat in silent protest while the rest of us stood to pledge allegiance to the flag.

In the seventh grade Bryan moved away. I mourned his leaving for a week then replaced him with Luke Warden, son of First Fundamentalist missionaries. We stayed after church to help fold tracts for the youth group to leave on restaurant bathroom toilet paper dispensers. He insisted we not kiss as it would lead us down the road to temptation so we held sweating hands with discretion—we spread the Gospel with more passion. He hoped to win his entire lunch table to Christ by the end of the school year, by which time I'd moved a table over to better study the way Jimmy McCreight's loose auburn curls fell over his forehead. Jimmy, the track star and homecoming king with whom I spoke twice, both times to invite him to church camp.

High school was similarly unsuccessful. First came Aaron Borke, chess club captain, talented swing dancer, homecoming date, and my first kiss. Then Charlie Smith, who led prayer around the flagpole every fall and spent the rest of the year in a state of borderline hedonism for which he would repent the following year back at the flagpole.

Twelfth grade was Seth Rieder, aspiring musician who was forever endearing for claiming that I had the knees of a supermodel, yet forever disappointing for liking breasts better. He stayed with Tiffanie Lewis who *had* breasts.

My college love affairs comprised a disappointing succession of altogether unattainable men: Leonard Brown, professor of literature, freshman year; Lawrence Green, roommate's boyfriend, sophomore year; Barry Jones, philosophy major and gay, junior year. After graduation, there was Dylan Jones, lead singer of the church band and my cubicle neighbor with whom I flirted for eight months, dated for six. I spent my twenty-fourth year of life in love, my twenty-fifth recovering from the break-up.

And then Adam Palmer, a relationship doomed from the start, made impossible due to problems of faith—in other words I had one, he didn't.

Of all the men I'd loved, I had relationships with four. That was an average of one relationship for every four years (if you only counted the court-able decades). Adam was the first I'd dated who neither believed in God nor made a front of being interested that I did. What had inspired me to think a relationship with a man who held every one of my beliefs in contempt could possibly be healthy?

Adam had been intriguing, his swagger a welcome change from the exhausting self-deprecation Dylan mistook for humility. And Adam made no attempt to hide his attraction or to keep his hands at bay. At first, it was exciting to be touched so boldly by a man who had none of the reservations that tortured the Christians I'd dated. I tripped along breathlessly, mistaking his flair for rhetoric for superior intellect and his sexual advances for romance. I ignored the growing conviction that I'd stepped out of line and suppressed the guilt in favor of the pleasure, a pleasure that grew more fleeting as Adam became more insistent.

At night, lying in bed alone, I relived the embarrassment of telling Adam I was a virgin, a fact I had revealed while standing in my panties and bra in the middle of his living room five seconds away from the worst mistake of my life. I told him I couldn't; he put his pants back on. This had only been two weeks ago.

I hadn't told Zoë. She only spoke cryptically of her own experience—or inexperience. While she and Michael did not sleep over at each other's places by rule, I had no idea what they did when alone. Sex for Marriage was our mantra, but Zoë tended to have more lenient interpretations of just about any belief we shared. She was the daughter of a travel writer and a nurse who had met through the Peace Corps. The Walkers listened to NPR; they voted Democratic; they were open-minded. I was the product of a culture that considered the phrase "open-minded" anathema.

My childhood was carefully policed by the powerful mandates of the First Fundamentalist Church of God, which discouraged fraternizing with nonbelievers. I had to save a boy before I could date him and even then there was little fun to be had without sinning, so I placated my hormones with fantasies and fueled my hopes with novels. I ascribed to the True Love Waits campaign without any real dilemma, having confused scriptural mandates with my own outrageous expectations: I believed God was the Divine Author and my life the story of an ultimate romance.

I quit the First Fundamentalist Church of God soon after attending college, exhausted by its stringent legalism. Leaving behind the church that had raised me was hardly a novel thing to do (it was, in fact, the one stab at independence I had most in common with my smattering of freshmen friends) and it was hardly difficult. But forsaking Christ himself was impossible. The basic precepts of the faith defined my life as the skeleton gives the body definition: I could as soon function apart from Christianity as sever muscle from bone and retain shape.

Particulars of its moral code, however, had grown increasingly tiresome. While I couldn't make love where I didn't feel love, chastity for its own sake had become pure drudgery. It had been fairly noble to champion virginity when I was sixteen, but the closer I got to thirty the more I began to worry. The more I felt like a baby-maker with a ticking egg timer.

3

Once I got around to telling them, everyone was kind about the break-up with Adam. Zoë said he didn't deserve me. Mom recited her usual litany of animal kingdom analogies: There were other fish in the sea; you had to kiss a lot of toads to find your prince; don't throw your pearls to swine. Valerie Powell came bursting into my office the next afternoon breathless and sweating. "He *broke up* with you?"

"In the cafeteria," Everett said from his desk without bothering to turn away from his computer.

Valerie was the only other woman from our graduate workshop who stayed in Copenhagen after finishing the program. While our friends moved on to finish Ph.D.s or write their novels in mountain cabins, Valerie promptly went about the business of getting pregnant. By escaping academia when she had the chance, she lived a sane and unhurried life. She was also a practiced gossip.

"Well what are we all doing here then?" She grabbed my coat off the filing cabinet. "You need to talk and I need carbohydrates."

Ten minutes later, we sat crowded into a Donut Shoppe booth, Valerie listening attentively to my now-detailed list of Adam's

inadequacies, and Everett who had invited himself along, interrupting to volunteer examples I'd forgotten.

"He broke up with me in the *cafeteria* of the student commons,"
I said for the third time. It had become the refrain of the story.

"It's sick," she muttered.

"And he had the nerve to be totally calm about it."

"Jerk."

"Not even an affectation of grief," Everett added.

"You want me to kill him for you?" Valerie asked. "Because I
could do it." She gave a wave of her arm over her very pregnant
belly, inviting us to examine her late-term physical prowess. She once
confessed to me that she'd spent all of junior high peeing in short,
quick bursts, having heard at summer camp that doing so toughened
your uterine walls for the birth process.

I was grateful that Valerie was back in my life. She and I had
been close in graduate school, our friendship the direct result of
similar schedules and shared workloads. Once we'd graduated, we'd
lost the common complaints that bound us together: There were
no more thesis abstracts to belabor or deadlines to dread. We spent
a year disbanded, living less than five miles apart but rarely seeing
each other outside of a random run-in at the farmer's market or
the library video aisle.

Valerie was the one who rallied us back together for a book club.
We invited neighbors and acquaintances, informing them we would
be reading serious novels by serious novelists: *Gravity's Rainbow* and
War and Peace and *A Portrait of the Artist as a Young Man*. When no
one else joined the club, we lost no time defecting from the booklist
we'd prescribed in favor of more indulgent forays into Jane Austen
and the Brontës. We had every intention of rereading the novels, but
the majority of our meetings consisted of watching the film adapta-
tions of books we'd already read.

Valerie finished a second raspberry-cream donut. At this point
in her pregnancy she couldn't wear her collection of handmade

silver rings on her swollen fingers and her usually curly hair had gone straight. "Hormones," she'd reply when people asked about the new do. I found the transformation exotic. She had the darker complexion of her Puerto Rican father and the voluptuous figure of her American mother. She was zaftig, thick-lipped and thick-thighed; on her, pregnancy seemed a natural shape.

"Well, I had my qualms about you dating a writer," she said, doctoring her coffee with a third creamer. "I don't know what I'd do if Jake was. We'd kill each other out of sheer competition. And at least you have time to focus on your writing now." She perked up, remembering: "Did you get any news from *Exatrope*?"

"Rejected."

"What? But your style is perfect for them." The sincerity of her surprise at this news endeared me to her forever. "Amy, this is *not* your week."

Everett said, "I'm beginning to think it's not her decade."

᠀

Everett had agreed to be my date for the poetry reading that night so I would be with company if Adam showed. The reading was held in the upstairs galleries of the Fuhler Art Building. As a member of the committee that had instituted the reading, I was obliged to attend. Three student performances were to be given simultaneously in three different galleries, the idea being that the audience changed rooms instead of the poets taking turns. I supposed it was meant to be interactive; mostly it reminded me of channel surfing.

"I can't stand it," Everett said.

We were sitting on folding chairs in gallery two. Fifteen rows up, a tall man with panty hose over his face was reading a sonnet. Behind him, a video montage of war headlines flashed on a projector screen. When it became apparent that the ten-minute recitation was only prelude to a second collection of poems, Everett began to fidget. He preferred rhythm, lyricism. These kinds of readings provoked him to panic, a minor detail I wished I'd remembered before demanding he come with me.

"Can we leave?"

"We can't leave while he's performing," I whispered.

Over our own poet, we heard three others; the walls separating the galleries did not reach all the way to the ceiling.

"I want to leave," he whispered back. His voice was petulant, like a child's.

"We'll wait until he's done."

He groaned under his breath, bent over, and started breathing into the program he'd folded into a tube. I noticed he was missing a button on his right cuff. He was typically dressed: old jeans and a white-collared shirt under a tweed jacket. At thirty-two he was completely bald up top. His glasses were horn-rimmed, his one stylish ornamentation. His intelligence eclipsed his social skills. Our friendship still surprised me.

When the panty hose performance was over, the emcee returned to the microphone. "All right, ladies and gentlemen, for your listening pleasure, please give a warm welcome to Jason Burkie."

"It's one of your students," Everett said unnecessarily.

Jason held the microphone, still in its stand, right against his lips. "I'm Jason Burkie," he said. "Can you all hear me?"

He held his poems up to his eyes, then paused. He spotted me over the rim of his paper. "This goes out to Ms. Gallagher, best-looking English teacher in Copenhagen."

There was a ripple of laughter. People turned in their seats searching the room. A few applauded, and one wolf-whistled. I nodded, waved tentatively, and slid down in my chair.

Jason was grinning. "All right!" He punched the air. "Power to the English teachers."

"He's a total moron," Everett said. "Do you encourage this kind of Neanderthal stupidity in your classroom?"

Jason read his work with unbridled pride. It was evident that he considered his performance superior to those that had preceded his.

Everett nudged me halfway through the fifth poem. "Do you know that guy?" He nodded his head toward the right side of the room.

I turned slowly to follow Everett's gaze. A tall man stood against the far wall, his arms folded across his chest. Our eyes met. Immediately he looked away.

"I've never seen him before."

"Well, he's been staring at you."

"I'm sure he wasn't doing it on purpose."

"Um, yes, well, the performance is up there, and his eyes were *here*."

"Everett, honestly, can you just pay attention for five seconds."

I glanced back, but the stranger had disappeared.

"Let's get out of here," I said to Everett as soon as Jason finished.

"Thank you."

We slinked off into the adjoining gallery to listen to a freckled freshman recite her haikus about dirty laundry and a cat named Fiasco. When the punishment was over, we stationed ourselves at the food table to eat Mini Gherkins and Ritz crackers. To my combined relief and disappointment, Adam never showed. It was unfortunate that he couldn't be there to see how well I was doing without him.

Everett poured us each a plastic cup of wine, a modest portion for me, a generous portion for himself. Everett thought better when he had something to sip—if not wine then coffee, if not coffee a cigarette. His graying teeth bore proof of this abuse.

"All I've had to eat since yesterday is a severely deficient powdered donut," Everett said. "And I have to say this spread is a decided disappointment."

"Everett," I said. "Can I ask you a question?"

He leaned over the table to pick at the platter of chocolate-dipped strawberries. "I'm all the proverbial ear, my dear."

"Would you write if no one listened?"

"I'm not sure I understand you."

"Should we keep producing work if no one ever reads what we write? If I never publish, should I just give up?"

He frowned, licking melted chocolate from his finger. "You're suggesting the worth of your work is contingent upon its readership."

"Isn't it?"

"If so, we're all screwed, honey." He patted me on the back and drained his cup. "Take my life as an example," he said. "Let's say, hypothetically, I write a groundbreaking essay on a previously overlooked line of stage direction given in Shakespeare's *Othello*. My work will be printed in *Shakespeare Quarterly*, where all of fifty academics will dissect it, gleaning from its overwrought prose some halfway singular thought to inspire their own overdue articles. Or worse, they'll photocopy the essay and assign it to undergrads as homework." He widened his eyes and dropped his jaw in mock terror.

"But you'd still be entering a public dialogue," I countered. "And you wouldn't have that without being published."

"It's disconcerting for me to hear you say *dialogue*. It's like when you say *text*. I feel as though we've tainted you." He examined a cheese cube. "I think these have jalapeños."

He held it up to my lips. I took a bite from the corner.

"No." I said. "It's fine."

While we were standing at the food buffet, I noticed the man who had been watching us. He stood in the back of the gallery, arms crossed, talking to Mrs. Haverson, newly appointed Dean of Arts and Sciences. He was dressed in black and wore rings on both hands. The way he pulled his hair from his face and twisted a rubber band around the ponytail was almost effeminate—it was certainly an overly casual gesture for someone talking to the dean. Watching him, I felt something different than attraction. I felt curiosity.

"You're being awfully quiet," Everett said. "Did I upset you?"

"I'm fine," I said. "Just thinking."

To my surprise, Zoë appeared beside the stranger. I felt a twinge of annoyance; had she told me she'd changed her mind about coming, I would not have dragged Everett along.

"No more talk of publishing and does it matter," Everett declared, shoving a plastic plate into my hands. "It will throw us into existential crisis. I say let's eat cheese and be merry."

Zoë was whispering something in the man's ear. I watched them, suspiciously; Zoë was a decided flirt, but she'd kept herself more or less in check since Michael had come along.

The man scanned the room until his eyes fixed on me. He smiled and waved. Idiotically, I lifted my palm in a brief hello. I sensed I knew him, but couldn't remember his name.

▸

Theoretically—ethically—teachers should be like parents, parceling out equal care for all their kids without favoritism. But truth be told, I loved my creative writers best. They came to class in their pajamas and didn't e-mail me much. On a particularly good day, they even raised their hands to talk in class.

Friday the students shuffled into class sullen and pale. We had reached the point in the semester where the novelty of being back on campus had worn off and the promise of Christmas break was still too far away to incite hope.

"The actual act of writing is a very private thing." I paced the front of the room, hoping the movement would wake them up. "But the private act of writing is only half the life of a story or a book. Its other half is the life it lives for its audience." On the board I wrote *imaginary audience*. "Who is it you see in your mind when you sit down to write?" I asked. "What faces—what crowds—do you write for?"

We discussed the many audiences we saw in our minds when

we wrote: editors in offices in great cities, professors with their red pens, peer reviewers, family, friends.

"Sometimes these people can hinder our voice," I said. "How many times when you are writing do you hold back for fear of what your mom would say if she read it? Or for fear of what a professor will say about your style? In today's reading, Lamott points out that you have to free your mind from the burden of that critical audience. To write what it is you need to write."

Lillian Finelley, a varsity cheerleader whom I suspected of taking the class for an easy A, raised her hand. "Who's our audience then?"

"Yourself. God. Someone kind and forgiving."

"But don't authors write for specific audiences?" Mary Beth asked. She planned to be a poet. It was clear that she resented having to agree with Lillian, but she kept on. "I mean, if you write for children you write for children, not for yourself. Or if you write romance, you write for a certain public."

"Of course we all write to audiences," I agreed. "And, yes, any given genre is compelled to meet its audience's expectations. But what I'm saying is maybe we get so busy trying to please a target audience that we miss the very story we have worth telling."

They were listening intently, but were skeptical.

"How about this," I said, regrouping. "Would you keep writing even if no one read your work?"

I studied each face in turn. One offered a sympathetic smile, another frowned to prove he was thinking. Few met my gaze. Lonnie Weis stared, but Lonnie always stared. Mostly at my breasts.

"I wouldn't." This from Jason Burkie, who only talked if he could be antagonistic.

"Why not?" I asked.

He shrugged his thin shoulders. "What's the use?"

His shrug tipped the debate. One after another, the students agreed with him.

"I think the whole point of writing is to be heard," said Lillian the cheerleader. "Like you write so you can have a voice in the world. You know, to protest evil and things."

Another student: "What good is it if you're just listening to yourself?"

And another: "Who cares about voice? If you want to entertain people you have to keep their expectations in mind."

On and on it went. One reason after another why an author should burn her pages and step off a ledge if unsuccessful at publication.

"But don't we write for more than just entertainment?" I asked. "What about writing for therapy? And doesn't a person who has been given the passion to make art have an obligation to use that talent no matter what attention he or she receives?"

Convinced I was now playing the devil's advocate, and that by opposing me they were doing precisely what I wanted them to do, they completely denounced any such notion. A writer should strive to be read. Writing that was not read was wasted paper. They rarely got this excited, but I didn't want to hear any more. I said it was Friday and we all needed a break: They were free to go early.

As they shuffled out of the classroom, I erased the day's notes from the board. It seemed a monumental task.

I turned to find Lonnie waiting at the front of the room.

"Lonnie! I didn't know you were standing there."

"I wanted to turn in my story."

"You know it isn't due for two weeks," I said.

His eyes, so intent upon me in class, were now fixed on the floor. "Well, you know, it was getting to me up here. I have deadlines for the paper, and I can only have one story in my head at a time."

Lonnie was the assistant editor for the *Copenhagen Campus Chronicler*, which said all I needed to know about the quality of that publication.

"I just need to let this one go," he explained.

I accepted the manuscript from his badly chapped hands. His

mouth was similarly red and chafed above the lip. During class he often ran cherry ChapStick over both his lips and his raw knuckles. He wore windbreakers everyday and never took them off. Altogether, his life seemed one constant battle against a secret gale.

"I'll try to read it over on the weekend."

"You don't have to," he replied, crossing his arms. He glanced up, blushed, looked back down. "I mean if you want to, but whenever is fine with me."

I said okay again, and he left the room with a hasty good-bye.

My feet throbbed. I sat down in one of the student's desks, having lost the motivation to collect my notes and the day's papers. Curious, I flipped to the first page of Lonnie's story:

> *Rinaldi: A Story of Love and of Rage*
> *Beneath a blistering fester of Remus's third sun the weakened Rinaldi was pacing his way fastly towards the tower. He was thinking one thing: of Roseanne and her hair like a flowing waterfall of ember flame. . . .*

I cradled my forehead in my hands. I felt a headache coming on.

4

Zoë's latest project was Eli Morretti, the boyfriend of an old college roommate. He lived in Cincinnati where he'd been working as assistant curator for Juxtapose Gallery. Though he never came to see Zoë during his visits to campus where his girlfriend, Jillian, was still a student, Zoë frequently drove downtown to Cincinnati to support one or the other of the many exhibitions he was particularly passionate about. These trips stopped in September when Juxtapose unexpectedly closed its doors, leaving the city without its more adventurous gallery and leaving Eli now three months out of work. This misfortune had been further followed by pestilence: In a matter of weeks his apartment had been overrun with an infestation of bedbugs. Just as quickly, Eli moved from an object of Zoë's affection to a potential recipient of her militant charity. How we should help him had become a frequent topic of conversation.

There were many aspects of the Christian faith that Zoë found troubling but the injunction to love your neighbor appealed to her humanitarian sympathies. When she opened our apartment to someone she was more than hospitable, she was downright altruistic. She didn't keep anything she could find a way to give or share. She had friends over for dinner and sent them out the door with the leftovers *and* the pots we'd cooked them in. She let people raid her closet for new outfits to wear to parties and never asked to have the clothes back. She gave her books away when she'd read them.

Having taken the long view on material objects and having found them rather meaningless, she was always baffled when I harped about condensation rings on the coffee table or missing DVDs. They were only *things* after all. What was mine was hers and what was hers was for everyone else to use. Whenever one of her friends had a crisis, something of mine invariably went missing.

She relayed the sordid tale of Eli's bedbug plague while I was writing lesson plans, a project that required my full attention and left me ill-equipped for conversation much less decision-making. She wanted to know if he could stay at our place. He was a good guy, a Christian, very fun to be with, wouldn't know how to be an intrusion if he tried, and besides it would only be for a few days, maybe a week—maybe over Christmas break to take care of the apartment for us—just until he could find a new place.

Unwittingly, I said I didn't mind.

~

It was Saturday and almost the end of the semester. My *To Must Do* list had grown exponentially since Monday. I forced myself out of bed at six and headed straight for The Brewery, a pile of student essays in hand.

The owner, Jimmy Barnes, had erected the popular shop from an old bar. The Brewery was so successful he had quickly made enough to open the T-shirt press in the adjoining building. Over the next decade, he systematically bought and renovated an entire section of the downtown strip. He did not own a car and preferred to walk the routes between his many businesses, leaning on the cane that counterbalanced the burden of his three hundred and fifty pounds.

On campus he was as familiar and beloved a caricature as a school mascot.

Despite the cheerful sunlight outside, the shop was dim, low-hanging Tiffany lamps casting cones of light on bowed, working heads. The bar could seat fifteen at a time. Jimmy had kept all the beer dispensers for decorative purposes, replacing the Corona and Bud Light labels with stickers for coffee liqueur flavors. The floors were finished with large black and white checkered tiles on which red and flower-print carpets lay here and there. Paintings from student artists decorated the walls, and the rich aroma of freshly ground coffee beans hung dense in the air.

I ordered a black coffee and took a table in the far corner. I had promised myself I would plow through the last of the composition essays, but when I opened my folder I found Lonnie Weis's story on top. I couldn't resist.

Rinaldi was an ambassador of the human race sent to negotiate peace with the enemy force of Zorgath. Roseanne was a daughter of a Zorgath lord and loved Rinaldi in return. Fortunately, the consummation of their love was made possible by her humanoid form.

I was so busy trying to absorb the story despite the awkward syntax and the atrocious metaphors that I was halfway through Lonnie's story before it hit me. Turning back to page three, I reread the description of Roseanne:

> She was tall, taller than most women but not so tall as to be unattractive but rather she was elegant. She had a cascading flame of red curly hair that billowed on her back. Her eyes were like two discs of blue, cloudless sky. And oh! the shape of her face, her round head, so perfect. Rinaldi ached to touch her.

Taller than most. Red curls. Blue eyes. He was describing *me*.

"Hey."

Zoë stood at my table, wiping her wet hands on her work apron.

"I have ten seconds." She took a chair and propped her feet up on mine, her black-and-white-checkered Keds studded with dirt-smudged *Hello Kitty* stickers.

"It's busy here today," I remarked.

"It always is once the cold sets in." She rubbed her eyes vigorously. Her nail polish had worn down to irregular blurbs of hot pink. "What've you been doing?"

"Grading."

"What else," she muttered, picking up Lonnie's story and leafing through the pages. "I talked to Eli this morning."

I waited. "And?"

"Do we have extra bedsheets? Towels?" Her voice trailed off and her brow furrowed as she read. "Amy, what is this?"

"A student's story."

I tried to take the story back from her, but she grabbed my wrist and held my arm over her head, turning in her chair to prevent me from reaching further.

Aloud she read, " 'Besotted, he gazed longingly into the starry night sky, his loins on fire with love.' " She laughed. "I haven't seen the word *loins* since Sunday school. This is *genius*."

"Zoë," I warned. "Come on, he's just a beginner."

"Oh, no. This is good."

I snatched the manuscript back. "You shouldn't laugh."

"I don't know how you read that stuff."

"What's this about Eli?" I asked, hoping to reroute the conversation.

"He just wanted to know if we had stuff to make up a bed. He had to throw all his sheets and pillows out."

"We have extras. We'll just make up the futon—if he doesn't mind."

"After what he's been through, I'm sure he'd be happy to sleep on the kitchen floor."

I perched my pen over Lonnie's manuscript, an indication that I needed to work.

"I should let you get back to the lover's loins." Her manager walked in the room. She stood quickly, wiping my already clean table with a wet rag. "I told her I'd work a double shift today so I need you to be at the apartment when Eli gets there."

"He's coming *tonight*?"

"He's coming now. He said he'd be here in an hour."

I glared at her. "Zoë, the apartment is a disaster—we don't have anything for him to eat, our laundry is everywhere . . ."

She pretended to restock the sugar packets at the next table. "He doesn't care."

"*I* care."

"Throw the laundry under my bed, leave the dishes in the sink, and I'll pick up something for dinner. Problems solved." She smiled her best customer service smile, turned on her heel, and walked briskly away.

⌒

He arrived in a green Volkswagen van that rattled so loud it was remarkable I didn't hear him until he appeared in my doorway. He was three and a half hours late.

"Sorry—I didn't mean to scare you." He jerked his thumb over his shoulder. "The door was open. Zoë said to come on in."

When I didn't say anything, he extended his hand. "I'm Eli."

I was taken aback by his appearance: He was the same man I'd seen at the poetry reading. He certainly wasn't the man I was expecting. The Eli I knew from Zoë's stories ran a gallery and a clothing drive, networked with artists, set commission, handled sales. He should have been shorter, heavier, dressed in khakis and a collared shirt, more like a thirty-year-old and less like a half-starved vagabond.

I accepted his handshake. "Amy," I said.

"I remember—from the reading. We waved."

"I saw you with Zoë. I just assumed you were a friend from campus."

"I was only down for the night," he explained. "Zoë meant to introduce us, but you disappeared with someone. A guy in glasses? Kind of balding on top?"

"That's Everett. He likes to sit in the back for quick escape. He doesn't do well at those things, for whatever reason. He's a friend from the office." I shut my mouth abruptly to keep from rambling.

"Not a boyfriend?"

"Oh—no, definitely not a boyfriend."

There was an uncomfortable pause. I considered his empty hands. Loops drawn with pen in tightly winding patterns stained the length of his fingers.

"Where are your things?" I asked.

From the screen door we considered the large duffel bag he'd abandoned on the driveway between his van and the porch. He eyed the bag menacingly as if it were a misbehaving pet awaiting punishment. He insisted I not let it in the house; he was burning it as soon as he'd rewashed all his clothes.

He wanted to know where he could find a laundromat so he could treat his clothes before bringing them into our apartment. Bedbugs and their eggs traveled in suitcases. I could have given him directions and kept the rest of the afternoon to myself, but my mother had forever ingrained in me the utmost importance of being the gracious host. I was inclined to help.

"You're sure?" he asked. "You really don't have to."

"They're not *in* there, are they?"

"They're in the bag if anything," he said. "But I want to wash the sheets for eggs."

He emptied the duffel bag of clothes directly onto the frozen driveway. Together we stuffed them all back into trash bags. His socks were worn at the soles, his jeans frayed, the fringe of each pant leg clotted with dirt. One by one I sifted through T-shirts that smelled of incense and turpentine. I also found a napkin on which someone had scribbled a phone number; a clipping torn from the newspaper in the shape of a heart; a Tupperware of buckeye nuts sporting drawn-on cartoon faces; and a tiny velvet string-pull bag that held two engraved silver rings.

"Are these important?" I held up the little cloth bag.

He tucked the jewelry in his back pocket, noticed the color-coordinated piles I'd been making. "You don't have to separate them. Just throw them in the bag."

"They'll bleed."

"The bugs?"

"The colors."

He shook his head. "We're not washing them. We want heat—just heat."

I held up a black T-shirt that had been starched to the point of rigor mortis. "Not even fabric softener," I stated.

"Not even fabric softener," he repeated. He crawled on his knees to grab the farthest of my piles, cramming it into the trash bag. "You know we'll have to be best friends forever now."

"We will?"

"You've touched all my underwear," he said.

That I blushed embarrassed me so much I blushed again.

At the laundromat he pulled an old Mason jar full of coins from his knapsack. When the last load had been stuffed into the dryer, he took the shirt off his back and threw it in for good measure. The undershirt he wore underneath was his cleanest article of clothing. The white cotton blazed bright against his dark complexion. He was tall with the lean but strong arms of a young athlete. A tattoo covered his right arm, the intricate pattern cascading from his right shoulder to his elbow.

We sat side by side on conjoined plastic chairs that lined the front window. To make conversation I asked about bedbugs. Companionably, he lifted his shirt to show me the damage. Red bumps rose in circles across his stomach and chest; some welts were large as quarters, others tiny as fleabites.

"They say you know it's bedbugs if they bite in a circle." He pointed to one particularly irritating ring. "Breakfast, lunch, dinner," he explained, pointing to spot one, two, and three. Beneath the raw rings of irritated skin, his stomach was flat and strong. A single black line of hair trickled down his chest and pooled around his belly button.

"Do they ooze?" I asked.

"No." He lowered his shirt. "Just itch to drive you crazy."

He caught me examining his tattoo. "You disapprove?"

I snapped my eyes away from his arm. "Why would you say that?"

"Zoë told me you come from a really religious background."

I found this an unfair indictment, considering Zoë had once said the same of him. I said, "Zoë says fish-oil tablets are a necessary element to a well-balanced diet."

He laughed.

"I like your tattoo," I went on. "I assume it means something?" The tone of the second comment canceled the approval I'd hoped the first would convey. I hated tattoos, but I flattered myself this dislike was an aesthetic preference rather than a religious conviction.

"It means something."

He stood up to check on one of the dryers. I took this as my cue to leave the subject alone.

⁂

The moment Zoë saw us pull into the driveway, she bolted from the front door to throw her arms around Eli. She leapt into his arms and wrapped her feet around his waist. Eli set her back down on the ground as effortlessly as he might a child.

She'd made a homemade dinner to celebrate his arrival. We ate whole wheat pasta tossed with organic dried tomatoes, and fresh, sparsely shaved Parmesan; whole grain toasted baguette; and bowls of arugula lightly spritzed with lemon and vinegar and olive oil. Zoë fussed over Eli the entire meal. How was his drive? How were his bites? Did he have to catch the bugs himself? Were they as disgusting as the pictures on the Internet? How was Jillian?

Jillian was fine, wonderful: she was in Germany studying painting until May. Her schedule was unconventional. They spoke when they could.

"Don't worry." Zoë slapped his knee. "Amy and I'll keep you company."

I had been entirely invisible up to this point. Eli made a rather obvious attempt to divert the conversation my way.

"Zoë says you're a writer." He leaned back so Zoë could clear his plate and glass away. "You're writing a book?"

"I'm lucky to write five pages."

"I'd love to read some of it."

"Amy doesn't like talking about her work," Zoë explained from the kitchen.

"Why not?"

"It's a private world, up there in my head," I said. "Talking about it with other people is like having a stranger come into your house and help themselves to your food, start rooting through your underwear drawer." I realized too late that this was a poor analogy considering the circumstances of our initial meeting.

Eli was not offended. "I promise not to go through your underwear drawer." He lifted his coffee to his lips. "Figuratively or literally."

This was the second time underwear had figured into our day's conversation.

Zoë set a cup of fat-free tofu pudding in front of each of us. Eli stuck his spoon in the center of the colorless, gelatinous mound. It stood upright on its own.

"You're banned from my panty drawer," I said to him, "but you can certainly eat all the food you want."

Later I wondered why I'd said "panty" instead of underwear, panty being such a frilly, flirtatious kind of word.

⁓

Arguably, Eli was attractive, with a face that belonged to someone younger than his thirty-two. Dressed more conservatively, his long hair trimmed and pulled back, you might notice the defined structure of his cheekbones; in the right circles, his narrow face and his deep-set eyes might be considered vogue, even beautiful. But you didn't immediately notice beauty. Too many other superficialities demanded your attention. His clothes were secondhand, well-matched but often stained with paint or plaster. He wore heavy jewelry, silver rings on his fingers and frayed hemp on his wrists and neck. Most distinct of all was the tattoo, a Celtic circular pattern that wound from shoulder to just below his elbow in dark green ink.

From his dress you could draw immediate conclusions that he made no effort to dispel: In high school he'd been a pothead; he'd grown up a kid who rode his skateboard on curbsides until the local police banned him from the harmless sport, and then he persisted anyway, with that air of martyrdom only an adolescent can achieve; he would have had parents with money who provoked a hatred of materialism almost as strong as his hatred of the government. He did not wear deodorant because he didn't believe in masking the body's natural functions with modern hygiene, which was really just another facade people put up. His girlfriend wore ankle-length dresses and did not shave her legs.

Not that any of this was true. He didn't talk about himself, so there wasn't a lot to go on.

During the last week of school he tried not to be an intrusion, and in return I tried not to notice that he was. He did little to upset the apartment. His furniture—what he'd salvaged of it—was

58

in storage. Aside from his duffel bag, he'd brought one extra pair of shoes and the military khaki green knapsack he carried on his shoulder wherever he went. He only ate the food we expressly made for him. He kept his bathroom things in a Kroger bag stuffed under the futon.

"You know there are some students on campus talking about opening a gallery," Zoë said. She was holding up the bottom of her mattress while I blasted it with Lysol. Every night since Eli had arrived, Zoë had scoured the Columbus craigslist for job openings and I'd scoured the mattresses for bedbugs. "I also saw an ad for lawn maintenance."

"It's December."

"True." She dropped the mattress and frowned. "Yeah, why would somebody post that?"

"Lift," I commanded. She lifted the other side of the mattress. I fumigated.

She said, "I wonder if Kathryn has any openings at the library."

I waved my hand in front of my face trying to dispel the antiseptic fog. "You're not telling the landlady, of all people, about Eli."

"Yeah. She wouldn't be too thrilled about the idea of someone living with us."

She said this as if it were news. Already we were making Eli park four blocks away so the sight of the old Volkswagen wouldn't rouse suspicion. At that moment I realized two things: (1) Eli was not just between apartments, he was broke; (2) Eli was going to be staying for a very long time.

"Zoë."

"Oh, sorry—lift." She lifted the mattress. I pushed it back down.

"What do you mean *living* with us?"

She feigned innocence. "I didn't mean anything. I mean he's living with us until he finds a new place."

"You said Christmas break. You said he just needed a place for the holiday."

"I know what I said, but it's just that everything's gotten a little more complicated."

"What about Michael," I countered. "What does he think?"

"Michael? Why would he care? It's not like I'm *attracted* to Eli." She frowned. "That would be so clichéd, to be in love with Eli. Everybody's in love with Eli."

We heard the front door open and shut. The subject was closed.

I found Eli in the kitchen, investigating Zoë's latest bulgur wheat soup experiment.

"Is it food?" he asked.

"It's edible," I said. "It's nutritious."

Tentatively, he lifted a spoonful to his mouth. The phone number written on the back of his hand was two days old. The ink had begun to fade, but I was willing to wager that the 9 and the 3 and the first letters of the owner's name—CAL—might last to the weekend.

Considering the fact that he'd spent the last four weeks as live bait, I hadn't minded his unkempt appearance at first; I'd begun to wonder, however, whether he hadn't been wearing the same variation of two outfits since arriving. Or maybe it was his scent that alarmed me, an odor pungent but seductive, like upturned, sun-baked earth.

⁀

"I want to meet this Eli." I held the phone an inch from my ear; Brian had my mother's volume. He was five years younger than me but insisted on acting like a big brother. "Are you charging him rent?"

"No, we're not charging him rent," I said. "I *thought* he was just visiting for the weekend."

"You need a timeline. A plan for eviction. You don't just let people come live with you. What if your landlord finds out?"

"She won't find out. You're starting to sound like Mom."

I hadn't meant to talk about Eli and I certainly hadn't meant to jeopardize my brother's good mood. He and Marie were registering for wedding gifts. "Amebuger!" he'd shouted into the phone when he picked up. "Vacuum cleaner with or without the central dust segregator?"

Direct contact with my brother had become a rare thing since he started medical school. When he wasn't in lecture, he was in the library. I couldn't remember the last time we hadn't held a conversation in whispers.

"How's Marie doing?" I asked to change the subject.

He asked her. "She says she's surviving, how are you? She's still in family med, so her schedule is good. She'd be better if Mom wasn't driving her crazy."

"Wedding stuff?"

"You'd think napkin anagrams were the be-all end-all."

"Monograms," I corrected.

"Whatever. She's making Marie nuts."

We discussed their honeymoon plans and our mother's relative insanity with all things wedding. When the conversation hit a lull, I worried the button on my blouse.

"Brian," I began, tentative. "I told the chair of the department I would teach again next semester."

There was a pause.

"So no planned escapes from Copenhagen?"

"I don't have the money—or the prospects. Do you think it's a mistake to stay?"

"A mistake? They pay you, right? And you get to write your stories, right? Sounds like a good setup to me."

"I don't think I'm any good at it."

"*Amy.* You're a great writer."

"No, I mean the teaching. I'm terrible."

"How do you know that?"

"Because I know it."

"That's enough. Those kids love you."

"Really?" I asked piteously; Brian was the only person around with whom I had no shame.

"If nothing else, at least you have all the time in the world to write." He spoke away from the receiver: "Baby! Rice cooker! We need this. *Need* it. No, I'm serious. Did you zap it?"

"I can let you go," I said. He didn't answer. I sighed and waited, twirling red circles on the back of a student's essay.

He came back to the phone five minutes later. "Marie wants to know if you heard about Mom's new boyfriend."

I made him repeat what he'd just said.

"Well, maybe not boyfriend yet. But they're going out. Every Friday night to Olive Garden."

When I pressed him for details, he said I should just talk to Mom myself. He had to get back to stainless-steel cutlery but would call again later. I hung up reluctantly knowing he was unlikely to make good on his word. I'd lost my brother in two phases: first to medical school, then to a woman. I was lying when I pretended it didn't affect me every time I called and got his voicemail.

Communicating with my family was like playing a game of telephone around a summer campfire, only there were no marshmallows and nobody was laughing. Approximately twenty-three hours after explaining the Eli situation to Brian, Mom called to inquire why in heaven's name Zoë was giving lifts to gypsies.

"Grandma says he has some kind of biblical name. Abraham? Micah?"

"Are you talking about Eli?" I asked.

"That's it. Eli. What's this business about Eli."

It took me half an hour to disentangle what Brian had said to Marie, what Marie mentioned to Grandma, and what Mom had chosen to hear from Grandma's final account. I told her that one of Zoë's close friends had come to visit for dinner, that he was attractive, educated, and talented. I did *not* tell her he had a tattoo, had flunked college before going back at twenty-eight to study art, and intended to stay at our apartment until he found a job, which was unlikely to happen anytime soon as he'd studied art. Under no circumstances would I allow my mother to know I was cohabiting with a man outside the holy bonds of matrimony, no matter how platonic or even antagonistic our relationship. This was the same woman who wouldn't let a boy within two feet of my bedroom all through high school, protesting that there was nowhere to sit but on my bed.

In an effort to rewrite my mother's first impressions of Eli, I was a bit too enthusiastic in my praise. Mom assumed I liked him, and immediately credited his visit to Providence: "It's just like it was for me. If I hadn't taken the job in Kentucky I'd never have hit your father on that exit ramp. I told you God still has you at that school for a reason. You were meant to meet this Eli."

This was exactly what she had said the night I met Adam; she had yet to recant that theory. And I hardly considered her meeting Dad a precedent, considering the ultimate outcome of that fateful intersection

"I have had my own providential run-in," she said coyly.

"Yeah, Brian mentioned something about this."

"I was in the shopping market, trying to decide whether I wanted Gala apples or Jonathan—the Galas have not been very good lately for some reason, and they're my favorites, but I finally had to switch to Jonathans—anyway, I had Jonathans in my bag and was just turning around to get more when I bumped right into Richard Moore. He said he was trying to get to the tangerines but had slipped because they'd mopped the floors, then I said I was trying to get apples but they were all so bruised and awful and *he* said the fruit has gone downhill since the new manager took over the store. You know he told the cashiers they don't have to wear those little paper hats anymore?"

"Who's Richard Moore?" I asked.

"The man from that little corner place that does my taxes."

"*Mr.* Moore, the financial advisor?"

"He's shaved his mustache. He's much less scary-looking now—he's actually almost handsome. Anyway, he's taking me to dinner tomorrow night."

Mom boomeranged back to the wedding colors, describing in detail the impossibility of finding a dress that properly matched the day's festivities without being a total imitation of the bridesmaid gowns.

"They're doing this greenish color. Something 'don.' Celadon, I think. It really is hideous in the right light. Almost sickly. It'll never do for my complexion."

"So buy a pink dress."

"You'll never believe what Marie said. I'm trying to help her pick out her makeup for the day, showing her the new Luna boysenberry line, which would look perfect with her complexion—she has that dark Indian skin you know, which is just beautiful—and she says to me, 'I don't think I'm going to wear makeup, Pam.' " Mom paused for dramatic effect. "I mean, can you *believe* that? Who doesn't wear makeup for their wedding!"

"Remind me to elope," I said to Zoë when I got off the phone.

She was curled up in her red reading chair, halfway through *Birds of America* and a Tootsie Roll Pop. Tootsie Pops were her dietary sin of choice. She said, "Do you know how many children you could feed with the money we pour annually into weddings?"

"How many?"

"I don't know," she replied, not turning her attention from the book. "A lot."

Zoë's parents had married on a beach at sunset, her mom in a blue dress she'd found at a local vendor's booth that morning. At the reception the in-laws coerced them into a month later, they requested that guests donate money to charity in place of gifts. She raised her Tootsie Pop in the air, gesturing with it to emphasize each word: "What Would Jesus Do, Amy? What Would Jesus Do?"

5

Rinaldi told Roseanne that she looked breathtaking, because she is.

"I want to run my fingers through your hair," he said. "I'm always taken by the urge."

Roseanne breathed hard. "I don't think we should." She said. "It would be wrong. It would be against everything we have been told."

"Please, Roseanne," he pleaded. "Please."

Rinaldi and Roseanne danced together. The burning suns of Remus set behind them, globes as hot and on fire as Roseanne's bossom. At first she pulled away, but he got the better of her.

Both were exquisitely ready for it to happen. It did happen; Rinaldi and Roseanne were experiencing ecstasy.

In my office, I struggled through Lonnie's story for the third time. We were critiquing "Rinaldi" in the next class and I had yet to write my response. With one last glance at the handwritten comments I'd made in the margins of his paper, I set the pages aside and cautiously began to type.

Lonnie,

Here we have, in a mere nine pages, a story of epic proportions: two lovers, destined to be together, whose happiness is thwarted by interfering parties (much in the manner of Romeo and Juliet). I appreciate the sweeping scope of the tale, and your attempt, in so few pages, to explore such complex relationships amidst an intergalactic war between the humans and the Zorgath. As a reader who spent the better part of her childhood and junior high years obsessed with science fiction, I particularly enjoyed the creative setting.

I do have to say that the brevity of the piece is, in this case, a handicap. The pacing of the story feels strained, as if too many plot points have been crammed into too few pages. Perhaps focusing on a more specific moment or scene would give the story a better sense of balance.

"Hey, Amy." Everett had entered the room. "Don't say hey back: I don't want to interrupt, I just want you to know that I'm not ignoring you."

"Actually, I have a question for you," I said, spinning around in my chair.

"Is it a long question or a short question?" He raised his forefinger. "Clarification: Is it an involved question requiring a long answer, or is it a simple question necessitating merely a brief, perhaps monosyllabic response?"

I cringed. "The former."

He looked at his watch. "I have a lecture to attend in twenty minutes, three e-mails to write, one to read in the meantime. You have two minutes. Go."

"What would you do if a student wrote a story and featured you as a main character?"

Everett smiled, a wicked, teasing smile. "You've got a student stalker, haven't you?"

"No," I moaned. "I don't know. Here, read this. Page three, paragraph two."

He scanned over the section quickly.

"Well?" I asked when he handed the story back.

"She certainly bears an uncanny resemblance." He shrugged. "Maybe it's just coincidence."

"I'm sure that's all it is."

"Yes, he probably had no intention of writing a character who looks *exactly* like you." He took his seat and pitched a tepee with his forefingers, tapping them against one another. "*Intention* being the operative word. He could have—unwittingly, mind you—written this—what's her name? Roseanne?—in order to purge his mind and body of his sexual obsession with you." He leaned back in his chair, clearly enjoying himself. "Yes?"

"Let's hope not," I sighed. "Or my love life has hit a new and abysmal low."

I returned to my computer and allowed Everett time to do the same, but he couldn't resist picking up the story again fifteen minutes later.

"Is this Lonnie Weis, that kid who works in the copy room?"

"That's him."

"Did you ever think maybe he noticed you before he signed up for your class?"

"Everett. This is not helping."

He scanned the story. "That's one heck of a Freudian slip," he said, dropping the story back on my desk. "Good luck with it."

By this point I had reached the conclusion of my review. I paused, unsure of how to continue. I'd once written a story about a short, balding widower who came to the door selling Girl Scout cookies for his daughter. Having prided myself on my originality, I was crushed when my mother read the story and said, "Oh, you've written about Mr. Tilney. What a peculiar man he was." The line between reality and fiction is a thin one for most writers—one better left unaddressed.

I finished typing:

In terms of character development, the descriptions of Roseanne were quite detailed but did not delve beyond the purely physical. She was easy to visualize, yet her motivation remains mysterious. Did she or did she not really wish to be with Rinaldi? This reader is inclined to think not.

All in all, an interesting extrapolation of Shakespeare's timeless plot.

Amy

On Monday the students were polite in their critique, but it quickly became apparent that they found nothing of merit in Lonnie's story. He spent the entire half hour writing in his notebook. I wondered if he was even listening. Inevitably, it was time to move on to the second story, which was about a sophomore in college who didn't know whether to stay in school and get married or break up with her boyfriend and pursue the life of the stage. The character pitched back and forth for twenty pages. It was unreadable, but as it did not take place in space or involve ray guns and burning suns, the students were much kinder. They liked accessible, familiar settings: This was the most disappointing failure of their imaginations.

When the class ended I handed Lonnie the copy I had personally marked up, my typed comments pinned to the top. He accepted both and fled.

⁓

When I returned to my office two hours later, I was surprised to find Lonnie standing outside my door, his story in hand. He was beaming.

"Lonnie, how long have you been here?" I asked.

"Not long," he said. "Just an hour and a half."

"You should have made an appointment."

"I was just leaving work. I work down the hall, you know."

"Yes, I know."

"Anyway, I just had to say thank you, Ms. Gallagher. This is great—this is so great."

"I'm glad I could be helpful," I replied.

"I mean, usually just my mom reads my stories. She has to like them because I'm her son."

I smiled. "My mom always did the same."

He kept his eyes carefully trained to the right of my head. It gave me the uncomfortable feeling of trying to meet the gaze of someone who was cross-eyed.

"So you like science fiction?" he asked.

"I adore science fiction," I said. "It was all I read in high school."

"I read science fiction like voraciously."

"I thought you might be a fan."

"I'm so into it." He folded his arms across his chest, fingers tucked tight in his armpits. He briefly caught my eyes before lowering his gaze. "So who do you like?"

"Who do I like?" I leaned back into the wall. "Where to start ... Douglas Adams, Isaac Asimov, Madeleine L'Engle, Jules Verne ... Oh, and of course George Orwell and Margaret Atwood."

"You ever read Neil C. Barker?"

"I haven't, no. Would you recommend him?"

"Barker is good stuff, premium."

"I have a pretty long reading list as it is," I replied, "but I'll be sure to write it down. What's the title?"

"It's not one book, it's seven," he said, almost impatiently. He ripped a scrap of paper off the corner of the response I'd taken such pains to type up the day before. Using his knee as a flat surface, he wrote down a list of titles in his indecipherable chicken scratch. "*Land of Doom* is the first, but you can read *The Flaming Arrow of Night* and *Brother of the Begotten* without it."

He handed me the paper. His hand trembled ever so slightly.

"Thanks." I slipped the notebook scrap into my coat pocket.

Simultaneously, we realized that he had used up all he had planned to say. He licked his lips; they were shiny up top from the cherry ChapStick.

The strap of my bag was digging painfully into my shoulder.

"You want to come in?" I asked. "I'm on my way home, but we can talk about your story for a few minutes if you like."

"I can't," he said, stepping back from the open door as if it were a trap. "I have to go—a thing—it's mandatory, so I have to . . . I'll see you next week."

He turned and hurried down the hall, backpack flapping against his pointed shoulder blades.

I was surprised that Lonnie had taken my critique as so overly positive. I'd been afraid it was too harsh. Now I chastised myself for inciting false hope.

I sometimes worried that my writing was bad and that no one would tell me. I imagined editors in New York offices passing my story around, laughing until they were teary-eyed. I imagined them photocopying my manuscript and reading it aloud at corporate Christmas parties for entertainment. It was all very disconcerting.

＝

The first week with Eli passed and I did not get bedbugs. I got the flu instead.

The annual Campus Plague descended the week before finals, crippling the student body with high fevers, running noses, and violent coughing fits. Though I swabbed my hands with Purell every hour on the hour, I was too sick to even attend the last day of class for which I'd bought three-dozen donuts and four gallons of off-brand cherry berry juice. Begrudgingly, Everett agreed to stand in my classrooms to collect portfolios and distribute Krispy Kremes.

"Have fun with that," he said, dumping the third crate of binders on my bed. "I left the other donuts in the kitchen."

He'd stuffed the rolled up Cheetos bag between the two remaining chocolate cream-filled pastries.

Monday evening the flu moved to my head. Out of pity, Zoë temporarily lifted the two-square-per-use toilet paper rule she'd instituted as part of her personal Save the Earth Campaign. She even returned from work with two boxes of tissues infused with aloe, tossing them to me on the way out the door for her now twice a week stint at the gym: When she wasn't running she was sweating at *Gavin's Glutes and Abs*. She reminded me that I wouldn't get so sick if I took the vitamin supplements she set out for me every morning. I would have taken pleasure in hating her, but they were very nice tissues.

When Eli knocked on my door I told him to come back later. "I haven't brushed my teeth all day."

"I don't care," he said.

"I haven't brushed my hair either."

He not only let himself in, he went so far as to sit on the corner of my bed.

"I brought something for you," he said. From a paper bag he produced a bottle of NyQuil, a bag of cough drops, and a set of stickers. *Great Job!* they said. *You're AWESOME!* I held them up questioningly.

"For your papers." He poured NyQuil onto a spoon for me. "I wanted scratch and sniff, but I couldn't find any."

I dutifully drank the NyQuil. "I don't think anybody's going to do so *awesome* on their papers."

"Then they can be for you. Didn't you ever have a sticker collection?"

"No."

"I thought all girls loved stickers. Stickers and ponies."

He peeled a *GENIUS* ladybug and stuck it to my T-shirt just below my right shoulder. "And men who ride ponies."

In spite of my headache, my fever, even my resentment at his presence, I laughed.

I graded in bed, essays fanned out to my left, grade book to my right. I drank NyQuil straight from the bottle. The syrup slid warm and viscous down my throat, the medicinal licorice flavor lingering in a film on my lips. Delirium set in. It was not unpleasant. The paper in front of me began to go fuzzy around the edges as I read the next student's thesis statement.

> *Since the dawn of time there have always been forms of entertainment. And like most everything else, entertainment has been criticized since there existed a Being knowledgeable enough to know how to do it. In ancient times, Jesus was criticized by many of the people and even went so far as to crucify him by nailing him to a tree in front of all his fans. More recently, The Internet has been going through a criticism war right now on whether the Government should be able to sensor what people do there. What I would argue and will argue in this paper is that that is not advisable because it is a violation of our Free Speech.*

Jesus had very fickle fans, I wrote in the margin.

I giggled until I got the hiccups. After a fifth read through of the paragraph that proved no more illuminating than the first, I threw the paper to the floor, crawled down under my comforter, and decided to sleep until New Year's.

❧

I woke from NyQuil-sodden dreams to find my mother sitting at my bedside, her Chantilly perfume and vanilla lotion thick in the trapped bedroom air.

"Honey," she said, cupping my face as she would a child's. "You look *dreadful*."

"I'b sick."

"I know. That nice groundskeeper told me you were in bad shape."

"The groundskeeper?"

"That young man with the ponytail out shoveling the driveway. He let me in."

I squinted up at her, forcing my eyes to focus.

"He's not a groundskeeper, Mob. That's Zoë's friend I was telling you about."

"*That's* Eli?" Her face went through a variety of contortions as she reformulated her previous impression of Eli. "Amy, you can't possibly be serious about him."

"I don't even know him." Rousing from my drugged stupor, I frowned. "Why are you here?"

"I had a Luna Landing in Columbus and was planning to do some Christmas shopping, so I thought, well, why not just come and pick you up to join me." She went to the window, opened the blinds. "And it's a good thing I did. You're in absolutely no condition to drive home."

I rolled over to avoid the sun. "I can dribe, Mob. I hab a cold. I'b dot paralyzed."

"I'll not have you driving under the influence." She lifted the half-empty bottle of NyQuil as proof. "You can't handle medications. Never could—your system is too sensitive."

She went to the bathroom to throw the bottle out. Her voice carried from the hall. "Whenever I had to give you those little blue pills for your ear infections, I'd find you sleepwalking in the basement searching for your Cabbage Patch dolls in the pantry. And then there was the time with the wisdom teeth."

She returned to the bedroom, her silver, sparkling Luna Lady makeup bag in hand. The front was emblazoned with the Luna emblem: black contours that suggested the figure of a woman holding a sphere in the crook of her robed elbow.

"What was that vile drug the dentist made you take? Viacon? You lay on the floor in the bathroom laughing so hard you couldn't breathe. I thought you were having a mental breakdown. Here. I brought you something for your Rosacea."

"I hab decided I hate by life," I announced.

"*Hate* is such a strong word. How about some soup?"

I examined my mother's Luna uniform: a pants suit with thick-set heels dyed a matching periwinkle. I still wasn't sure if it was morning or afternoon. My mother's schedule had been anything but routine since she'd become a salesperson.

As a Luna representative, it had been my mother's duty to travel the tri-state with her toolbox of colors, painting women in wrinkle-reducing, sunray-blocking cosmetics while peddling Luna Lady philosophy:

A Luna Lady never forgets she is a celestial body.

A Luna Lady is like the moon, beautiful but inconspicuous, a reflection of the natural beauty shining around her.

A Luna Lady lives in rhythm with that heavenly body's monthly cycle.

It was feminine mystique with boysenberry lip gloss at fifteen bucks a pop, hardly the material for a First Fundamentalist. My mother enclosed a tea-stained scrap of paper quoting Proverbs 30:31 in each complimentary blush compact to redeem all business transactions of any of That New Ageism. I assured her I didn't think her morals compromised; all that mattered to me was that she had finally found work she loved.

She made herself busy in the kitchen while I showered. Washing with Luna Bubble Grit was like using sand for soap. I came out of the shower scratchy and red.

"I feel sunburned." I accepted the bowl of soup she'd heated.

Zoë was at the table already halfway through the bowl my mother had heated for her. "You look sunburned," she confirmed.

"That's how it's supposed to work," Mom said. "The exfoliating bubbles create microscopic abrasions on the skin that scrape off all the dead cells. When you wake up in the morning, you wake up to a whole new you!"

We argued about my holiday plans. She insisted I come home with her. I argued I could drive myself. As I threw up the tomato soup and crackers five minutes later, my argument did not prove convincing.

I lay in bed while she packed my suitcase. This consisted of her holding up blouses and pants from my closet to which I was to nod yes or no, an arrangement reminiscent of childhood when she helped me pick out my clothes for elementary school every morning while I lingered in bed as long as physically possible.

"How about this black jacket?" Mom asked.

"Old."

"You have some nice sweaters."

"Not from the top row. Those are going to Goodwill."

She raked through the hangers. "You should wear that little pink blouse I bought you last year. The one with the little white buttons."

"Absolutely no blouses."

"This?"

"No."

"This?"

"Okay, that."

Zoë sat at my desk chair watching our little operation. I eyed her suspiciously. I sometimes feared she was taking notes.

Growing up, Zoë had lived in New York City, D.C., and Chicago, where she graduated from high school. Her personal geographic bearings were far encompassing, the borders of Ohio proportionally insignificant. As if Zoë's wanderlust hadn't been enough, we now had Eli, who'd spent six weeks backpacking through Europe and an entire semester studying art history in Italy. I felt positively provincial sandwiched between this tête-à-tête of expatriates. Both my brother and I lived within an hour's drive from home and were always visiting. I'd naively believed that if I were geographically close to my family we'd stay emotionally close. Our mutually single lifestyles had kept that illusion alive temporarily. Now Mom had Mr. Moore and her new career as a Luna Lady, Brian had Marie and his textbooks, and I had the feeling I'd missed something.

It wasn't that I'd never dreamed of travel. I'd indulged fantasies of living a more exciting life in the city by applying to schools in Boston and Pittsburgh and Chicago, but they all rejected me. Once settled in Copenhagen, I was resigned, happy with my small-town routine like a cat or a retiree. But now, watching my mother reorganize my underwear drawer while explaining that I wouldn't get those fuzzy balls on my silk panties if I let them air out instead of putting them in the dryer, I wondered if the closeness of family wasn't a little suffocating.

⁓

"I should warn you," Mom said, taking the exit that led home. I blew my nose. "Ward me what?"

"I've been doing some reorganizing."

"In the house?"

"Well, yes. In your room, actually. Sally Linden called last week requesting an order for Luna Lady Bubble Gum Bubble Bath, and when I went over, she actually ordered a whole anti-aging facial set. Then she calls me a week later wanting to know if I'll do a Luna party. Ten women came—that's twice as many as usual. I've been so busy I don't even have time to substitute teach anymore."

"What does that have to do with my room?"

"It's a mess. I meant to clean it, but I got so busy this week with the wedding. Marie wants to hang bulbs from trees at the reception—so we went to Internet for ideas."

My mother always spoke of the Internet as though it were a being one should consult with deference and awe.

"I have just the bulbs she needs. The wedding planner wants her to rent them, but what they charge for every little thing is *outrageous*! So I tell her that I have these bulbs in the attic, and I was going to try to get them, but I can't get up there without moving everything in your closet."

"You went into the attic?"

"No," she said, offended that I would suggest such a thing. "I wouldn't go up there. I was waiting for you."

It had snowed in my hometown the night before. Battery-powered candles lit each window of our house, casting slants of buttery light onto the square bushes, the square patch of lawn. Mom paid a man to manicure our bushes year-round. She took pride in appearances.

The aroma of cinnamon, the striped wallpaper, and the ticking of the kitchen clock were so familiar I felt as if I were a little girl again. The nostalgia was a reflex, a brief but pleasant emotion that took me by surprise every time.

Upstairs, the sentiment quickly vanished. Madame Luna had pitched camp in my bedroom. My bookshelves had been cleared, their contents relegated to cardboard boxes lined up on the floor. A filing station had supplanted my old nightstand, and deliveries bearing the Luna Lady emblem covered my bed. The bulletin board that used to hold pictures from high school and then from college now displayed work orders and invoices.

I was completely taken off guard; in all the years I'd been gone, my mother had never touched my room, except to vacuum the carpets and wash the sheets in preparation for my visits. I'd never asked her to leave my room alone, but I'd grown accustomed to it. For years my bedroom had been a carefully preserved shrine to my childhood and a reminder that my mother's calendar revolved around my homecomings.

She set my suitcase in the doorway. "You can sleep in Brian's room tonight if you want—I'll have this stuff off your bed tomorrow." Even as she spoke, she began to fuss, picking boxes off the bed and shoving them against the back wall.

"It's fine, Mob," I said. "Honest. Clean it later."

"I'll get in here early in the morning." She kicked another box beneath the bed and shuffled loose mail on the filing cabinet into a neat stack.

"*Mob.*"

"Tomorrow!" she declared, raising two pointer fingers in the air and tiptoeing over the mess to escape down the hall.

Evicted as it were from my old room, I spent three days convalescing on the couch. Doped up and slack-jawed, I revisited old favorites: *Singin' in the Rain, Alien, My Fair Lady, Spaceballs.*

Brian was on break as well. His arrival made things better. When Marie wasn't on call for her ob/gyn rotation, she was sleeping, which meant I had my little brother all to myself.

The night he came home, Grandma joined us for dinner. Over dessert, Mom made her big announcement: She'd been promoted to Regional Director. In the two years she'd worked as a sales representative, she'd supplemented her income by working as a substitute at the local elementary school. Now, to her relief, she would never have to step foot in a classroom again.

We congratulated her on the promotion. Grandma wanted to know if this meant she'd be getting more free samples. Brian said he needed some wrinkle reducer. And I said no, I didn't mind that she needed my old bedroom for an office (though it took considerable self-control to resist asking why she'd chosen my room over Brian's, which was decidedly larger).

Brian and I pitched new products:

Mooning, a perfume aphrodisiac

The *Moonwalk* foot bath

Crater Cream for acne

Rover, the battery-powered razor for women fighting that pesky mustache

Brian even invented a jingle: *"You'll rave when this Rover shaves!"*

"You all think it's funny," Mom said. "Mustaches on women is more a problem than you'd think. You remember Mrs. Priory from the supermarket? She looks like Uncle Lynn now."

Grandma said, "Uncle Lynn looks like Hitler."

After dinner I took a book to the living room. Brian came in to sit beside me.

"Just to warn you: Mom knows about your little live-in boyfriend."

I dropped my book to my lap. "What did you tell her?"

"Nothing. She brought it up."

"*Brian.*"

"It's not my fault you've lost all common sense."

He took my foot and popped my toes, trying to irk me. He was always popping things. Knuckles, gum, bubble wrapping.

"Did you read those books I sent you?" I asked, kicking my foot free.

"I don't have time to read, Amy."

"You should make time. It's good for you. Like exercise is good for you."

"I'll read this one." He took the book from my hands.

"*Love in the Time of Cholera,*" he read. "That's like titling a book, *Love in the Face of Massive Diarrhea.*"

His tastes had never been literary.

While Mom and Grandma finished their holiday shopping, Brian and I killed two days with PlayStation and managed five games of Monopoly. Laughing with my brother, I gained some perspective: Introductory composition was not purgatory, and thirty was not so old.

⁓

The day before Christmas Eve I was well enough to walk without experiencing vertigo, so Mom drafted me to search the attic for the elusive glass globes. Holding on to the low-hanging rafters, I stepped cautiously from beam to beam. The air smelled of wood and dust, an almost sickeningly sweet potpourri.

My mother never got rid of things; she simply reshuffled them, which gave her the illusion of cleaning house. When the closets filled to capacity, she used to make our father redistribute the clutter to the attic. When my father left, I took over the chore. The trapdoor opened from my closet ceiling; I'd always considered the attic an extension of my room and felt a kind of ownership over the mysterious, dark place. I carried boxes of old Tupperware, crates of used Matchbox cars, and bags of winter sweaters up the rickety ladder, frightened of the shadows lurking in the corner, determined to overcome my fear so I could enjoy the solitude such a private place afforded.

The attic had two gabled windows overlooking the front lawn. One was directly over my bedroom, providing a view identical to the one I saw from my dresser, but from higher elevation. I pushed an old desk against this window to create my secret office on the small square of weight-bearing floor, partitioning the space off from the rest of the room with a tall discarded bookcase placed three feet opposite the desk. For increased privacy, I braced dowel rods between the shelf and the wall on each side, hanging a shower curtain on one and Brian's old Superman bedsheets on the other.

The attic was stifling in summer and unbearably cold in winter. I alternated a desk fan and space heater accordingly. In summers I sat in my church slip; in winters I wore long underwear. I considered the harsh conditions romantic. Writers were meant to suffer. In an age of electric light bulbs and jet printers, suffering was hard to come by.

For years, no one suspected my hideout, and even when my mother did find out, she didn't tell me. Without ever speaking directly of the matter, we came in time to the quiet understanding that no one was to go into the attic without my permission. If she and Brian thought my behavior strange, they didn't say.

From my window I tracked our neighbor, Mr. Matlon, who came and went from his house in the early hours of the morning. I imagined he was a spy. Also, I imagined the red blinking light of the radio tower was actually a beacon to help invisible aliens direct their course as they flew in the skies, watching over us like guardian angels. I wrote short stories and poems and began work on a novel. I cut people from magazines to use as characters in my plots. The door to the attic was my wardrobe into Narnia, my portal into the strange dreams of Wonderland.

Now I sat down at the old desk, my knees bumping against the edge of the tabletop. It had always been too short for my long legs. The items on the desk were still carefully arranged in preparation for a night's hard work. Sheets of paper were stacked at my right. The pencils in the plastic Disneyland cup were sharpened, the pens capped. To my pleasure, the reading lamp clicked to life.

A family photograph sat on the left corner of the desk. We were on summer vacation in Austin, Texas, for one of Dad's business trips. Though he was only in his mid-thirties, his hair was turning white. In the photo he's standing beside Mom, who holds one-year-old Brian propped on her waist. I am between them, a spindly six-year-old in a flower-print jumper, hair a fringe of friz around my face, overbite smile proud. Dad has one hand around my mother's waist, the other resting protectively on my shoulder. It was this protective gesture that made the photograph one of my favorites; I liked the way he spread his broad arms to encompass all three of us. He left one year later.

My parents' separation had been abrupt and final: My father was home and then he was not. He stayed at a Motel 6 for a month, then moved into an old house in Cleveland. Brian and I spent every other weekend with him until my freshman year of high school, when he moved to Atlanta to live with his then-girlfriend, Linda. He appeared at holidays and at our high school graduations, his life tethered to ours by a thin bloodline.

As the years passed, I absorbed information about his life the way I took bad news about foreign countries: with a stirring of abstract sympathy but with no real concern. Linda got pregnant. They married; they bought a house; they divorced. Over the years he changed houses, jobs, and girlfriends with alarming frequency. Now he was living near the beach with a pharmacist named Penny, who rode a Harley and volunteered as an EMT for the county. She drove everywhere with a portable siren in the back seat of her jeep.

I popped the Austin picture from its frame and held it up to the lamp. It was one of the few photos of my father I'd managed to salvage. My mother was a revisionist. Under the guise of scrapbooking projects, she had systematically removed him from our family photo albums. By the time I realized what was happening, he had been erased from our documented family history.

Turning, I ran my fingers along the notebook bindings lined along the bookshelf. They came to rest on the smallest of the journals, a ratty notebook with its spiral spine undone and sharp at top and bottom. I had used an eraser to etch the title *Space Adventure* into the purple ink of the notebook cover.

Chapter One: The Wograt Invasion

Once, in the blackness of space, the human race was a people without a land. It had been taken from them by the Wograts.

Wograts are hideous, ugly, and stupid. They have pig noses that stick out of their hair and usually stand between 6 or 9 feet tall. Their ears are hardly notisable since they are covered in hair. Their little black eyes get very large and red when they're mad or in battle.

If you were ever to meet a Wograt and if you, let's say, shot off one of the two larger horns on it's head, you probably wouldn't live to see what the Wograt looked like without that horn. Wograts consider their horns their only pride and joy, exept for a capture or a prisoner. One Wograt named Barthogly-Nud, grew 3 horns. That's why he is now the main leader of the Wograts. Some people say that his brain turned into another horn, because Barthogly Nud is not only considered (by the Wograts) the greatest Wograt, but by humans is considered the dumbest.

All Wograts think that they should be in charge of everything and everyone. Although the only races that they control are like small fish or little animals.

The novel was written entirely in pencil. The graphite had begun to fade, the words blurring and softening the pages. I'd written to the very last page and then some, chapter four spilling over onto the cardboard backing of the notebook where I was forced to resort to pen. The novel ended where the cardboard ended. I couldn't have been more than nine.

I ran my hands affectionately over the manuscript, before setting the notebook aside and reaching for another. My penmanship had changed. I'd retrained the broad, fat loops of childhood stories into a self-conscious cursive scrawled in pen. Behind every pinched curl and carefully crafted sentence, the torment of being a freshman was raw on the page. In junior high, all my girlfriends traded dolls and dress-up clothes for bras and tampons. They took pride in their budding breasts and whispered complaints about their periods with martyrdom many women spend their adult lives exploiting. And the boys watched as they sunbathed, as their still narrow hips switched back and forth in hot pink bikinis, in silky sundresses.

I was just as admiring of their beauty. I grew up, rather than out. My padded bra vexed me almost as much as my gangly height. I despised the Time of the Month, as my mother hygienically called it. Hormones roared in my body like too much alcohol in the blood, clouding my judgment, and puberty coiled my hair into tight ringlets so thick my ponytails snapped hair twisties. I fell in love with a new boy every semester, but only ever adored them from a distance. I worked hard, with hopes of studying chemistry in college, but I had no talent for science.

Then toward the end of my sophomore year, our English teacher read one of my essays to the entire class, to my combined pleasure and mortification. I wasn't particularly bright in other classes, so people forgave my talent for English. Within a week, fellow students were calling me for help with their papers, and I was invited to write editorials for the school newspaper. Both improved my social standing. Senior year I was voted Best Personality. I wore the title like an invisible badge into my twenties, when life kept me too busy to worry about being myself and I began to take having a personality for granted.

A car door slammed outside. Grandma's car sat in the drive below. I clicked off the desk lamp so she wouldn't notice the light in the attic window. Before me, the last high school journal was open to an entry in which I had written:

Things to Do Before Thirty

See the Sistine Chapel

Have own apartment

Read all of Austen, Tolstoy, and Chekhov

Complete first novel

Skinny dip in ocean

Wear size 6 jeans

Publish (short story or novel, but preferably a novel)

Find decent and, if at all possible, tall man to marry . . .

"Find anything?" Mom's voice called.

"Hold on," I said. I slipped the family photo from Texas into the notebook to mark my place.

"Walk on the beams," Mom demanded at the sound of my footfalls. "I don't want you sending your foot through my ceiling!"

There was something unabashedly territorial in the way she'd taken lately to referring to everything in the house with the possessive singular ("My ceiling!" "My kitchen!"), as if my brother and I had been intruders our eighteen respective years living in the house. She had taken my room. The attic would be next.

"What on earth have you been doing?"

I peered down at my mother. "I got distracted. Which boxes did you say you put them in?"

She wrapped her sweater tighter around her body, shuddering at the onslaught of winter air. "They should be in the one marked *glasses*."

In the far corner I found three sealed boxes marked *kitchen-wares, Kitchen 2,* and *glasses.* The one marked *glasses* contained elementary school papers, popsicle-stick Jesus puppets from Vacation Bible School, and shoe boxes plastered with construction paper hearts for Valentine's Day card exchanges.

"Did you find them?" she called.

"It's all junk."

"What?"

I teetered back toward the hole in the floor. "The boxes are labeled wrong," I said. "I don't know how you're going to find anything."

"Did you look in kitchen-wares?"

"It's just bowls."

"What are you nuts doing?" Grandma's head appeared around the corner.

"Mom wants glass globes."

"For the wedding," Mom explained. "You know those flickery lights we saw on the Internet?"

"Oh, those were lovely."

"I don't think they're up here," I insisted.

"You sound terrible," Grandma said. "Pamela, tell her to get down from there before she comes through the ceiling."

To date I'd broken two windows, one vase, three glasses, and an antique chair at Grandma's. Justifiably, she had no faith in my sense of balance.

"You'd better get down," Mom said, exasperated. "I could have sworn they were up there."

I was slow coming down the attic ladder. Grandma floated her hands to the right and left of my body to spot me. Mom had disappeared.

"What's the matter with her?" I asked.

"She's nervous," Grandma said. She was wearing a bright purple and orange silk wraparound, a sort of sari-muumuu hybrid. Her earrings dangled flirtatiously over her shoulders. She winked. "Guess who's coming to dinner."

⁓

Mr. Moore arrived at six, bearing meticulously wrapped presents and what appeared to be a giant blue diaper bag. He was a little shorter than I remembered, a stout man with a bushy pompadour of gray-white hair. His face seemed naked without the old matching mustache.

"Amy." He nodded his head in greeting.

"Come on in," I said.

Mom was upstairs applying her lipstick for the third time since he'd called to say he was on his way. We stood in an uncomfortable silence until Brian came bounding up the stairs. "Richard!" he called. He'd been running on the basement treadmill and was naked from the waist up. His arm, more flesh than muscle, jostled as they shook hands. I wished he would put a shirt on.

"How's school?" Mr. Moore asked.

"I'm getting by, getting by," Brian said. He was panting. "One day at a time." He took what I now learned was an insulated Crockpot (hot cider spiced with cinnamon sticks, a recipe from Sandra Lee) and directed Mr. Moore to the living room, talking with him like an old college roommate who'd come to rehash the golden days.

"I didn't know you could make drinks in a Crockpot." I said it to be good-natured, but Grandma shot me a warning look.

"Oh, you can make all sorts of goodies in those things," she sang.

All through dinner, Mom chattered so incessantly Mr. Moore never got a word in edgewise. This seemed to suit him perfectly. He ate slowly, methodically working his way through his plate of food. This proved a difficult task, as Mom and Grandma alternately spooned a new heaping of mashed potatoes or beef or green beans onto his plate whenever its rose pattern became visible.

"Richard, we need your help," Mom said. The dinner dishes had been cleared. We worked slowly on our banana cream pie. "Amy has a boardee we're trying to talk her out of."

"Boarder, not boardee," I said.

"*Boarder*." Mom winked at Richard as if sharing a private joke with him. As if I weren't sitting directly opposite her. She rested her chin coquettishly on her hands. "Some man who knows her room-mate. You've simply got to help us talk her out of it."

He cleared his throat. Rumpled his napkin on the table. "Well, let's see. I don't know that I'd be much help with that."

"But we need a man's judgment!" Mom declared. "Look at us: three women with only Brian to serve as the voice of reason."

Mr. Moore took advantage of this segue to defer to Brian, who managed to change the subject via some stealthy route. Soon he was telling the story of an ill-fated accident in the dissection room that involved a scalpel and Mr. Body's testicle. Mr. Body was his cadaver. We'd heard the story before, but Mom and Grandma laughed riot-ously anyway, eager for Mr. Moore to find it funny.

The laughing set the conversation back on a harmless track. Mr. Moore only joined in when pressed. He was reserved to the point of timidity, polite and neat. He was, in every way, the direct opposite of my father.

When Mom stood to clear the dishes, Mr. Moore insisted on helping. The way she colored, you'd have thought he'd paid her the most extravagant compliment. As they walked to the kitchen, he placed his hand on the small of her back. The rest of the night I couldn't help thinking of this tender gesture.

6

Christmas Eve we drove together to Grandma's for the Karrow family Christmas. Mom's older brother, Lynn, and younger sister, Patty, were already there when we arrived, along with their children and in some cases their children's children. Now committed to join the madness, Marie was obliged to come. Mr. Moore was not and did not. He not only failed to be a Fundamentalist, he went so far as to be Catholic. While Grandma had accepted him, she suggested warming the family to him slowly. Grandma had always been faulted for her open-mindedness. *She* had liked Bill Clinton, thank you very much, and *she* did not think the New Ageism so vile. Really, meditation sounded very relaxing.

At dinner I was placed next to Aunt Patty, who spent the entire hour recounting to me her caloric intake for the previous day, meal by meal. She had been on a diet since the mid-nineties. She ate no more than 1,200 calories a day on weekdays, then ate whatever she wanted from five o'clock Friday to noon Sunday. On the Aunt Patty Diet, all holidays counted as Saturdays. A decade of this self-prescribed regimen had succeeded in making her the largest of the Karrow women.

"I'm happily satisfied," she said at the end of dinner, "but not bloated." She lifted her shirt to show me the elastic waistline of what appeared to be her oldest daughter's recently retired maternity jeans.

This conversation was topped only by Uncle Lynn's misconception that I was dating a college professor, as opposed to working as one.

"How's the professor doing?" he asked.

Assuming he meant me, I replied, "Getting by."

"You guys have any serious plans?"

"Plans?" I asked, bewildered. "With who?"

"This professor guy."

"I'm not seeing anyone, Uncle Lynn," I explained, thinking briefly and not without chagrin of Adam. "I'm just teaching at the university."

"Pamela!" he called.

"Lynn!" she said back. She was perched on the floor, playing with one of the babies. (It had not taken her long to find the nearest baby to hold.)

"I thought you said Amy was dating a college prof?"

Thankfully, she didn't mention my ex-boyfriend. "No, she *is* a professor, Lynn."

He crossed his arms and leaned back to consider me in this new light. "College professor, really? That's impressive."

"I'm adjunct slave labor, actually." I darted back to accommodate the two-year-old that had bounded into my lap.

"They take good care of you then? Dental? Vacations? The works?"

I smiled meagerly. "It pays the rent."

"Get down, Lynn," Uncle Lynn commanded, picking up his namesake from my lap.

He had promised to open a trust fund for the first grandchild to bear his name. My cousin, Lauren, never cared for the name Lynn, but she had always been opportunistic. She was planning on a big family; she had names to spare.

"That's Lynn?" I asked.

"I know. Seems like she was just born yesterday." He nodded at Lauren. "I wouldn't be surprised if they started working on numero quatro soon."

"They're not wasting any time."

"It hits you. You'll see. That biological clock is not some story. Won't be long before Brian and Marie start to make announcements."

I studied my brother. He was sporting a Reese's peanut butter cup shirt and snapping pictures of his own knee.

As the recipient of student loans that more than covered his rent three times over, Brian was the most extravagant gift giver of the night. He bought each of the little girls a new collector Barbie, bought me a new DVD player, and bought Mom her first cell phone.

She turned it in her hands, suspicious of its size. "It's so tiny!"

"I've started you on the same plan as Amy and I," Brian explained. "Now you can call us for free."

"For free?"

"Anytime, anywhere, and it won't cost you a cent."

When he said it like that, it didn't sound like such a good idea.

Brian explained, "You only have one hundred minutes to use between nine and five on weekdays, but *after* five you can call anyone you want for free anyway. Or on weekends."

"Oh, I see." Mom said, uncomprehending.

"Does that make sense?"

"Yes, of course."

"I thought with your converting the house line to business you could use another phone for personal use."

"But it's so tiny! Lynn, look at this. Can you believe how tiny it is?"

Uncle Lynn could not be impressed. He himself Facebooked.

⇌

Before leaving that night, I helped Grandma clean the kitchen.

90

She set me to work dividing the leftover cookies for everyone to take home. While I was busy lining a row of gingerbread men atop the peanut butter blossoms, she brought up what she perceived as the precarious state of Brian's virginity. A First Fundamentalist Sunday school teacher raised during the Depression by men who kept pornographic magazines under every other couch cushion, she was an unpredictable mixture of wholesome innocence and bawdy street smarts. Conversation with her was like shaking the Magic 8-Ball: You never knew what maxim would pop up.

"Do you know that Marie is staying over at his place a lot?" she said.

"I didn't know."

"Do you think he's all right?"

"I'm sure they're fine, Grandma. It's a half hour drive from her apartment to his, and there's a lot of ice and snow this time of year. And you know the sort of schedule they keep. He probably doesn't want her driving on bad roads when she's tired."

Grandma considered this. She didn't believe Marie slept on the couch any more than I did. "He's nearly twenty-five, the poor boy," she said. "Men can't help it. God made them the way they are. It's not like us women have to do anything. We could just walk into a room and they're ready to get it on."

I ripped a long sheet of aluminum foil across the silver razor teeth of the box rim. That Grandma forgave Brian's behavior in advance bothered me. Why was a man's impatience for sex biologically justified, while a woman's virtue was a matter of course? I had yet to hear the church forgive a woman's lust for being a mere matter of crossed wires and chemical misfires.

By the time we left the house I was exhausted from the imaginative strain of making conversation with my family. I crawled into the backseat of my mother's sedan and gratefully rested my forehead against the window.

"See you at New Year's! Love ya! Have a good night!" Mom

shouted out her car window, cheerfully waving to Aunt Patty and Uncle Lynn. She slammed the door. She said with steel in her voice: "Amy, you cannot have a stranger living in your apartment." She glared at me through the rearview mirror. "You call Zoë right now and you tell her that you want that man out of your house."

"Here we go," Brian sighed.

"It's not a problem, Mom."

She explained that Aunt Patty had told her how in Cleveland, just this year, a young girl had been kidnapped from her home and chained up to the back of a van to be used as a sex slave at every truck stop between Detroit and Louisville.

I didn't tell her Eli had a van. I reminded her, instead, that Eli was a long-standing friend of Zoë's and not a stranger.

"Blood runs thicker than wine," was her response.

"First of all, Mom, that's nowhere near the correct application of the phrase," Brian said. "And secondly, that's not even how the saying goes."

"What are you talking about," Mom protested, acting indignant. "Everyone says that."

"No one says what you just said. It doesn't mean anything."

"It does—it means you can't just trust anyone."

Brian laughed. "What does comparing blood to wine have to do with trust? What does that mean? Better a brother than a drunkard? It's like you're speaking another language."

"Isn't that the truth," Mom muttered. She either agreed she spoke another language or thought it was better to have a brother instead of a drunkard. It didn't matter; now she was being purposefully ridiculous and found her own act entertaining. I always took my mother's exasperation seriously, but Brian knew how to disengage in just that way that made her laugh. Watching him interact with Mom was like watching a skilled ballplayer fool his opponent with a head fake.

At home, I took inventory of my old bedroom now that Mom had cleaned. The walls were still pink but for irregular squares of white where the tape from posters had ripped away the surface layer of paint. A crate of Barbie dolls crowded the door. They were, suspiciously, naked. I picked up a Ken doll, considered his hairless, shining perfection. Disturbing that Ken came with underwear drawn directly onto his plastic body while Barbie went commando. Another of society's provisions for the male sex drive: permanent underwear, impenetrable, to keep Ken's desires in check.

I reached to place the crate of Barbies with the other dolls that crowded the uppermost ledge of my white bookshelf. The shelf beneath housed boxes brimming with the remaining clutter of my growing up. The one beneath that held two crates of novels. The juxtaposition of childhood play objects and my high school library struck me as emblematic. Dolls to novels: from one romp of imagination to another.

I pulled a heavy sweatshirt on over my pajamas and put on an extra pair of socks before lacing up my tennis shoes. With the flashlight I'd stolen from the kitchen junk drawer clenched between my teeth, I climbed the closet ladder back to the attic and my secret office.

By the watery light of the desk lamp I finished *Love in the Time of Massive Diarrhea*, systematically chewing the flavor out of the pack of cinnamon gum Mom had put in my Christmas stocking. It was late when I closed the last page. I set the book aside, massaged my jaw. Across the way I could see the neighbor's television playing in the otherwise dark living room. The commercials flashed on the TV screen, the Christmas lights on the tree beside it chasing one another around the four walls. Together they cast a spinning kaleidoscope of color on the snow where a plastic Rudolph and plastic Santa worshiped a plastic Jesus. Mr. Matlon had passed away while I was in college. I resented the current owners for the garish display they had made of the old man's house, a reminder that life went on without me in places that I'd once felt I owned.

Without any real purpose, I reread the *Things to Do Before Thirty* list. My progress had not been good. I had read all of Austen's novels, but found it unsettling that I'd assigned her name to a list as if she was or could ever have been a chore. No, had not yet skinny-dipped in the ocean. Yes, had kept my own apartment, which had been nice while it lasted, but I was too broke to live alone, much less tour Rome. I didn't care to take further stock of the remaining ambitions.

Why the urgency to achieve my life's goals before thirty anyway?

And why was marriage at the end, as if globe-trotting served only as prelude to romance?

My mother had always instructed me to live life before settling down, settling down requiring a seismic shift in one's energy, from adventure to nurture. The fault in her admonition was the assumption that meeting a man marked the end of the journey. I grew up thinking the single life was the rising action and marriage the climax. Every writer knows climax is followed by dénouement: in other words, it's all downhill after the wedding

Maybe I would never marry or have children. For the very first time, this future struck me as entirely plausible, if not inevitable. Many women lived alone. I was no more entitled to marriage than the next person. Maybe I belonged to the world of the celibate saint, granted a life of solitude and free to explore the inner world of my imagination while inspiring young minds to greater intellectual and spiritual heights in introductory composition. I thought of my students and was overcome with a feeling of affection. It was very easy to like them when they were miles away.

Yes. To serve the students was my mission, and writing my love.

I thought vaguely of Adam, but didn't dwell on him. He was like any other of my endless infatuations: the product of too much romanticism stirred by restlessness and indulged to remedy boredom. So much for real men. Men in books were so much more fun.

I picked up a pen; I began to write.

part 2

7

"What *are* you doing?" Zoë asked.

I had wedged myself behind my bedroom dresser and was attempting to unscrew the television cable cord.

"I've made a New Year's resolution," I said. "No more television."

"None?"

"None."

"Never?"

"Never."

I stood triumphant, the dismembered cable in my hand.

Zoë gave me a disbelieving frown. "What will you do with yourself?"

I lifted the television from its stand and toddled toward the hall closet. "Stop wasting my life," I managed.

"You're really getting rid of it."

"Yes, Zoë. I'm serious."

"Then can I have it?"

"I thought you didn't watch TV."

"I like watching the news," she said defensively.

We swiped a spot clear on her desk and set the television on top.

"Turn it to the right." She bounded to her bed. Sitting cross-legged, she made a window frame of her forefingers and thumbs. She squinted an eye at the screen. "Perfectamundo. Thank you, dear."

"Enjoy."

I spent my first week back in Copenhagen dedicating the hours typically spent on television to writing. I'd hoped for a short story and instead found myself experimenting with the relativity of time. Thirty minutes in front of *Friends* is no time at all. Thirty minutes in front of a blank laptop screen lasts approximately four hours and six minutes.

Zoë was enthralled by my new diligence. If she found me writing, she wrote too. Though we both had laptops and were mobile, we remained in our separate rooms for some semblance of privacy. Through her open door I could hear her typing, which meant she could hear that I was not.

I resorted to copying out old stories from my *Great American Short Stories* collection. An author once told me she copied one of Chekhov's stories every morning so she could feel what it was like to write the story of a master.

Zoë came to check on me around ten. "How's it going?" she asked.

"Fine." I smiled.

"I brought cookies. A midnight snack."

The "cookies" were made with honey, whole grain, and raisins. Dense as stones, both before and after digestion.

"Thanks."

The next night was the same, and every night that week. I typed, she typed, and at some point she came into my room uninvited to check up on my progress.

How was it going?

Did I want something to eat?

Did I need something to drink?

Fine, no, no.

Friday night she appeared with a printed manuscript. "Can I read you what I have?" She proceeded to read without waiting for a reply.

"It's good," I said when she finished half an hour later.

"That's all? It's good? I mean, is the dialogue real? Does the premise seem too outlandish? I feel like Mrs. Sander's motivation is unrealistic."

I chewed the end of my pencil. "No. It's working."

She twirled her hair around her finger and leaned her head back to peer up at me, still sitting on the floor. Today her nails were lacquered in shiny polish the color of orange soda. On her forefinger she wore a plastic ring mottled with glitter and large as a bottle cap. "What did you write?"

I snapped my laptop closed. "Nothing."

"Let me see."

"No—please—Zoë, it's not very good."

She took the computer from me and read: " 'The hills across the valley of the Ebo were long and white. On this side there was no shade and no trees and the station was between two lines of rails in the sun. Close against the side of the station there was the warm shadow of the building and a curtain, made of strings of bamboo beads.' Well. It's good. But the syntax is repetitive—all the unnecessary expletives are distracting—'there was' and 'there were'—all over the page."

"Good. It's Hemingway." I held up the *Great American Short Stories* I'd concealed beneath my leg.

"Oh. Well, he was a pig anyway." She got up to sit in my lap. "Maybe it's not a writing day today."

"I thought you said there's no such thing as writer's block."

"You're beginning to make me a believer."

Zoë prescribed somatic antidotes for my writer's block. She suggested I eat more protein and less empty carbs: The brain functioned on sugar and needed steady fuel to keep it running. She recommended vigorous exercise.

"I don't need exercise," I protested. "I need inspiration."

"Once you get the blood flowing, you can hardly tell the difference between the two."

I doubted working out would benefit my writing. I wasn't opposed to the good it might do my post-Christmas waistline. Though I'd long ago resigned myself to the fact that I would never be Michelle Pfeiffer, it wasn't too late to avoid becoming Aunt Patty.

Copenhagen's student recreational center stayed open eighteen hours a day, seven days a week, and most holidays, meaning even when you couldn't find an open library you could find an open treadmill. The three-story multimillion-dollar complex was the newest addition to campus; the year it was finished, student enrollment spiked ten percent.

The cardiovascular machines lined the perimeter of the weight room. Each faced either a mirror or a window. The mirrors were warped at the center, strategically, I assumed, just enough to exaggerate whatever part of your body you felt most sensitive about, assuring you it really was as grotesquely disproportionate as you'd feared and thereby securing your patronage to the gym forever. The walls that did not have mirrors were lined with windows; where you could not see yourself and judge, you could rely on everyone walking by the sidewalk outside for a verdict.

When I got to the gym Monday, the sunrise was a line of pink spilling upward. I'd hoped by arriving early I'd avoid seeing anyone I knew, particularly my students, who did not get out of bed before ten if they could help it, but I wasn't even there for half an hour before Michael sidled up to my machine. He held either end of a towel draped around his neck in his clasped fists. Zoë must have ratted me out.

"Look at you!" he said in the tone parents use to celebrate their baby's first steps. "Working out. I don't think I've ever seen you here before."

"Thanks for reminding me."

"You shouldn't be self-conscious. Lots of people have a hard time making room for exercise in their schedules."

The StairMaster shifted to a more difficult level. I tightened my grip on the handles. I was sweating profusely. "Are you working today?"

He shook his head. "I've got Mondays off. Just came to pump some iron. I am teaching cycling starting next week, though." He nudged my arm with his elbow. "You should come. I'll get you half price."

"I'll think about it," I lied.

He gestured to the book I'd propped up on the machine's screen. "You know the worst thing you can do is to get focused on something other than your workout. I've trained girls who only spend half the energy exercising when they bring notes to study."

"A shame to exercise the mind and not the body," I said.

Whenever I said something Michael didn't understand, he just pretended I hadn't said anything. "Well. Better get to it. Call me about that class." I said I would, and he left me with a muscular, cheerful "Keep up the good work."

I shared the locker room with two willowy angels, women whose bodies were flawless and underdeveloped as children's. I splashed water on my cheeks, my complexion an animated illustration of continental drift theory: a pangea of red on my cheeks and forehead breaking apart into floating splotches. The room was lined with adjoining stalls, each partitioned into two sections, one for showering, one for dressing. Dorm life all over again. I left my folded towel and underwear carefully tucked into the far corner of the dressing stall shelf. When I emerged from the shower ten minutes later, both had fallen on the floor and were drenched through. I waited, naked, until the other women had vacated the bathroom before running to the hand dryer and standing beneath it.

I reached the English office forty-five minutes later. My hair crackled toward the roof in a cumulus cloud of static and frizz. I half ran down the hallway to the copy room but was stopped by a folding table set up to block the entrance. Lonnie sat at the table, order forms lined in neat rows along its edge.

"Lonnie!" I said. "What is this?"

"Hey, Ms. Gallagher." He hazarded a glance at me. "Did you get a chance to read *Flaming Arrow*? I left it in your mailbox."

"I haven't, actually, but I'll be sure to check my mailbox tonight. Right now I really need to get into the copy room."

"I think you'll like it," he said. "I struggled with whether to give you the books chronologically as they were published or chronologically according to the story. It's very *Star Wars* like that."

"Lonnie, I'd love to talk, but I really, really need to make some copies."

He raised his eyebrows. "Did you want to place an order?" He pulled a work order sheet from the stack of paper at his left. "Name?"

"You know my name."

Despite my protest, he sat waiting, pen poised over the paper.

"Amy Gallagher," I said. "G-A-L-L-A-G-H-E-R." I set my bag down on the floor. "I could just fill the form out myself."

"Code?"

"*Lonnie*."

"I need your code, Ms. Gallagher. Mr. Benson's orders." He tapped his pen against the notice on the wall.

Effective January 8th
COPY ROOM PRIVILEGES SUSPENDED
Teachers: this means you!!
ALL ORDERS MUST GO THROUGH A STU-
DENT WORKER OR THROUGH ME
NO EXCEPTIONS, EXEMPTIONS, OR
EXCUSES
Please include NAME, CODE, and DATE NEEDED
on ALL forms
~Neil Demetrius Benson, Second Secretary to the Chair
and Copy Room Manager

"Is he serious?" I asked.

Lonnie was waiting again, pen ready. He glanced nervously at the line forming behind me. It was the first day of class. The copy room would be backlogged with work requests in half an hour. "Code 2468," I sighed.

"Date needed?"

"Now."

Lonnie checked his watch. He marked the box for Morning.

"Number of copies?"

"Fifty of the first, twenty-five of the second. Front and back for both, stapled—"

"You're making two orders?" he interrupted.

"I have a different syllabus for Creative Writing than for ENG 102," I explained. "Can't I just place one order?"

"I'm sorry, Ms. Gallagher, but we need separate work orders for every document being reproduced." He pulled a second work order sheet. "Code?" he asked.

I left the copy room in a fury. Turning the corner, I ran directly into Adam's chest. His eyes scanned my body up and down, catching a moment at my breasts. He grinned. "In a hurry?"

"You're in my way." I hustled around him quickly. I didn't want to waste time noticing how handsome he looked in a new blazer and starched white shirt.

"Mr. Benson is going to have a riot on his hands," I said to Everett when I finally reached my office.

He was sitting at his computer, a stack of freshly printed syllabi on the desk.

"How did you get those?" I asked.

"Kinko's."

"Kinko's. You know," I said, "I have this theory that you're secretly rich."

He stood and reached behind me for his coat. "Is that why you're my friend?"

"You should take me out more often. For real food. Not just to graze open house buffets. What? Why are you looking at me like that?"

"Amy," he said slowly, his eyes on my chest. "This will sound utterly ridiculous, but I do believe you're lactating."

I looked down. The blue polka dots of my bra were floating hazily beneath two wet splotches, left and right on my cotton blouse.

⁋

The rest of the week was no improvement. I typed seventy-nine pages of *Great American Short Stories* and moved on to *Wuthering Heights* for variety's sake. Inspiration did not come. In the meantime, Zoë had finished one short story and outlined an idea for a second *UrbanStyle* proposal. She planned to analyze makeup as a means by which a woman hid her true essence: "How much does concealer conceal?"

"You wear makeup," I pointed out. By this, I meant the characteristic blue eyeliner and pink Mary Kate and Ashley lip balm she donned for work at The Brewery.

"I wear it to draw attention to the fact that I'm wearing it, which defeats the purpose," she explained. "I wear it ironically."

I needed photocopies for Wednesday and Friday, which put me

in constant contact with Lonnie, who insisted on delivering the work orders to my office instead of placing them in my mailbox as was protocol. When I wasn't avoiding Lonnie, I was hiding from the dreaded Ex. Adam had been assigned a Monday, Wednesday, Friday class that met on the first floor just when my ENG 102 ended. After class I wiped the board down slowly, waiting to hear the sound of his morning monologue through the wall adjoining our classrooms before leaving.

Despite my better judgment, I was tempted to go to Adam for help, particularly when I started having disciplinary problems with a student. The entire first week of class, Ashley Mulligan shuffled into my creative writing class late, tiptoeing to the back of the room to hide behind the enormous linebacker who sat in the second to last row. The second week she missed all but the last fifteen minutes of our first workshop. She was unnaturally thin, a stylish girl whose designer jeans hung loose on her hips. She brought a diet Voltage energy drink and a Fiji water bottle with her to class, sipping them daintily and in turn, as if they were delicacies. Despite the ginseng and caffeine, she fought to stay alert. I was certain I had an anorexic.

When she earned her fourth tardy, I decided to speak with her. To my surprise, she took the initiative.

"Could I talk to you a second?" she asked.

"Of course."

She hugged her books to her chest. Her ponytail was askew in that way that looked messy but had become fashionable. Blue rings lined her eyes.

"I'm really sorry I'm late," she began.

"I'm afraid I can't count you present for coming half an hour late to a class," I replied.

"I know."

"Three tardies is an absence—and too many absences could really hurt your class standing."

"I really am sorry, Ms. Gallagher. I promise I'll do better. I just came up because I thought I should explain . . ." She lowered her eyes. "My little sister died four months ago. I know it's been a long time and I should, like, be getting on with it, but sometimes I just have trouble getting out of bed. I just thought you should know."

I was thrown off guard. "I'm sorry," was all I could think to say.

Numb to this response, annoyed by it, Ashley shook her head. "No, it's okay. It's not a big deal or anything. I mean it is, but it shouldn't affect my studies." She pulled at a hot pink hair twisty looped around her tiny wrist. It snapped back against her skin. "It's hard to stay motivated sometimes. I wanted you to know it's not because I'm not interested in the class—I am, honestly, I just might miss sometimes for . . . unrelated reasons."

"Thank you for telling me." I thought a moment. "Why don't we consider your absences excused in advance? If you can e-mail me the days you can't come, I can write back a description of what you missed, be sure you get the right assignments."

"I don't want special treatment."

Before she left, I promised I would remember our conversation and that I would be happy to talk with her if she ever needed a listening ear. She was as uninterested in my listening ear as she was in my special consideration.

Though the rest of the day went on in its usual blur of lesson plans and student e-mails, I couldn't stop thinking of Ashley. I regretted how hastily I'd found refuge in a label. Knowing that she had just buried a sister, I saw every detail of her appearance differently. The rings beneath her eyes were evidence of sleeplessness and weeping, not hunger. She wrapped her arms around her body for comfort, not warmth.

⌒

That afternoon Mom called to report two deaths at Kent State.

"It was a fire. Caught while they were sleeping, all of them in their beds completely nonsuspecting. There were ten people in the house total—they all got out but those two. Died of smoke, we can only hope."

"That's awful."

"The girl was in the *boy's* bed," Mom explained. "They weren't even dating, just together for that one night. I'll tell you what, that girl didn't know what she was in for: You give a boy an inch he'll take a foot, that's what your grandmother always told me. But then it doesn't seem like people much care about that kind of thing anymore. When *I* was growing up you didn't sit on a boy's bed without sending the wrong signal. Now nobody seems to care. Everybody's about this booty call, is that what your students are calling it?"

"More or less," I said, switching my phone to my left ear and hiking the strap of my heavy bag higher on my shoulder.

"It just goes to show you."

"Show you what?"

"So how's Eli?" she asked brightly.

"He's fine."

"He's at the apartment?" Her voice strained with the effort of sounding nonchalant.

"He's at work," I said vaguely, careful to imply this was not a new development. Monday he'd had a phone interview with Zoë's boss that lasted all of three minutes. He was hired to work at The Brewery on the spot. I had every suspicion this was Zoë's doing; the coffee shop was a popular place to work and had been turning down applications for weeks.

"Is he helping with the chores?" she asked, unimpressed and undeterred. "If you're going to have a man in the house you might as well make him useful. Have you changed the batteries in your smoke detector?"

"Our landlord takes a look through our place every year," I said. "I'm sure we're fine."

"You really ought to check them anyway. Those batteries can die."

"Mom, I'm sure we'd know if they died."

"I'm just saying. You go check them, and if they're not working, I'll buy the replacements."

"They don't need to be replaced," I said, slowly counting my breath with each word.

She punctuated the ensuing silence with a sigh. "With this wedding and with Brian leaving us, I just don't need more worry."

I promised I would check the smoke detector and hung up.

∽

I told Zoë about the situation with Ashley. "One of my student's sisters died."

"Really?"

She didn't look away from the television. We were in her bed watching a PBS special on killer whales. Since declaring my sabbatical from television, I only watched when she watched and she only watched what qualified as educational. Michael was at her desk, bidding on eBay and chewing a Bic pen cap. He was hoping to win a new Hydr8r Ultralight Hydration Water Bladder.

"She didn't say how, just that it was recent and that she thought I should know in case she didn't make it to class sometimes."

When Zoë failed to respond, I said, "It's hard for me to wrap my mind around. I don't give these kids enough credit. I get sucked into this stereotype that they're spoiled middle-class grade-grubbers, not even thinking what they might have been through in their lives. Hey—are you listening?"

"I'm listening."

"Well." I stared at her profile. The blue then white then yellow light from the television flashed on her cheek. "What do you think I should do?"

"What can you do?" she murmured.

I pinched her arm. "Zoë to the land of the living."

"What?" she scowled. "It happens, Amy. People die. Her sister will always be gone, and there's nothing you can do about it."

Michael and I shared a look. While Zoë was generous with her things, she was less generous with her sympathy. The years Zoë's mother had spent in and out of the hospital had done more damage than good to her capacity for compassion where illness and death were concerned. When confronted with someone in pain, there was always an unspoken competition: had said person suffered more or less than her own family?

Silently, we watched the whale masticate its prey, the blood blossoming beneath the water in a pale pink cloud.

To dispel the tension, Michael asked me, "Did you go to the gym this morning?"

"I went."

He winked. "Atta girl."

Atta girl. Michael's verbal equivalent of a firm slap to the butt.

Zoë squeezed my thigh. "Feel the burn?"

I lifted my leg, considering it as though it were a separate creature from my body. "Nothing yet."

"What have you been doing?"

"The recliner bike thing."

"The recumbent," she corrected.

"Sounds political. The machine you can't vote out. "

I was glad to have a name for the thing I despised. It felt perfectly asinine to sit in a chair pedaling ninety miles an hour and going nowhere. Too much like a bad analogy for my life.

"I'm trying to get her to take one of my classes," Michael said.

"You *should* take a class," Zoë said. "It's more rigorous than just working out by yourself."

"I don't think I'm up for that."

"I'll take one with you," she said. "It will be fun. Kind of a roommate bonding thing."

"What do you think we're doing here?" It was rather intimate, the way we'd squashed our bodies into her tiny twin bed.

"Being lazy," she countered.

Combined, Zoë and Michael's zeal for physical fitness was nothing short of evangelistic. Though they never succeeded in drafting me for group fitness, I finally agreed to train for the spring 5K they were both running for breast cancer research. I could hardly turn down the chance to support Zoë's mother in some small way. And running seemed the one exercise suited for the writer's life, the solitude, the pain. (Wo)Man vs. Nature. It always seemed spiritually invigorating on the Gatorade commercials.

⌒

Saturday afternoon, Eli found me stretching in the kitchen. He poured a cup of coffee and eyed me curiously over the rim as he drank.

"Joining the madness?"

"Don't discourage her," Zoë said. "You really aren't going to want that." She tugged on the scarf I'd wrapped twice around my neck. This was in addition to the turtleneck and the Ohio State hoodie I was wearing over my brother's old Buckeyes T-shirt.

"It's negative ten degrees," I said. "It's freezing."

"I'm telling you," she warned, "five minutes and you'll be burning up. You don't want to sweat too much anyway."

"That's easy for you to say, you're insulated."

She wore form-fitting Spandex black pants and a green windbreaker specifically designed for runners. I was the Orphan Annie to her Nike Goddess.

I turned to Eli. I held out my arms. "Do you think I'm overdressed?"

Even when invited to look at my body (however padded and overdressed), he kept his eyes fixed on mine. In a moment of clarity, I realized this marked a defining difference between men like Michael and men like Eli.

"I'll be on the couch," he said. "Come join me when you give up."

Outside, Michael and Zoë were arguing about whether to take me for an interval walk/run or whether to just start out at a slow pace. She wanted to start me off slowly. He wanted to just see me run. They bickered until she gave up and went off on her own, leaving me alone with Rocky. We jogged out of the neighborhood and alongside University Way. Immediately I wished Zoë had won the argument. Michael slowed his steps to a leisurely pace, but I struggled to keep up.

"Don't hold your breath," he said. "Breathe consistently: in, out. In, out."

I nodded. It was difficult to hear him over the roar of blood in my ears. Zoë had been right about the layers. Though I could feel the cold wind numbing my nose and chafing my cheeks, I was sweating profusely. Beside me, Michael's body moved with the seeming effortless grace of a trained athlete. His arms swiveled easy and loose at his sides. His feet padded buoyant on the sidewalk, the rubber soles of his shoes bounding off the cement. Somewhere to my left he spoke with the maddening calm of a husband coaching his wife through labor. "That's good. In, out. In, out. Watch your step. You're doing great!"

At the edge of campus I stopped and bent over, resting my hands on my knees. "I don't think . . . I should overdo it . . . the first . . . time."

"Walk it off," he said. "Head back to the apartment on Collins Street. I'll do a loop through campus and catch up with you."

I nodded in agreement.

It took two blocks for my breathing to slow and my legs to unwind. Once Michael was out of sight, my power walk slowed to an amble. Campus was quiet. Occasionally, a student passed on the sidewalk or drove by talking (or, more alarmingly, texting) on a cell phone. I imagined students bunkered in their dorm rooms, sleeping off the previous night's party or cramming anxiously for an early Monday exam. I heard girls' laughter behind the bathroom doors and could smell the pungent funk of the men's hall: dirty socks, sweating bodies, and the miasma of trapped hormones.

Somewhere in that crowd, Ashley was trying to pioneer her own life. She had hours and days to spend; I wondered if the absence of a loved one left any capacity for the normal. When she'd said her little sister died I'd pictured a child, a miniature version of Ashley with pigtails and baby cheeks. But I still called Brian my little brother, and he was twenty-five.

I made it back to the apartment without seeing Michael again. Eli met me at the door with my ringing cell phone.

"Third call you've missed," he said.

"Mom."

"Hey, honey," she chirped. "Just calling to ask if you returned that sweater yet."

"I haven't had time."

"Don't keep it just because I bought it for you. I don't like it when people keep things they don't like to be nice, you know that."

I kicked off my shoes. "Honestly, I just haven't had a chance to return it."

"I put the receipts in the boxes before you left, so make sure you don't lose them." Her voice tapered off. I thought I heard Richard in the background. "Amy—are you still there?"

"Ye-es."

"Did you check those batteries yet?"

"No."

"You girls live on the second floor. Smoke rises, you know."

When I hung up I could hear Eli in Zoë's room one wall away, talking to Jillian. She was the only person he talked to on the phone for more than five minutes. Sometimes he emerged from these conversations cheerful. Other times they put him in a black mood that didn't lift for hours. From the low, frustrated murmur of his tone I predicted tonight would not be a good night.

I showered, dressed, began dinner. The three of us ate separately. I took a book to bed, in need of distraction.

⁀

In the middle of the night I woke with a start, the book *Empire Falls* flat on my face. I was sweating as if I had just come inside from a long run. There had been fire, someone screaming—had it been my brother?—but the details of the nightmare had vanished upon waking. I stared at the ceiling, palms flat against the mattress, feeling my heart pound.

When I'd calmed down I got up from bed and crept into the living room. The minute hand on the bookshelf clock clicked its way around the hour. Eli lay on the couch, still dressed, his arms curiously folded over his chest as if disapproving of something in his sleep. The apartment was blue with moonlight. The curtains threw shadowy patterns intricate as doily cloths on the cold hardwood floor.

I dragged a dining room chair to the hall, climbed on top, and pressed the red button on the smoke detector.

A high-pitched ring pierced the silence. I released my finger, but the alarm did not stop. As I scrambled to remove the battery from the machine, Eli ran to my side. He pulled me down off the chair, climbed up in my place and expertly popped the battery out of its plastic cradle. The siren stopped. Zoë had stumbled from her room, stark terror on her face. Seeing me, her fear turned to exasperation.

"Well that was exciting," Eli said. He set the batteries in my hand.

"Just take the steak knife to my heart the next time you want to kill me," Zoë said. "It would be less traumatizing."

Despite her irritation, relief washed over me, as if the cry of the alarm had frightened away any possibility of danger.

8

Once we'd all grown accustomed to the idea that Eli's stay was temporarily permanent, he wasted no time getting famous.

Leaving the coffee shop with Zoë and Eli one afternoon, we were stopped by a middle-aged woman in a full-body sweat suit who let Zoë pet her new puppy while she asked Eli what to name him. "You're so good with that kind of thing," the woman gushed.

Without pause he said, "Name him Fargo."

"Who was that?" Zoë asked when the woman had safely power-walked out of earshot.

He stroked the growing beard that now covered his chin. Whether it was purposeful or the result of neglect was anybody's guess. "I have no idea," he said.

People began showing up at our apartment asking for him. Several were Jillian's friends, who knew Eli from his previous job at Juxtapose. There was Diedre with dreadlocks the exact frayed blond of old ropes softened by use; she had somehow talked Eli into helping her collate two hundred handmade chapbooks she planned to scatter across the country. For a week they lay scattered across our living room. Amber and Lynn, Jillian's housemates, liked to sit with him on the roof, chain-smoking and gossiping, even though Eli declined to participate in either activity. Kevin McCormick was the most frequent guest. He was a graduate student working on his MFA in sculpture, a painfully shy man who began every conversation with a comment about the weather. He and Eli spent whole days scavenging at junkyards and welding found objects. Because he was helping Kevin, because he worked after course hours, and because he was so amiable, no one bothered to ask Eli whether or not he had jurisdiction to use or even be in the campus studios. He returned to our apartment late at night, carrying freshly fired ceramic pieces and newly printed lithographs in ink-splattered hands.

He had a creative energy that would have been medicated with Ritalin in someone half his age. His hand trembled when he drew, from excitement or from caffeine. He drew on his jeans or his hands if he couldn't find paper. He didn't eat at home if he could find someone who would go out, and just about anyone would do: He handed out his friendship indiscriminately.

The Volkswagen was partly to blame for his notoriety. The van looked innocent and playful crowded between the bullying SUVs the students favored that year, a clown car infiltrating military camp. It bounced through Copenhagen's narrow old streets like Mr. Rogers' cheerful trolley. People honked and waved.

His new and many friendships, however, were a direct result of his job at the coffee shop. He hosted poetry night, introducing each artist with one-minute bios he'd drafted from brief interviews conducted beforehand. The menu marker board featured quirky Morretti illustrations. Because Jimmy, The Brewery's owner, had created Eli's position, assigning him to shifts that did not need a third barista, Eli was essentially paid to sit at The Brewery six hours a day hopped up on espresso and practicing Foam Art: the delicate making of patterns in people's lattes. He could make a branch of delicate leaves, a wobbly star, and—most endearing with the women—a floating heart.

~

The first thing Eli did when he got his paycheck was offer to pay his share of February's rent. He stocked the kitchen with things frozen and dyed, novelties our fridge hadn't seen since Zoë's dietary takeover: Tombstone pepperoni pizzas, salami, banana freezer pops. Because he was a guest, she didn't protest.

Eli was mindful of our space and of our habits. If friends came over, he asked our permission before herding them all out to sit on the roof. Once outside, if he found out Zoë and I were writing, he stopped his friends' intermittent guitar strumming or hushed their near hysterical tirades against the war. He didn't mind that I blessed my food before eating it, and bowed his head in respect if not accompaniment. (Zoë had never participated.)

Though he had no interest in seeing the sanctuary of Copenhagen Baptist, he gladly came with us for one of our first of the month Saturday grocery giveaways. We drove together in his van to the edge of town to deliver turkeys and children's coats to families who couldn't afford either. I enjoyed seeing the children, but always felt awkward around the parents. Eli talked to them as if he were visiting his own family. He got into a discussion of baseball with Mr. Jones that went on so long we had to leave him behind to get to two other homes. He prayed for five minutes straight with Lawrence Kennedy, the resident alcoholic. And Bertie Lewis adored him. Bertie was a widowed black woman who weighed all of eighty pounds, had been on an oxygen tank for as long as I'd known her, and called me Honey. On seeing Eli with his long hair and beard, she grinned and announced it was like having Jesus come hisself to deliver her milk.

As we were leaving she clasped my hand in hers. Her palms felt dry and fragile as autumn leaves. "You hold on to that one now," she said. "That's one of the good Lord's better creations. Don't you let him outta your sight."

Instead, I took to avoiding Eli altogether because I couldn't talk to him without betraying the fact that I found him incredibly attractive.

⁓

Zoë was upset. She wanted to know why I didn't like Eli.

"Who says I don't like him?"

"No one says. It's obvious to anyone who's in the room when the two of you are forced to share it. You do everything in your power to avoid him." She reached into the last of the remaining grocery bags and stacked the leftovers on the shelf with the twenty other cans of peas and kidney beans. "When I asked him what was up, he said he didn't know how to talk to you; he said you're a nervous person."

"I like him fine," I insisted. "I treat him just like I treat you."

"No, you treat him like an infestation. He's our guest." She slapped the empty bag against her knee to deflate it. "It wouldn't kill you to treat him like one."

"He's not our guest, he's *your* guest. And I've never treated him any different than I treat you."

I rotated the cans she'd just put away so their labels faced outward.

"He said I was *nervous*?" I asked. "That's a terrible thing to say about a person. Do you think I'm nervous?"

Zoë watched me situate the last can so the Green Giant on the carrots stood identical to the Green Giant on the corn. She answered carefully. "I don't think you're a *calm* person."

"Eli doesn't even know me."

"Right." She shrugged, already resigned to the fact that he and I would never get along. "So why should you care."

"Sometimes I worry that people think I worry about what people think of me."

She'd looked at me plaintively before rolling her eyes and leaving the pantry.

The next night she had to work the closing Sunday shift, leaving

Eli and me home alone. I carried my stack of textbooks into the living room. He was sitting on the couch with his legs crossed the way women do, a posture that highlighted the length of his body to admirable effect. His reading glasses were wrong for his face, too square and thin-rimmed and out of decade.

"Mind if I work in here with you?"

"Sure." He got up to flick on the second lamp. He returned to his magazine, the first of a stack of sloppily piled *Art in America* magazines. He flipped through each quickly. He was looking at the pictures.

"Anything interesting?" I asked.

"Some," he murmured.

I made a few more gentle attempts at conversation. He met each with a succinct reply. I finally gave up. I worked; he read pictures. Had a stranger walked in the room, she might have found the situation companionable, but I felt acutely aware of his silent rebuttal.

Around eleven he tossed the last magazine aside and wandered into the kitchen. The fridge door open, shut. He returned to the living room empty-handed.

"Are you at all hungry?" he asked.

I hesitated. It was late, a school night, and all I really wanted was to sleep.

"I could eat," I said.

꩜

We took his van, driving slow over the mounds of accumulating drifts, fat flakes of snow getting mashed in the windshield wipers. I suggested Bailey's Bistro or the Chinese restaurant, but both were closed.

"The Lucky Tavern?" he asked.

"Sounds good to me," I replied as enthusiastically as I could manage.

There were more bars than restaurants on the downtown strip. I hadn't been in a single one since the last time my graduate workshop had met to celebrate Valerie's thesis defense. I counted The Lucky Tavern among my least favorites. It was the hot spot for upperclassmen jocks who came in droves to watch The Big Game. It was crowded and dark and perpetually damp. Everything came with grease: fried pickles, oily onion rings, and soggy menus.

While the waitress led us to a booth, Eli eyed me skeptically over his shoulder, as if his first glance around the room had been enough to tell him how little such a place could possibly have to offer and how unlikely it was that a person like me would actually prefer it. His skepticism rallied what little school spirit I had. I resolved to have a wonderful time. I resolved Eli would have a wonderful time.

"All burgers are good here and the curly fries are superior to the French fries," I said as he reached for his menu. "But I wouldn't recommend the veggie burger. It's a patty of beans squashed between toast. The taste is bad and the texture is even worse."

"Anything burger, no veggie," he echoed.

I considered the menu without any real interest. I couldn't think of what Eli and I could possibly talk about for an hour and a half. And there was the problem of what to drink. I never touched beer, but it seemed wrong somehow to order wine in The Lucky Tavern.

When the waitress returned, I ordered the cheeseburger and a Guinness. Eli ordered a grilled cheese sandwich and a Coke.

"You don't drink?" I asked.

"I don't." He pulled a Sharpie marker from his back pocket and began drawing on his napkin. "So I hear you typing away all the time. What are you working on?"

"I have a few stories I'm revising." This was an exaggeration. Aside from my slavish transcription of every classic on my shelf, I'd been retouching one story—the one I'd been farming out to rejections since last summer. This mostly involved swapping limp words for synonyms and reshuffling commas. Since graduate school I'd lost the faith and enthusiasm that serious revision required. "I haven't been making much progress," I admitted.

"That's all right," he said. "As long as you're working."

"Teaching's the real work."

He glanced up from his drawing. "I've tried to imagine you as a teacher. I can't see it."

I tried not to feel offended by his remark. "Why not?"

He thought before he spoke. "Maybe I just never had a good English teacher."

"Maybe you were a lousy student."

"Unfortunately, that's a distinct possibility."

The waitress returned with a pint of beer as black as coffee. The glass was enormous—I'd meant to order a bottle.

"How long have you been at it? The teaching," he clarified.

"Two years? I lose track. It feels like so much longer . . . I think people who teach age in dog years."

I was surprised to hear him laugh.

"Sometimes in the middle of class I'll suddenly realize where I am and what I'm doing," I said. "It's like I'm waking up in the middle of someone else's life."

He tried to return to the subject of writing, but I told him I didn't like talking about my stories.

"Why not?"

"It's a little self-absorbed, don't you think?"

"Not if someone asks."

"Why don't you tell me about *your* work." I nodded at the napkin he'd now covered in ink caricatures and hatch-marked clouds.

"This," he said with an affectation of pride, "is Pew Art." He signed his name on the ribbed margin of the napkin and slid it over to my side of the table.

"Pew Art?"

"That's what my Aunt Jenny used to call the drawings I did in church when I was supposed to be listening."

"I didn't think you went to church," I said.

"I didn't think you drank Guinness," he replied.

Apparently, I was the only one at the table trying to make an impression, and I was making entirely the wrong kind. I already felt guilty about the beer. It had taken years to drain a modest, ritual glass of wine from an accompanying sense of transgression. Walking around at parties with a plastic cup of five-dollar Merlot, I sometimes felt that I'd switched teams in the middle of a very important game.

We were two of five people in the entire pub, but our food took forty minutes. In that time Eli managed to cover three napkins with drawings and inquire about everything personal: how I'd voted in the last election, why I wasn't dating, who I'd last dated. To my surprise, I answered every question at length.

"Am I talking too much?" I asked.

Laugh lines framed his smile. "I think you should talk like this all the time."

He ate like he hadn't seen food in days. I imagined the calories burning on impact, like water evaporating on contact with a hot, greased skillet. You had to admire such a body.

I said, "So you still haven't told me what your tattoo means."

"I thought I did."

"No. You told me I disapproved of it and then you didn't say anything else."

He wiped his fingers on his one still-blank napkin. "You want the long version or the short version?"

"Whichever's better."

He sat back in his seat. "I was in a car accident when I was twenty-three. It was on an old country road. I don't remember seeing headlights behind me, but right after I wrecked the car, a man in a pickup truck driving around the corner saw the fire from the accident and came running to pull me out. If he hadn't gotten me out, I'd have been badly burned, at the very least. He was a total stranger. I couldn't tell you a thing about the accident, about this guy's face or what he was wearing or what he said to me in that ER, but I can see the tattoo on his arm like he lifted me up out of that car five minutes ago." He examined his arm. "It was this same pattern."

I admitted that was an amazing story.

I asked if that was the short version or the long version.

He considered the question. "If I tell you the long version, you may not want to talk to me again."

I crossed my arms. "I hate to think what Zoë's told you about me."

"Only good things."

"She's right that I grew up in a strict environment," I said. "The First Fundamentalists."

"Never heard of them."

Remembering a jingle Grandma liked to sing, I said, "They don't smoke, chew, or go with girls that do."

"Sounds like about every denomination I know."

We were talking about me again.

I said, "So you grew up in church . . ."

He wiped bits of salt from the table onto the floor. He folded and unfolded his napkin. "My Aunt Jenny was a Methodist," was the unlikely beginning of the long version.

~

Eli's parents despised the church almost as much as they despised each other, but he'd grown up under its influence nevertheless, his aunt and uncle being devoted Methodists charged with the duty of civilizing him.

Aunt Jenny and Uncle Rod lived across town from Eli's family in a ranch house with a steep front yard they decorated with porcelain ducks dressed in raincoats for April, polka-dot frocks for May and June. In winter the ducks were replaced with a plastic Mary, Joseph, and Baby Jesus who glowed. In texture and color the nativity figurines reminded Eli of Nik-L-Nip wax bottle candies, the Virgin Mary's cheeks two cherry dots floating beneath her milky complexion.

He understood Virgin to be synonymous with Queen and always thought the word lovely and holy, even when, in the fifth grade, he was educated as to its true meaning.

Eli and his brother, Aden, never saw their father after the divorce. Weekdays their mother worked as a housekeeper for the Marriott and on weekends she took a second job cleaning house for a well-to-do family whose garage was bigger than two normal-sized houses. By rule, his mother did not bring her work home; it therefore fell to Eli and Aden to throw the beer bottles away and empty the ashtrays the mornings after late night parties and poker games. Eli topped off whatever beer was left in each of the bottles before finding inventive ways to make his little brother clean them up. They played Monopoly or poker, betting their chores, Eli winning easily every time. When bets didn't work, he resorted to sheer physical intimidation: locking Aden in the closet, pinning him down and threatening to drip loogies on his face until he gave in.

Their mother had boyfriends, one the same as the other. They got drunk, stayed over, slept it off. There were a few who showed kindness, treated the boys to playing cards, gum, little gifts of recognition. The truck driver (Eli couldn't remember his name) had been a decent man. He let them sit up front in his big rig just to drive to the grocery store, just to rent a movie. That was a good summer.

When the brothers were alone, Eli was in charge by virtue of being older and a handful of inches taller. He protested this arrangement every morning, cussed at his mother, said he shouldn't have to waste his time taking care of a baby. He complained so he wouldn't look like a sissy girl; really he liked the responsibility. He made Aden do his homework. He made him SpaghettiOs and grilled cheese sandwiches. When there wasn't any food they walked to the nearest Kmart and slipped Twinkies and Snickers bars and M&Ms in their coats, a feast they shared on the living room floor, laughing riotously, the sugar rushing through their skinny bodies and out their open mouths, molars packed with half-chewed candy.

When their mother met Carl Roker, this comfortable routine changed. Roker was different than the other men, enormous and unkempt, with a temper that flushed his cheeks a blood red. He made them stay in the house even though he never wanted anything to do with them—he didn't like their running around. He brought their mother novelties, new highs to take her where the alcohol couldn't. Eli knew the little baggies of white for what they were—he wasn't stupid—and the sight of the powder on the living room table gave him a sinking feeling of dread. The school had presentations on the campaign against drugs regularly. He was everywhere accosted with his mother's sin: "Just say no," the smiling teachers singsonged. *Just Say No*, the high school students' T-shirts declared.

Roker and their mother snorted lines of coke from the living room table. They watched television for hours, never ate, had sex. One night they forgot to shut the door. Eli only wanted the remote control. He'd thought they were sleeping. "Little perv," Roker said, laughing. Eli ran from the room, his cheeks burning with shame. Roker pulled Eli aside the next day, wrapped the impossibly fat weight of his arm around the thin boy's shoulders. His breath was sour with cigarettes and alcohol. In the other hand he held two magazines. A different woman on every page, each exposed in creative and gymnastic ways, a world Eli had never known existed. "You want to watch?" Roker asked. "You're gonna have to study." And then, the only gesture of affection between them, he tousled Eli's hair.

Eli took the magazines to his room and locked the door. He read every page, studied the pictures slowly. The next morning, sick with the same burning heat on his face that he'd felt at the sight of his mother's nakedness, he stuffed the magazines into a trash bag and set fire to them in the backyard. Roker saw the flames from the kitchen window. He ran out of the house, doused water on the fire. When Eli tried to run away, Roker grabbed his arm and twisted it behind his back. He twisted the arm until Eli cried out in pain, terrified his shoulder would pop from its socket. Roker dropped him to the ground, kicked him twice in the stomach, and returned to the house without looking back.

Eli took the beatings. He never let himself cry out again. In the bathroom, after brushing his teeth, he sometimes dug a razor blade into the flesh of his shoulder, making neat bloody lines in careful rows, learning to feel the pain without fearing it. Roker at least did him the service of keeping the bruises in easily hidden places. Eli sometimes wore long sleeves, but he never had to hide his face. He told no one: He didn't want Them to take Aden away.

Eli liked school inasmuch as it gave him an eight-hour reprieve from anxiety. During school hours he could relax, knowing Aden was safe. His teacher, Mrs. Davis, was nice and very pretty. She let him draw in class, a rare privilege. ". . . from a broken home . . ." he'd heard her admit, somewhat smugly, to a fellow teacher in the hallway.

Mrs. Davis liked art. She did her bulletin boards in Monet lilies and Van Gogh shapes. She took the students on a field trip to a local art museum. Eli stared at the paintings. Like the magazines, the men had clothes, the women didn't, but these pictures were different. He couldn't explain why. He wondered why there would be naked women in the same paintings as Jesus, and he stared five whole minutes at the wounds in Jesus' side, the sliver slits of blood, like the engravings on his own arm. He didn't believe Mrs. Davis that someone had made them with so much pencil and paint. He wrote the names of the artists on his hand intent on investigating the matter for himself. The next day he got a hall pass to use the bathroom. He walked out of the school and hiked the five miles to the library. He could only find pictures from one of the painters, but the librarians wouldn't let him take the book home: It was expensive and it was *inappropriate*. He kicked the librarian's desk. "Young man," she warned. He ran home, surprised to find himself weeping.

He didn't get home until seven. The house was empty. The television was still on, the table dusted with scattered white powder.

He found Aden crying in the bathroom, a welt across his back and another across his legs. Eli examined the wounds. He turned to the toilet and threw up. It was his fault: He'd left his brother alone. He thought of the Jesus in the painting, the rivers of blood. He imagined his brother beaten and bruised, wrists sliced through with razor blades. No one touched his brother.

The next week when they learned Roker was coming to stay, Eli instructed Aden to invite himself over to a friend's and personally escorted him to the neighboring house after school. When he returned home he gathered beer bottles from the kitchen sink. He put three in a Ziploc bag, carried the bag to a rock in the backyard, and used a hammer to smash the glass to pieces. He waited until Roker and his mother were asleep before sprinkling the shards of glass on the mattress beside the grown man's naked hulk of a body, and on the floor where his feet were likely to land in the morning.

Roker received thirty-two stitches. Eli received a year in Sunday school.

"Your Jesus works miracles?" his mother asked Aunt Jenny, hauling him up to her sister's doorstep that Sunday morning. "Ask His holiness to civilize this one."

Eli's mother didn't believe in church, but she did believe in capital punishment.

Aunt Jenny was thrilled: She'd been begging to take the children to church for years and was happy to provide the service no matter her sister's motivations for allowing it. Every week for a summer Eli was to attend Sunday school. He was also to stay after to wash Uncle Rod and Aunt Jenny's cars and to mow their lawn. This was on top of his usual chores cleaning up at home, a duty that now fell entirely to him as further punishment. He continued to finish the night's old beers left in the kitchen and, to spite his mother, smoked her cigarettes while he cleaned. He arrived at Aunt Jenny's for church every Sunday smelling of Corona and menthol.

"You smell like the devil," she would say, not without good humor.

He was wound too tight for the soft-spoken old ladies who taught children's church, so he sat beside his aunt in the adult sanctuary, chewing Wrigley's or sucking hard candy while he amused himself drawing unkind cartoons of the minister farting at the pulpit. Rather irreverently, Aunt Jenny kept her favorite Pew Art on the fridge.

She rarely made him do the chores his mother had demanded he complete. She explained her lawn mower was too unwieldy for a boy to handle. She decided the car wasn't so dirty it needed immediate washing. Most afternoons she made Eli sit with her at the kitchen table, eating sugar cookies and playing board games. Eli loved the way her kitchen smelled of sweet things freshly baking. He loved how all her furniture matched. He liked to sit on the love seat in the living room and run his sensitive, quivering hands up and down the edge of the seat cushions, the crushed velvet slick beneath his palm if he pushed in one direction, the fibers resisting when he pulled his hand the other.

When summer was only half over, and carting Eli to Jenny's house became more a punishment for his mother than it was for him, she announced he'd served his time and informed Jenny he wouldn't be coming back. He took a month off church. Things were better. Roker was gone. The new boyfriend was an idiot, but gentle. Eli had his usual Sunday pastimes to keep him busy, fishing and harassing his brother. Some nights he still locked himself in the bathroom, took secret satisfaction in drawing blood from his own arms with unwound paper clips and kitchen paring knifes. He worried about Jenny: Who would she play Monopoly with? Who would eat her cookies? He got his church clothes back out in resignation: He just couldn't be worrying about her all the time. He didn't want her to feel lonely, he explained to her on their way to service. She nodded and said she agreed that she wouldn't know what to do without him.

Aunt Jenny was no missionary, but she did her bit. She taught Eli to bless his food before eating and to recite the Lord's Prayer before bed. She answered his theological inquiries as best she could: why God was invisible, why He was so angry in the Old Testament, why the churchgoers drank grape juice and called it blood.

The way he described his childhood, Aunt Jenny was an anchor of sanity in his otherwise chaotic world. Even in high school, when he only went to services to stare at the uniformly gorgeous back row of the junior high all girls choir, he still spent whole afternoons at Jenny's, sleeping on her couch, mowing her lawn, eating the food she cooked only for him.

Eli had Jenny all to himself. Aden would have nothing to do with her. Aden had friends and clubs. He had been labeled Gifted and reaped all the rewards that came with the title. The teachers loved him. Their mother sobered up enough to attend his parent-teacher conferences, basking in the praise. He was soon being courted by costly private schools that offered to pay his way.

Aden's intellect eclipsed Eli's more practical talents: Eli could put anything back together in better shape than it had been in when he took it apart. He was terrible at math but had an innate skill for carpentry. He knew cars. These talents merely impressed upon teachers the need to keep Eli under close surveillance. Whenever he was sent to the principal's office for gluing the teacher's pens to her desk or drawing dirty pictures on desktops, the principal wanted to know the same thing: why couldn't he be more like his brother? Eli didn't mind. He loved that people loved his brother. And when it did bother him, there were bottles from the pantry to silence the unwelcome thoughts and endless blades with which to cut and mask the hurt.

He couldn't say when the drinking began in earnest. He'd been sipping from his mother's beer bottles for as long as he could remember. He could get liquor when he wanted it. But somewhere between his third and fourth year of high school the pictures in his memory begin to blur. Faces fade at the edges. The order of events is vague, the line of chronology tangled.

At eighteen he applied to a state school to study engineering. To everyone's surprise, he was accepted; unfortunately, it took him less than two semesters to justify his most avid critics' doubts. After a string of D's and F's, he dropped out. He followed his girlfriend to Michigan, where he worked at GM until his perpetual delinquency cost him his position. In four years he went through as many jobs. When his girlfriend left him for someone else she cited his drinking as the problem. He argued otherwise. She'd slept with his neighbor. That seemed like a pretty good reason to him.

He'd loved her, and her departure woke in him some innate sense of self-preservation. He knew he didn't have an addiction, but was willing to admit he drank maybe a little more than was necessary. He could ration his drinking, cut back some. He traded whiskey for beer. Every evening after work he stopped at the Exxon station for a six-pack and for cigarettes. The first night the beer lasted until nine. The next night until eight when he decided he couldn't be expected to go from constant drinking to a few bottles of cheap beer without weaning himself carefully. He walked to the bar down the street for a drink—just one—and had five. For two months he rationed his drinking in this way, promising he would only have the six-pack, finding himself at the bar by ten.

The night of the accident he'd found one of his brother's letters buried under a month's worth of unopened mail. Aden only wrote because his new wife, Rebekah, made him. Eli had missed their wedding, passed out at home on the couch while his flight took off down the runway. Rebekah had sent pictures. Every year he received a birthday card containing gift cards for local restaurants (Aden wouldn't let Rebekah send money) or typed, printed letters recounting the news of their lives: his promotion, their first child. Eli didn't own a phone. With her elegant penmanship, each letter as carefully scripted as her message, Rebekah did the brothers' talking for them.

But the letter that night was in Aden's crisp, square handwriting, the message without Rekebah's practiced kindness: Their mother

129

had been found dead in her apartment. Her manager discovered her after she'd missed three days of work. An accidental overdose, they claimed. The funeral would be held on the seventeenth.

He read the letter on the thirty-first.

Eli drove to the nearest liquor store and bought a bottle of Jack Daniel's. He drove to the field ten miles from his apartment where he sometimes liked to lie on the ground and stare at the stars, feeling their brightness buzz all the way to the back of his skull. He felt God best when in the field, exposed to the elements. He could feel the holiness of things humming in the trees, roiling the ground. He felt these things more clearly when he'd been drinking.

Lying on his back, staring up at the night, he tried to feel some pain at the loss of his mother. He tried to feel grief, if only to feel something at all. But the memories that battered him were merciless in their specificity, and they only inspired a pure, unadulterated hatred: his mother on her bed, half naked and passed out, the welts on his brother's legs, nights crouching by the toilet, overcome to gagging with its stale odor as he set another razor blade to his skin. He stood up, threw out his arms, and screamed. He screamed until his spit was froth and his throat raw. Until he was empty.

Usually he walked home—he knew enough to walk when he'd been drinking—but that night he wanted to sleep in the field, under the stars. A ceiling over his head would be too suffocating. He needed to feel ample air around his arms and legs, to know he could run if his anger overwhelmed him. He woke to a storm. It was midmorning, dark and cold. He ran to his car, anxious to escape the rain.

Four miles down the road he ran his car off the road and wrapped it around a sycamore.

He remembered very little of the actual accident, except for the panicked realization that he was trapped. He did, however, remember waking up in the ER, feeling the shock of being completely sober for the first time in four years.

He was twenty-three, a college dropout and an addict. He went the only place he knew to go.

When Jenny opened her door and found Eli standing there, duffel bag in hand, face battered by the accident, she began to weep. She had been as affected by the years: Since he'd run away she'd lost her husband to a heart attack and the better use of her right hip to an icy curb outside her church. She had never fully recovered from either.

"You smell like the devil," she said, and welcomed him back into the house.

Jenny informed him he could stay if he worked. With only a high school diploma and a stubborn refusal to cut his hair, his job opportunities were limited. He could easily have worked full time as a bartender, but Jenny wouldn't allow him within arm's reach of alcohol. He worked part time at a custom car design factory where he showed marked skill with a welder, supplementing the physical labor with another ten hours at a family-owned grocery where he stocked shelves and mopped floors.

His aunt kept a regimented life. She woke every day at seven, kept lists, and had not missed a church service for fifty years. But she gave Eli his freedom, providing he stayed away from bars and attended Wednesday night prayer meeting. The structure of her life was a refuge for Eli, whose tyrannical cravings and unpredictable temper had left him without any sense of stability. She lived for his stories, humored his mood swings, and fueled his emaciated body. She never asked for an explanation of his past behavior and she made it clear she did not condemn him for it.

His conversion to the faith was as slow and methodical as the fight for his sobriety. On his days off he sometimes drove to the art museum to sit and mediate on the Crucifixion paintings that he had first seen as a child. He studied the rivulets of blood running the course of the dying Christ's body, fascinated by the idea of a suffering

Savior, seduced by the liquid flow of paint. He copied pictures of the painting for hours. Church was far less interesting, but he went, he listened, and then he took what he'd heard and turned it in his mind while he sat studying the face of Christ. Over a Saturday breakfast of eggs and toast he tried to articulate to his aunt how his love of art and his love for Christ would be forever overlapped in his mind, irrevocably intertwined. She worried he was perhaps idolizing the paintings even as he explained the difference between the worship of an idol and the appreciation of an icon. He was not as good at talking about art as he was at making it. She only nodded, and prayed, believing God was good enough to honor this young faith however peculiar its inception.

They lived in shared quiet routine for two years until Eli began to talk of school. She didn't laugh when he said he wanted to study sculpture. That was all the encouragement he needed.

He was accepted to the art academy on academic probation, a cautionary action that proved entirely unnecessary. He excelled. In his painting class he met the first person who could replicate on paper the tattoo he described from memory. She drew the pattern on his arm and sat with him at the parlor while the tattoo artist carved the image into his skin with blood and ink.

He unveiled the tattoo to Aunt Jenny at Christmas. When she recovered from the sudden onset of heart palpitations, her only complaint against the tattoo, which her church and personal faith expressly forbid, was that it was "so big." Had he needed one so big?

When he explained that the tattoo was meant to remind him of the angels who had pulled him from the wreck, who had kept him from getting burned, she went as far as to be flattered that he'd thought of her—she was glad that at least he hadn't done something as foolish as print her name in a heart on his shoulder or something as sentimental.

By the time Eli finished his story, the bar had closed. Outside the snow had stopped. The snow-covered trees stood elegant as ladies dressed in white stoles. Eli wanted to walk.

"But what about your van?"

He shoved his hands in his pockets. His only protection against the cold was a blue pilot jacket that was an inch too short at the wrists. "I'll get it in the morning."

"They'll tow it if they find out you left it here all night."

"I'll get it early. It's too nice out to drive."

It was two in the morning and not quite twenty degrees. Nothing a reasonable person would consider "nice." I joined him on the sidewalk anyway. A sheet of ice intersected our path, and when I reached it he took my arm to guide me over the most treacherous part.

"Why did you stay on campus for Christmas?" I asked. "Why didn't you visit your aunt?"

"She passed away two years ago. A stroke."

"I'm sorry."

He lifted his shoulders, a very gentle shrug of resignation. "She didn't suffer. And she was lonely as a widow. I visited as often as I could, but there was nothing I could do to fix that loneliness.

"I haven't seen Aden in years. He's never quite forgiven me. . . ."

He left the thought unfinished. Eli was always surrounded by a crowd. I had never thought of him as someone moving through life alone.

"You know I've lived a lot of my life at the hospitality of other people," he said. "And I never accept someone's hospitality without appreciating it. It's good of you to let me stay in your place until I get things sorted out."

"Of course—it's nothing."

"Don't say that. I know it isn't nothing. Well, maybe it's not for Zoë—she couldn't care less—but I know it matters to you. You're kind of a cat person."

"A what?"

"You're one of those people who likes things the way she likes them. You're structured."

My expression must have amused him. He asked, "Am I right?"

"It's not a very flattering description."

He was nonplussed. "I don't mean it as an insult."

Turning the corner to my street, we had no choice but to walk directly over a large frozen puddle. He toed forward, inch by inch, his hands perpendicular to his body for balance.

"What are you doing?" I asked.

"It's slippery."

"It's just ice."

"I don't want to fall," he protested. "I've seen people really fall. You can nip the tip of your tailbone right off."

I laughed. I was happy and full and glad to be out in the night air, talking to this man who never failed to surprise me.

At home, I fell into bed half dressed and wide awake.

There was a bang on the wall as the futon fell against the wall.

"Sorry," he called.

"It's all right."

I waited for him to say something else—Good night or See you in the morning, but there was only silence.

The next morning Zoë thanked me for taking Eli out to dinner. I didn't know what version of the story Eli had given her, but I went along with it.

"We had a good time," I said, reaching for the coffee, hoping it would magically compensate for a meager four hours of sleep.

"Well, just for the record, I appreciate you loosening up."

I said you're welcome, sure that if Zoë knew just how much I'd loosened up—how much I'd said and how much he'd confessed— she'd be more concerned than grateful. There was Eli's girlfriend to think of. Jillian had been her old roommate, after all.

I did not intend on loosening up around Eli again.

9

I went to Valerie's baby shower reluctantly, knowing I was the only one from our graduate class who'd been invited. I didn't know the woman hosting or the women attending, and three hours of sharing cheap cake with strangers was not my idea of a fun Saturday afternoon. The house was new and smelled of paint and wood, of still settling construction. During lunch I held my fruit punch with both hands, nervously eyeing the white carpet while the ladies swapped stories of losing their virginity with the pride of veterans recounting battle wounds. The youngest in the group was getting married in a month and wanted to know whether she and her fiancé should stop having sex now or just give it up for the last week. She wanted the wedding night to be amazing.

"Good luck," one woman said. "We collapsed. You'll be too exhausted to even think about it."

"How many times did you do it on your wedding night?" Valerie asked the host.

"Nada."

"Seriously?"

"Are you counting night or night and the next morning?"

"Wedding night," someone piped.

"Both," another protested. "If your wedding goes late, you don't have much of a window of time. Morning should count as part of the wedding night."

"Yes, exactly."

"All who vote to keep the morning after as part of the wedding night, lift your punch."

I escaped to the bathroom, locked the door, and sat on the toilet to wait out the conversation. The yard outside the window to my right was too nice, square allotments of sod clumped together like patches of a quilt. A single sapling stood in the lawn, supported by wires knotted round its trunk and plugged into the ground. The wires were so taut you could imagine things the other way around: the wires held the tree down, not up, and if you clipped the strings, the sapling might escape.

By the time I returned to the party, Jake and another husband had returned from the gym, and on their arrival the subject of wedding nights had been temporarily suspended. Everyone moved to the table to admire the bassinet cake that said *Congratulations, it's a girl!* in sweating curls of hot pink icing. We stood in the kitchen eating slices off paper plates. Valerie raised her shirt to show off her rounded belly. Jake gazed at her with a doting adoration I had only seen in teenage boys and in grooms.

At home, I stuffed a pillow in my shirt and considered my newly rounded figure in the bedroom mirror. Too light. Babies weighed seven to eight pounds and that wasn't counting the fluids and what-not. I would probably need a bowling ball.

"You've been busy."

Zoë stood in the doorway. I held my cupped hands an inch from my chest. "My breasts would have to be bigger."

"Your everything would have to be bigger."

I pulled the pillow out from my shirt and tossed it at her.

"How was the shower?" She sat on my bed.

"It was all right. Valerie seems happy; she was quite literally glowing."

"Michael told me that he finds pregnant woman incredibly sexy," she said.

I sat beside her on the bed. "Do you ever think about having children?"

"Occasionally, but it never seems real to me that I could be a mother. I guess I imagine myself with older children—teenagers. Five boys, all football players. But I can't see myself with a baby. Can you?"

I didn't say anything. I lay down on my back and ran my hand over my stomach, wondering at its latent power.

⁐

Mom called at six thirty Monday morning to say there had been a kidnapping at Harvard and I should be on my guard.

"Mom, it's not even light out yet."

"Turn on channel nine."

"It's Harvard. In *Boston*." I pressed my face into my pillow.

"You can't be too careful these days. Apathy killed the cat."

I sat up, propping my elbow on my knee and my forehead in my hand while Mom relayed everything the Channel 9 News anchor said: ". . . Police canvassing the neighborhoods . . . no news from the campus . . . woman at the supermarket says she saw a man who fits the suspect's description . . ." She turned the television down. "I should call Brian."

"Mom," I sighed. "Why do you keep calling?"

"I don't want to waste my minutes," she said.

"You don't have any minutes. They're *all free*," I said. "Anytime you call me it's free."

"Precisely!" she exclaimed. "I don't want to waste free minutes!"

"I'm going now."

I felt more than saw Zoë listening at the open door.

"That Mom?" she asked.

"Yes. Someone should have performed an intervention when Brian decided to buy her that phone."

"I told you it was a bad idea."

"You said no such thing."

"Get up. We can argue about it on the way to campus."

I squinted at the clock, then at Zoë. She was carrying a pair of running shoes.

"Your morning run," she stated.

I'd forgotten: today was trail day. I pulled the blanket back over my head. "I would prefer not to."

"Come on, Bartleby." She threw my shoes on the bed. "Michael's meeting us in ten minutes. He hates it when people are late."

"Us?"

"I'm coming with you."

Michael was outside the student union checking his watch when we pulled into the parking lot.

"Ready to go?" He stood with his legs spread wide, his arms extended. Swiveling his hips, he stretched this way, then that.

"I don't think I'm up for it today," I said.

"You'll feel better once your blood gets flowing." He pecked Zoë on the cheek, then gave her a spank. "Let's go, baby."

It was a long, hard run. When Michael and Zoë got ahead of me I didn't try to keep up. Michael had taught me how to pace myself, how to breathe correctly and how to keep my mind focused. When I ran I tried to visualize the work my body was doing, the pumping of the heart and the oxidation of cells, the contraction of muscle, puppeteer of bone. When a sharp jab of pain stabbed my side I pretended I was carrying a baby that felt the need to announce itself with a swift kick to the ribs.

Only a month without cable and I'd fallen off the wagon. After Valerie's shower I'd spent five hours watching a marathon of *A Baby Story: Xena Princess Warrior* meets *Alien*. It made me want to scream and push, to be a part of a miracle. It provoked cravings for the sweet powder smell of a baby's hair. I told myself this was a biological phase on par with the hormonal revolution that made prepubescent boys ache at the sight of breasts and bucks chase doe tails right into oncoming semis. But still.

I'd tried praying about these feelings, but had a bad habit of praying tangentially so as not to appear too shallow in my desires. (As ministers were fond of reminding me, *God is not concerned with your happiness but your character.*) All the years I'd wanted a husband, I prayed God would make me content as a celibate, confident that if He saw my willingness to remain forever His chaste servant, He would see fit to send me an unexpected blessing of a very handsome man who would make love to me the way Daniel Day-Lewis made love to Madeleine Stowe in *The Last of the Mohicans.* And now whenever the desire for a family of my own began to gnaw at my heart, I prayed for my students and thanked God for the brood He'd already given me.

Meanwhile, Valerie, who had never waited on God for a blessing in her life, was in the third trimester of her pregnancy and looked positively Rubenesque. Her rounded figure made me hate my flat stomach and my empty breasts, parts of my body I'd mistaken for ornaments.

Zoë's shriek broke my train of thought. She'd baited Michael. He was chasing her into the forest. I hurried to catch up with them. At the tree line, the trail narrowed to a thin, meandering path of dust mottled with stones and roots. For fifty feet it ran parallel to a steep drop-off before winding down the hill, turning sharply to realign itself with the creek, and heading back up to the forest in the opposite direction. Zoë and Michael were just to my left yet some twenty feet down and running the other way. They stopped when they saw me.

"What are you doing way up there?" Michael called.

"Get your boo-tay down here," Zoë commanded.

139

I raced to join them. Some strange freedom had come over us. They whooped and cheered, uncivilized and dirt-splattered as kids at summer camp, and halfway down the hill I threw my hands out and hollered along with them. I shouted in frustration and hope and desire. For two and a half seconds I felt entirely alive.

Then my foot stopped and my body kept going. There was a loud pop and a searing heat shot up my right leg to my eyes in a quick flash of white. I think I cried out but it didn't much matter, Zoë and Michael were raising such a ruckus. I fell to my knees, rolled, and landed on my side.

Zoë was dancing with her knees locked so she wouldn't pee her pants. "Oh, I'm sorry, I'm so sorry," she gasped. "Oh, it's not funny."

I squeezed my eyes shut as a wave of pain overwhelmed me. Somewhere Michael was talking: "Zoë, stop. I think she's really hurt."

"Michael, I swear, don't mess with me. Are you messing with me?"

I opened my eyes and saw Michael's face. He said, "Let me look at it."

I shook my head.

"Amy, let me see it," he demanded. "We have to make sure it's not broken."

Zoë knelt beside him, sobered by the word *broken*. "Amy, are you okay?"

I straightened my leg hesitantly.

"Can you turn it?" Michael asked.

He took my ankle in his hands. With his help I turned my foot ever so slightly to the right, then the left, wincing as I did so.

"It's not broken. I think she just sprained it," he said to Zoë. "But we need to get her on ice."

"Can you walk if we help you?" she asked.

"I think so," I managed.

Together they lifted me up from the ground.

"Don't put weight on it," Michael said. "Use us as a crutch."

With one arm around Zoë's shoulders and another around Michael's back, I hobbled slowly up the trail. It took us fifteen minutes just to get back to Leonard Field, and by that point I was sweating and close to tears from the pain.

"Wait," I said. "I need a second."

I hobbled to the bench that sat half sunk in the mud just outside the trail.

Zoë gaped at the size of my foot. "Come on, Amy, we have to get back," she said. "It's freezing, and your foot is getting huge."

"I know, just give me a few minutes," I pleaded.

"There's a bus stop ten minutes away."

"She's too hurt, Zoë," Michael said. "She can't do it."

"I can so do it," I muttered. I stood back up to prove it, balancing my body against a nearby tree and willing myself to stare directly into his eyes, though the pain blurred my vision. "I'm fine."

"Get on my back," Michael said as if he hadn't been listening.

"What?"

"I'll carry you."

I said no, but he knelt down on the ground and waited. Humiliated, I climbed onto his back and wrapped my arms around his neck. He sometimes carried Zoë this way, but I was a good five inches taller and more than a few pounds heavier. I pressed my face against his shoulder, praying desperately that none of my students would see us.

At home, he untied the laces of my shoes and delicately peeled my sock from my swollen ankle. I was sporting a carpet of blond leg hair fit for a Viking, but he didn't seem to notice. He sandwiched my bare ankle between two bags of ice, setting a pillow on the coffee table on which I was to keep my leg suspended. Zoë watched the operation from her reading chair.

141

"Keep your foot on ice until the swelling goes down," he told me. "And don't put any weight on it."

"I have class at ten o'clock."

"You're going to have to cancel."

"Yes, doctor."

"Swear you won't walk on it."

"I swear," I said.

I smiled at him reassuringly despite the pain. The scent of his cologne lingered on my clothes.

⌇

When the swelling did not go down by the next afternoon, I told Zoë to call Eli—I needed to go to the emergency room. I gingerly tugged on a pair of jeans and hobbled down the stairs, leaning on Zoë to get to the car.

"What are you doing?" I asked when she sat down in the driver's seat.

"I can't get ahold of Eli and Michael's at work. I'm driving you."

"I don't think that's a good idea."

"Look at your foot!" she said in exasperation.

She held the key aloft, searching the dashboard, staring down at the pedals, the gearshift.

I pointed to the right underside of the steering wheel. "The ignition's there."

"I've got it," she said.

"You *can* drive, can't you?" I asked.

"Of course I can drive." She pressed on the gas so that the engine revved. "Oops. *Not* the brake."

I reached for my door handle. "I want out."

"Here we go." The car lurched two feet and stopped. The sudden change in motion forced the passenger door I'd just opened to slam shut.

"Stop, Zoë. We're not doing this."

"Would you chill out?" She started laughing. When we hit and dragged one of Katherine's rubber Hefty trash cans, she whooped out loud. "Oh, she is going to *kill* us!"

"If you don't."

We crawled out of the neighborhood but hit Main Street like it was the Indy 500. She full-stopped at the first four-way for a complete five seconds, then proceeded to run a red light in town. The hospital was only ten minutes off campus; by the time we arrived I wanted to kiss the ground.

At the desk, I was given a work sheet featuring the drawing of a unisex figure on which I was to circle the places that were giving me pain. On the right margin was a chart numbering the severity of pain, 1 being mild, 10 being the worst pain I had ever felt in my life. Each number came with a corresponding smiley or frowny face.

"Why would I have a whole body to choose from?" I asked. "It's my foot."

"Circle the head and see if they ask you about depression," Zoë said.

We were moved to a private room immediately, but it was an hour and a half before I saw the doctor. He walked through the door reading my chart, glancing up long enough to offer a hearty handshake. His name was Dr. Santini. He looked nineteen.

"Swelling and sharp pain?" he asked.

My pant leg was already rolled up. I had taken pains to shave that morning, though vanity seemed beside the point considering my ankle had swollen to the size of a cantaloupe. Dr. Santini's examination was far more brutal than Michael's had been.

"Probably a sprain," he murmured. "But I'd like to get this X-rayed. Better safe than sorry."

I wondered how often he practiced his tone and delivery. It was hard to talk with young physicians without seeing my brother.

While we waited for the X-ray results, Zoë pulled a chair up to my bed and belabored the inefficiencies of the hospital. She dismantled everything from the outdated chart system ("they're all online now") to the outdated yellow curtains ("an offense to the patient's sensibilities").

"It's not a resort," I reminded her.

"It's not the UC medical center, either."

Zoë was a very devoted fan of the oncology centers that had administered her mother's treatments. She stood beside these hospitals, like an alumna eternally defending her alma mater.

⁖

Dr. Santini's verdict was that I had very badly sprained my ankle. His recommendation was that I stick to a careful regimen of RICE.

"**R**est, **I**ce, **C**ompression, **E**levation," he explained.

"But I work on campus," I said. "I walk everywhere."

He shook his head. "Best way to let it heal is to stay off it as best you can. Crutches the first five days, some exercises as follow-up. You'll be in an air cast for at least four weeks—maybe as many as six."

"Don't worry, dearest." Zoë laid her head against my shoulder. "I'll drive you."

"That doesn't worry me at all."

Dr. Santini wrote me a prescription medication for the pain, along with specific instructions on what exactly I was and was not to do. Zoë, who loves being needed, wrote everything down in her Hello Kitty notepad.

10

News of my malady spread through the ranks. Mom called to inform me that the First Fundamentalist Church of God prayer chain had been alerted to my condition; Grandma FedExed a Ziploc bag of crumbs that had once been homemade oatmeal cookies; and Brian called to ask if the painkillers had had any adverse effects. I was touched, though I suspected he only wanted to test his memory of pharmaceuticals.

My brace was plastic instead of plaster, but Eli drew on it anyway. A cartoon old man holding a bundle of balloons rode a bicycle on the left side of my ankle; a field of overly large flowers sprouted on my right. Over the Velcro straps he wrote *Feelings Happen* in fat bubble lettering.

"I broke my leg when I was twenty-one," he said. He was coloring the daisies in with a hot pink marker he'd bought just for the occasion.

"What were you doing?"

"Being an idiot." He set his foot on the couch and rolled up his pant leg. He had thin legs covered in wiry black hair. A scar ran up his ankle, lines of tender pink skin in a row neat and orderly as the dotted punches of perforated paper. "I was trying to jump off the roof of a shed onto a trampoline. My leg broke my fall and the fall broke my fibula. Worst pain I've ever felt in my life."

He rolled his pant leg back down. The silver charm of his hemp bracelet caught the light and winked.

"I suppose it would be predictable on my part to ask why you would be trying to jump from a rooftop to a trampoline."

"It was a dare." He'd returned to his drawing. "And I wasn't exactly sober."

"Was there ever a time in your life when you weren't abusing your body in every way imaginable?"

He pulled the reading lamp over my foot. "Sit here at least half an hour—until the ink dries."

When I went to bed that night I was startled by a blur of light at the foot of my bed. It darted erratically like a stage Tinker Bell dancing. The pink daisies on my cast were glowing in the dark.

⁀

The next morning, Mom called to update me on her progress with Mr. Moore. This required a half hour conversation clarifying the difference between dating and going out.

"I just don't understand why you say 'going out.' You're not *going* anywhere."

"It's an expression," I said. "It's the modern equivalent of being pinned. It means you're together."

"I still think it's unsensical."

"Are you trying to tell me that you and Mr. Moore are going out?"

"Well, we're not just holding hands at the park," she laughed.

I had no idea what this was supposed to mean.

"How's your ankle?"

"It's fine, but I have to wear this ridiculous air cast."

"You're not walking on it," she stated in disbelief.

"Not everywhere."

"Amy Gallagher! You go tooling around campus on a hurt leg and you're libel to mess up the other one. Make That Eli drive you."

My mother had more or less accepted the fact that Eli was a long-standing guest. She'd recommended we make him sleep in the garage beneath us. I told her that was a great idea, then did nothing to discourage her belief that I'd acquiesced. Despite her erroneous faith that there was now an entire floor between her only daughter and the traveling vagrant, she had not yet given up her right to disapprove. She only referred to him as "That Eli" and only when she'd come up with some new chore he should do for us.

I promised I would stay off my feet as much as possible. With the air cast I managed a stilted kind of walk. Driving, however, was out of the question since it was my right ankle. The bus that passed down our street went directly to campus, but I still had to make it to the stop some four blocks away and then hobble another ten minutes through campus, the bus stop outside the Humanities Building posing the impossible challenge of a steep hill. When it came to getting to work on time, I was forced to beg rides.

Eli was the first to volunteer. Wednesday he not only drove me to class, he insisted on walking me all the way to the Humanities Building, even carrying my books up to the classroom where his presence caused no end of excitement. Students love any interruption. One with a tattoo is even better.

He stood at the front of the room while I set up the day's Power-Point. He asked questions about the Spanish verb conjugations left on the board by the previous professor.

"I thought this was English class," he said. "*Voy, vas, va, vamos, van* . . . You guys know this stuff?"

Some of the students laughed. A few stared at him skeptically.

"Dude, who *are* you?" one of the boys in the front row asked, nervously eyeing Eli's many bracelets. Today he wore one with spikes.

"I'm here to observe," Eli said matter-of-factly.

Of course, on this day my slide show would not play. I ejected the flash drive and tried again. I tried to reboot the classroom laptop. Eli kept the students entertained by attempting to read the chalkboard dialogue: *Para celebrar su aniversario de bodas Juan lleva a su sposa a un restaurant muy elegante.* When he learned that one of the students spoke fluent Spanish, he talked her into giving an impromptu translation of the novel in my bag for the entire class. He sat in the front row to listen and seemed frankly impressed.

"I think that's enough," I announced.

Eli told them they should pay careful attention and not give me a hard time and then walked out the door, leaving me to shut them all up. The girls wanted to know how long had we been together and why had I never said anything before, and the back row fraternity contingency wondered aloud if he belonged to a fight club.

I asked Eli to drop me off at the front door in the future.

Unfortunately, Eli had less and less time to taxi me to campus. He had been assigned a few shifts at the T-shirt press to help supplement his meager income at The Brewery. I was left entirely dependent on Zoë to get around town.

Zoë's schedule was as unpredictable as Eli's, and she'd grown uncharacteristically penurious with her time. Thursday I had to limp directly from my third-story office to the parking lot where she sat waiting in my car, painting her fingernails to placate boredom she made no effort to hide. Friday I was forced to linger at the office as late as seven, more and more frustrated every time she called to say one more thing had come up, could I give her five seconds. Saturday she informed me we had two hours in which to complete my day's errands, a list that had grown typically long as the week dragged on:

To (MUST) Do

SCHOOL
grade AT LEAST 10 papers
lesson plans
photocopy orders for ENG 101
upload new grades
read creative writing stories for Monday

HOUSE/ MISC.
grocery: essentials, plus tampons (not cardboard kind)
post office: mail new submissions, book of stamps, postmark bills
~~shower~~

FINANCES
balance checkbook
file bill invoices

FUN
shower

I always scrambled on the weekends to keep up with class and complete piling lists of chores, which I listed by priority from most important to least. Generally speaking, school took precedence over finances (as it was the means by which I *had* finances) and finances over house. Everything took precedence over leisure.

"Where are we going first?" Zoë slid the key into the ignition and clicked her seat belt into place. I'd insisted that she wear it.

"First the store, then the office, and we'll swing around the coffee shop on the way back," I said.

She took the piece of paper I was holding. "What is this?"

"A list," I said innocently. It had continued to grow.

"Amy! This is thirty things long."

"It is not."

"We are *not* going to all these places."

"What do you want me to do?"

"We only have two hours."

"I don't have to get it all done. Just the things underlined in red—those are priority."

She looked at me in disbelief. Or disgust. It was difficult to tell.

"You color-code these?"

"If you're going to make fun, I'll have Everett help me."

"No," she said, taking the list from me with barely restrained resentment. "*I'll* help you."

She couldn't stand the thought of being a bad Samaritan. She would drive me if I needed it, she would do the chores that usually fell to me (meaning all of them), and she would wait on me hand and sprained foot. She had admirable motivations, but inadequate compassion. In her resolve to be of Christian help, she became a tyrant.

I didn't blame her; you couldn't help the personality you were born with. But I hated that my schedule was contingent upon her goodwill and availability. I hated that suddenly everything I did annoyed her.

While waiting for me to finish dressing Monday morning so she could drop me off at school, she surveyed the many to-do lists scattered about my desk. "Have you ever thought about living one day in your life without plotting it all out beforehand?"

"Zoë, I told you. If I don't write things down, I forget."

She snatched a sticky note off the wall. "Quiet time—5:20. You schedule prayer?"

"You make appointments for dates, don't you? Why not schedule prayer?"

The argument did not appeal to her.

Added to the burden of helping me around town, her writing wasn't going well. She was constantly locked in her room either talking to her parents or writing. She typed all night, only to delete everything first thing in the morning. She would never admit to writer's block. It was all I could do not to gloat.

At night I peered around her door. "Can I get you anything?"

"I'm not hungry," she said without looking up from her laptop.

"I can make coffee," I added sweetly. "Some caffeine might help your thoughts flow."

We both knew I was rubbing it in.

⁂

"Is the power out?" Everett asked when he found me alone in our office reading by flashlight. It was nearly five and neither Zoë nor Eli had called to inform me who was picking me up from work. I was busy hating both of them.

"Shut the door," I said. "I'm hiding from Lonnie."

"Amy—*honestly.*" He wandered in, leaving the door wide open. "The kid's not there. I just walked by the copy room, and it's just Mr. Benson today."

"Oh, he's here. He's waiting. Turn that light back off."

It wasn't half an hour before someone knocked on the open door.

"Lonnie," I said, pretending to be pleasantly surprised. "Come in."

Lonnie shut the door behind him. I glared at Everett. Everett gaped at me, perfectly baffled.

"What's up, Lonnie?" I asked.

"I was wondering if I could ask a favor, Ms. Gallagher." He held a clipboard to his chest. "I'm doing an article for the school paper on the dangers of campus life and was wondering if I could interview you about your accident. I e-mailed you three times about it. And I left you notes."

I chose to ignore his mention of the unanswered e-mails. "I tripped," I said. "I hardly think that qualifies for campus danger."

"I did some research." He handed me three stapled photocopies. The print was so fine it was almost illegible. "The Copenhagen University Grounds Keeping Manual states that 'all grounds must be kept in prime condition, including but not limited to the trails and parks within a two-mile radius of the academic lawns.' It's in Section 2B ii." He pointed to the specific line. "Right there, where I underlined the words in red."

Everett read over my shoulder. "Amy, you could sue. You could quit your job. Buy a condo in Florida and drink margaritas."

I handed the photocopies back to Lonnie. "I'm not suing anybody."

"It's only a small article," he persisted, his eyes nervously following Everett back to his desk. Lonnie was one of those students who never caught sarcasm in a teacher; he took everything a superior said literally. "It would really help me. No one else has agreed to an interview."

"They really asked you to write an article about this?" I asked.

Bashfully, he replied, "Well, I was supposed to interview Jessica Baily Barts, the girl that broke her femur in that hit and run last year. But she transferred."

I hesitated.

"Fine," I said. "I'll do the interview."

"Thank you, Ms. Gallagher, thank you. It will only take ten minutes, I promise—quick and painless. I mean, I wouldn't want to inflict more pain on you, seeing how you have enough and all."

He took a chair and produced an old tape recorder from the nest of crumpled papers in his backpack. I sighed. I hadn't realized Lonnie meant *now*.

"Strictly for the sake of notation," he informed me. He hit Record, then pitched forward in his chair, notepad balanced against his knee. "Ms. Gallagher, ma'am, could you tell me exactly what happened on that trail that day."

I gave him the short version. He scribbled a row of indecipherable hieroglyphics. "Which trail were you on?"

"I don't know for sure. We took the trail that starts right outside Leonard Chapel."

He nodded. "Tell me about the conditions of the trail that day."

"I don't know," I said. "It was like any trail. It wound, got narrow in some places."

"Were there an excess of protrusions?"

"Pardon?"

"Were there roots and rocks and such?" he clarified.

"Oh, almost everywhere. Pebbles, rocks, some thin roots."

"How large was the root you tripped on? Was it blocking the path?"

"To be honest, I really can't remember, Lonnie—it all happened so fast."

He waited.

I said, "I think it might have actually been a very thin, wiry root—it was like tripping over a taut rope."

He nodded quickly, jotted something down. "What is the extent of your injury?"

"A bad sprain. I'm in a brace for a month. Maybe longer."

"And does the university health-care policy cover this?"

Everett said "Ha!" so loud that Lonnie jumped.

"*I* pay for my health insurance," I said.

Flustered, Lonnie ran his pen up and down the list of questions he'd composed beforehand. "Has the injury significantly hindered your ability to perform usual activities?"

"It's a hindrance, of course. I can't drive. I can't walk. Not well at least. But that seems beside the point once I'm in the classroom."

"How did you get into teaching?"

I frowned. "Is this really pertinent?"

"Biographical background," he explained.

I hesitated, but was anxious to finish this unexpected conference as soon as possible. "I got into teaching by default. I finished my master's degree here. They offered me a teaching position. I was too worn out from grad school to consider anything else at the time, so I stayed." I paused. "I like the trees."

"You don't like teaching?"

"Oh, no, I like teaching just fine. It's challenging and varied. I enjoy getting to know the students. It's just not what I expected to do."

"What did you expect?"

"The usual. Flight attendant, ballerina. Astronaut."

He tapped his pen at the air, boldly maintaining eye contact for an entire twenty seconds. "Off the record, you could have been a superb ballerina."

"Doubtful."

"You're very tall."

He looked down again, but he wasn't taking notes anymore. He crossed his arms. He examined the Garfield on my desk. He asked if I'd ever taken dance lessons. I said no. He replied that he had.

"Really?"

"But only until the second grade. Now I do tae kwon do. I was two days from my black belt when I had to leave for college."

"So this is recent," I said.

"This is *now.*"

"Are you going to get your black belt?"

"I can do these tricks."

He stood, braced his hands on his hips, and slid effortlessly into the splits, knocking his chair into the desk and the tape recorder onto the floor.

Everett stared.

Lonnie pressed his nose to his knee.

"That's impressive," I managed.

"Very impressive," I said.

"You'd better get up now," I practically pleaded.

Lonnie got up from the floor and calmly took his seat as if nothing had happened.

"I'm a little out of shape," he said. "But I practice in the dorm when my roommate's gone. It keeps me limber."

"I'll bet," Everett said, grinning.

"What the heck are you guys doing in here?" Michael stood in the doorway. "I can hear you all the way down the hall."

I introduced Lonnie to Michael, who waved his hand, perhaps to say hello, though it was the same gesture a person might use to swat away a bothersome fly. "Are you ready to get out of here? Zoë sent me to get you."

Lonnie's eyes darted from Michael to me. His face fell.

"Maybe we can finish later?" I asked.

He nodded and silently gathered his recorder and papers.

"That one of your special-needs kids?" Michael asked as he helped me down the sidewalk to the car he'd left running at the curb.

"Don't make fun," I said.

"Let me carry that."

He took my bag and slung it over his shoulder, then opened the car door and helped me inside, his hand lingering on mine just two seconds too long. In the months I'd known Michael, he'd shown me about the level of affection due a punching bag. I was someone he could playfully abuse with an occasional kick off the couch or a swift slug to the arm. Since the afternoon he'd carried me out of the woods, his attitude had changed entirely. If we happened to touch, the contact was gentle. He held my arm to steady my balance. He set ice on my ankle. His hand brushed mine. These moments were too frequent to be accidental.

I would have to put an end to it eventually, but for now it was harmless. It felt good to be noticed, however fleeting the attention.

꙾

Lonnie's story appeared in that week's edition of the *Copenhagen Campus Chronicler.* The only good thing about the article was that it ran on the lesser-read Community Life page, tucked neatly beneath "Dorm Kitchen: Recipes for Microwavable Rice Krispies Treats."

INJURY SLOWS PROFESSOR
by Lonnie Weis, Assistant Editor

AMY GALLAGHER, SELF-PROCLAIMED tree lover, was of late felled herself by a tree root of insidious intent. Running along the unkempt trails outside Leonard Chapel, unsuspecting, Professor Gallagher's foot caught beneath an invisible root strewn across her path. The accident resulted in a serious sprain that has left the professor handicapped by a cumbersome cast for a minimum of six weeks. The injury has significantly hindered her ability to function on campus. "I can't walk, I can't drive," she says.

Article 2b ii of the Copenhagen University Grounds Keeping Manual states that "all grounds must be kept in prime condition, including but not limited to the trails and parks within a two mile radius of the academic lawns."

Is Professor Gallagher's accident proof of violation?

Professor Gallagher is decidedly humble. She had great plans of being an astronaut or a ballerina. Instead, she has sacrificed these dreams to become a lowly instructor of freshmen minds. It seems unfair that she should be repaid with injury. Particularly when it becomes evident the university does little to provide her with health insurance. "Out of pocket" she laughs good-naturedly, though there is a tinge of regret in her voice.

Now she can thank heaven it was only a mild injury which she can afford. What if the root had pierced an aorta? You cannot put a price on an aorta.

When questioned about the accident, Professor Gallagher admits "it was like tripping over a taut rope." Though highly doubtful that professor Gallagher has any real enemies, the suspicion in her statement cannot be denied: she implies that someone laid the rope to trap her. Someone failed to care for the grounds and as a result a beloved teacher has been dangerously wounded.

Did the grounds people lay a trap for this unsuspecting professor? Of course not. But an act of inattention makes a party guilty. Is not one bolt out of place enough to explode the Challenger? I ask you, are there not sins of omission? Inaction is as much a crime as action. If the people of Copenhagen do not demand better grounds keeping we can expect to hear more where this came from.

When I arrived in my office Friday, I found a bouquet of flowers waiting on my desk. The card read *Get Well Soon* and was signed *The Grounds Committee.* This was followed by four e-mails from the president for the Board for Student Rights, who wanted to know if I would come speak at a lecture on their weekend conference devoted to the Health Care Crisis on Campus.

Everett encouraged me to milk the incident for all it was worth.

"These are just flowers," he said. "Think what you could get if you actually pressed charges. There's money in litigation."

" 'The love of money is the root of all evil'," I recited.

"No, the root is evil," he said. "Actually, I believe *insidious* was the word."

11

February took its time. The clouds promised snow but delivered ice. The days blurred together like watercolor brushstrokes bleeding into one pale stain. Though I hated Ohio winters, I was a veteran. Zoë suffered from the lack of color; she dyed twin skunk streaks of fluorescent pink in her hair to compensate.

Her mood as the month went on gave new meaning to the phrase *under the weather*. She hadn't written a successful page in weeks, and as a result the energy that she usually channeled into writing had no outlet. She stayed up until five in the morning baking four dozen whole grain, almond raisin granola bars she never ate. She painted our kitchen yellow. She ran seven, eight, even ten miles a day, until her shins throbbed in protest. Michael recommended total rest. At night he played nurse, rotating Ziploc bags of ice from my ankle to her shins and back again.

Though Eli, Zoë, and I spent almost every night together in the small apartment, I gravitated away from Zoë's company and toward Eli's as a plant naturally strains for sunlight, grateful that at least one of us remained immune to the ubiquitous gray.

He was applying to artist residency programs on the coast, filling out applications that piled in disorderly stacks. He sometimes talked of moving out. Though the traffic of artists through our apartment had dwindled with the inclement weather, Kevin, the ever-shy sculptor, still appeared every now and again and lingered, a quiet shadow in the background of our busy days. The money he'd poured into his graduate thesis exhibition had left him struggling with rent payments. He lived in a loft over the Chinese restaurant on Main Street and had all the room we lacked. His kitchen consisted of a microwave, a coffee maker, and a hot plate set up on a folding table, his living room of a flower-print velvet couch and a halogen lamp arranged in the corner. He used the rest of the single open room for making and showing artwork.

I told Eli I thought his moving in would be a good thing for both him and Kevin, inwardly surprised by the disappointment I felt at the prospect of his leaving. But it was only talk. There was always one or another reason why this weekend wasn't ideal or the next weekend wouldn't work. Every night he was in our living room, sitting at his desk preoccupied with another project.

The desk was an old drafting table he'd found discarded on the curb and talked Zoë into helping him carry to our living room. In the last week he'd entertained himself by dissecting and reassembling into collage the twenty-five *People* magazines he'd bought by the crateful at the used bookstore.

The collages were expertly detailed and unpredictably bizarre. They featured whimsical landscapes populated by strange little people, segmented celebrities reassembled into disproportionate figures. There was a young man and young woman holding hands against a hot-pink striped wallpaper backdrop. In the next a preacher atop a skyscraper-high pulpit shaking his red tight fist at the city grotesques shopping below. And (his favorite motif) an old man on a bicycle riding through blue skies and puff paint clouds.

Since spraining my ankle I'd gained seven pounds. I blamed Michael, who felt personally responsible for my accident and apologized with ice cream. I accepted each gift with more resignation than appetite. Apparently, injury is the shortest route to love handles.

Saturday he arrived with two pints of Ben & Jerry's.

"Scoot," he demanded.

I made room for him on the couch. He handed me the Chunky Monkey and a spoon. We took turns eating from the ice cream and the leftover oatmeal cookie crumbs Grandma had sent. His temples pulsed while he chewed. Ironic that the more muscle a man has, the more energy he seems to exert for even the slightest exercise.

"Let me have a look at your ankle." He rubbed his hands together to brush the cookie crumbs from his palms.

"But I'm all mummified."

"I want to make sure it's all right."

He sat on the hassock, facing me, his legs straddling mine. He propped my sprained ankle on his lap. Unlatching the Velcro that held the boot in place, he gently slid it from my foot.

"Looks a lot better," he murmured. "Are you still icing it?"

I thought of my toes decorated in fondant and chocolate. I nodded. The slight pressure of his hands on the arch of my foot made me feel somehow undressed, a Victorian lady scandalized by her own exposed ankles.

"So how's Zoë holding up?" he asked.

"She's been icing her legs every night. I think she feels better. I don't know, she hasn't talked to me much."

He reached for the brace. "I mean how's she holding up about her mom."

"What do you mean about her mom?"

"She's back on the drip."

I was stunned. (And annoyed. *On the drip*. Only Michael could make chemotherapy sound like a street drug.)

"Why didn't she tell me?"

He looked as surprised as I felt. "I just assumed you were the first to know."

When Zoë walked in the room my ankle was still on Michael's lap. Her eyes flashed. I quickly put my foot down.

"Was just checking for swelling," Michael said.

But I saw his ears go red.

～

"I didn't know Michael could be so sweet," I said to Zoë.

We were at the kitchen table. I was grading quizzes. Zoë was painting creek rocks. She had curious ways of dealing with writer's block.

"There's a lot more to Michael than people give him credit for," she said.

I remembered how she'd once told me she would never be able to marry a man who wasn't physically attractive. I'd assumed she was joking, but whenever I pointed out one of Michael's particularly dense comments or dim-witted philosophies, she would always come back with, "I know—but he's *sooo* good-looking."

I asked, "Do you think you'd be with him if he weren't so handsome?"

"A person can't be responsible for good genes any more than responsible for bad ones. It's such a double standard. Everyone says not to judge a person on their appearance, but they judge good-looking people all the time. Nice body, handsome face, ipso facto: vapid meathead."

"Don't get so defensive. I was just joking."

"No. You were serious." She dabbed polka dots on the rock with a detail brush. "If you really got to know Michael you'd see him for what he is. All that macho stuff—he does that because that's the way he thinks he's supposed to be. That's what people expect of him."

"The fact that he plays to people's expectations shows just how self-conscious he is. He should be himself."

"We all play to people's expectations, Amy."

"Not like he does."

"Really?" She twirled her brush in a Mason jar of water. "Why do you pray before all the meals you eat?"

"Because it's a gesture of gratitude."

"No," she said. "You do it because people are watching. You rarely pray for your food at home. You only do it in public."

I frowned. "So."

"So, it's a performance." She gathered blue on her newly cleaned brush. "You do it because you think that's what makes people think you're a good Christian."

Where was this coming from?

"Zoë, I don't do it to look like a good Christian," I countered. "I do it to *be* a good Christian."

She groaned in frustration. "That's my point. You try so hard to be a good Christian. It's not about being *good*. It's not about being *Christian*."

"I don't know what you mean," I said.

She turned to face me. There was a streak of white paint on her eyebrow. I checked the temptation to laugh.

"Everyone's so obsessed with acting right and saying the right things and praying at the right times and in all the right ways. That's all surface stuff; it has nothing to do with anything."

"Are you saying I'm a hypocrite because I don't pray over all my meals?"

"Actually, that's a complete misinterpretation of what I'm saying."

"It would help if you would stop talking so abstractly."

"I'm not trying to be abstract—" Reaching across the table for the red paint, she'd accidentally tipped over her rinse water. She hastily set the jar aright and ran to the kitchen for something to clean up the mess.

"We need some more napkins," she said, trying to dab up the blue-stained water with the only two left.

Automatically, I got up and clomped to the kitchen to add napkins to the pad of paper on the fridge.

"What are you doing?" Zoë asked.

"What?"

I knew *what*, but I said it anyway.

"Don't write it down."

I wrote it down. She stormed off to her room.

⁓

I waited for the clacking of the laptop keys to stop before knocking on her door. She was belly flat on her bed, earphones on.

"Hey."

She hit pause on her iPod. "Hey."

I sat in her office chair. I twirled right and left.

"Sorry about all that," she said.

"It's all right."

She rolled over on her back, laying her arm over her forehead.

"Is it the writing?" I asked.

"Yes. Sort of." She twisted the earphone cord around her forefinger.

"Why didn't you tell me about your mom?" I asked.

She didn't even pause to think. "You didn't ask."

"So I'm asking now."

She sat up. She set her iPod on her *Starry Night* nightstand. She'd painted the homage to Van Gogh so thick that the paint peaked in custard-soft tips. "She's on a new chemo regimen and she's reacting a lot worse than usual. It used to be she could get over the nausea after two or three days, but now she's doubling over every time she takes a bite of a cracker."

"Is it a new drug?"

Zoë shook her head. "She's been on this before."

I waited for a further explanation. She didn't offer one. Her silence was a slap in the face. I realized that she wasn't annoyed with me and she wasn't just being moody. She was *angry*.

"I'm tired of feeling like you don't take us very seriously," she said. "And that hurts, you know? I know what you think of him." It took me a moment to understand we were talking of Michael and not of her mother. "I know you write him off as some pretty boy toy. But he's a good guy. And we're not high school kids fooling around. We're playing for keeps. I wish you'd respect that."

Whether it was my failure to inquire after her mother or my failure to stiff-arm Michael's new, ridiculous flirtation, I'd taken her affection for granted and by virtue of my nonchalance, and without a single conscious intention to do so, I'd lost it.

"I'm sorry," I said without knowing for sure which offense I was apologizing for.

⬎

Zoë's mom was violently ill. She couldn't eat without agony. A sip of chicken soup left her in bed for hours. A bite of fish sent her retching in the toilet. Walking from the bathroom back to her bed required all the energy she had.

As bad as Fay's health was, it was Zoë's appetite I worried about. She couldn't eat a slice of fruit without feeling guilty that she could so readily enjoy a pleasure that had been robbed from her mother. For the first time I noticed the rings beneath her eyes, how her once tightest pants were now falling down at the waist.

Eli offered to drive her home for the weekend, but she didn't want to inconvenience anyone. She took the first available bus to Chicago.

"You'll be all right?" she asked as she tossed makeup from her vanity into her suitcase.

"Shouldn't I be asking you that?"

"I mean you two. You're not going to be weird about being left

164

alone with him?" She eyed Eli as he walked by the open doorway. He was pacing. Jillian had called two hours ago and he was still on the phone, a new record.

"Of course not," I said.

He glanced in the room and grimaced. I grimaced back. I'd never spoken to Jillian, but I imagined her voice shrill and piercing like the sound of his phone and its incessant ringing.

~

Zoë called the next night. "Inflammation of the bowel," she said. "I think it's a tumor."

"Did they say 'tumor'?" Eli asked, leaning unnecessarily toward the speaker on my phone.

"They didn't have to. What else could it be?"

"What can they do?" I asked.

"Surgery."

We only spoke for a few minutes. When I hung up, Eli ran his hand over his mouth. "It's bad, isn't it?"

I nodded. The fear in her voice had been unmistakable: She was terrified of what they might find if they opened her mother up.

~

The only thing that cheered Zoë was the prospect of a party. Her *UrbanStyle* article was set to print the first of March, one day before my thirtieth birthday. Eli decided that as soon as she got back we should have one big party to celebrate both. The way Zoë beamed at the idea, I wished I'd thought of it.

I tried to drum up excitement, for Zoë's sake and in gratitude to Eli, but I wasn't thrilled about turning thirty. I made my mother promise she wouldn't do anything extravagant for my birthday. She mailed gifts anyway, a sunlamp to counteract my seasonal affective disorder and a Luna Lady Pro X1000 Hair Straightener. There was a note taped to the box:

*I know you have no luck with your hair, but this is a
brand new, top of the line product and it works! You can see a
demonstration on Internet! TRY IT!! It will make your hair
smooth like Lindsay Johnson's! Love XOXOX–Mom.*

"What is this, to iron your sleeves?" Eli asked. He clamped the
flat iron on his shirt cuff.

"To iron your hair," I explained.

"What's wrong with your hair?"

While I tried the Straightener, Eli sat on the bathtub ledge to
watch with equal parts fascination and horror.

"Will it go back?" he asked.

"It's not permanent," I said. "You just wash your hair and it goes
curly again."

I pressed the iron down on a plait of hair. There was a sizzling
sound, like steaks on a griddle. Eli winced.

"Can't you burn your hair?"

"Of course not," I said, worried that I would.

While I worked my way slowly from one side of my scalp to the
other, he worked on talking me out of it. He said my hair reminded
him of a Pre-Raphaelite muse. He also, for a fact, knew plenty of
girls who worked hard to have hair half as wild as mine.

This was the first time I'd heard the word *wild* applied to my
hair in a positive way. Wild curls—"your father's" my mother was
fond of saying—were public enemy number one. We tried to cut,
to dye, to perm, but you didn't style curls like this. You could only
bushwhack. I'd made my peace with it; for my mother, however, the
sheer obstinacy of such hair was an affront. She was forever sending remedies in the wild hope that one day I would return home
looking less like the Bernadette Peters of Broadway and more like
the Andie MacDowell of *Four Weddings and a Funeral*, a movie she
loved, despite all the premarital sex. (Such was the power of Hugh
Grant's adorable bumbling.)

Eli gave up and left me to the business of tormenting my hair into submission. The Straightener straightened, but the quality of the final result was questionable. I went to him for a verdict.

He was in Zoë's room, sitting at her vanity, her curling iron in hand and the entire left side of his beautiful black hair sprung into a bouncy Shirley Temple bob.

"You're a stupid man," I said.

"You don't like it?"

"I think you look ridiculous."

He turned toward me slowly, careful not to upset the curling iron hot near his cheek, and informed me he wasn't washing his until I washed mine. I said that was fine with me, because I didn't believe him for a minute.

When I saw him at The Brewery the next morning taking orders and serving coffee, his hair still wound in loose but persistent curls, I laughed loud enough to turn heads. Everett was at the bar working his way through a stack of books and a bottomless mug. He looked from my hair to Eli's.

"What is this?" he asked, exasperated. "Performance art?"

From the other end of the counter, Eli winked.

⌒

That night I washed my hair. I Googled *Pre-Raphaelite*.

The Pre-Raphaelite brotherhood comprised a group of nineteenth century English poets, painters, and critics who believed the art of their day was polluted by academic standards. There was mention of the compositions of Raphael, the purposeful mimicry of Quattrocento Italian and Flemish art. But I didn't have the vocabulary to understand the essays I'd found. I took, like Eli, to studying the pictures.

I recognized *The Lady of Shalott* from a print framed and hanging in my aunt's living room, but the other images were only familiar inasmuch as they alluded to classical stories and mythology. My favorite was *Proserpine* by Dante Gabriel Rossetti. In the painting, a tall woman wearing pale green robes stands before a square shaft of blurred light. Her dark hair falls in heavy plaits down her back. There's an almost masculine strength to her brow. Or maybe it's her stern gaze, shaded with mourning, that lends her face the appearance of a man's hardened features. She looks down and into the distance. In one hand she holds a pomegranate. Her other hand clasps the wrist of the first, as if she is torn between taking a second bite of the fruit or leaving it to drop to the ground. In her indecision, she reminded me of Eve, sorrowfully cradling the remnants of a forbidden fruit.

According to one source on classical mythology, Proserpine was the daughter of Zeus, king of the gods, and Ceres, goddess of agriculture. Struck by Cupid's arrow, Hades fell in love with Proserpine and carried her to the underworld to be his wife. When Ceres learned that Zeus had conspired to marry his daughter to Hades, she stopped the growth of all crops. She searched for her daughter, leaving deserts as footprints. Finally, Zeus intervened. He and Hades reached an agreement: Proserpine was free to go providing she had not eaten during her captivity, for those who ate the food of the dead cannot return to the land of the living. Unfortunately for Proserpine, she had eaten the nectar of four pomegranate seeds. Abiding by the terms of the bargain, she was condemned to the underworld four months of every year, to serve as the wife of Hades. The painting portrayed a period of her captivity.

More interesting: According to historians, Rossetti was in love with his model, Jane Morris, who was already married to a fellow artist. It was left for debate, then, whether he'd painted Proserpine's sorrow or his own.

As a character, the woman in the painting was the beautiful daughter of a powerful goddess; as a model, she was merely a pretty, married woman. In both, a marriage held her captive.

12

It snowed the night of the Happy Birthday Publication Party. We piled coats by the doorway until they formed a formidable barricade on the stairs. People arrived pink from the cold, then flushed red in the warmth. The air was heady from the singed oil of jalapeños and the breathing of wine. Zoë had outdone herself in the kitchen. We had spicy pot stickers and vegetable kabobs and pitas spread with fresh hummus. Everett brought music. A very pregnant Valerie brought cake.

Amber and Lynn, Jillian's housemates, brought a pervading sense of Jillian's presence.

"You remember Amber?" Eli asked. She had been to the apartment to see him several times so it was more than a little unnecessary that I set down the drink I was pouring to offer a handshake.

She accepted, quickly looking me up and down. Her appraisal made me self-conscious of the efforts I'd taken that night. I was wearing blush and had carefully chosen a tighter than usual sweater. I'd taken similar care in not touching my hair. It billowed on my shoulders in haphazard curls. Amber's hair was neatly gelled in place, a shiny implacable helmet.

Eli took her coat—a formidable ankle-length red velvet—but she remained planted at my side.

"You know you don't look at all thirty," was the first thing she said to me. "You don't have a light, do you?" was the second.

I gestured to the matches we kept in a jam jar beside the stove. She kept her cigarettes in a hot pink handbag. I didn't have the courage to tell her not to light one in the apartment.

"So you guys are pretty good to let Eli stay here like this." She cupped the palm of her hand around the flame, waiting for the cigarette to light.

"We don't mind having him around."

"I know, right." She was watching him. "He's adorable."

Amber wore a black dress with cobweb-patterned lace sleeves. While she told me at length about Jillian and Eli and the minutiae of their seemingly complicated love life, I wondered if her arms didn't itch terribly. In the seventh grade I'd been accosted every morning on the school bus by a Larissa Spregg, who invited herself to sit with me and then spent the fifteen-minute ride to school detailing how she'd spent the previous night debating whether or not to kill herself. She knew I was a Christian and confessed to me in the hopes I would entertain her by attempting to witness. I spent all of junior high and high school desperately uncomfortable around people who dressed Goth.

"Do you think they're pretty serious?" I asked when she stopped talking long enough to light a second cigarette.

"Jillian doesn't do relationships that aren't serious. She's one of those woman who was just born for serial monogamy."

I turned the oxymoron *serial monogamy* over in my mind, adding it to the brief list of things I knew about Jillian.

"Unfortunately for her, she's like a magnet for the desperate and the loser," Amber said. "Eli's the first guy she's had in a while who treats her right. She's been in relationships—serious ones—since she was in like the sixth grade, but she never realizes how much it weighs on her, the problems, the resolutions, the constant need to give and take. It's existential for her; she gets like really large with it when it's actually really—" she tapped the ash of her cigarette into a plastic cup left on the counter—"micro," she finished with satisfaction.

Jillian deserved a good man. She had issues with men, mostly with her father, issues that had spawned new problems, bulimia for one. She and Eli both planned to move to New York when she returned.

My head ached. I found it difficult to focus on a thing Amber was saying. In the living room someone accidentally broke a glass on the hardwood floor. At the sound of the splintering glass, I gratefully begged off to help clean up the mess. I did my best to avoid Amber the rest of the night, but she kept appearing within arm's reach, her conversations bleeding into mine. Or maybe it was the unchecked volume of her voice, the fact that I could hear her across the entire apartment that made her seem omnipresent.

Late in the evening a copy of Zoë's story finally began to circulate. People sat on the couch in a tight-wedged row to read the magazine over each other's shoulders. Zoë couldn't hide her pleasure at the attention. I worried I would be as unable to hide my jealousy. I took myself out to sit on the roof, just to be on the safe side.

Down below, Valerie and Everett were sitting side by side on the old picnic table that sank a little more into the lawn each month. At least Everett had the decency to smoke outside. They were arguing good-naturedly about constellations. Valerie's husband was too soft-spoken and passive for argument. She liked to disagree with Everett once in a while to get the fight out of her system.

"There's no Orion's Oxen," Valerie said.

"It's right there. By his belt."

"I don't see it."

He leaned over until his head was aligned with hers and pointed with the burning butt of his cigarette. "Follow the left star there, over five degrees, and you're at the tip of the horn of the giant water buffalo, otherwise known as Orion's Oxen. Why would he have that belt if not to whip his beast of labor into submission?"

Valerie asked if he was on crack.

I sat on one of the lawn chairs scattered on the porch and leaned back to consider the stars. I closed my eyes, rubbed them vigorously until constellations of red blossomed on the backs of my eyelids. I should take an Advil for the headache. I felt irritable and tired. Maybe I just felt thirty.

"Forget something?" Eli handed me my coat.

"Thanks."

"You all right?"

I sat up. "I'm fine. Why?"

"You've been quiet all night."

"I just need some air. It's so crowded and loud. I guess I got a little claustrophobic."

Below us, Valerie was laughing. No one could make her laugh like Everett. For a moment I entertained the idea that Eli and I could be comfortable with each other like that. There wasn't anything wrong with his having a friend outside of Jillian. I had to tell myself this quite often.

"Amber's talkative," I said.

"She's something." He pulled up a lawn chair, unfolded it, examined its torn and frayed underside, and set it aside in exchange for another. "I shouldn't have left you alone with her. Sorry about that." He sat down with a quiet, contented sigh. "Jillian's girlfriends are very *vocal*."

"She was worried about Jillian."

"Amber doesn't worry about anybody. She likes drama; it makes parties more interesting."

"She doesn't have to open her mouth to make things more interesting—she could just walk in a room."

"I'm glad I caught you alone," he said to change the subject. "I haven't had a chance to wish you an official happy birthday yet." He reached in his pocket and produced a small gift wrapped in baby blue paper, tied neatly with a delicate white bow.

"You're not supposed to get me a gift."

"It's not much, but when I saw it I thought of you."

Inside the blue wrapping paper was a jewelry box, and inside the jewelry box, on a bed of cotton, lay a pair of glass earrings shaped like flowers. The pit of each had been made of tiny, golden beads that together resembled a sunflower's eye.

"Kevin's ex makes jewelry," he explained. "Do you like them?"

"They're gorgeous. But they're almost too pretty. I usually don't wear things like this."

"Put them on."

The earrings were heavy. I tilted my head to model. The way he looked at my hair, eyes following a ring of curls from my brow to the nape of my neck to my chest, it was as though he'd reached across and touched me ever so gently.

I hurried to take the earrings off.

"Thank you," I said. "These are the nicest thing anyone's given me in a long time."

The screen door flew open. Amber shouted, "Eli *Morretti*, what are you *doing*! We are bored to death in here without you!"

"So come out here." He folded the blue wrapping paper and hid it in his pocket.

Amber came and sat right in Eli's lap. He allowed it, but kept his hands on the armrests of his chair.

"Lynn and I have been having a little discussion," Amber said. "And we've come to the conclusion that in light of your work and ambitions and the very length of your body, you are in need of a larger bedroom."

"Or a bedroom at all," Lynn volunteered.

"So . . . maybe—if it's okay with Amy—you could come live with us!"

"And make us cappuccinos!"

"And T-shirts!"

"But there's one condition." Amber raised her finger and waited for Eli to focus his eyes on it. "Under no circumstances are you to fall in love with us."

I excused myself. In the kitchen I opened the freezer door and stuck my face inside. The heat sloughed off my cheeks in waves.

Zoë's manager from The Brewery was leaning against the counter, reading Zoë's *UrbanStyle* article. She slapped the magazine against my hip playfully.

"It was good of you to let her write about this," she said.

"Write about what?" I asked.

"Haven't you read it?" she asked.

"No, we just got it today. Why?"

"Well, you might not be having much luck as an author, but I think you may have found work as a muse."

No luck as an author. It surprised me how abrasive the woman could be.

"It's good." She handed me the magazine and began skirting her way around me to return to the party. "Something every woman should read."

I flipped back to the first page of Zoë's essay. In boldface the heading read: *Making a List, Checking It Twice.* Beneath ran a subtitle: *Getting to the Bottom of the Modern Woman's Obsession.*

Under the two-page heading, a woman sat at a white desk in a white room. Thousands of identical yellow sticky notes plastered the walls, the chair, the nondescript desk—even the woman. She sat at a table with her legs primly pressed together, her back straight, and her eyes staring upward at the enormous pile of chores littered about her head. In her left hand she held a smartphone and in the right a red pen poised over the Franklin Day Planner lying open on the desk.

At the bottom of the page, the article began:

*A few weeks ago, while scavenging for a working pen
(an abnormally rare commodity in an apartment of aspiring authors), I found a rather telling scrap of paper beside my
housemate's computer. Or, I should say, several rather telling
scraps of paper. In piles around her desk, hung from the bulletin
board over her bed, lining her computer screen in sticky notes
were to-do lists. Not one, but many.*

*These to-do lists were categorized in various ways, the
chores organized by location, by day, or by priority. For example, there was one list of things to do while in the downtown
area (drop off laundry, buy stamps, pick up library books) and
another for things to do by 5:00. She had taken pains to carve
out ten-minute slots for eating and even a twenty-minute slot
for showering.*

*My housemate is a textbook addict of multitasking produc-
tivity: the belief that the worth of one's life can be measured in
the efficiency with which one completes the highest number of
chores. But is this any real way to live? Are we killing ourselves
with our need to be productive?*

*My friends and co-workers keep checklists. So did my
mother—until the day she was diagnosed with breast cancer.
Standing before my housemate's extensive collage of chores, and
thinking of these women I know who've struggled in one way
or another with the same compulsion, I began to wonder if it's
possible that in spending our days in the systematic elimination
of perceived obligations, we are actually missing out on living
itself. . . .*

"Do you have more ice?" Everett asked. He held two empty
cups in his hands. "Rations low."

"Up there." I gestured toward the freezer absentmindedly, excus-
ing myself through the crowd to my bedroom. I locked the door
and turned to page 223, where the article went on to explain that
checklists were symptomatic of a woman's need to feel productive. It
then delved into a brief lesson on history, tracking the evolution of
the Franklin Day Planner to the present-day smartphone, detailing

how digital calendars had only increased the dependence on a false sense of productivity.

Throughout the essay Zoë used "we" and "our," lumping all women, career-driven and homemaker alike, into one homogeneous, guilt-tripped class of multitasking do-gooders. Despite her best efforts to maintain a consistently plural and sympathetic voice, I did not hear "we" in my head as I read. I heard "you." *You, Amy Gallagher, are killing yourself with your need to Get Things Done. You, my poor Ms. Gallagher, believe your life's worth can be measured by the efficiency with which you complete the greatest number of chores.*

Though I was more or less aware of this compulsion, I've never considered how visible it was. I kept grocery lists tacked to the fridge; people to e-mail lists stuck to my computer screen; *Books to Read* and *Books Read* piled in ratty notebooks on the living room shelves. And she didn't even know about the lists from childhood: *Potential Careers, Boys Kissed, Stories Written, Things to Do Before Thirty.*

I forced myself to read to the conclusion:

> *The opportunities we have today are still somewhat new for the female sex (and I am grateful for them. God bless the 14th Amendment, the tampon, and Title IX!). It seems, however, that the knowledge of all these opportunities leaves us feeling as though our independence and self-sufficiency are precarious. We are always striving to be the best at home, at school, and at work, trying to prove we can do it all. Sooner or later we have to admit that "it all" is too tall an order.*
>
> *I'm not trying to depreciate the value of hard work. But I am a firm believer in "all good things in moderation." We must learn when to put the lists away—when to stop and watch a sunset, enjoy a bubble bath, laugh with a friend, take a walk without the need for a destination.*
>
> *The first thing my mother did on getting her breast cancer diagnosis was burn her Day Planner. Has she missed appointments? Yes. Has she bowed out of more than one potentially career propelling opportunity? Yes. Has she lived every day as*

fully as possible? Most definitely yes. Her cancer has come back in sundry and vile ways, but every time it does, she's prepared with an arsenal of freshly lived memories to give her strength and to remind her that life is worth fighting for. Watching her struggle for even the smallest pleasures the healthy take for granted, I've learned the hard way that life is too short and the world too varied to fit into carefully drafted rows of check-boxes.

So at the risk of being trite, I say: Ladies, burn the checklist, and smell the roses.

I was insulted by the unrelenting optimism of women's magazines, by the willing suspension of self-respect required to read such nonsense. I stared at the photograph of the young woman and her sticky notes. It was one thing to see your weaknesses brought to light by a loving friend, but to be exposed in a national publication? I was so angry my hands trembled. It was ten minutes before I trusted myself enough to the party.

"There she is! Miss America," Everett sang. He put his arm around me. "We were just going to cut the cake without you."

"I had to go to the bathroom," I said.

He patted me on the back. "Well, we hope it all came out okay."

He led me to the kitchen, where everyone had gathered around the cake that read *Happy B and P Day!* beneath a haze of lit and quickly melting blue-white candles.

Zoë stood at the center of the circle, a birthday hat on her head. Valerie held the glowing sheet cake, beckoning me to help blow out the candles before the wax ruined the icing. Eli and Amber and Lynn were not in the room.

"Hurry!" Zoë cried, strapping a paper birthday hat on my head; it sat lopsided on my curls.

"On three!" she said and took my hand. "One, two—"

Together we shot out all thirty of the flickering lights.

⌐

"That was not a bad party," Zoë said.

It was nearly three in the morning and we were alone. At some point in the evening, long before everyone else had begun the mass exodus, Eli had left without saying where he was going or when he was coming back. He hadn't spoken to me the rest of the night. It mortified me to think he'd read the article.

Zoë had been in the living room for the last two hours, lying on the floor with her feet propped on the couch, lazily talking to Everett, the last of our guests. I'd left them alone when it became obvious the three Red Bulls he'd had were not going to wear off anytime soon. In my room, I'd listened to their occasional bursts of laughter, irate with Zoë and annoyed with Everett for delaying my opportunity to let her know.

I was sitting in bed reading when she came in.

"I will be full until Thursday." She threw herself long-ways across my bed, setting her head in my lap. "Everett is hilarious. Have you heard his theory on *Sixteen Candles* and adolescent rite of passage?"

Her spontaneous kindness, a stark departure from her general attitude toward me in the last week, only made me angrier.

Peering up, she caught my expression and stopped. "What's wrong?"

"I want to talk to you."

"Something the matter?"

"You wrote about me," I said.

"What?"

"You used me," I repeated. "In your article." I picked up the magazine and read the first paragraph aloud. Her back stiffened. "You wrote this about me. And, to be honest, I don't exactly appreciate it."

Zoë sat up. Staring at the bedspread, she said with carefully checked frustration, "I don't understand what the problem is."

"You can't just write about your friends in national magazines and not expect them to be upset!"

"I didn't write *about* you. I was inspired by you. There's a difference."

"You've humiliated me in front of everyone we know."

She laughed disbelievingly. "No one we know is going to read that stupid magazine. It's *UrbanStyle!*"

"Oh, really?" I counted on my hand: "What about Valerie, Eli, Everett. This article's made you a local celebrity."

She stood up. "You're totally overreacting."

I followed her to the living room, where she began stacking plastic cups from the coffee table and smashing them down into the wastebasket.

"I want to talk about this," I insisted.

She raised her eyebrows, passing me for a second round through the living room for the paper plates. "So talk."

"Did you have to use me as a case study? Couldn't you have dug up something more profound from your own life? Why me?"

She smashed the paper plates down in the trash can, then threw up her hands. "I don't know! Why do writers ever do what they do? It just came to me. It's not like I sat down with the intention of publicly humiliating my roommate and best friend."

I was surprised to hear her say "best friend." It made me think of elementary school.

She stepped into the trash can, pushing the discarded plates and cups and napkins down with her glitter-bedecked sneakers. "Writing doesn't work that way, and you know it." She stomped her foot on the ground to shake off the debris. "You sit down, you start to write, and things from life just creep in. It's not on purpose. And it's not like I used your name or anything."

"*My housemate*," I repeated. "Great cover. How many of those do you have again?"

"You know, I really thought you were different from this," she said. "I thought living with another writer would be good for me." She marched past me, stacking the bowls beside the couches. "You'll have to forgive me, but I had all these crazy ideas that we would be sitting around talking about books and ideas. That we would be up late, editing each other's work, brainstorming characters, throwing ideas back and forth—and *sharing* them. It's not like there's a copyright on creativity. I say something, you use it; you say something, I use it. That's the way it works."

She threw the dishes into the sink.

"Let's not go there," I said. I felt her anger snowballing, gathering debris from every minor disagreement and artistic difference. "That's not what we're talking about."

"That's what I'm talking about." She threw the cake pan into the sink over the other dishes, sprayed it with a zigzag of dish soap. "I don't see how everything between us has to be a competition."

"When have I ever competed with you?"

"I stand up for you, you know," she went on. "I praise your work; I tell people what a good teacher you are; I practically make you out to be a saint. And then you go and you act like a schoolgirl around Michael."

"Now you're just being ridiculous," I muttered. "I have only ever been friendly with Michael."

"It would be courteous for you to work on being a little *less* friendly."

"You think I want to be with Michael?" I laughed. "Michael. Who thinks New England is a country."

I turned my back and wiped down the counter. Zoë dropped the pans in the sink one at a time, louder with each pan.

"What I don't understand," she said as if we hadn't paused at all, "is how you make all these resolutions but never get around to fulfilling them. That's what your lists are. Unfulfilled resolutions."

"Name one."

"Writing," she answered immediately. "You move the television and promise you're going to devote yourself to writing, but you spend more time pitching fits about writer's block than fighting it. If you spent half the time at your laptop you spend complaining to your mom and brother about teaching, you'd have an epic novel by now."

"I write."

"When?"

"When I get the inspiration."

"When is that?"

"I can't schedule inspiration," I said. "There's something you failed to mention in your little article: I never make checklists for writing."

We locked eyes.

"Except to catalogue rejections for stories you know aren't good anymore."

I really hated her for those two seconds.

"That's different."

"Your work hasn't moved on since graduate school." She said it gently, but the kindness in her voice was condescending.

"You can't just sit down and write a novel like it's a nine-to-five job."

"You can't sit on the couch eating bon-bons and waiting for a story to hit you over the head either. You have to exercise talent if you want it to work for you."

"So, what, you think I'm a waste of talent?"

"No." She paused. "I think you're a flirt, Amy. I think you're a hypocrite."

We were both surprised at what she'd said. I walked out, because I knew I would say something I'd regret if I stayed. I sat on my bed. Zoë slammed a cupboard door three times until the latch finally caught. Dishes rattled. I stood back up, paced, tripped on a T-shirt left in a pile on the floor. I tried kicking the shirt away with my sprained ankle, only to get it wrapped around the brace.

With the T-shirt still tangled on my foot, I crawled into bed and buried my face into my pillow. I didn't know which was worse: that Zoë might actually believe I was a hypocrite or that she would say such a thing just to hurt me.

⌐

Eli was in the kitchen, carefully balancing his burnt toast on the windowsill to cool off. He wanted to know where Zoë was. He'd never seen dirty dishes left overnight; he feared imminent disaster.

"She left." I poured myself a cup of coffee. I added three heaping tablespoons of sugar and a generous pour of cream.

"Where to?"

"I don't know. Michael's, I think."

I took three gulps of the coffee, carried the rest to my room. Kneeling down, I pulled the stacks of manuscripts I kept in a box under the bed. I dumped its contents, loose-leaf paper, stapled manuscripts, the dozens of workshop critiques from friends I'd highlighted and annotated.

Eli came in the room. "What's going on?"

"We fought."

"About . . . ?"

"The article—the fact that I'm a frantic, compulsive overachiever. Everything."

"The article?"

"You haven't read it?"

I yanked the *UrbanStyle* magazine off my desk and tossed it at him.

"It's about me," I explained. "And it's humiliating."

He sat on my bed, opened to the article and read. I was reminded of what a terribly slow reader he was. Before he could turn to the last page, I closed the magazine shut on his hand.

"You get the idea."

He opened the magazine again. He tapped the picture. "So this is you?"

I covered my eyes with my hands. "I alphabetize my checklists."

"So."

"I have a list of every book I've ever written."

"Not a big deal."

I dropped my hands in my lap. "I have one of every boy I've ever kissed."

He raised his eyebrows. "Written?"

I nodded.

"Well." He set the magazine on my desk. "You're conscientious of your commitments."

"I'm neurotic."

"Sure. But only a little. No more than is normal. Did you ever think maybe Zoë's exorcising her own demons? She's the one who keeps a daily page quota; she's the one who runs five miles a day. She's one of the most compulsive overachievers I've ever met. Maybe she sees something of herself in you and maybe she doesn't like it. I really doubt she meant anything by this. She admires you."

He picked up a sheet of paper from the floor. "Is this your stuff?"

"My stories. From grad school." I piled a stack together. "Trash."

"Why would you say that?"

"No one wants it. One rejection is okay. Twenty is understandable. But when you start counting the failures in months it's time to get a clue." I sat in my office chair, took a sheet of paper from the stack and folded it over on itself. "Do you know how many articles Zoë's printed since she graduated? Five. And every time to a wider audience. I've never published a single story."

"Publication's overrated, Amy. It's just words on a page. You should write for yourself, not for the critics."

"You don't understand," I said. "It's different for you. You make something and it can exist on its own and people can take it or leave it. But a story isn't finished until someone reads it."

"Why don't you 'publish' it yourself then? Start a blog."

I pressed the origami I had created onto my knee. "I don't blog. I write fiction."

"So make it a fiction blog: one story a week." The idea excited him. "Or you could publish serial chapters like they used to do with magazines. You could easily find an audience for that."

"I'm not interested in propping my work up on my own possibly exaggerated opinion of myself." I pinched the tip of my paper airplane to a point, flew it at Eli. "Editors exist for a reason."

He caught the airplane, unfolded it in frustration. "There's no magic to books, Amy."

"But there is! I love the idea that someone else could for a moment live in a world I created, make it their own. I might have a mental picture of a character, but everyone else who reads the book will see that character a little different. If I invent and then publish an Annie Smith, I've created a hundred or a thousand Annie Smiths, each different from the other imagined, but all of them as real as a real person to the reader who falls in love with the story. How many people talk about Mr. Darcy or Scout or Jo March as real people they've known? And isn't that magic? To make something real out of thin air?"

I was so caught up with my own argument it took me a moment to notice the peculiar way he was looking at me. For the first time it occurred to me that perhaps he found me as exasperating and as fascinating as I found him.

"It's the only childhood magic I still believe in," I confessed softly.

"Fine," he said, but the strain in his voice had gone. He waved the now-crinkled sheet of paper in the air. "Can I have the rest of this one?"

I shrugged. "Take them all."

To my surprise, he did.

As the morning passed, so did my sense of victimization. What Eli had said made a kind of sense: Zoë *was* the one who kept a writing schedule and a workout regimen that were nearly militaristic. Even if I tried to stay angry, I found it too exhausting. I had grown up in a home where misunderstandings dissolved into laughter almost of their own accord, my brother too good-natured to fight and my mother too easily distracted to remember an offense.

Zoë was of prouder Appalachian stock, the kind that carried grudges through generations, sparking family feuds fueled by moonshine and loaded hunting rifles.

"I'm going back to Chicago," she said when she returned to the apartment that night.

"How long will you be gone?" I asked.

She walked right past me, calling for Eli.

He opened the bathroom door. He was toweling his wet hair.

"You can have my room," she said. "I won't be needing it for a while."

"Where are you sleeping?" he asked.

"I'm going back to Chicago. You can sleep on my bed. But"—she pointed at his chest—"you'd better wash the sheets before I come back."

"When are you coming back?"

"When I find a new apartment."

I rolled my eyes.

She stood in her closet and threw clothes into an open suitcase on the floor. Michael, who had come with her, watched from the living room. He'd left his coat on. He seemed both uncomfortably hot and embarrassed, regarding Zoë's temper with the amused forbearance of a married man who had learned it was better to side with his wife despite the eccentricities of her so-called logic. I wondered if he knew he was one of the things we'd fought over. No doubt it would give him pleasure.

She was in and out in half an hour. She slammed the door behind her.

Eli was taken off guard by the entire spectacle.

I actually found myself defending her behavior: "She gets irrational when her mother's sick."

Worriedly, he stood at the living room window and watched as she walked resolutely away from us.

13

After a month of stomping around, one part human and one part Clydesdale, I was finally given permission to shed the cumbersome air cast. Eli drove me to the doctor's office and sat in the waiting room reading *Highlights* while I had my last examination.

"You'll have some residual pain," the physician said. He was the third I had seen throughout this ordeal. I couldn't even remember his name. "But for all intents and purposes, you're back on two feet." He smiled. He couldn't resist the pun.

On the way home we bought a sleeve of Toll House easy-bake cookie dough to celebrate. I had the very best intentions of baking the cookies. Instead, I put a dozen in the oven and ate the rest of the dough raw while watching *Sense and Sensibility*—a fitting film, I explained to Eli, because the spraining of an ankle served as major plot point in the romance between the beautiful Marianne and the dashing rogue Willoughby.

Eli sat on the floor, his back to the couch on which I was rather unceremoniously camped with the cookie dough to my left and my liberated ankle enjoying its perch on the armrest. As Edward Ferrars began to fall, in an ever so endearing and awkward way, for Elinor

Dashwood, it occurred to me that I'd seen this movie at least eight times and wasn't tired of it. But then I'd always had talent for repetition. As a little girl I played Amy Grant's "Thy Word" until Mom threatened to donate my Fisher-Price tape player to the church poor box. I read favorite books until I could recite them from memory. In one year I watched *Return of the Jedi* one hundred and twenty-three times. Writing turned my childhood love of repetition into a professional skill. When working on a story I could envision the same scene and the same characters a dozen times, perfecting or changing a minor detail with each replay.

My fantasies of men were similarly nuanced and rerun. In my mind's library of catalogued romances lived men famous, men ordinary, boys I knew, and boys I watched from a distance. The conversations I had with these men, the kisses and otherwise we shared in dark rooms, comprised a collection of ideas taken from cinema, from magazines, and from the novels I'd read burrowed beneath my bedroom blankets, cheeks flushed with vicarious excitement.

I knew better than to expect much from love, from romance. But to expect and to fantasize are not the same thing.

I watched Eli trying to watch the movie, studied the line of his profile, the concentration furrowing his brow. We hadn't been acting any differently than we had when Zoë was around; he only ever treated me with the friendly detachment of a roommate. When he moved to the couch to sit beside me, I knew better than to expect him to take me in the crook of his arm or to even notice that I was wearing perfume. I never wear perfume.

He fought sleep. His head bowed lower and lower as his eyes grew heavier, until, gently, his cheek came to rest against my shoulder. My breath caught. I closed my eyes, wondered if his lips would taste as spiced as the scent of his skin.

The credits rolled. I turned the volume up to startle him awake. He was only a little bewildered to find the ending had made me cry.

Late that night Valerie went into labor. By the time I got home from work the next afternoon, Jake had posted pictures of mother and baby on Facebook. They'd named her Rachel.

When the young family returned from the hospital, Everett and I drove to her house to visit and deliver food. Jake met us at the door, wearing sweatpants and a T-shirt on which a smiling taco said *Hola!* The house was small, crowded in a comfortable way. The living room smelled of baby powder and tomato soup. It had the closed-in feeling of a happy family absorbed in their private world. Valerie let us take turns holding Rachel. I was mesmerized by the tiny white line of her fingernails.

"She's beautiful," I said. In the moment it felt like a novel thing to say.

Selfishly, we stayed an hour, a good forty minutes after Valerie lost interest in our company.

When we got in the car I started crying.

"Why are you crying?" Everett said. "She's fine—the baby's fine. Everybody's fine."

"I think I want one," I said.

"Oh, honey."

This was my second breakdown of the week and I didn't even care this time. I had lost all dignity. Everett drove directly to the Donut Shoppe where we ate bear claws and coffee for dinner. He tried to cheer me up with gossip about Eli.

"So that was some drama, the other night."

I'd managed to stop crying. I wiped my nose on a napkin and asked what he was talking about.

"Eli and Jillian. They were arguing on the porch at your party. Well, he was on the porch, on *the phone* arguing with her. I don't know what she had her panties in a twist about, but things look bad for our hero."

"You could hear them fighting?"

"I heard his end, which was more than enough. Trust me, barbs were thrown, rejoinders met with sarcasm."

"How can you tell?"

"I'm a writer. I know dialogue."

"You write criticism."

"Then I know character development. Whatever." He lifted his coffee as if to make a toast. "It's curtains for Jillian."

⁕

It was too hot for March. We suffered a weekend of rain that only amplified the humidity. When the sun returned Monday, it seemed an earnest, unwanted newcomer at an already out of control party. It shone eerily over the wind that throttled the windowpanes and whipped the trees into a frenzy. Girls walked sideways. Dead leaves, blackened from months under snow, stirred and spun in mini-twisters. On the field, the men's soccer team kicked the ball toward the goal only to wait in suspense as it lingered in the air eight, nine, ten seconds before falling back to the earth and directly at the opponent's feet.

At the office, I closed the blinds and shut the door. I was too busy working to notice the increasing violence of the wind. When I checked my e-mail several hours later I found four campus security messages waiting in my inbox.

To: gallagham@copenhagen.edu
From: campussecurity@copenhagen.edu
Sent: Monday 3.12.07 10:37 AM
Subject: Wind Advisory

Students and faculty:

A severe wind advisory is in effect for Copenhagen University from 3:30 PM to 8:14 PM. Winds have been clocked in at 40 MPH with corresponding gales at nearly 60 MPH.

There have been power outages on South Campus. If you are without power, you may stay in the Student Commons for the night. Bring a sleeping bag and pillow. The Student Commons and Laws Dining Hall will be open for meals. Campus security requires that all individuals not moving to the student commons REMAIN INDOORS until further notice.

~Campus Security

Similar messages had been sent at 11:21 a.m., 12:15 p.m., and 3:12 p.m. Each insisted that students and faculty remain indoors so, like the students, I went outside to see what was going on.

The sky had yellowed. Somewhere wood splintered, the spine of a sapling snapping in two. The clouds moved quickly, each a part of a larger tapestry pulled quickly on a reel. In the parking lot, a group of boys took turns sitting in wheeled office chairs, using dormitory bedsheets as parachutes to rocket themselves back and forth across the lot. I drove home at a crawl, mindful of falling debris and blacked-out intersections.

Eli forced the door open for me with both hands.

"You all right?" he asked.

I shook leaves from my coat. "The traffic lights are out."

He took my bag and ran up the stairs ahead of me. "Everything's out. We had to close The Brewery—Kevin says the whole downtown has shut down." He returned from Zoë's bedroom cradling the flame of a cinnamon candle. "Do you have any more of these? It'll be pitch-black in half an hour."

We found one flashlight, three jar candles, and twelve tea lights I'd kept stashed away in the closet with the Christmas decorations. We lit them all. The many flickering lights cast the living room in soft shadow.

I shone the flashlight into the almost empty kitchen cupboards, wishing I hadn't skipped lunch to work. "I'm assuming all the restaurants are closed."

"We have hot dogs," Eli said optimistically.

We cut the hog dogs into half-inch slices and laid them on white bread, smothered in mustard and ketchup. We ate at the table facing the open screen door so we could enjoy the show. Heat lightning had begun. The cold hot dogs tasted good. They reminded me of home, of Friday nights with my brother playing Monopoly. We'd eat box macaroni and rubbery, cold hot dogs dipped in ketchup packets snatched from McDonald's. We loved hot dog night and were oblivious to the guilt our mother felt serving us dinner on paper towels, how she'd stood in the grocery aisle an hour before doing math, thinking of the electric bill and the rent.

After dinner, Eli and I worked together at the dining room table, sharing the glow of the single flashlight. Eli was finishing a drawing he wanted to eventually commit to lithograph. I wrote in an old notebook, something I hadn't done since before graduate school when I'd had time to leisurely draft the edges of a story on paper, take my time working toward a cohesive center.

"Do you always write in such pretty rows?" he asked.

"Do you always draw in such ugly lines?" I asked back. I watched his hand skittishly jump here and there on the page. "What's it like in your head when you're drawing? I've always wanted to know what it's like to be able to draw."

"I don't know. I don't really think about it. I just make something and keep making it until a pattern or a figure or something emerges. And it becomes pleasing to me."

"You love it, don't you?"

"I don't work when it's not enjoyable."

This struck me as somehow profound. "Can you call it *work* then?"

A smile tugged at the corner of his lips.

I said, "I doubt there are very many things I hate more than writing."

"Then why do you do it?"

I chewed on the end of my pen. "For that one moment of inspiration," I decided.

He stopped drawing, leaned his chair back on two legs in that way that so exasperates junior high teachers. "So it's one moment for you—the light bulb going off over the head?"

I considered the image. "More like a million light bulbs going off at the same time. Like paparazzi. Then nothing—silence for weeks. It only ever comes in bursts for me. The rest is pure drudgery."

"Sounds daunting."

I gathered my courage and asked what I'd been meaning to ask for days. "You never said what you thought of my stories."

He let the chair fall back on all fours. "I liked them."

"We're not allowed to say 'like' in our critiques."

He continued drawing. "Can I say I really liked them?"

"Much worse. *Really* is an empty modifier."

I imitated his expression, eyebrows raised in theatrical alarm.

He worked silently, feverishly, at the corner of his notebook for a full five minutes without speaking. When he'd finished he showed me the drawing: cartoon me being pulled into the sky by a dozen light bulbs like helium balloons. Cartoon me looking desperately down at the ground as if unsure the sky is where she wants to be.

"Your characters seemed real to me," he said finally, setting the sketchbook back on the table. "Can I say *real*? Is real an emptying or whatever modifier?"

I laughed. "You can say real."

I pulled my hair into a loose knot at the top of my head. Eli watched the careful operation, and I pretended not to notice. The wind smelled of rain that never came, but when the trees gave up their first spring growth and the baby green buds shot like pellets across the yard, the sound was like sleet on the rooftop.

A complete happiness came over me like the heat of a blush to the cheeks. I had a vision of the two of us together always, sharing the little apartment. I would write and Eli would cut and paste and paint, while the rain pattered and the night closed us in. This would be a quiet contentment so wonderful I wouldn't need anything else. I didn't even need him to touch me—not anymore than this brush of the hands. Our affection would be pure, platonic, simple. I just wanted to wake up and spend every day near him.

The light of the flashlight faded until our eyes were heavy with the darkness and strain. We took turns in the bathroom. Just like any night, he spread a sheet on the futon. He said good-night.

⌒

It was nearly one in the morning. In bed I lay wide-eyed, an energy in my chest and belly humming.

Eli came to my room.

"Was just wondering if you were asleep."

I sat up. "I can't."

He came and sat on the bed, his face close to mine. Shadows pooled beneath his brow and his cheekbones until his face was almost like a stranger's.

"Are you all right?" I asked.

"I can't sleep either."

We were whispering. I moved over. He crawled into the bed beside me. He put his arm under my head and I pressed my face into his neck. I breathed in his smell.

He kissed me on the forehead; his lips lingered at my brow. Then he pressed his mouth on mine. He wrapped his arms around my waist as he said my name. The wall beams creaked, and I felt a fleeting sensation of falling, a dizziness, as if the room itself rocked in the wind.

14

I woke up to the sight of Eli's abandoned pillow, to the sound of the shower running. It was nearly ten already and the sunshine hot in the room. Eli had left a note on the alarm clock. Classes had been canceled due to power outages.

I closed my eyes, wishing I could return to sleep, indulging for a few moments in memories of the night before. But the guilt had already planted itself, a sickening nausea that forced me out of bed. I imagined explaining myself to Zoë. To say something happened or nothing happened depended entirely on a person's sense of sexual morality: We had only slept holding each other. We hadn't been thinking; it had only been once; he was miserable with Jillian—anyone could see that. I didn't know why Zoë was the one I felt I owed the apology.

I checked my reflection in the microwave. I ran my fingers through my hair and splashed water on my face from the kitchen sink.

"You're up," Eli said. He walked over to me, hesitated slightly, then kissed my cheek. It was a rough, dry kiss, heavy with self-conscious effort. He'd been in the bathroom forty-five minutes. A shower never took him more than five. "Kevin called. The downtown area has power. He and Diedre are getting together for brunch and wanted to know if we'd meet them."

"I'll get dressed," I said, angry that I hadn't already.

We walked with a good foot of sidewalk between us. I hoped he would reach for my hand, a public gesture to redeem what I already knew had been a mistake, but he couldn't even bring himself to meet my eyes. We mourned the damaged trees and said nothing of what had or hadn't happened between us.

Thankfully, Kevin and Diedre were already at the restaurant when we arrived. Kevin smiled, offered me a croissant, and asked how we'd enjoyed the storm. I blushed severely.

Eli went to work straight from brunch. I was relieved to see him go.

                                          ⌒

I knew I'd lost him for good even before he told me he was moving out. It had been a stupid mistake, a thing that happened when good friends who liked each other well enough got a little lonely, got a little too close. I said these things to him after he'd announced he was leaving. As with Adam, I regretted that I hadn't been the one to initiate the inevitable. Two days of careful politeness and outright misery; I should have kicked him out.

He knelt on the living room floor to pack his clothes. I remembered the first day we met, how thoughtlessly he'd tossed them onto the driveway. Now he took his time, wrapping his shirts into little cocoons he then tucked into his duffel bag in rows.

"Zoë can't be gone for long," he said.

"No, I'm sure she'll be back by the end of the week."

"You'll call me if things get bad with her mom."

"You'll still be working with her," I pointed out.

I showed him to the door, promising I would be back from class by four to help him move his desk and artwork. Back upstairs

I leaned on the kitchen counter, dreading the day. I cringed as the Volkswagen revved to life.

Classes were terrible. I left my notes at the office and had to struggle blindly through my lessons. By the last class I gave up and made the students write in their journals. They lost interest quickly and whispered to one another, drew pictures in their notebooks. One fell asleep, but I didn't have the energy to make a spectacle of him. I stared out the window and remembered the peculiar, pained expression that had flashed across Eli's face when I told him he hadn't hurt me, if that was what he was worried about. It was a revelation to me that I could lie so effortlessly; I had almost succeeded in deceiving myself.

I dismissed the students early and rushed home, but his things were already gone. I searched the apartment up and down for a note or an explanation. An apology. He'd left without so much as a drawing.

It took three days of phone calls to get ahold of my mother. After months of nonstop phone calls, my mother had abruptly stopped harassing me. We had only spoken briefly about the fight with Zoë (she was on my side, naturally) and the return of Fay's cancer (it was in God's hands, of course). I had been the one to hang up, impatient with her easy answers. Now I regretted being so rude. I was frustrated with myself, worried about Zoë, distraught about Eli. I needed to talk to her.

"Is everything okay?" she asked. "You sound terrible."

"I'm fine," I said. "But what about you? How are you? I haven't heard from you."

"I know, I know, I'm so sorry—I *have* been meaning to call, but things are so busy here. I've been working every day of the week, and I've got two new salesladies to train. Things are piling up like you wouldn't believe."

"You could have at least e-mailed me."

"Oh, honey, I really am sorry. You sound bothered. Are you sure you're doing all right?"

I updated her on school and tedious Copenhagen news. I had hoped to circle conversation toward Eli eventually, but Mom was only half listening, her eyes on the kitchen television or a newspaper. I changed the subject to one I knew she could carry. "How's the wedding planning coming?"

"Oh, it's madness. We've been trying to decide on a restaurant for the rehearsal dinner, but you know Brian and Marie—so indecisive. It takes me hours to get them to say what they really want. I keep telling them we have the money now, so we can do things nice, but Brian says he wants to have it at the Roadhouse Steak Pit. Honestly."

As she continued to talk, I realized that this "we" she spoke of referred to her and Richard. It soon became apparent that he had offered Mom money for the rehearsal dinner and the various components of the wedding she had wedged herself into organizing.

"Are you sure you want him to help?" I asked.

"If I'm going to be indebted, it might as well be to someone I know."

"That actually sounds like the worse kind of debt to be in."

"I've been meaning to tell you," she replied. "Richard and I are going away."

"Oh?"

"Well, he has these frequent flyer miles adding up, and he's practically won himself a free trip to Napa Valley. We're going next week—it's completely last minute. The house is an utter disaster. I have clothes all over the living room and in the kitchen, and I've been trying to get my mail forwarded to Grandma, but I don't know if they'll only do that for just seven days. Do they do that for seven days? I think they do."

"Seven days is a long time," I said.

"I know, I've never been on a vacation for more than three, and your father always insisted on going to old historical sites. He liked to see those cemeteries and war statues—Civil War this and that. I'm beginning to think I didn't know myself then. I don't know why a body in their right mind would want to walk around a lot of dead people and call it a vacation. If *I'm* going on vacation I'm going to enjoy myself. I know those men died for us, and don't get me wrong, I *am* grateful and all, but if it's my vacation I don't want to be moping around thinking of a lot of men dying on some field for the slaves."

"Where will you be staying?"

"The Meridian," she answered. "They have a pool and a downstairs restaurant, where we can get free breakfast and pool towels. *And* they have AA discounts."

"What, rewards for alcoholics?"

She missed the sarcasm entirely.

"Richard only drinks red wine, Amy. It's good for his heart."

Since Mom had started seeing Richard, I'd maintained a tedious picture of their weekend courtship. Saturday would be spent at Sam's Club, buying bulk birdseed and making lunch of the sample stations. When he accompanied her to church, they would linger at the Sunday school donut table, nursing weak coffee and discussing the contemporary relevance of Habakkuk.

I had only just reconciled myself to the fact that my mother had a steady boyfriend while I didn't; it was a testament to my selfishness that I'd never considered the possibility she and Richard might actually fall in love.

There was one benefit to living by myself again. Free from the tyranny of Zoë's moods and from the constant awareness of Eli's presence, I finally began to write.

The first story I finished was about a twenty-something sculptor who returns from her honeymoon to a one-bedroom apartment in the backwoods of Kentucky. This new life is four hours from her friends and studio in the city where they met. Her husband's work mystifies her. While he's explained what he does many times, she can never understand it, so she tells people he is in business management.

As soon as they return, he has to leave for a business trip. He unpacks his suitcase, only to replace swimwear with business suits. For an entire week the young bride is alone. She washes the honeymoon laundry, the slinky lace lingerie still smelling of perfume and lovemaking, the string bikini still saturated with Coppertone and sunshine.

She cleans. There is nothing else to do. She sweeps, mops, dusts. She burnishes the sink faucets with an old toothbrush. As she works, the acrylic nails she had glued to her fingers for the wedding begin to peel and chip. She never wore fake nails before meeting her husband. Before, her nails had always been dirty with clay and chipped at the edges. The acrylic nails tell her that she had sold out, that something she valued has been lost. Her husband comes home the following Sunday to find her at the sink, weeping and trying to rip the nails off her fingers.

The story ended abruptly. I had never been good at conclusions. Reading over the ten pages, I wondered if the symbolism was overwrought and the conversation between the man and wife melodramatic. I knew about loneliness; I could only imagine loneliness in marriage. Of all the disappointments in life, the failure of marriage wounded me most deeply.

I saved my story and slipped off to bed, but I couldn't sleep. I felt personally responsible for my loneliness. Zoë and Eli had both left because of me, because I'd flunked, on both counts, the principal rules of friendship.

"Maybe Zoë's right," I told the ceiling. "I spend more time planning my life than living it. I love the attention of men I can't have. I really have no idea at all what I'm doing. I try so hard to be the kind of Christian I was raised to be, but I'm starting to wonder what that really looks like."

I listened to the silence.

"Or if it matters at all."

⁀

I didn't know what woke me. The room was pitch black. As if from a bird's-eye view I saw my body in a bed that stood in the middle of an empty room attached to an empty apartment. I mapped the trajectory to Eli, who slept blocks away. I flew over the town, past the cornfields and the checkered plots of farmland to the trafficked streets of the suburban fringe, to my mother, and farther into the busy city to my brother and then to Zoë in Chicago. My father was so far on the horizon he disappeared.

I had never been more painfully conscious of the fact that I slept alone, but the awareness of my solitude was followed by an equally profound awareness of an invisible Presence in the room, filling the corners, over my bed, protective and jealous. The knowledge that I was not completely alone comforted me, like the arms of a mother or the familiar nearness of a lover.

15

It has been my experience that when you ask God for help, He often responds by asking you to help someone else.

Since our conversation about her sister's death, I continued to worry about Ashley Mulligan. Though she'd been a contributing member of workshop since the first half of the semester, her attendance was becoming a problem. She came to class late or left early. She crossed her arms and sank her chin down to her chest so that the red ball cap she now wore to every class concealed her tired eyes. She seemed intent on vanishing from sight.

The day her fiction piece was due, she managed to arrive on time. She walked slowly and silently through the room, dispensing copies of her story to fellow students, who said "thank you" more politely than was usual. I scanned over her story on my way back to the office. I was so struck by the elegance and simplicity of the prose, I didn't put the manuscript down until I had read it all the way through to its end. The story followed a high school girl through the night she finds her parents have been in a car accident. She's taken to the hospital to say good-bye to a father whose body is alive, but whose mind is dead. Between the night of the phone call and the funeral, she walks along the bay, trying to wrap her mind around the reality of his permanent absence.

> . . . *Natalie stood at the entrance to the hospital feeling her heart pound in her chest like a bird that could not escape its cage. She felt the walls of the hospital shrink back and the reflection of her face looked hollow to her as it stared back from the many windows of the long hallway. She did not recognize herself. She didn't belong in this life. She had seen it before in movies and had read about it in books, but it was a life twice removed from reality, a world she had thought only existed for others and never for herself.*

> . . . *They say time is relative. Natalie had even heard it said that any teenager knows this principle: four hours on a couch with a lovely girl is a second to an enraptured love-struck boy. Thirty seconds with your hands on a burning oven is an eternity.*

> *People often speak of eternity when they speak of the dead. But, Natalie wondered, why do they only speak of it in terms of the dead themselves? Anyone who has watched their loved one buried in the earth knows eternity. Eternity is the hours of the Sunday afternoons spent at a table without your husband of fifty years; it's the long, forced cheerfulness of birthday parties without the little sister you shared a bed with growing up. Eternity is the way a minute becomes an hour and a lifetime becomes unbearable at the thought of being without someone.*

I read the story a second time to provide criticism, but I forgot I was reading. In other words, this was a story.

⸻

Though Ashley had demanded that I treat her like the other students, I had yet to give her demerits for missing class. I noticed when she wasn't there Monday, but, as usual, I didn't pencil in the absence. Wednesday I was so distraught about Eli leaving, I forgot to take roll. Friday she didn't show, even though we were discussing her story. Realizing she had been gone an entire week, I panicked. She'd never missed more than one class a week, and I'd never thought that failing to mark her absences would lead me to forget them entirely.

I e-mailed her directly after class:

To: mulligaaj@copenhagen.edu
From: gallagham@copenhagen.edu
Sent: Friday 3.16.07 2:24 PM
Subject: Class

Noticed you haven't been in class the last few days. Was just wondering if you were doing all right. Please let me know if I can provide you with any information about what you've missed.
If you'd like someone to talk to, the offer still stands.

Sincerely,
Ms. Gallagher

Standing at the stove cooking dinner that night, I had a strange conviction that an e-mail was not enough. You hear about the professors who noticed their best students had missed one too many days only to read about the suicide later in the local paper.

I got Ashley's phone number from the online campus directory. The phone rang six times, but no one answered. I hung up and worked on dinner, but couldn't shake the nagging feeling that something was wrong. I dialed again, nervously tapping my pen against my thigh.

On the seventh ring, a girl's voice answered. "Hello."

"Hi. Um, I was wondering if I could speak to Ashley Mulligan, please?"

"Just a minute."

The stranger murmured something in the background. "Can I ask who's calling?"

"Tell her it's Ms. Gallagher."

"Ms. who?"

"Her English teacher," I supplied.

"It's your English teacher." I heard amusement in her voice.

In the five seconds it took Ashley to cross to the dorm phone, I realized that (a) she was fine; (b) she was most probably not going to kill herself; and (c) she might actually be very uncomfortable with the fact that I'd called.

"Ms. Gallagher?" She sounded puzzled.

"Hey, Ashley," I replied. "I'm sorry to call you like this, but I'd noticed you hadn't been to class in a while. I just wanted to make sure things were okay."

There was a pause on the other end of the line.

"I'm fine," she said.

"I still have the story you turned in to workshop. It's very good. The best I've seen all year, actually." I was struck with a sudden inspiration. "We didn't critique the story since you were absent, but I'd still like the chance to talk with you about it. I think you could submit it for one of the upcoming student writing awards."

"I didn't know they did that sort of thing."

"They have competitions at the end of every spring term. There are several categories: best argumentative essay, best expository, best fiction. I think there's a money award. And they publish the best creative writing pieces in the school's literary journal."

"I'll think about it."

"Maybe we can get together after class sometime to talk about it?"

"I have another class after yours."

"Just let me know. We can always make an appointment to talk in my office at a more convenient time."

Voices picked up in the background. Ashley said something away from the receiver. Her roommate spoke back.

"I don't want to keep you," I said.

"Sorry. They were asking me something."

I smelled something burning just before the smoke detector went off. "Well," I said quickly. "I'll see you in class tomorrow."

"Okay."

I ran to shut the smoke detector off. Staring at the blackened chicken plastered to the blackened skillet, I actually missed Zoë's nonfat, vegetarian, organic cooking.

⌒

Apparently, I had underestimated the power of a roommate's presence. In my office, Ashley was an entirely different person than she had been on the phone. She was excited about the prospect of seeing her work published in the school lit magazine. Timidly, she fished for compliments.

"Do you really think it's good?" she asked.

"More than good," I said. "It could use revision, but it's well-paced and full of rich detail. Despite the subject matter, you manage to avoid being melodramatic."

"Thank you," she said, genuinely grateful.

"I was disappointed that we couldn't workshop the piece in class," I ventured. "In fact, I've noticed you've missed a lot of classes lately. Is everything all right?"

She averted her eyes, twisted the cap of her Fiji water bottle. "It's all right. I'm getting by. It's hard, you know, but I manage."

"Do you have anyone on campus you can talk to?"

She shook her head. "My roommates know, but they don't bring it up unless I do. I go home every weekend, so I see my dad a lot."

In a freshmen dorm, weekends determined social status: If you braved every weekend on campus, you passed the litmus test. Those who went home frequently to medicate homesickness or to be with high school sweethearts were eventually looked down upon for their confused loyalties. Added to her frequent trips home, Ashley was quiet, a personality trait frequently mistaken for snobbery in pretty girls. Unfortunately, it was not hard to imagine her roommates disliking her on every count.

"Do you have other siblings?" I asked, wincing to hear myself say "other."

"I have an older brother and an older sister. They're both married and have kids. They come home for Christmas and summer breaks, but we're not real close. Mostly it's just Dad and me."

I decided not to ask about the unmentioned mother.

"How's he doing?"

"He's okay. He works a lot. Do you think we could maybe not talk about this?" she said. "I came to talk about my story."

"Of course. Let's talk about the story."

I was grateful to get back on a subject on which I was proficient. I couldn't tell Ashley how to alleviate her depression, but I could tell her how to make the imagery of a metaphor fit its emotional context. I could teach her how to organize sentences for improved rhythm. I could show her how to take the mess of emotions in her head and create a work of art, a thing she could control and craft, though the grief itself remained unyielding.

We read through the story aloud, discussing my suggestions for revision page by page. At first, I worried that certain sections would surface emotions neither of us would know how to handle, but she remained the aloof and divested artist, picking at the presentation of emotion while completely divorced—at least momentarily—from the emotion itself.

"Why don't you rework it as we've talked about," I said when we'd finished. "Then we can meet again before you submit the application. I'll e-mail you the guidelines for the competition; you can fill all that information out yourself."

"Thanks, Ms. Gallagher." She buttoned up her coat, picked up her bag.

"Ashley . . ." I hesitated. "I don't mean to catch you off guard with this, but if you ever want a place to get away, to find people to talk to, I go to this church—the one across from the local library. We'd be happy to have you."

She said she'd think about it. She didn't seem at all surprised by the invitation.

It had shocked me.

I dreamed about Eli. We were walking along campus. He asked me to come to his place. "What about Jillian?" I asked. "Oh," he said. "She died." I went to the visitation with him, but the person in the casket was not Jillian at all: It was my father. "I wasn't ready for this," I told Eli. He was juggling bowling pins. I was angry with him for not caring more. "Nobody is," he said.

Oddly, I felt no sorrow at seeing my father in a casket. I only felt a slight twinge of regret. How sad for someone else; his girlfriend, I knew, would miss him.

Outside of my conversations with Ashley, I took efforts to avoid my students. I made myself scarce in the office. I graded at home and did my lesson plans at The Brewery. If I needed copies, I sent my work orders through Everett to keep from interacting with Lonnie. Since the fateful *Copenhagen Campus Chronicler* interview, he'd begun leaving things in my mailbox: copies of the newspaper, fliers announcing student activities in which he participated, Hershey's kisses. These gifts came with the fifty handouts I'd requested for ENG 102 or with the Greenberg story I'd needed copied for my creative writers. Eventually, they came of their own accord. One day a pack of Orbit gum, another day a follow-up installment of Neil C. Barker. I took the gifts without saying thank you or even acknowledging their presence. It was like being courted by Boo Radley.

So Friday when I checked my mailbox and found a manila envelope merely marked *Amy* I was more horrified than pleased. I picked it up with forefinger and thumb, threw it in my bag, and returned to my office to open it in the dark.

To my surprise, the envelope contained artwork, a delicate intaglio print of a young woman walking a narrow path through a forest, her gait sprightly despite the enormous white cast on her right foot, her hair billowing up in intricate curls, which mimicked the stylized patterns of the surrounding trees' leaves. Eli had titled it, *Amy Takes a Break.*

On the back in pencil he had written:

> *It was my fault so please don't punish yourself. Guard your ankles; beware of ice. ~ELI*

Between the office and home I read the note a dozen times, trying to tease meaning from between the lines. Did this count as an apology? And if so, was he just sorry for betraying Jillian or was he sorry it happened at all?

Distractedly, I put my key in the back door only to find it had already been unlocked. Someone had turned the kitchen light on. Zoë was sitting in the living room, waiting for me.

"Hey," she said, standing. Her cheeks were streaked with tears. Balled-up Kleenex lay scattered on the coffee table. "I'm so sorry."

I set the collage down on the kitchen table, my bag on the floor.

"No," I said. "I'm the one who's sorry."

"It's my mom."

Something cold washed over my head.

"What happened?"

She began to sob. "They don't think she's going to make it."

16

When Fay's doctors stopped telling her what she wanted to hear, she went to another oncologist for a second opinion. With frightening conviction, he recommended she transfer to palliative care immediately and enjoy the weeks she had left with family and friends. Fay returned to her previous team of physicians; she returned—stubbornly—to chemotherapy.

Of course, in a fit of solidarity, Zoë shaved her head.

She e-mailed me a picture, her and her mother wearing colorful scarves wrapped about their heads.

I wrote back:

> You know, you really are the most darling bald person. Like a Halle Berry.
> Like *A Midsummer Night's Dream*. A freckled Navy Seal.

Zoë had an aversion to cell phones that even rivaled Eli's. We corresponded by e-mail. She wrote:

> . . . no one who knew my mom would have thought she cared a great deal
> about appearances. She tanned easily but the sun imprinted her skin in
> irregular patterns, white lines at her arms and legs, a halo of her gardening
> T-shirts and high-rise shorts. her nails were always dirt-stained from potting

and tending houseplants, and her hands were always dried out from hours washing dishes at the food pantry. she hated makeup. sometimes she'd dab a bit of Vaseline on her lips for shine and pinch her cheeks for color—that was it. but she LOVED her hair. i'd never noticed it before, but even in my earliest memories, she wouldn't leave the house unless her hair was neatly braided and pinned. i didn't recognize this as vanity because it was so unstylish. it was a good braid—thick as climbing rope—but a waste of hair, I thought. but she had to have it just so. not a strand out of place during her first chemo treatments, Dad and I went with her to buy her first wig. she hated that thing. said it looked nothing like her real hair. for a week, she refused to leave the house. she washed that wig, she tried ironing it into submission. no matter what she did, she couldn't get it to braid like her hair did. Dad finally told her she was coming out with him. his new book was out and she was coming to his book signing, whether she liked it or not. of course, everyone praised the new look. The wig was more stylish than she'd ever been. from then on it was an obsession. she collected wigs like some women collect purses . . .

Zoë ranked the doctors according to attractiveness and avail-ability, promising to give my number to anyone worthy of me. She praised the nurses' kindness. She reported the conversations she and her dad had about the general state of things. Both were avowed pessimists, and the world provided no lack of things to criticize. They talked long into the night every night, distracting each other from the inevitability that as pessimists they were obliged to accept, but as family could not discuss.

⌒

I should have been grading papers. I should have been cleaning the bathroom or replying to e-mails. I should have been doing a lot of things, though I couldn't remember which and by when. Since Zoë's article, I hadn't made a single checklist. Consequently, I missed one student conference, incurred ten late fees at the local library, and forgot to file a copy order for my creative writing students. But the student rescheduled, the late fees were paid, and the writing workshop benefited from one fewer reading on dialogue. We talked that day of symbolism instead.

I had stopped making lists, and there had been no insurmountable calamities. This was more a surprise than it should have been.

I spent a lot of time with Valerie, who was having difficulty recovering from Rachel's birth. Since I didn't work a typical nine-to-five, I was the only one of her friends available to help out during the day.

"You don't know how glad we are for your help," she said. "Jake especially. He worries too much when he's gone."

"It's nothing," I said. "Honestly. Without Zoë around I'd just end up home moping all day."

Rachel farted.

"Are you making music back there?" Valerie asked, peering over her shoulder into the bassinet.

The baby let loose again. Valerie and I laughed.

I tickled Rachel's taut baby belly. "What do you feed this child?" I asked.

"Just one hundred percent Grade A breast milk," Valerie said. "She has my eyes and her father's indigestion."

Valerie and Jake were the kind of couple who made you believe in marriage. They were kind to each other in public, getting each other drinks and taking each other's coats, doing all the little favors people normally reserve for first dates. He was a logical, quiet man, very reserved. She talked enough for the both of them. Their home was practical but artistic, an extension of their respective personalities. Abstract paintings hung in the living room and bedroom. They were the kind of abstractions that calm, not agitate.

"Are you still mad at her?" Valerie asked. Aside from the new baby, Zoë's unpredictable moods had been our most frequented topic of conversation.

"Of course not. How could I be? All this time I thought she was upset with me and she was waiting for the doctors to give her mother a death sentence."

"But she didn't have to take it out on you."

212

I set my tea bag on a spoon, twisted the string around the pocket of leaves. "I want to be supportive, but she's so bent on her independence, she won't let me."

"She has to let her guard down first," Valerie said. "It's hard to love a person who won't let you."

Valerie considered Zoë judgmental and difficult. Which she was. Somehow this didn't make me miss her less.

Valerie lifted Rachel from her bassinet. "I heard Eli's living with Kevin."

"He moved out last week."

"That has to be a relief, both of them finally out of your hair. I know you missed having that apartment to yourself."

I sipped my already lukewarm tea and agreed, yes, a relief.

～

After dinner I went for a walk. I didn't need to be anywhere. I just needed to move.

The sidewalks were laced with salt. The smallest tree limbs overhead had frozen, their new spring buds encased in ice like beads in glass. When the wind blew, the branches clattered as if the forest were giving a hand of applause.

I walked to campus and up the hill that led to the Humanities Building. I hadn't left with any intention of visiting the studios, but found myself walking toward the front entrance of the Fuhler Art Building and stepping inside. A few students sat on the floor at the end of the hallway, drinking coffee from heavy handmade mugs. An open office door cast light on the tile. Otherwise, the building was relatively empty, abandoned for the weekend. Dust covered the floors, and the hallway stank of strange chemicals. Cafeterias aside, there were two campus buildings identifiable by smell alone: those devoted to the sciences and those devoted to the arts.

I walked the second and first floors, taking time to patiently consider the prints and clay sculptures displayed behind glass cases.

In the basement, I followed the sound of music to the single lit studio. Two long tables covered in canvas ran parallel in the center of the room. Throwing wheels lined the tables in place of chairs. Behind the tables, shelves of stacked bowls and cups ran the length of the back wall. Most of the objects were still the wet gray or red of unfired clay. On the tallest rows sat mysteriously bagged shapes resembling sculptures of human busts. They oversaw the activity of the room with their haunting, silent presence.

Eli sauntered in from the adjoining classroom, whistling and carrying a slab of gray, wet clay in his equally gray, wet hands. He held the lump in both open palms, his elbows pressed into his hips for balance. Kicking a stool into place with his foot, he straddled an already dirtied wheel at the head of the table and, with more force than I had expected, smashed the ball of wet earth onto its center. He pumped the floor pedal, and the wheel began to spin.

With his elbows anchored on his knees, he pressed his hands firmly around the clay. It resisted, its irregular surface jostling his hands and his arms. He let his hands ride the dimpled contours of the clay, layers of silt slipping slick between his fingers. When he had caught the rhythm of the wheel, he leaned forward and braced his hands, every muscle in his upper arms tensing. The clay fell instantly into form.

He began to work the now-cylindrical tower of clay, forcing it flat into a disk, then up into a towering cone, higher and higher. Just when I began to guess what he was making, he pressed the materials down again into a nondescript pile of spinning earth. The appearance of concentration on his face was misleading. He wasn't working: He was playing, content as a kid in a summer sandbox, his pant legs rolled up, his toes exposed in flip-flops. I loved him for his naked toes, for such a small and harmless rebellion. Let the rain freeze; he would have his private summer.

Without interrupting him, I walked quietly down the hallway, up the stairs, and back toward home. It was no good pretending: I'd

wanted this man from the moment he stepped unwelcome into my
living room, carrying everything he owned on his back. I loved him
for every seeming defiance—the tattoo, the jewelry, the untamed
wanderlust. Near him I began to believe I could share in his light-
ness, walk freely in and out of the constructs of my religion, my
fears, and my habits, as if they were rooms I could quit with a few
confident steps.

17

Eli came to my office the very next day.

I was kneeling on the floor, fishing for the grade book that had fallen behind my desk. He peered under the desk, startling me, and I hit my head on the keyboard tray in my rush to stand.

"Do you knock?" I asked.

"The door was open." He helped me up. "Maybe I should have made an appointment."

He sat exactly as my students did, facing me directly, the corner of the desk between us. He crossed his legs. He looked around the room.

"I don't think I've ever been on this side of a teacher's desk without being in trouble."

I arched my eyebrow.

He smiled faintly. "Maybe this is no different."

"How did you know I'd be here?"

"I was leaving the studio and saw your car." He rubbed his thumb ineffectually against a spot of white paint staining the worn knee of his jeans. "So were you by any chance out by the studios last night? I thought I saw you out the window."

I hesitated just long enough.

"It must have been someone else," he rushed to say.

"Probably."

Thankfully, Everett returned to the office. Eli said hey and shook Everett's hand, a gentlemanly quirk he had with people he was particularly fond of.

"Anyway." He slapped his knee, giving up on the paint. "Kevin and I are having some people over tomorrow tonight. I was wondering if you wanted to come." He turned to Everett. "Both of you," he added quickly.

A warning in my head told me to say no. "When?" I asked.

"Eight-ish."

"Will there be student poetry, is the question," Everett said.

"No," Eli assured us. "There'll be a film if we can get things rigged right, but no student poetry, I promise."

I told him I would think about it.

He stayed long enough to inquire after Zoë. He stayed long enough to be polite. And then, as if overcome with a sudden change of emotion, he left abruptly with a hasty "See you."

His unexpected visit bewildered me. He'd never called. For two weeks I hadn't seen or heard from him and now he asked me over as casually as if I were one of his dozen studio acquaintances.

"What's new with our ever-wandering hero?" Everett asked. "He looked almost peevish. The drama unfolds with Jillian?"

"Everett," I said wearily, "shut up."

〜

Zoë's father mailed me a check for two months' rent.

"He didn't have to do that," I told her, having talked her into a phone call. "I'm sending the money back."

"He wants to give it." She was breathing hard into the phone. Leg lifts. Her shin splints were worse, and she hadn't been able to run since returning home. She did hours of calisthenics to de-stress.

"It makes him feel useful. He needs something to make him feel useful."

"If it makes him feel good." In reality, I'd needed the money. Summer was coming and I'd been trying to save for the long months with no paycheck.

She finished her exercises, greedily drank a glass of water.

"How are Valerie and the baby?"

"They're fine."

This was the part of the conversation where Zoë would want Copenhagen news. She would inquire after everyone, indulge a moment in the normalcy of our lives. I provided detailed if not overly enthusiastic updates on Everett, on Lonnie, on the worst sentences from my students' essays. When she asked about Eli I finally told her he'd moved out.

"What? When?"

I told her.

"Why?"

"He needed more space to work."

"You didn't kick him out." It was more a warning than a question.

"Of course not. It was mutual. It was getting awkward, the two of us alone in the apartment together. I don't think Jillian would have liked it."

That last bit about Jillian was particularly deceptive. I'd practiced telling Zoë everything, but I couldn't bring myself to make an issue of what I was trying so hard to pretend hadn't happened.

"I guess it's for the best," she said.

When I asked how her father was doing she was quiet a moment. "He acts like he's all right. But I know he's not. It's the way he stares sometimes, completely checked out. Hold on, he's in the room." She said something to her father. There was a pause. When she returned she spoke louder. "Amy, I found a manuscript. He keeps it in his desk drawer and it's nearly a foot thick."

"What's he working on?"

"The story of his life? I don't know; I didn't read it. He usually writes quickly. It's not like him to hold on to something like this . . . He hasn't published for years."

She'd spent most of college dealing with the idea of losing one parent, a fear she could share with the other; she'd always been close to her father. Over the last three weeks, however, she'd developed a new anxiety, the fear that the cancer would take them both.

∽

When Eli said he was having "a few people" over he meant all of The Brewery staff and half the sculpture class. Kevin had arranged what furniture they had in rows before an old projector screen. People sat wedged hip to hip, girlfriends sat on their boyfriends' laps. The movie was French and in black-and-white, two things that promised a long and tedious night.

I arrived late and sat in the back. To my right a folding table had been spread with pizza and plastic bowls of Cheez-Its and popcorn, the food men buy for Super Bowls and art openings alike. While Kevin cued the second film, I picked at the food. Beside me an undergraduate wearing a jumper intended for a seven-year-old was trying to impress a fellow artist with a description of her latest installation piece. I felt suddenly tired of the college scene: the same events recycling themselves over again, the flirtation masquerading as professional discourse.

As the lights went out a second time, Eli took the seat beside me. I kept my eyes on the screen.

"I'll warn you now," I whispered. "From back here it's impossible to read the subtitles."

"Trust me," he whispered back. "It wouldn't help."

He smelled of incense, of paint.

I pointed out that he'd invited all of Copenhagen.

"Yeah, well, you know Kevin; he has a way of drawing a crowd."

219

He winked. Kevin was the shyest man I knew.

As the film began, he leaned in to explain the plot, his head bowed toward mine, even when the rising volume of the room made whispering unnecessary. Ten minutes into the screening everyone was talking as if the film wasn't playing at all. Two students from Kevin's sculpture class came to sit with us. Reluctantly, I moved from the couch to a folding chair to make room for Art Major Number One, who asked if I had seen other work by the director. I said no. Did I like French films? I didn't speak French, I replied shortly. Art Major Number Two was a young woman, tall, with the legs of a Versace model. Her bony knees knocked against Eli's. She was doing an imitation of one of her professors, one hand on her hip, the other gesticulating wildly. Eli laughed. They talked half an hour before he thought to introduce me.

He introduced me as the friend of a friend.

"Nice to meet you," Art Major Number Two said. I reached to shake her hand, but she only raised herself ever so slightly off her chair, forcing me to stand and cover the distance between us. Since I'd already abandoned the couch to conduct this little greeting, I announced I would be back and escaped to the stairwell.

Eli found me digging for my coat on the pile that had collected by the door.

"You're leaving?" he asked.

"I have class tomorrow," I said.

"Let me give you a ride."

"I'd rather walk," I replied.

He followed me down the stairs. "Amy, what's wrong?" he asked.

"Nothing's wrong."

"Something's wrong." He opened the door for me. "If I did something to offend you, tell me. I want to know."

I turned to face him. "I'd like to know why you go out of your way to invite me over only to spend the entire night ignoring me."

"I sat right beside you."

"And proceeded to talk to everyone else." I tried to walk away, but still he followed. "You introduced me like you don't even know me."

"I introduced you as a friend," he said, his tone defensive. "I thought that's what you wanted: friendship. I'm having a friendship with you."

"We had our friendship, Eli, and it was perfect the way it was. Why did you have to ruin it?"

He didn't respond immediately. "You said what we did was a mistake," he said slowly. "That our friendship was important and that it was best I leave so we could keep it. That I hadn't hurt you."

It pained me to hear all the things I'd said.

"I left," he said. "I waited, and I figured it had been long enough maybe we were over the whole thing." He shuffled along to catch up with me. "Will you slow down?"

"Well I'm sorry, but two weeks isn't long enough for me to just 'get over things.' "

He was baffled. "It never once occurred to me that you felt anything more for me. You never let on that you wanted anything else."

"Why would I? You're *with* Jillian, Eli. You're taken."

"That's not working and you know that as well as I do. Amy! Would you please *slow down?*"

We had reached the corner of the downtown park. I walked to the bus station and sat obediently on the nearest bench.

"Thank you," he said in exasperation. He remained standing.

The park fountains played to our left. A tower of water shot into the air, then twirled as it fell, a pirouette of liquid beads dissolving. Just as the first fell, a second jet of water shot up a foot from the first, swirled in the air, folded in on itself. On they went, one firing off as the other fell in the orderly succession of a Rockette kick line.

"I got the print you sent," I said quietly. "I really appreciated it."

"I'm glad." He didn't sound glad at all.

"What do you want, Eli?"

"I thought that was obvious." He joined me on the bench. "Do you really think I slept on that futon because there wasn't another bed in town that might be more comfortable? Because I couldn't afford my own place?"

"Then why didn't you leave?"

"Amy, I didn't think anything would happen. I always thought you generally disapproved of me, that you put up with me. But that didn't change the fact that I wanted to spend time with you. I would never have stayed if I'd known . . ." He paused. "If I'd thought you felt anything for me."

"Well, I felt things for you. You're funny and sexy and talented." I sounded so angry the compliments sounded more like indictments. "You even like my stories."

He smiled. He looked at me the way every woman wants to be looked at. "Amy Gallagher, you are the most interesting woman I have ever had the misfortune of living with."

"What about 'you're beautiful'," I said. "Or 'I'm deeply attracted to your intelligence.' "

He told me I was beautiful and gently touched my cheek, ran his thumb across my lower lip. He told me he was very attracted to my intelligence. He would have kissed me if I'd let him.

I told him to take me the rest of the way home.

We walked side by side. When he reached for my hand I let him. He laced his fingers through mine. The streets were empty, and in the moment's anonymity I was free to enjoy what it would be like to belong to Eli. All our other many walks through campus, hands in pockets and cautious distance between our bodies, seemed unnatural in retrospect.

I asked what he was going to say to Jillian.

"I don't know," he said. "I haven't quite figured that out yet."

"You have to tell her."

"Of course I have to tell her." He let go of my hand, slipped it back in his pocket.

"Look," I said. "I'm not interested in anything that's not going to be serious from the beginning."

"Neither am I."

"I don't want to date and I don't want to mess around."

"We're in total agreement then."

I crossed my arms. "There's no way you and I would ever work."

"Why not?" He shrugged, half laughed, as if I'd given him reason to hope.

"We don't want the same things," I said, exasperated by his good humor.

"Try me."

I tried to imagine Eli holding a child or balancing a checkbook. With complete honesty I confessed, "I don't even know where to start."

"I promise you, I'm breaking up with Jillian."

Of all the things he could have said. That he would so fervently offer her disappointment as foundation for my happiness made me sick to my stomach.

"That's too convenient, Eli."

"Why does it have to be hard?"

"Shouldn't it be? Shouldn't breaking up with someone you've been with this long at least be a little hard?"

"That's not what I meant."

"Jillian adores you," I said. "You have to at least try to make it right with her."

"You've become quite the expert on someone you've never met." He began to say something, stopped, then said it anyway with a spitefully calculated superiority: "Don't flatter yourself that you're the only problem we've been having. You have no idea what she needs."

"What she needs? Isn't this about what you need? You live like there's no consequence, like you can walk away and live your own life and no one's the better or worse, but nobody lives like that, Eli. When you leave you hurt people, and there's nothing you can say about your work or your art or your needs that will justify it."

He was taken aback. "What are you talking about?"

Beyond his pretense of innocence I recognized the likeness of my father, the ever affable, the ever apologizing, the man whose love wasn't enough. What kind of idiot would I be to make myself the moving target for the same misery Jillian would suffer tomorrow?

The torrent came easily, and each spiteful word filled me with relief: "You don't care what people think of you and you think that gives you license to do whatever you want without consequence. You're done with Jillian? Walk out on Jillian. You're done with your aunt? Walk out on her, leave her alone after all she's done for you."

"Amy, wait a minute—"

"You're not as independent as you'd like to think you are, Eli Morretti—you just delude yourself into thinking that just because no one follows your long meandering quests no one cares or misses you."

"You don't know anything about my family." I had never seen him angry before. "My family," he said fiercely, "is *my* business."

"I know that you haven't spoken to your brother in years— that your aunt was lonely and you left her. You leave, that's what you do. And I can't be with someone who thinks he can walk out when it suits him."

"Sometimes I run. I'll admit that. But you should think twice before you point your finger, Amy. At least I'm living my life. You bury yourself in books and papers and hole yourself up where no one can mess up the safe little world you've made for yourself."

"First Zoë and now you." I glared at him. "I'm tired of being told what I should be and what I'm not."

"Amy!" He grabbed my arm just as I turned away, grabbed me

so hard it hurt. Before I knew what was happening I had slapped him across the face.

He dropped my arm, his hand flying to his cheek.

"I'm sorry," I stammered, shocked by what I'd done. "I don't know what I was thinking—"

"You hit me," he said in disbelief.

"I didn't mean it, but you grabbed me. Eli, I'm sorry." I ran my hand over his cheek. "Are you all right? Is it bad?"

This time when he grabbed my arms, just below the shoulders, I felt the restraint in his hands, how careful he was to hold me gently but hold me nonetheless. "Don't presume, Amy Gallagher, that you know what I mean or what I need—or what I want." He dropped his hands. "I wanted you."

He turned his back to me.

"You can walk yourself home," he muttered.

I would have called after him, but the shame of my own broken-ness overwhelmed me, burning as hot as the imprint of his face, pulsing, on the palm of my hand.

part 3

18

I was checking out at the student commons food court when a man dressed in a styrofoam ice cream cone costume walked by, advertising the Alpha Delta Phi ice cream social fund-raiser being held on the lawn outside.

"Get the milk shake!" someone shouted. A dozen students appeared from nowhere to stampede the ice cream cone out the door and across the quad.

"Some kind of relay," muttered the cafeteria lady. She shook her head and took my money. "Kids will be kids."

She did not need to explain. The weather had finally taken a turn. The sunlight was like Ecstasy crop-dusted over Copenhagen. Runners and dog-walkers appeared at dawn and dusk. Fraternities threw lawn parties just for the excuse to get half naked and beer-buzzed in the middle of the afternoon. Downtown, parents set their children to run wild in the park fountain, and students wearing flip-flops on their already tanned toes sat outside The Brewery to indulge in books that had nothing whatsoever to do with school.

Mom came by to celebrate another successful Luna Landing in Columbus. We sat on the porch roof, watching the commotion.

She'd been talking me deaf since she walked in the door. She was so relieved Eli was gone, she spoke of him all afternoon, saying what a nice man he was and how good it was that we'd had some help around the apartment while he was there. I smiled and said nothing. I hadn't seen him since our fight and had no desire to see him ever.

"What's all this racket?" she asked. "Is there some big event on campus?"

"Yes," I said. "Spring."

⁓

Zoë wrote saying she needed a few things and asking if I could ship them to her. There had been days when her mother could eat without pain or vomiting, and they were packing their bags in anticipation: the next good day, they would make a trip to the beach.

I drove to UPS for bubble wrapping. I packed Zoë's sequined slippers, her second pair of running shoes, and her favorite red string bikini. I packed a dozen pieces of specifically requested jewelry. She also wanted beach reading, including her well-worn copies of *Tess of the D'Urbervilles* and *The Handmaid's Tale*.

I made an exaggerated list of everything she wanted, checked each item off with bold red check marks, and put the checklist inside the box so she would find it first. I threw in a bag of Tootsie Pops for good measure.

You will all get through this, I wrote on the bottom of the checklist.

I knew better. Brian warned me that the doctors had probably helped Fay maintain some semblance of normal life as long as they could, but curing the disease had not been an option for years. Despite his warning, I held out for a miracle. Fay had baffled physicians before.

Of course, the improved weather might have tainted my expectations. My hopes were expansive, for despite fears to the contrary, winter had ended after all.

As if to combat the feelings of seasonal optimism, Pastor Maddock chose to begin a five-week series on the book of Ecclesiastes.

Pastor Maddock was a towering man. He had a booming voice but rarely employed it. That was what I liked about him: For all his potential powers of intimidation—height, sonorous voice, extensive knowledge of Scripture, among others—he taught rather than preached, mitigating his passion with a kindhearted professor's concern. It required conscientious effort on his part to speak slowly and gently, with words that would not impress his congregation, as he disapproved of their adoration of ministers. And this was a congregation that very much liked to be impressed.

That Sunday he concluded his sermon by reading from Scripture: " 'What has been will be again, what has been done will be done again; there is nothing new under the sun. . . . There is no remembrance of men of old, and even those who are yet to come will not be remembered by those who follow.' "

He took off his reading glasses and set them on the pulpit ledge. "Listen to me, people: If you don't believe in an afterlife, and all you have is—at most—a good eighty years on this earth, then your life is so small in proportion to the great expanse of space and time, it might as well not have happened at all. We don't have to think in eons to see proof of this. Each generation forgets the preceding.

"Recently, my wife and I visited Civil War battlegrounds while vacationing with friends. We stood there overlooking this beautiful field, trying to imagine the tragedies that took place on the very same soil and not that many decades ago. Now, like many of you, I have mental pictures of this war that transpired before I even existed; I have memories of a thing that happened before my time. Who hasn't seen a Civil War documentary? Or read a Civil War story? Or seen a Hollywood film that portrays the conflict in one way or another?

"We may commemorate the Civil War in books and films, but

both are frequently colored in a romantic light, washed in a nostalgia for a lost time. The specific story of each boy, father, and brother, the specific strife of each wife, slave, or child, is lost, buried, as each generation forgets a little more of their parents' parents' parents' parents' stories.

" 'There is no remembrance of men of old,' Solomon said. 'And even those who are yet to come will not be remembered by those who follow.' " Pastor Maddock paced the platform slowly. "Folks, we will pass from this earth, and this earth will forget us. Oh, we may be remembered by our family and by their descendants, but for how many generations? And even if you are remembered, you will be known only by a name on a family tree or by a single accomplishment or, worse, a single mistake.

"Yet that is not who we are. We are more than a single accomplishment. We are more than the accumulation of mistakes. Something in us craves to be recognized, to be seen and heard—and, most important, to be affirmed."

He walked to the end of the platform, wiping his forehead with the purple handkerchief he'd pulled from his front pocket. He perspired as if the sermon required strenuous physical exertion.

"This desire to be known is all around us." He folded the handkerchief back into a square. "Go home and turn on your television. You'll find men and women crawling all over themselves to be the best, the most honored, the most awarded. You'll see teenagers who can't sing their way out of a paper bag standing in line for hours to make fools of themselves in front of judges on national television, all for that chance to be seen by the millions, even for just those fifteen seconds of fame.

"But folks, even the 'immortality' of fame cannot preserve the life of a man or woman forever. Who knows the name of the man who erected the obelisk in D.C.? Or the name of the artist who sculpted *The Ecstasy of St. Teresa*? How many people do you know who can recite the names of all the presidents of the United States?

And even if they can recite their names, do they know anything more than a brief biographical sketch of each man?

"If we are known only to those who know us now and are forgotten soon after they too pass away, what do we have to give our lives weight and meaning?

" 'I have seen the burden God has laid on men,' says Solomon in Ecclesiastes. 'He has made everything beautiful in its time. He has also set eternity in the hearts of men; yet they cannot fathom what God has done from beginning to end.' "

He returned to the pulpit, shuffled the notes he hadn't consulted once. "Now, I know you all can't stand much more of this. 'Pastor Maddock,' you want to say, 'we've got dinner in the oven.' Just hold on to your seats, I'm almost done. And believe it or not, this is a message of hope. Because if you notice, the Scriptures say that *God* has set eternity in the heart of man."

He braced his hands against either side of the pulpit. "That aching in your body that feels almost like a physical hurt. God has made it so. That passion to be known and loved not as a name or by an accomplishment or by a mistake—that desire to be known as you, yourself, in all your individual thoughts and dreams and worries and hopes and foibles—God has made it so. That need to wrap yourself around Time, to defeat death, to outlive this life—God has made it so. He has made it so that you will find recognition in Him."

The pianist began to play. In automatic unison, we stood to sing the closing hymn. I was deeply stirred by the things Pastor Maddock had said and blinked back to the present moment feeling somewhat outside myself.

Dazed as I was, it took me a few moments to recognize a familiar looking girl slipping out the back doors after the last prayer had been said and the congregation began to file orderly from their pews. I hurried to the foyer and searched over the crowd of bustling families, but I'd no sooner seen Ashley Mulligan and she was gone.

⁊

After a lunch at the deli across the street, I took the bus to central campus and followed the sidewalk past the academic buildings to Leonard Chapel. The chapel was a whitewashed room with a steeple and narrow rows of many-colored stained-glass windows. It did not inspire religious feeling, but it was quiet and isolated, a good place to think. My thoughts wandered to Eli, but I quickly corralled them back. I refused to dwell on our fight; I didn't want to consider the possibility that what he'd said about me had been true. I prayed, instead, for Ashley and then for Zoë and her parents. I prayed until I was sure I'd been in the chapel an hour. My phone informed me it had been exactly seventeen minutes. Prayer usually had this effect on me.

I took the trail down into the woods, following the creek until the path crossed the water by way of a rickety wooden bridge. I was skeptical of Pastor Maddock's message. The need for popularity or fame or recognition had always been a point of guilt, not of hope; I had never before considered the possibility that the desire to be known was Spirit-inspired.

The well-worn trail wound and divided. When the path finally met an open field I was surprised to find myself on north campus, a soccer field away from the crowded neighborhood of underclassmen dorms.

It began to rain while I waited at the nearest bus stop. When the bus finally appeared ten minutes later, I was soaked to the skin, my arms covered in goose bumps. I didn't mind the rain. It felt good, God's opened arms throwing liquid blessing into mine.

⁊

Michael's car was in the driveway when I arrived home. I hadn't seen him since Zoë left. He ran to meet me under the porch awning.

"Where have you been?" he demanded, as if I had no right to be out alone past dark.

"Out." I was cold and wet and quite aware that my body was broadcasting both of these facts through my shirt. I crossed my arms over my chest. "Why are you here?" I asked.

"I need to talk to you about something—to ask a favor, really."

"Okay."

"It's serious."

I sat on the porch to take off my shoes. I wrung out my socks one at a time.

Michael grew impatient. "Can we go inside?"

"Just give me a minute."

He sat in one of the lawn chairs. He clasped his hands. He leaned forward, wiped his mouth, clasped his hands again.

"Michael, what is wrong with you?"

"It's about Zoë and me," he said. "I need you to talk to her for me."

I picked bits of gravel from between my toes. "Why can't you talk to her?"

"It's complicated. You know, she's already upset about her mom. If I try to tell her how I feel, she'll freak out. But she'll listen to you."

"Tell her what, then?"

"Amy, look, don't think I don't care." He turned to me with the most wounded expression. "We're just not working. She's way out there, I'm here. We never talk—and when we do—I don't know, I never know what to say . . . I just can't do it. Our lives are different now."

I stopped rolling my pant legs up. "Her mom has *cancer*. She doesn't need you to talk; she needs you just to be there."

"But I can't be there, that's the thing."

"Your boss would give you a few days off. You could visit."

"I can't just cancel everything and be always driving to Chicago."

"That's exactly what you can do."

A series of faces passed before me: Adam, the narcissist; Eli, the delinquent; and now Michael, the ever moronic. The men I knew seemed different enough at first, but ultimately one proved as fickle as the other, and the plot never varied: men showing up, men exiting.

I asked if he was leaving her.

"I'm not cut out for this kind of stuff."

"Michael, no one knows what to do in times like this. There's no right or wrong thing to do or say—you just need to be there."

He shook his head.

"You can't do this to her," I whispered. I didn't trust myself to raise my voice. "Wait until her mom gets through these last treatments. Wait until she's home at least, so you can talk to her in person."

Michael studied the side of his shoe. Mud from his sprint to the porch had sullied his fresh white soles. He wiped them clean on the edge of the porch. "I think we need to end things now while we're ahead. We had a good run, you know? We were good for each other for a while. Now we need to move on."

He'd already made up his mind. And here he was, trying to use me to buffer the blow.

I stood so fast I hit my head on the wind chime dangling from the porch roof. He reached the door first, insisted on holding it open for me.

"Does that mean you won't talk to her?"

"Tell her yourself," I said, slamming the door in his face.

⌒

I considered calling Zoë, but decided against it. Michael was above all a fickle person. There was always the chance that he would change his mind. Secretly, though, I wished he would break up with her, so she could find a pleasant, intelligent man who deserved her.

To calm myself down, I made a cup of tea. I sat at the kitchen table, intent on organizing the week's unopened mail. I saved the envelope postmarked from the *Southwest Literary Review* for last.

> *Dear Author:*
>
> *THANK YOU for your submission to the Southwest Literary Review. We find, however, that your manuscript does not meet our current needs. We wish you the best of luck placing your work elsewhere.*
>
> *Sincerely,*
> *The Editors*

I sat at the table, stewing in my irritation, staring until the tea went cold. The envelope included a brochure for an upcoming writers' conference, *Getting Published for the At Home Writer*. It was a $700 overnight workshop.

I scribbled out *the At Home Writer* and then wrote *Dummies* in bold caps. I stared at the phrase.

I went to my bedroom, opened my laptop and typed:

GETTING PUBLISHED FOR DUMMIES
Writer's Creed:
With my pen
(laptop, word processor, or otherwise)
I will pursue truth and beauty
for the improvement of my mind and the edification of
humanity.
If this results in personal fame and glory,
I am resigned.

Chapter One: The Inflatable Ego

So you want to navigate the slush pile (which in your mind resembles a very large pool of pink Icee) to that great pot of glittering gold success: publication. Aspiring author, this book is for you!

We at Getting Published for Dummies believe that if given the right tools and pointed in the right direction, any and every striving writer can publish their fledgling manuscript to become king of the hill, Oprah Winfrey Show-*bound stars. No more late nights wondering if your sorry flesh will amount to anything! No more counting your greasy tips and rejection slips!*
Turn to page two, buckle up, and kiss anonymity good-bye!

I stared at the blinking cursor. In workshop we frequently complained (with no trifling satisfaction) how everyone we knew wanted to write a book. We were like Americans in summertime Paris, bemoaning the rush of tourists, guilty of the very trespass we found so distasteful. We were in competition, always. We forgot why we'd started the entire journey in the first place.

I couldn't pinpoint the exact moment when being recognized for my work had begun to matter. There'd been a time when I cared only about the work itself, when I'd have spent hours happily sweating in the corner of an old attic just for the joy of seeing my thoughts materialize on the page. Back then it had been play. As a child I would have recited my tales to a brick wall for the pleasure of storytelling.

When had my being heard become such an imperative?

. . . If the author has deluded him- or herself into believing that writing is a selfless act of discovery or a vehicle of human communication or the expression of the soul's deepest longing etc., s/he cannot deny that s/he also hopes the book will become a ticket to the Interesting Life.

It behooves us at this point to define the Interesting Life

*(IL). For the aspiring novelist, the IL is a vague conglomera-
tion of things, most commonly consisting of flights to great cities
(which, to date, the author has only ever seen in pretty night-
scape posters), interviews on television talk shows, book sign-
ings, and the endowment of a glistening aura/radiant beauty
and importance upon his/her person, the kind paparazzi
photograph.*

*The IL is analogous to and interchangeable with the Tragic
Life, the Rags to Riches Life, the Inspirational Life and so
forth. While it should be noted that each has its identifiable differences, they all spring primarily from the greed of the competi-
tive ego . . .*

I wrote with the rejection letter open on the desk beside me. I
debated taking the letter to work and recording it in my blue binder
along with the other carefully tabulated rejections.

Instead, I walked to the sink, shoved the letter down the garbage
disposal, and chunked the form up.

19

From: gallagham@copenhagen.edu
To: spenceev@copenhagen.edu
Sent: Thursday 4.19.07 12:04 PM
Subject: Final Excerpt
Attachment: Getting Published for Dummies part2

Elements of a Publishable Novel
In alphabetical order

Character: Any person who plays a part in the narrative
Also, what you stand to lose in becoming famous

Climax: The turning point or point of highest interest in the plot

Complication: A problem or host of problems. Example: the apartment in which you are working burns down, your laptop and files smoldering with it. And/or your spouse threatens to file for divorce, on grounds of indecent exposure, i.e. that you are writing about his/her personal life, thereby exposing him/her to public censure and shame.

Crisis: When complications become overwhelming

Denouement: The unraveling or untying of the complexities of a plot. Derives from the Old French *denoer*, "to untie." Sprinkle generously in party conversation to impress non-literary acquaintances.

Omniscient: Literally, "all knowing." The ability of an author or narrator

(usually third person) to tell the reader directly about the events that have occurred, are occurring, or will occur in the story, and about the thoughts and feelings of the characters.
Also, God.

Plot: Looks like a witch's hat: $\bigwedge$

Conclusion: A Happy Ending. Boy gets Girl (or vice versa), protagonist saves the world, and, when novel becomes a success, the author's Interesting Life begins.

————

From: spenceev@copenhagen.edu
To: gallagham@copenhagen.edu
Sent: Friday 4.20.07 1:30 PM
Subject: Dummy's Guide

Amy:
Read your piece. Whimsical form for a cathartic rant. And funny. Enjoyed the "dictionary" definitions excerpt in particular.
My theory: you have been reading Vonnegut and receiving rejections. A courageous first attempt at pomo metafiction, yes?
Will leave my formal response on your desk.

Ever so sincerely,
Everett

P.S. Lonnie sends his love

————

From: gallagham@copenhagen.edu
To: spenceev@copenhagen.edu
Sent: Saturday 4.21.07 11:37 AM
Subject: Ugh

Everett:
Thanks for your response. It was, as always, brilliant. I'm recycling the manuscript as we speak.

You really think I am trying to be Vonnegut? Am I that sophomoric?

Sincerely Dejected,
Amy

———

From: iheartofu@writersnet.com
To: gallagham@copenhagen.edu
Sent: Sunday 4.22.07 2:00 AM
Subject: story

Beloved Aimeeeee:

everett is a chump. really, he didn't like it? then don't listen to him. i think the whole thing is hilarious straight through and that you should send it out with your next batch of submissions. you're still submitting, right? tell me you're submitting. you have to write for two now. . . . i haven't read or written a page since coming out here to be w/mom and feel perfectly wretched about it. it's like this weight on my chest—except, crap, that's a terrible cliché. see, even my e-mails are clichéd now! and I'm using exclamation points (!!!!)

Zoë, the illustrious

———

From: spenceev@copenhagen.edu
To: gallagham@copenhagen.edu
Sent: Monday 4.23.07 9:03 AM
Subject: IMPORTANT

The Intergalactic Gateway Convention is coming to Columbus May 12th through May 14th. Tickets on sale now at 1–800–345-SPACE. Informational flier attached below. Costumes sold separately.

———

From: gallagham@copenhagen.edu
To: spenceev@copenhagen.edu
Sent: Monday 4.23.07 9:07 AM
Subject: Re: IMPORTANT

If you want me to respond, then turn around and mock me to my face. I'm sitting three feet away from you.

Amy

P. S. And please put that out, you know you can't smoke in here.

———

From: gallagham@copenhagen.edu
To: iheartofu@writersnet.com
Sent: Wednesday 4.25.07 8:45 PM
Subject: home*sweet*home

Zoë,

Am at home tonight b/c Mom insisted I go with her to buy a dress for the
wedding and this was her only night free. I should have gone out myself,
but she wanted to buy the dress for me and I couldn't very well afford
anything new on my own. I think this is compensation for the fact that I'm
not a bridesmaid, which offends her to no end. I hope Marie believes me
when I say I'm glad to be free of the obligation. I'm at that age where being a
bridesmaid is a dangerous gamble: "always a bridesmaid . . ."

I can't seem to escape this house. I lie in bed and examine why I'm so tied
to home (which is not really home anymore—I have worn out my welcome,
as the boxed journals and bedclothes indicate), but I feel like it's out of
my hands. I can't help that Brian is marrying—that you are gone. That I
don't have the money or inclination to be elsewhere. Or do you think those
are poor excuses? Am I in danger of become a hopeless, tragic townie in
manner of Ethan Frome, my hands tied by impersonal fate?

Amy

————

From: iheartofu@writersnet.com
To: gallagham@copenhagen.edu
Sent: Thursday 4.26.07 10:03 PM
Subject: Naturalism Sux

A:
what's all this ethan frome business? i don't ever want to hear you mention
him again. no more of this fatalistic pessimism. gather the coins from
the couch cushions and fly away little bird! flee to a place warm and free
where men are your servants and it is Christian to lie on the beach merely
contemplating the lovely idea of God.

i asked michael if he could come visit this weekend he said he was going
to try then called back to say he couldn't get away from work. this whole
cancer thing totally freaks him out.

Zoë the illustrious but increasingly exhausted.

————

From: gallagham@copenhagen.edu
To: iheartofu@writersnet.com
Sent: Thursday 4.26.07 11:45 AM
Subject: (none)

Zoë the illustrious:

Have been praying for you and promise that I will continue to do so. I meant
to say so earlier, but it felt kind of trite. Know that you're in my thoughts every
second and that I beg God to keep you sane.

I've been wondering lately what would happen if I really prayed. All the
promises in Scripture seem to imply we are entitled to the same miracles
Christ performed.

Did I ever tell you that when I was a little girl I tried to walk on water? Dad had
rented a paddleboat for our family vacation. I don't know what came over
me, but out there in the very middle of the lake, I just stepped off the back of
that paddleboat and slipped right under the water. It was, and remains, the
greatest spiritual failure of my life.

So my question: was I being foolish or was my faith smaller than even a
mustard seed?

Amy

———

From: iheartofu@writersnet.com
To: gallagham@copenhagen.edu
Sent: Thursday 4.26.07 7:02 PM
Subject: Re: (none)

who's to judge?

what i want to know is why miracles are things you always hear about but
never see. it's always a story someone heard from a neighbor who saw it
happen to a cousin. as a believer, i am always catching the aftereffect of
the miracles, the last ripple to roll out from the place God comes down and
touches the earth. why can't i see an angel? water to wine? your faith was
big enough: why didn't you walk on water?

the year mom was diagnosed with cancer i prayed every day that God would
heal her—miraculously heal her. what kills me is that I really believed it could
happen. the expectation only increased daily because a part of me feared
that if I didn't expect Him to help her, He will have no choice but to fail me . . .
that's so messed up it almost sounds like something you'd do.

244

it's exhausting to keep the hope engine running. i'm like a kid pinching her eyelids open to stay awake for the end of the show: certain that if i let my hope fall even for a second, i've failed mom, God, myself.

don't tell anyone this. esp. the Baptists. they will just tell me to read Psalms.

love
Zoë

———

From: iheartofu@writersnet.com
To: gallagham@copenhagen.edu
Sent: Thursday 4.26.07 2:07 AM
Subject: news

back in the hospital. wanted to call but is late. mom in bad way: high-grade small bowel obstruction. she's up for early morning surgery. pray it goes all right.

———

From: gallagham@copenhagen.edu
To: iheartofu@writersnet.com
Sent: Monday 4.30.07 11:56 PM
Subject: Re: news

Zoë,
I've been trying to call. I know maybe you don't want to talk. I just wanted to write, to say I'm sorry.

Waiting to hear from you.

Love
Amy

20

Brian once told me that when a person has cancer, they always have cancer. However aggressive the treatment, however meticulously a surgeon disentangles the tumors one by one, a single stray cell flicked from the scalpel is all the root a metastasis needs. Some patients are fortunate; for whatever reason the remaining cancer cells never grow and the body carries them along unwittingly. Others aren't so lucky.

It was Brian's first year of med school and he was always relaying facts he found fascinating. But what fascinated him typically horrified me. Cancer, for example.

Fay's surgery went well, but the physician suspected a perforation in her bowel. A hole in her intestines would be inoperable. The cancer had grown throughout her lower digestive tract and further surgery would do more harm than good.

They fed her a mixture of charcoal and then they waited. When the black matter appeared in the bag affixed to the wound in her abdomen, the hospital cleric gave Jerry prayer and a handful of brochures for hospice.

⌐

I called Zoë morning and night, but she never picked up. I was grateful for my busyness, how it distracted me from imagining her grief. It was the end of the semester and tension filled the air. No amount of hard work leaves a teacher or a student prepared for May. My freshmen balked against writing their last essay. The creative writers scrambled to complete revisions for the final portfolio I'd assigned the very first day of workshop.

I rushed to finish overdue recommendation letters and counseled worried freshmen through grade anxiety. *Please be kind*, one student wrote on the bottom of his final paper. *I need an A in this class to get into law school. And I need my dad to not kill me.*

Everett and I went to every end-of-the-year reading and graduate student presentation hosted by the English Department. We attended Middle-Class Morality, poems by Dr. Janine Madison's creative writing class; Leslie Boyle's dissertation presentation on *Women's Rhetorical Transformations of the Discourse of Domesticity*; and Jennifer Donally's *Mirabel LeAnne Johnson's Circus Feline: Renegotiating Models of the Other*. We sat quietly through the presentations before slinking back to our office, stolen soda pops under either arm, one plastic plateful of hors d'oeuvres each.

Amidst end-of-year festivities, the English Department also hosted its annual undergraduate award ceremony. Ashley was the only student I had nominated. She won a $2,000 scholarship for her story about Natalie, which, for lack of inspiration, she ended up titling "Natalie."

The assembly was held in the ballroom of the student commons building. They could call it a ballroom, but it more resembled a hotel lobby—wallpaper with cream and white stripes, a dizzying flower-print carpet. Dr. Lindbergh, the presenter for the evening, wore a paisley silk blouse so like the curtain behind her, the competing patterns made my eyes cross. All those in attendance not receiving an award had nominated the winners, who were for the most part overdressed and self-conscious.

Ashley had been thrilled when I told her about her win, but she was positively white at the ceremony. She took her certificate and returned to her seat without once glancing up to acknowledge the applause.

"What's wrong?" I asked her afterward.

"I don't know." She folded the corner of the certificate between her forefinger and thumb. "It doesn't feel right."

"What doesn't feel right?"

"I feel like I made money off of something personal," she explained. "Like I'm a sellout."

"You didn't write that story to make money," I said. "You wrote it because you had to. Besides, this is an academic scholarship. What's two thousand dollars to the cost of one year of school? It's like getting two dollars really."

"I guess."

I took her out for dinner to celebrate. We ate at Dinah's, the greasy spoon of Copenhagen, where the waitresses wore blue uniform skirts with white tennis shoes and every meal came with a blueberry muffin the size of a small cake. We managed to talk for half an hour about writing and books and school and grading.

When we hit a lull in our conversation she confessed, "So I stopped by your church the other day. I went to the service, actually."

I debated telling her I'd seen her, but decided against it.

"It was kind of weird to be in a church," she said. "I used to go all the time as a little girl, but it's been a while."

I smiled. "It can be a strange experience if you're not used to it."

"No, it wasn't that weird. Well, sort of weird. But not too bad. I'm Episcopalian," she stated, as if this explained everything. "I've been thinking about the things Pastor Maddock said. About eternity and life as meaningless without an afterlife. A depressing outlook."

"He was posing a rhetorical question, though. Obviously he believes in eternal life and hopes we will consider it a possibility by asking us to imagine existence without it."

"Well, yeah." She pursed her lips. "I'm in this art history class. We've had to study all these paintings about hell. They're totally gross: people being disemboweled and roasted on pits by demons." She wrinkled her nose, as if hell were merely distasteful, a poor concept she could not approve of. "It's all, like, really demented."

I had seen pictures of the paintings Ashley was talking about, church ceilings depicting the damned in a wild assortment of creative agonies. Paintings commissioned to terrorize the poor into buying their relatives out of purgatory.

"A lot of those paintings were intended to educate an illiterate public," I said. "They relied heavily on symbolism. As does Scripture."

There was a script, a tract, things I should say: That hell was a nonnegotiable, that she needed Jesus to save her from her sins, but in this moment it wouldn't translate. For the first time in my adult life, I forgot what I was supposed to say and said what I meant.

"The imaginative failure of fearing hell as fire and, conversely, of expecting heaven to consist of clouds and harps is that both depend on the assumption that we will have the same bodies in the afterlife that we have now. Christianity asserts we will have bodies, but they will be as different as a walnut tree is from the nut it grows from. If you'd only ever seen the seed, you would have no idea about the intricacy or strength or longevity of the creature that it evolves into."

Ashley picked at the lid of her coffee cup. "I want to believe there's more than this. The day we buried Chelsea I wondered, you know? I couldn't help it. It doesn't seem real that a person could be with you one moment and gone the next, like they never even existed. But it's too abstract. How can you know it's not just another ignorant superstition? You're a Christian, but you'd discount all these other religions that have their own versions of the afterlife."

"Maybe belief in an afterlife is something many religions share because they're all man-made. Or maybe it's the opposite. Maybe there's a truth buried subconsciously in each man, woman, and child and that truth is projected out into the many religions people practice."

She swirled her coffee in its mug. "So you believe in heaven?"

Of course I said yes. But in moments when I really considered my faith I was sometimes alarmed by all of it—by what odd and miraculous things Christians believe. I pushed my plate aside, crossed my elbows on the table. "This will seem off-topic, but I've always been fascinated by science—anatomy, quantum physics, space and time theory. I don't understand these things, but the mystery is a part of what attracts me to them.

"That the world I live in now is complex beyond my under-standing only encourages me to believe that there are wild possibili-ties in creation beyond even the things of this dimension of time and space. If this universe has alternate dimensions outside of our understanding, isn't it possible that we might exist in a life beyond this one, in another kind of dimension that is fuller and more alive than the one we know?"

She smiled at me. "My dad would like you. He's a total science geek."

It was her way of steering the conversation back to safer ground.

When I pulled up to her dorm half an hour later, she lingered in the car, hesitant to say good-bye. Three girls were walking on the sidewalk in our direction, sundresses brushing high on their thighs, hand-bag straps bright against their tanned shoulders.

"They're from my floor. Leslie and her band of loyal admirers," Ashley said. "I'm sorry, but I hate them. Leslie goes to the tanning bed three times a week. She gets in completely naked except for a towel she puts over her chest." She rolled her eyes, a sardonic smile tugging at the corner of her lips. "So she won't get breast cancer."

We laughed together.

The girls' chatter grew louder as they walked by the car.

"They talk about me," she said. "I told my roommate about Chelsea and asked her not to tell anyone else. I didn't want people treating me different. But sometimes when I walk in the room, they all stop talking and look at me like they're guilty. They accused me of being antisocial."

"No one can know what you've been through unless they've gone through it themselves," I said. "It doesn't matter what they think."

"Yeah, I know, but it's not easy." She traced the rubber weather strip of the window with her thumb. "So I've been meaning to thank you."

"It was nothing. The story deserves the attention it received; you shouldn't be ashamed of it."

"No, not for the story. You know that night you called, a while back? It was my sister's birthday." Her hand fell to her lap. "It meant a lot to me that you called that day. I wasn't doing so well."

The night air had cooled. That wasn't why she shuddered, but I flicked the floor heater on anyway.

She stared out the window. "I think about Chelsea every single second of every single day. Sometimes I just want to go and be with her. I think I would do anything to be with her."

I considered this young woman who knew a grief I couldn't imagine. I thought of Fay and of Zoë.

"Ashley—you've never thought of hurting yourself."

She turned to face me, sincere or very well-rehearsed shock on her face. "I wouldn't, I swear," she said. "Ms. Gallagher, I couldn't do that to my dad." She ran her hand through her hair. "Look, forget I said it. It was a stupid thing to say."

"It's all right. I believe you."

She was the one to break eye contact. "I should get going." She reached for her bag and stepped daintily onto the sidewalk, but before leaving she peered back down inside the car. "Ms. Gallagher? I'm really okay. Honest."

"I said I believed you."

"Okay. See you around?"

See you around. Verbal clutter for good-bye.

She walked up the sidewalk, heels forcing her to walk with a decided strut. She could pass for a Leslie, for any of her self-conscious, vapid girlfriends, and I wondered how many people would take the time to see past the pretty face and recognize what lay beneath.

I knew she wouldn't come back to the Baptist church, that she and I would probably never talk again like we talked now. We might see each other once, maybe twice, only from a distance, and only if I stayed in Copenhagen long enough.

I couldn't save Ashley. But I hoped I was the first of many people who would lead her step-by-step until her fledgling wonder turned to faith and took flight, one of the many believers burning in rows like lights illuminating the length of an airplane runway.

21

I made Brian promise to come and stay with me in Copenhagen for a night. Class was over and I had grading and more grading to finish by the end of finals week. The prospect of spending hours alone in the apartment, slogging through the mountain of paper was unbearable.

On the phone, we negotiated the terms of his visitation.

"I have to study," he said.

"I know. I have to grade."

"You can't distract me."

"I'll be quiet as the grave. Circumspect as a monk."

"And I need to sleep."

"You can have Zoë's bed. I promise, you'll sleep like a baby."

"And I have to get up early."

"Done."

He arrived Saturday afternoon, laden with equipment: a computer bag slung over his shoulder, a thirty-pound book bag on his back, and a duffel bag stuffed with dirty laundry he hoped he could wash at my place—he was flat out of quarters. He unloaded his books on the kitchen table and set to work. I separated his darks and lights and made popcorn for brain food.

"What are these?" I pulled two bridal magazines from his duffel bag where I'd been searching for the dryer sheets he insisted he'd brought.

"Oh, I was going to take those back to Marie. She keeps leaving them at my place. You watch out," he warned. "Those magazines are poison. They bite."

"I'll be careful," I said solemnly.

The first magazine was two inches thick. The woman on the cover smiled with Julia Roberts wattage. She was sitting in a field of sunflowers, crowded by shouting headlines:

450 New Gowns
LOOKS YOU'LL LOVE FOREVER
REAL ADVICE FOR HOW TO DEAL WITH
IN-LAWS
Best Dressed Moms
GLUTES, THIGHS, AND ABS
the ultimate pre-wedding workout!

I read about Jessica and Brad's "modern and elegant" nuptials in the luxurious Ritz-Carlton resort in Naples, Florida. I read about Melanie and Mike's carved melon toothpick holders and how the air smelled of lavender and eucalyptus at Chloe and Jerome's outdoor sunset ceremony.

I drew a beard on Jerome with a black pen, which improved him significantly.

The men in bridal magazines were practically invisible in their uniformity, the same JCPenney underwear models in the same tux, the features of their smiling faces symmetric and attractive in a completely underwhelming way.

"These men all look alike to me," I said to Brian. "Is it the same when guys see women in magazines?"

He didn't move.

"Brian," I said.

"Mmm?"

"Do you think the women in these magazines all look the same?"

"What?" he said, annoyed.

I held the magazine up for his inspection. I repeated the question a third time.

"I guess." He went back to his studying.

Identical. Not the miraculous resemblance of twins, but the frightening uniformity of genetically enhanced clones.

"Like clones," I said.

"I'm studying, Amy," he warned.

I traded *Modern Bride* for *Robbins Pathology*, studying the pictures of anatomy and of cells, mystified by the charts and hieroglyphic equations. I'd always envied Brian's talent for science. In high school I loved chemistry but barely managed a C- and that by half copying my lab partner's homework. I studied hours for anatomy, but skinned by with a D, given not earned. Dr. Brown said I got an A for effort as if it would soften the blow.

All these years later, I still looked longingly at Brian's books, an illiterate toddler, limited to illustrations.

⌢

The call came that night. It was Valerie. She said she'd been trying to get ahold of Zoë to ask about the last surgery, but Jerry picked up her phone instead. Fay had passed away that morning, earlier than anyone had expected.

"I guess she was just ready to go," Valerie said. "Jerry sounded shocked."

Brian found me sitting on my bed in the dark, the phone silent in my lap.

"I thought you were talking to someone," he said.

"Zoë's mom is gone. She died this morning."

He ran his hand over his head. He sighed. Sitting beside me, he grabbed my hand, and we were back in elementary school, sitting on the bus together, my hand safely tucked in his.

"Have you talked to her?"

"She won't want to talk."

We sat in silence, staring at the rug.

"She'll need you," he said finally.

He made me a cup of tea. I didn't know my brother could brew tea. Marie taught him, he explained. She drank it compulsively while she studied. We sat on the roof, sometimes quiet and sometimes talking. The night was pleasantly cool. In the distance we could hear the hum of students partying. A group of freshmen walked by on the sidewalk. The boys wore pastel-colored shirts paired with plaid shorts. In their eagerness to dress well, they looked as fragile and colorful as Easter eggs.

"Has Marie ever seen a patient die?" I asked.

"She saw a kid die her second week in the clinic. He was only sixteen. She said it was real surreal. Like you knew it was happening but couldn't quite wrap your mind around it. She's had to see other patients go since—she doesn't have time to get to know them, but it's still hard. You can't just leave the hospital and step back into 'normal' life."

"Do you think it gets easier?"

"I don't know," he said. "A part of me hopes not."

Brian spent one summer interning in the ER. His resilience mystified me. How could a person stand it—watching people stream in night after night, torn, bleeding, and broken?

When I asked how Marie was doing with her clinics he couldn't say enough. He was unabashedly admiring of her skills and intelligence.

Maybe my difficulty with Marie was not sibling rivalry. Maybe it was jealousy over a career as opposed to jealousy over my brother: She was becoming the scientist I could never be. I would have to come to terms with this.

We talked about their plans and dreams and even about the wedding. Brian said he'd invited Dad to the rehearsal dinner. He was apologetic about it.

"I didn't want to invite him, but Marie said we should," he explained.

"Is he coming?"

"I don't know. We've been leaving each other voicemails all week. He's always vague: 'Be there if the weather permits, kiddo' or 'Juggling a few things, will get back to you.' "

"I hope he doesn't come," I said. "For Mom's sake."

"For all our sakes," he agreed.

I leaned back in my chair and tried to spot the stars. Tonight they were hidden beneath a purple scrim of light pollution. Or the fog of caffeine blurring my vision from the inside out. Pulling the quilt I'd brought with me tighter around my body, I closed my eyes. I couldn't remember the last time I'd seen my father.

The next thing I knew, Brian was gently nudging me awake. "You'd better get to bed."

It took me a moment to remember why he was here, why we were on the porch.

"What time is it?" I asked.

"Nearly three."

"I don't want you to leave."

"I'll stay the weekend," he assured me. "C'mon. You're exhausted."

I slipped into bed still dressed. The tears came easily. Not so much for Fay as for Zoë—and for shame that deep down, were I to admit it, my relief overwhelmed any sorrow. You played the odds in life. Statistically there were only so many bodies that succumbed to cancer a year. I wept in gratitude to God that my loved ones weren't the victims of chance this time around.

In the morning, while Brian was in the shower, I took *Robbins Pathology* out of his bag and searched the index. I flipped to the given page and stared at the photograph of a single breast cancer cell. The cell comprised an irregular, spherical mass, its surface riddled with interlacing strings of light like those writhing on the surface of the sun. It was aware of its power, fecund, cunning arms reaching to embrace its host.

⌐

We sent our condolences by mail. Everett and I signed our names to a card Valerie had made. I called a Chicago flower shop and asked to have an arrangement of flowers delivered to the Walker house. The florist asked what I wanted on the card.

"There's a card?" I asked.

"Of course," she said. "We pin it to the center of the arrange-ment."

"Can I skip the card?"

"We have balloons instead."

"This is for a funeral, not a birthday party."

"They're very tasteful," the clerk said.

"I don't want balloons."

"You can only order one balloon."

"I don't want *any* balloon."

Zoë specifically asked that none of us make the trip for the funeral. I considered calling but didn't want to be a burden. I tried to send an e-mail. The blank computer screen proved as insurmountable as the sympathy card. In the end I gave up trying to piece together my condolences. I wrote Zoë a brief message, asking if she would want company. She wrote back saying yes. I packed a book bag and a suitcase, the book bag for overnight clothes and a toothbrush, the suitcase to hold the essays I hadn't yet graded.

The drive to Chicago was more tedious than I remembered. For hours, the Indiana fields stretched gray to the right and left. By the time the automated tolls appeared to signal the nearness of the city, my back and eyes had begun to ache. I called Zoë to say I was ten minutes away. Three wrong turns and two hours later I called to say I was ten minutes away again. When I finally arrived she stood waiting for me on the porch.

She was pale and too thin.

"Tired?" she asked.

"I'm exhausted."

"Well," she said, bending down to lift my overnight bag from the trunk. Her hair stood on end, spiked and coarse and smelling of sleep. "You're in good company."

The house was exactly as I remembered it from the one time I had visited: old, simply furnished. Books everywhere. The photographs on the mantel sat in purposefully slanted rows, Fay smiling happily in three of the five portraits. The sameness of the house surprised me. I wanted the drinking glasses on the tables and the plants on the windowsill to acknowledge what had happened, but they just sat there oblivious, safely mired in their thingness.

Zoë led me to the kitchen. The sun had begun to set, tipping the clouds in gold, casting neon slants of orange light from the row of tall windows to the floor.

"Are you hungry? There's macaroni and cheese, spaghetti, lasagna, spaghetti, spaghetti." She leaned over the open refrigerator door. "Anything that could possibly be casseroled, we have."

I chose the dish that would cause the least amount of trouble.

"I'm glad you didn't come to the funeral," she said, spooning the spaghetti into a bowl. "The sanctuary was packed. They said we had over four hundred people at the visitation. The line to the cemetery was long enough for some political dignitary. *I* had to comfort people."

She spoke matter-of-factly, a newscaster giving her report. They dressed her mother in her favorite spring blouse. The bagpipers who played at the burial site performed beautifully. The people from her parents' church were so kind.

"Everyone's been great. We have so much food. Food and flowers. I'm sick to death of flowers."

Thankfully, I hadn't asked if she'd received mine. We sat together at the table while I ate. She pulled her legs up to her chest, tucking her knees inside her oversized T-shirt, which made a small hole in the upper left shoulder rip wider.

"It's hot," she warned after I'd already burnt my tongue and spat the noodles back onto the plate.

She shook her head. "I can't take you anywhere."

I was to sleep in the spare room, the space they'd allocated for the flower arrangements. The odor of decaying blossoms was suffocating.

"Sorry there's not much room," she said. "I told you: flowers."

"I don't mind," I said.

I found my arrangement on the center of the dresser. A small bunch of white lilies, and planted in the center—exactly as I had not requested—a silver balloon that read *With Sympathy* in blue cursive.

In high school I read a book about a Jewish family that sat shiva to mourn the loss of their adult son. They covered the mirrors in black cloth, and they didn't cook or clean or wash themselves. For seven days they had no business but grief. Visitors were to console the family, but were not to speak unless the family initiated conversation.

There were no such clear guidelines for Christian grieving. In my eagerness to project the right spirit, I'd only packed dark clothes.

I'd come prepared to sit, to listen, to cry. But Zoë, like her father, dealt with grief the same way she'd dealt with the cancer itself: She worked. When I got up at seven, Jerry had already left for the local paper where he worked as assistant editor. Zoë was in her parents' bedroom, sorting labeled boxes.

"Her clothes," she explained. "She'd already boxed the summer ones."

She'd known.

"Can I help at all?"

We dismantled Fay's closets for hours, Zoë all business. These pants were to go in this bag, and those shirts were to go in this pile. The jewelry would be auctioned; anything with stains we would rip for the ragbag. She was as ruthless as she was careless. One by one I folded and bagged and boxed the precious artifacts of a mother and a wife.

"Zoë, don't you want to keep some of these things?" I asked, hesitating to force yet another beautiful shawl into the already over-stuffed bag of scarves and hats.

"For what?" Zoë asked shortly.

"You could keep a few for yourself," I suggested gently. "Something to remember her by."

"Dad's selling the house. He can't afford this place, let alone storage for me to hoard junk for some sentimental whim."

Of course: the price tag for chronic disease. I finally connected the seemingly unrelated comments she'd been making about auctions, about the housing market, about the insufficiency of her father's salary. He would live the rest of his life under the financial burden of his wife's prolonged illness. I worked without saying another word.

When I returned from carrying the last box to the car, I found Zoë sitting on her mother's bed staring at a framed photograph of her parents. They were standing on a beach, Fay in a blue dress. Their wedding day.

Zoë started when I stepped forward, as if caught doing something shameful. Then a change came over her expression; there was a glint of mischief in her eyes. "Want to see something?"

She took me to her old bedroom. It was tidy, simple: a bed, a rug, an elegant oak dresser. On the dresser sat a glass canister of cotton balls and decorative bottles of cheap lotion.

Beside the lotions sat a mannequin head.

"The wig head, for the wig of the day," Zoë explained. She opened the closet to reveal a shelf that housed several such mannequins. Each wore a wig of real human hair. Auburn, blond, short, long, curly, straight.

"You weren't kidding about it being an obsession," I said.

"Somewhere along the way, she gave up trying to look like Fay and enjoyed being a new Fay every day."

"What did your dad think?"

"He put up with it." She picked up the auburn wig, twirled her fingers through its curls. "She tried to pass the collection off as ironic, a purposeful exaggeration of women's coping mechanisms."

This sounded like someone I knew: Zoë came by her flair for theatrics honestly.

"I think deep down she was genuinely horrified by her appearance." She carefully set the wig back in its place. "I guess every woman has her vanity."

"Vanity? Zoë, you really think it was vanity?"

The disease took Fay's breasts; it ravaged her skin and robbed her of her beautiful hair. A body was a machine that could function without a number of disposable parts, and as Christians we'd adopted the lofty belief that a person's spirit could exist distinctly separate from this biological vehicle so susceptible to temptations and to breakdowns. But you couldn't dismantle the body piece by piece and expect the spirit to escape unscathed. You couldn't call it vanity, the loss of the breasts that had nursed your child, or even of the hair that had once seduced your husband.

"I know—I know you're right, I didn't meant it," she apologized, guilty for the careless comment. "It scares me, though, to realize that who I am is so inexorably linked to my body."

I rubbed my ankle, which now ached when the humidity changed. I'd always thought that was an old wives' tale, the trick knee or arthritic elbow that could predict a coming storm.

"It's terrifying," I agreed.

⌒

Fay's closets were empty. The chore Zoë had been dreading was over. In her relief, she grew talkative. We sat on the porch swing, her legs on my lap. I rubbed her feet with Luna Lady Peppermint Foot Lotion. The evening sunlight shot through our glasses, illuminating the amber tea. Across the street, three little boys were running around the lawn. The tallest wore a SpongeBob SquarePants bedsheet as a cape. Zoë watched their game intently.

"I dumped Michael," she said.

"When was this?" I asked, surprised.

"Before Mom's operation. He wouldn't come up to be with me. Said he had work." She shook her head, muttered "jerk" with more spite than the word could carry.

I rolled my knuckles in the arch of her foot. "Why didn't you tell me?"

"I don't know. It didn't seem to matter at the time, all things considered."

The neighbor boys shot at each other with pretend ray guns. "You're dead!" one shouted. "I killed you!"

"How do you feel about it?" I asked.

She shrugged. In the bright sunlight, her eyes were red-rimmed and bloodshot, though I hadn't seen her cry since arriving. "I can't even care right now. I'm assuming it will hit me later."

"You'll be over him so quickly you won't know what happened." I switched to her left foot, kneading it from the heel up.

"I should never have gone out with him in the first place."

I rallied, "He was your Adam Palmer. As Adam was to Amy, Michael was to Zoë."

"And what is that?"

I squeezed fresh lotion into my hand, thinking. "A good-looking diversion, but not the final destination."

"A vacation, but not home."

"Exactly." I tried to remember Michael's exact words. "You 'had a nice run' was how he said it."

She rolled her eyes.

"Derision." I smiled. "That's the spirit."

Without warning she started to cry. She lay down on the swing, crumpled into a ball like a child, her head in my lap. She sobbed until I feared she'd hyperventilate. I ran my fingers through her coarse hair, coaching her to breathe.

She used her overly long shirtsleeve to wipe the snot and tears from her face.

"Amy."

"Yeah?"

"I wasn't ready for this."

"I know."

I rocked the swing back and forth. There really wasn't anything else to say.

That night we slept together in the spare room. I waited until the lights were out, conversation stretching to its second hour, to tell her about Eli. It seemed wrong to call attention to the trivial melodrama of my own love life the week of her mother's funeral, but all evening she had been so uncharacteristically transparent, so full of intimate confessions, that I felt inspired to reciprocate.

She had been telling me how when she was a child they were always moving from one place to another, her parents never interested in settling down. How she'd learned not to get too attached.

"I was fine on my own and I learned to be proud of it," she said. "But I forget sometimes how lonely it was. Even now, this awful lonely feeling comes over me. Like no one knows me. That I'm unknowable. I live my life constantly preparing for that moment when a person I love will look at me and realize I'm a stranger."

She propped herself up on her elbow.

"It's like I prepare myself to be disappointed, or to be misunderstood. That's what worked about Michael and me. He made me feel safe, because he never looked that deep. If that makes sense."

I told her it made sense.

After a long pause I said, "Zoë, I think I'm in love with Eli."

It was the first time I'd heard her laugh in weeks. "*Really*," she said.

She was less entertained when I explained he was not only attracted to me but had acted on the feeling.

"You *think* you're attracted to him," she repeated sarcastically when I'd confessed everything. "So that's why he moved out."

"It was only the one night."

"Has he told Jillian?"

"I don't know. I think so."

I begged her not to hate me.

"Why would I hate you?"

"Jillian is such a good friend. I guess I felt like betraying her was betraying you."

"So you made a mistake. You made it right. He moved out, anyway. And you haven't seen him since? Then it's up to him to make things right with Jillian. That's not your responsibility.

"I like Jillian," she added. "Her various neuroses aside. But she's not like you—we never had what you and I have." She looped her arm through mine as she said this, an unselfconscious, automatic gesture. I realized Eli had been right about our friendship: She would never have hurt me wittingly.

"Eli," she mused. "I would never have thought Eli your type."

"Do I have a type?" I asked, more worried than curious. I was picturing youth pastors with crew cuts, who carried Palm Pilots on their belts and listened to early nineties' Christian rock.

"I suppose saying a person has a type flattens them unfairly."

Her own statement struck her as important. She was wired enough to elaborate, to take a little mental trip away from thinking another second about how to survive without her mother. She talked until I couldn't stay awake, her voice even and analytical, her open eyes fixed on a thought she was determined to articulate. Something about her and Michael, about the fundamental flaw of their relationship, about the impossibility of loving someone wholly and sincerely.

"You should write a book," I murmured.

"Based on the life of Zoë Walker?" she asked.

"I hear memoirs are all the rage."

"All right." She rolled over on her side. "But just remember you said that when you show up on page five."

⌒

The next afternoon Zoë packed me a Zoë lunch: hummus and cucumber on rye with two organic Jonathan apples and a bag of dried pineapples. In the driveway she kissed my cheek good-bye. She made me promise to write at least once a day.

I hated leaving her in that house. As I drove home, the burden of unfinished work compounded the depression I'd felt since arriving in Chicago. Final grades were due Monday, and I hadn't even made it through half the essays I had to mark. At this point, it was hard to care. In light of the past week's events, very little I'd ever worried about seemed that important.

I tried to pray, but even the simplest prayer was impossible. Talking with Ashley about her sister's death and then living two days beside Zoë's grief had made me acutely aware of God in a way I'd never experienced before. This was a God silent and terrifyingly other, the unknowable force that knelt down to blow the dust in motion and then ascended back to His throne to watch the drama, the universe like a top set to the ground spinning. Particles blowing apart and cleaving, birthing suns, stitching babies, sprouting cancers. It was chance, the one missing gene; chance, the single cell that decided to stage a coup.

The impact of the accident woke me from my daydream. I was in the right lane veering to the left when, from distraction or caffeine deficiency or pure negligence, I failed to check my blind spot. I felt the impact before I registered the shrieking scrape of metal on metal.

The brief sideways collision knocked the driver's side mirror clean off, but otherwise my car was unscathed. I pulled over. The other driver begged me to settle down, to please stop crying. He insisted his truck wasn't worth the trouble. It was halfway to the junker already. When I saw the two-foot-long dent that had stripped the paint from his truck, I cried harder. On a scrap of paper I'd found in my purse, we exchanged information quickly. He sped off, leaving a cloud of exhaust in his wake.

In the car, I set my trembling hands on the wheel and tried to make the world stand still.

⁓

I bypassed the exit to Copenhagen and went straight home, certain I needed nothing more that moment than to feel my mother's arms around me.

I'd hoped for sympathy; I was given censure. She was angry that I hadn't told her I was in Chicago. That I had been in an accident only confirmed every suspicion she had against highway driving.

"Fortunately, his information is bogus," she said, returning to the kitchen with the wrinkled scrap of paper I'd handed over to her at the door.

She was dressed in a hot pink jumpsuit, her skin an orange tan and her hair frosted blond, an ensemble incandescent against our yellowing kitchen wallpaper.

"This isn't a real insurance company," she said. "That's probably why he was so eager to get out of there."

"If you'd have called the police, he would have lost his license," Richard explained needlessly.

Mom propped her hand on her hip. "I still don't understand why you didn't call the police," she said.

"I don't know—I wasn't thinking. Thirty years old, and I forget what to do in a state of emergency."

Richard made an admirable attempt to cheer me up: "I'm fifty-one, and I don't know what I'm doing half the time."

"That's reassuring." I spun my coffee cup around and studied the rainbow on the front. Bubble letters read *Virginia Beach or bust!*

"I've had worse with the old Dodge. It'll be taken care of. 'Don't be anxious about anything,' " Mom recited, joining us at the table. " 'But in everything, by prayer and petition, with thanksgiving, present your requests to God.' "

"I think He has more to worry about than dented fenders," I said.

"If He has the hair on your head numbered, He has your fenders counted."

I gave her a look.

"What?" she asked.

She was too excited about Brian's Big Day to share in my misery.

The wedding was a week away and already our house was as bustling and chaotic as Zoë's had been silent. Dresses hung in plastic, corsages chilled. There were rehearsals and scripts and props. Everyone had their part and seemed comfortable with their lines, while I stood mute at center stage, staring at the waiting darkness, hoping for a cue.

22

Mom's church friends Sandy Baldwin and Mrs. Jenkins drove over the afternoon of the wedding rehearsal for a complimentary Luna home-spa treatment. I had been coerced into attending. To my mother's endless distress I'd pulled two all-nighters to finish my grading. Lack of sleep was *terrible* for the complexion: She would not have *her* daughter wearing eye bags to *her* son's wedding.

I sat across from Grandma and to the right of Mrs. Jenkins, my third grade Sunday school teacher, who liked to take personal responsibility for the fact I'd turned out so well. I traded surreptitious glances with Grandma over the table while the women talked: I was still weightless from the first euphoria of summer vacation and had patience enough for the both of them.

"I have eight grandchildren now," Mrs. Jenkins answered to my polite query. "Seven by blood; the eighth from my Robert's wife's first marriage." She dipped her hands in the warm wax Mom had mixed up in our old popcorn bowl. The old lady's manicured red nails had terrified me as a child. Though her hands had wrinkled and shrunk with age, the pointed red nails had not changed. It gave me an almost physical jolt to see them.

"It's not a good situation. He's nearly twenty now. Into all sorts of things that are of no benefit to anyone. But I guess every family has one of them." When she lifted her hands, the wax gathered to a point at her fingertips. "Not my business."

"That's why there are so many problems with the youth today," Sandy said to me. Her expression was one of desperate concern. She was wearing cucumber slices on her eyes; the round whiteness of the cucumbers made her appear all the more alarmed.

"These young children don't have the Lord in their hearts," Mrs. Jenkins said. "We need to make a great effort to teach them while they're young."

"Oh, I don't know," said Grandma. "We do right by some. What's Lisa up to now? She was always a bright girl."

"Still in Europe," Sandy said. "You know Lisa. Impossible to keep track of. One minute she's here, the next she's flying to Paris. That girl wears herself out."

"When is she set to come home next?" Grandma asked.

She was being overly polite. Behind Mom's back she referred to Sandy and Mrs. Jenkins as "Those Cats."

"Christmas, or so she says now," Sandy said. "Give it two weeks and she'll have changed her mind."

"I thought she'd already been to Paris," Mrs. Jenkins said.

"Well, she went once with the class trip. This is her second go, only now she's working there the whole time, teaching English."

"Meeting any Parisian men?" Grandma winked at me.

Sandy said, "That would mean some profit for all this running around. Now, I'm not one to pressure a girl, but land sakes, she'll be thirty-one this July!"

She sounded shocked, as if her daughter had not been progressing steadily toward her next birthday month by month like everyone else.

"A woman can't just live life as if age doesn't matter."

Mom stood abruptly and snatched the bowl of wax from beneath

Mrs. Jenkins's still suspended hands. In the kitchen, she refilled the bowl, her back to us.

Mrs. Jenkins raised her eyebrows. "She won't be young forever. I hope she realizes that."

"These girls are so different now. They're so—so *entitled*," Sandy said.

The cucumber on her right eye fell in her lap. She picked it up and, after a momentary hesitation, sniffed it. I hoped she would take a bite.

"They're admirably ambitious," Grandma said.

"I had two babies and a third on the way when I was her age," said Mrs. Jenkins.

"I had two children, a mortgage, and an ex-husband," said my mother. She shut the microwave door with more force than was necessary.

This was the first time Mom had spoken in half an hour, which in and of itself was strange. Moreover, it was the first time I'd heard her admit to the divorce in front of Mrs. Jenkins. Ever.

Sandy and Mrs. Jenkins had always accepted my mother as a friend, but their silence surrounding my parents' separation kept any real intimacy at bay. My mother acted as though she were indebted to them for their resolution to ignore what they perceived as her greatest failing as a Christian and as a woman. Most peculiar of all, they now seemed as blind to her new boyfriend as they had been to her failed marriage. When Richard had come by an hour earlier to drop off some dry cleaning, Mrs. Jenkins blatantly ignored his presence.

I waited in suspense for Mrs. Jenkins to acknowledge my mother's statement.

Instead, Sandy made some oblique comment about the difficulties of raising very young children.

"It is not easy," Mrs. Jenkins agreed.

Sandy reached for the lotion. She did not eat the cucumber after all.

~

In the late afternoon Grandma went home to nap before the rehearsal. The rest of us drove with Mom to the chapel. Mrs. Jenkins had agreed to play piano for the ceremony at no cost; Sandy was present for moral support. The ladies' shins bumped up against cardboard boxes of votive candles and plastic ivy. I sat shotgun next to my mother, uncomfortable in pantyhose and a dress, my cheeks exfoliated, red and tight as the skin of a newly blown-up party balloon.

"Weather's looking dreary," said Mrs. Jenkins, eyeing the dark clouds through the minivan window. "You'd better tell Marie to say her prayers."

Sandy added, "The weatherman says it'll be a fifty percent chance of rain tomorrow."

"The Lord wouldn't do that to me," Mom said. "I've been asking for sunshine six months now. He's promised it to me."

Sandy grabbed the sides of Mom's seat and peered around the headrest. "It's a left here," she said, pointing.

"I know where I'm going," Mom snapped. Her hands were tight on the wheel, her knuckles white.

"It will be beautiful," I said to her when we began unloading at the church. I expected rain, but I wanted to show a sign of solidarity.

"Sandy doesn't know what she's talking about," Mom replied. "That woman sits home all day watching the weather channel like it's the greatest thing since Lawrence Welk."

Mom: 2; Sunday school women: 0.

I took the boxes she was unloading and followed her across the parking lot, intrigued by this woman who was playing my mother.

The chapel was smaller than I had expected, narrow with a crowded aisle leading to a crowded platform. A stained-glass window featuring the ascension of Christ loomed over the little sanctuary. There was a piano to the right and a pair of candelabras at either side of the communion table. The place might have been pretty but for the garish purple carpet. It smelled musty, with the lingering odor of cleaning detergent used to polish blond wood furniture that had been all the rage in the seventies but now appeared tawdry and worn.

Brian and Marie had arrived earlier with two of her bridesmaids, who were already busy folding bulletins for the next day's guests. Marie's father had been charged with setting candles on the windowsills. Cousins were tying bows to every other pew, Marie's mother following to undo and more perfectly retie every single one.

Within the hour, the rest of the bridal party arrived, the minister second to last, and—to everyone's surprise—my father last of all.

"Darren," Mom exclaimed.

I looked at Brian, alarmed. *Don't look at me*, he mouthed.

Dad strode to the front of the chapel. He wore sunglasses on his head, sandals on his feet, a tourist stumbling onto what he hoped would be a good beach party. Though I had known there was a chance he would show before the wedding, his presence was scandalous. Perhaps it was the nonchalance of his entrance, the way he so casually interrupted the lives we'd made for ourselves without him.

Mom met him halfway down the aisle. "How are you?" she asked.

"Doing all right." Chewing his gum, he surveyed the pews, the candelabras, the altar. "The place looks good. Real good."

"When we didn't hear from you, we assumed you couldn't make it."

Dad said, "I wouldn't miss this for the world."

"Well, you can sit in the back," Mom instructed. "We're just getting started."

He obligingly sat in the very last pew, a safe distance away from conversation with anyone involved in the wedding.

I walked purposefully to his pew. "Anyone sitting here?"

"Hey, sport," he said, rising to give me a hug.

Tall and thick-shouldered with a mane of white hair that hadn't diminished over the years, my father was what some women might consider handsome. Brian and I had our father's bold features: long nose, expressive eyes, full lips. But taking a seat beside him, I couldn't help noticing he had changed a great deal since I'd last seen him. He was heavier, his waist wider and lower, his now-full cheeks bristled with a pepper-and-salt beard. He was crumpled and weary. Old.

"We're glad you could make it," I said.

"I'm real proud of your brother. He's a fine kid."

Dad often spoke about us as if gossiping to a neighbor about someone else's family. It was particularly unnerving when he did this while addressing one of us directly.

The wedding planner corralled the bridesmaids into place at the foyer doors.

"How's school going?" Dad asked.

I told him that other than the weekly desire to jump off a cliff, I did all right.

"I couldn't do what you do." He shook his head wonderingly. "It takes a special kind of person to be a teacher."

"I'm not a teacher, Dad. I'm a writer."

"You're still on that?" he asked, frankly surprised. This from the man who filled my early childhood with incessant monologues on the fundamental virtues of the American Dream, social mobility, and the chasing of falling stars. He had changed, maybe more than I thought.

"Where's Penny?" I asked, fully aware it was a loaded question. You never knew if Dad was on his way in or out of a relationship.

"Couldn't make it. Work's been riding her tail real bad this year."

"I haven't seen her in a while."

274

"What's it been now?" he asked. "A whole year?"

"Since the Christmas before last."

He whistled. "Hard to believe. You ought to see Marjorie now."

"Is she in high school?"

"Freshman year of college," he corrected. "Eighteen going on twenty-five."

He retrieved his wallet from his suit jacket and opened it to a picture of Penny's daughter, a product of her first marriage. She was a masculine girl, hair like yarn, braces barely restraining a fierce overbite. "It's an old picture, of course," he said. "She's a real beauty now. A total heartbreaker."

I imagined him showing a picture of me to Marjorie, saying *She's a real beauty. A total heartbreaker.*

The rehearsal was well under way. It was too rude to talk without whispering. Brian and Marie recited their vows. The minister told Brian he could kiss his bride. He dipped Marie down toward the floor and raspberried her cheek.

When the wedding planner demanded a second run-through, Grandma drafted me to photograph the event with her camera, complaining that in the chapel's dim light she couldn't see well enough to do it herself.

As soon as I stood, she took my seat beside Dad. She kept him busy with whispered conversation the remainder of the rehearsal. This could have been a gesture of kindness; however, she seemed more to be controlling the situation than enjoying it, like a small woman walking a very large dog, mindful of the energy on the other end of the leash but fully capable of restraining it.

At dinner afterward I saved a seat for Dad. He never showed.

From: gallagham@copenhagen.edu
To: iheartofu@writersnet.com
Sent: Friday 5.18.07 11: 05 PM
Subject: the Big Day

Zoë:

Eve of the wedding. Brian is with his groomsmen at the hotel and Marie is sleeping at her house. Is very quiet here now that the Sunday school ladies have left. Mom's downstairs ironing her shawl for the third time. She's been worrying this one particular wrinkle since noon.

Amy

_____

From: iheartofu@writersnet.com
To: gallagham@copenhagen.edu
Sent: Friday 5.18.07 11: 20 PM
Subject: Re: the Big Day

Amy,
weddings are beautiful and lovely and overrated.
above all, be faithful to me. if some man sweeps you off your feet, remind him you already have a housemate.

love
Zoë

_____

I had grown up in a world that lived in perpetual anticipation of the marriage of Christ and the Church, the glorious Bride without spot and wrinkle, the wedding that would kick off eternal bliss. In this world, sex is a union of souls and every wedding a microcosm of the Great Consummation—a mystery belied by the daily mechanics of most every relationship I had ever seen and by the failure of my own parents' marriage. And so Brian and Marie's wedding ceremony (lovely, romantic, flawless even) seemed like just another rehearsal, a shadow or reflection of the great thing it aspired to be.

Afterward I rode with Grandma to the reception. Brian and Marie had chosen to rent out the public park beyond the schoolyard, where he and I had attended elementary school. I laughed when he told me. In my mind, the park was as it had always been: a muddy field with a rickety merry-go-round and a dandelion hill only good for dizzying, consecutive somersaults.

My skepticism was unwarranted. Over the years, the swing set had been replaced with a cast-iron sculpture of birds in flight. Carefully cubed shrubs had been planted in place of the rusted jungle gym. Now the park was pure magic. White candles in glass votives had been hung from the overhanging tree branches with white ribbon. The lights swayed in the breeze. Beneath the pavilion, the DJ had begun to play a round of classical dinner music. We ate platefuls of chicken and salad and bread. Laughter burst out overhead.

I worried that enjoying the reception would be a betrayal of Zoë, but despite my best attempts to remain ironically aloof, the festivity worked its way into my blood. Soon I was laughing, enjoying myself. My brother was charming in his tux and well-gelled hair. Marie had lost the anxiety that shaded her face all through the day's preparations and the aftermath of the ceremony. Everyone seemed happy and relaxed. Everyone was, for that fleeting moment, beautiful. The sun set, but we were too busy to notice. Our plates were miraculously cleared away, carried off, perhaps, by fairies from the trees.

The dancing began shortly after sunset. The crowd was small, most guests married and thereby consigned to one partner, the rest faithful members of the First Fundamentalist Church of God and therefore forbidden to dance at all. As such, there was a severe shortage of male partners. I sat on one of the folding chairs lining the pavilion, watching the fun and trying to be philosophic about it: Elizabeth Bennet didn't have anyone to dance with either, and look what that started.

Grandma came and sat beside me. "The ceremony was lovely, wasn't it?" she asked.

"It was."

For a moment her smile faltered. "It's all over so quickly."

"I know. Say a few vows and you're married. Hard to believe how much work goes into half an hour."

"That's not what I mean," she replied. "Look at Brian."

He was dancing with the flower girl, who stood with her feet on his. I used to dance that way with my father. It gave me a fleeting vision of Brian with children of his own. *Aunt Amy*, I thought, trying it on for size.

"I always knew he was going to be a romantic," Grandma said. "It was the way he cared for your mother even as a little boy. Remember how he always bought her flowers on Valentine's Day? All the way up to high school?"

I spent a moment remembering.

"He will make Marie a happy woman," she concluded.

"Grandma, can I ask you something?"

"Sure, Sugarpie. What is it?"

The blue balls dangling from her earrings swayed on her old earlobes. They made me think of little planets.

"Did Dad make Mom happy? Ever?"

My grandmother did not reply immediately, blindsided by the question. No one in my family discussed my parents' marriage. Ever. A part of me wanted to take it back, to apologize for ruining the evening. But there was my father, eating cheddar cubes off toothpicks and presiding over the wedding with a certain kind of pride despite the fact that he'd missed every other monumental moment in my brother's life. And as always we accommodated his presence. We remained somehow righteous in our indifference, as if silence were sufficient absolution for the sins of the past.

Grandma leaned back in her chair with a heavy sigh.

"Your mother was very much in love with Darren once," she said.

"Did he make her happy?"

"Sometimes."

"She never talked about him," I said. "All my childhood. All through high school. And she was aloof at best when he came by— like he was a stranger from the church who had come to visit. She never seemed shaken by his presence."

"That's because she didn't want to worry you kids," Grandma

said. "Don't underestimate your mother. It took a lot of work for her to hold it together back then. *A lot* of work."

"I just don't understand why she refuses to talk about the past. We have a right to know."

"Did you ever think that maybe this isn't about you?"

But something in me protested: To some extent it was about me. It was *my* mother who had been left, and *my* home that had been abandoned. He left me too, and after all these years I wanted someone to acknowledge the hurt, to let me know it was only natural to find myself still daily dressing a childhood wound.

"Maybe she just wants to be happy," Grandma said. "After all these years, it's finally her turn."

We were both thinking the same thing.

"She's really fallen for Richard, hasn't she?" I asked.

"He worships the ground she walks on. You can't do much better than that." She watched the party with a wistful glint in her eyes. Parties made her miss our grandfather. They'd always thrown the better steak-fries and birthday dinners. But she was never one to indulge her grief if there was something brighter to think about. She quickly turned playful. "So. How about it? You ready for your turn?"

"Someday, of course," I replied automatically, though I wasn't sure it was true. I thought of Brian, dealing with a confusion between his mother-in-law and the minister; our family suspicious of the dancing; Marie's family bewildered by mine. The scene of barely contained chaos and strained diplomacy seemed discouragingly representative of the married life.

An old friend stole Grandma's attention, and I took the chance to slip away. The caterers had already begun to clear the dinner dishes. The bare tabletops glowed opalescent in the moonlight. I traded my shoes for my shawl, stowing the heels beneath my dinner chair. The grass felt cool and wet against my blistered feet.

As I returned to the pavilion, I saw my father cross the dance floor with purpose to his step. He stopped when he came to my mother, who sat talking happily with some second cousin. He extended his hand. After a momentary hesitation, she accepted.

This was unprecedented: She did not dance, by rule.

My father led her to the dance floor, placed his arm around the small of her back, and together they began to sway in time. She let him lead, but barely. Her back was stiff, and they stood just close enough to manage a stilted sort of rhythm, the way I'd danced with boys at the junior high prom, elbows stiff and shoulders back. He made conversation. She spoke with the same polite economy with which she danced, calm but wary.

The song had not yet ended when Richard stepped in. My mother beamed at him. A new song began, lively and loud.

To the alarm of the watching Fundamentalists, my mother *danced*.

23

Monday I returned to Copenhagen. I spent the entire day in my pajamas eating cereal for breakfast and lunch, sleeping off the emotional upheaval of the last two weeks. By evening I was wide awake and restless. I got dressed, grabbed *To Kill a Mockingbird*, and locked the apartment behind me. The insects were loud, their invisible metropolis hustling in the trees. Downtown Copenhagen was all but abandoned. Occasionally a car passed. In the sandwich shops and liquor stores the cashiers leaned against their counters reading magazines, not expecting interruption. The entire town had the empty feeling of a house just cleaned from a long, overdrawn party: The crowds were dispersed, the beer bottles thrown out, and the hosts glad of a long-awaited, quiet sleep.

I walked the empty streets to The Brewery. A young man sat in the back corner writing on his laptop. Two older women were talking on the couch beside the front window. I took a seat at the bar. I didn't recognize the barista who made my drink and was glad I didn't have to talk to any of Zoë's friends about how she was doing. Slowly, Harper Lee and the mocha worked their magic. I was tucked away in Alabama, pocketing treasures from a tree with Scout, when a hand bumped mine, startling me back to reality.

Eli stood behind the counter. He was wiping down the bar with a wet rag, the rag he'd collided with my hand. I was more than a little surprised to see him—I'd been keeping track of his schedule, strategically avoiding the café while he was working. And he wasn't supposed to work nights.

"What are you reading?" he asked.

I showed him the cover.

"I read that in high school," he said.

"Me, too."

"You're reading it again?"

"I read it every year."

He walked to the other end of the counter, dragging the wet rag behind. "To be honest, I never finished it."

"Well." I opened my book up again. "Maybe we can still be friends."

He grinned, his eyes on the counter where a spot of spilled coffee kept him momentarily busy.

I read two pages without remembering a word.

Within the hour the other customers began to leave. I debated whether to follow suit. I didn't want it to seem as though I'd come to see Eli on purpose; I didn't want him to think I was avoiding him either (even though I had been, for weeks). After standing at the door in a moment of indecision, I went back to the office to say good-bye.

He sat at the desk, the blue light of the computer screen high-lighting the hollow of his cheeks.

"Hey," he said.

"Hi."

"Finish your book?"

"I can't seem to concentrate."

He gestured to the calendar on the wall. "Zoë's on the work schedule," he said.

"I know." I ventured over, took a seat beside him. "She's planning to come home next week."

"How is she?"

"As well as can be expected." I paused. "So you're here for the summer?" I asked conversationally. Hoping.

"Uh, no, actually—" He glanced at me, then quickly looked back to the computer, minimizing windows on the screen. "I've been accepted to the Pendleton Artist Residency—upstate New York. I leave Friday."

He brought up the website, began flipping through a number of photographs, studios, galleries, paintings. But New York? I was so disappointed by his news I overcompensated. When he asked what I was doing for the summer I announced I had no plans with such enthusiasm it was almost grating in my own ears. "They don't need any more adjuncts for the summer so I'm essentially on vacation with my students. Which would be splendid except for that little problem of money."

"Maybe they'd hire you here—they'll need to fill my spot."

"I could never work here," I said. "I need somewhere to sit and think that's not my desk."

There was an uncomfortable pause. I said I should get going.

"I'll let you out."

The chairs had been stacked while we spoke, the lights in the coolers switched off. Outside, the streets were just as abandoned.

"I told Jillian the truth," he said. "I wanted you to know."

"How did that go?"

His expression said enough.

"Eli, I'm so sorry. I should never have said the things I did about you—about your family."

"Stop apologizing, Amy."

He held the door for me. "You want me to walk you home?"

"I don't know. That didn't work out so well for you last time." We both laughed in a forced kind of way.

He let the door shut behind him. The noise of insects buzzed in the night air. I studied his feet. He desperately needed new shoes; how insane to fall in love with a man who couldn't even afford shoes.

"I hate good-byes," he said, all of a sudden awkward.

So stay, I thought.

I said, "So, let's just say 'I'll see you around.'"

He leaned in closer. He lifted my chin to his face and kissed me, a gentle kiss, a chill down my spine. His hand lingered a moment on my cheek.

"See you around, Amy Gallagher."

With a definitive click, the bolt latch locked behind him.

24

Eli left.

To the last minute, I held out hope he would come to the apartment to say good-bye, but he disappeared from Copenhagen as unobtrusively as he'd appeared. I went to The Brewery Saturday, ordered coffee and sat at the bar reliving our last conversation, stunned by the permanence of his absence.

My only consolation was that Zoë had finally committed to a plane ticket. She would arrive Monday, and her return was the only thing that made Eli's leaving bearable. She had not stipulated how long she planned to stay in town, but there was never any talk of her moving out and both our names were on the summer lease. I washed her bedsheets and stocked the fridge with nonfat yogurts and organic spinach. At Wal-Mart I bought a cartful of cleaning supplies, intent on scrubbing the apartment from ceiling to floor, on distracting myself from the terrible loneliness that threatened to ruin the long summer vacation hours I usually enjoyed alone.

Grandma called while I was in the home-goods aisle comparing prices for Swiffer mops.

"I wanted to talk to you," she said.

"About?"

"Let's talk in person. How about dinner?"

She drove up that evening. The limited list of Copenhagen eateries did not impress her, so we went half an hour out of town to an Italian place she and Grandpa had frequented before his doctor outlawed complex carbohydrates ("complicated carbohydrates" as she and Mom called them). I ordered what I wanted without attention to price. Grandma hated to treat cheap people.

"So what did you want to talk about?" I asked, unfolding the cloth napkin in my lap.

"Your father had an affair," she said without prelude. "Two actually."

I blinked in shock. "What?"

"I'm sorry, I don't know any other way to say it but to say it."

I stared at my grandmother, trying to get my bearings. "Mom said they loved each other but couldn't live together."

"She told me the same thing, until you were both in high school. Eat your soup, Sugarpie. It's getting cold."

I stirred the soup, but I'd suddenly lost my appetite.

Grandma cut her salad, cross-hatching with her knife until the lettuce had been reduced to a pulp. Her earrings—big orange O's—dangled as she worked. "Amy, I know this comes as a surprise. I never thought I'd be the one to tell you."

At the sight of my confusion, she sighed. She set her silverware down, dabbed either corner of her mouth with her napkin, and explained: "I never knew about his cheating. She told me the same thing she told you, that they loved each other, but couldn't live together. Of course, that wasn't enough for me. You love someone, you make it work, that was always my theory. The Lord knows I couldn't live with your grandfather sometimes, but as I saw it, that wasn't reason enough to throw in the towel. It was all I could do to hold my tongue around your mother those weeks. The divorce was quick. Over. Just like that.

"Then, years later, there was an incident at church—I don't know if you remember. A choir member committed adultery with the music director. Rumors about the affair circulated for months. Your mom was so bothered by it; I couldn't figure it out. Then she came to the house one day, all shook up and crying, and she finally told me the truth about what happened between her and your father."

"He cheated on her," I repeated in disbelief.

"He had his first affair the second year they were married and the second several months before the divorce. Your mother said she could only guess at the first, but she found letters the second woman had written to your father, and caught them talking on the phone on more than one occasion. She never actually saw them together, thank heavens, but the letters broke her heart. When she confronted him, he said he'd end things, but that wasn't enough for your mother. She said she couldn't live her life wondering when he was going to do it again.

"Your mother left your father, Amy. Not the other way around."

My breath felt shallow. Why had Mom lied to me?

"You know you can't tell this to a soul," Grandma warned. "Especially not to your mother. She's wanted to tell you, but she doesn't know how." Careful to keep the billowy sleeves of her hot pink blouse from dipping into her salad, she reached across the table for the salt. "She has this featherbrained idea that she should wait until some big defining moment—first it was your high school graduation. Then it was your college graduation. Now she's decided it would be best to wait and tell you before you get married."

"Did she tell Brian?"

"Of course not. This whole 'waiting for the right moment' is nonsense."

"I just don't understand why she would lie to me."

"I have my theories. To admit he cheated is to admit she wasn't good enough. I think she decided having a husband up and leave his family for no good reason was preferable to living with a husband who had a wandering eye. So she told everyone he left her. And that's the story she tells herself."

Grandma contemplated the striped wallpaper to the side of our booth.

She said, "I for one would rather be a widow than know my husband preferred another woman."

～

At home I ran to my room. I reached under the bed for the shoe box I kept hidden beside the box of old manuscripts (which, I remembered with annoyance, Eli had never returned) and behind the Tupperware of off-season clothes. Inside were carefully organized piles of photos I'd rescued one at a time from Mother's burial of all things that reminded her of my father. I studied the latest photograph I'd salvaged, the picture of our summer vacation in Austin that I'd taken from the attic at Christmas. I held it up to my face until the colors of my father's face blurred. He almost looked happy.

I cleaned the apartment in a silent rage. I swept and mopped the hardwood floors, scoured the scum from the bathtub with scalding water, worked the dust motes and dried spaghetti sticks out from beneath the refrigerator. I needed to feel the hatred for my father in my arms. I wanted to feel it as a pain in my back. Standing on the bathtub ledge to clean the shower head, my hand on the curtain rod for balance, I slipped and fell, taking the shower curtain with me. I cussed at the curtain, threw it into the bathtub, and hobbled to my bed, my butt and thigh throbbing.

I slept fitfully, feverish with bizarre dreams. At four in the morning I gave up on sleep. In front of Zoë's vanity mirror, I pulled down my pants to examine the purple bruise blooming across the back of my thigh.

"That's going to be there a while," I said.

As a child I'd sometimes wondered what it would be like if a body could survive even if it lost the ability to repair damaged tissue.

What if every scratch, bruise, and abrasion remained, a permanent blemish, an unrelenting pain? The mental pictures I'd entertained were horrific: men and women zombies by the age of twenty, skin tattered as old clothes, broken limbs forever askew. Aging would be nothing more than a series of unfortunate, ever debilitating accidents and the fully grown adult a grotesque.

It was a silly horror I invented to flip my own switches, to set my pulse pounding quick with dread. I might not have been so casual with my fears had I known there was some legitimacy to the nightmare. For what were adults if not an accumulation of internal injuries still festering? What were our bitter memories if not wounds still bleeding?

I stared into the open fridge, then out the kitchen window, then at my laptop. And as I sat waiting for my laptop to give me an answer, the story began to write itself.

Linda wakes up one morning to find a form letter in the mail. It reads:

Dear Wife:
THANK YOU for your submission to Mr. Charles Andrew Plumb. We find, however, that you do not meet his current needs. We wish you the best of luck placing yourself elsewhere.
Sincerely,
The Proxies

Linda folds the letter and places it back in the envelope. She glances across the street. Her neighbor, Mrs. Alconbury, is pulling weeds with the same cool, calculated vigor with which she gossips at prayer meetings. She makes a visor of her hand and waves to Linda, who forces herself to smile while waving back.

Inside, Linda goes to her bedroom, locks the door, and lowers herself slowly to her knees. She pulls the shoe box from beneath the bed. She is forty-two. She has been stowing secrets under this bed since sixteen, but it's getting harder on her body. Gingerly, she stands, sets the box on her dresser, and gently lifts its lid. She lays the new rejection on top of the others that have been tied together with white string.

Linda, maiden name Pendigrass, has been rejected twenty-seven times: by three husbands, ten one-night stands, and fourteen boyfriends. Charles's letter is her twenty-eighth. She keeps the form letters the men have sent in a manila envelope stashed under her bed. In a college-ruled notebook she painstakingly records the date each relationship began and the date each form letter arrived to terminate it. She prefers the delicate blue lines and skinny white spaces of the college-ruled paper. She has never been to college. Writing on college-ruled paper gives her a feeling of accomplishment.

Linda can recite the contents of each rejection. Her work was unsuitable, as were her dimpled thighs and deflated breasts. Or the grievances were confined to trivialities stored in secret against her: that she sometimes left her fingernail clippings on the bathroom sink or confused continents with nations. One husband rejected her because she failed to provide adequate meals at an appropriate time. Another because she failed to perform adequately in bed: there were things even she would not subject herself to.

Linda numbers the twenty-eighth line of her notebook pad and records this, her latest rejection, from Mr. Charles Andrew Plumb, who did not even deem it worthy of his time to outline the specific reasons for his rejection. Somehow, the form letter's generalized complaint is more wounding than the specific critiques made by previous lovers. Without specific reason for his departure, she feels it is not one particular habit or physical trait or personal flaw that he cannot stand, but rather her whole person that he abhors. Such comprehensive rejection makes her weak in the knees with grief.

Seven pages in, I stopped, unsure of how to end. Pencil lines of pink dawn seeped through the window blinds.

I went to the roof to watch the sunrise, carrying the shoe box of photographs with me. There was the yellowed picture of my first birthday, me sitting on my father's left knee while he balanced the two-tiered chocolate cake he'd made for the occasion on the right. The first day of kindergarten, the last day of summer camp. Both of us on either sides of my bike the day he taught me to ride without training wheels. Two envelopes of pictures, barely enough for one album—never enough for a lifetime.

A cool wind blew. The leaves of the maple tree slapped against one another, like a hundred decks of cards flap-flapping as they shuffled. I loved our tree. It reminded me of the old gnarled oak that grew in my backyard as a child, its delicately veined leaves good for catching my attic daydreams, its limbs strong for climbing. I could feel, vividly, where the bark left abrasions, skin flicked back in thin strips like ash.

One particular summer day would always be with me. I was six and four months old as I would proudly inform anyone who asked. I could smell the funk of picked dandelion stems on my palms and, on the air, burning charcoals from the grill. We were hosting a picnic. All the Karrows had come. I was wearing my favorite jumper, the one with five pockets in front, two in back, every one of them stuffed with treasures: my one-dollar allowance money, worn soft as silk from its long-term investment in my pocket; two marble-colored rubber balls that sparkled; one flattened specimen of Bazooka bubble gum I was saving for a special occasion; and a fistful of tart red berries picked from the front lawn bushes and intended for Uncle Lynn's balding head. I was sweating and hungry, but I climbed without slipping, even though dizzy from the height. I had climbed the tree a dozen times before but never this far up. I didn't know what was goading me, but I felt a terrible urgency to find the top. When I reached the highest weight-bearing limb, I stood on its bending arm and shouted *"He-ey!"* to everyone below. A crowd collected. I heard a boy—probably the one who told me I couldn't do it—telling his friend that he'd been to the top of much higher trees, and I heard my mother shouting at me to get down, and my grandmother crying out *"Lord, have mercy"* while she held her heart in her chest. They appealed to my father who was happily grilling and whistling and blithely unaware. He turned, he looked, he spotted me three stories up. Then he threw back his head and laughed. He was impressed by my achievement. He would no doubt brag about it at the next family event. I grinned. With only one hand pressed against the trunk for balance, I bowed, little histrionic creature that I was, and then shimmied back down, swinging faster and faster, imagining myself an Olympian gymnast windmilling her body effortlessly around the parallel bars, building momentum for the final landing! But of course I didn't land. I fell, the wind flying out of my chest so fast and hard I felt momentarily breathless and deaf from the shock. There, floating over me, was my father's face. *"Amy, Amy,"* he said, shaking his head, carrying me into the house. *"Amy, my little battering ram . . ."*

I could recall every nuance of that afternoon more clearly than I could remember a single thing I'd done last summer.

If you studied stories long enough, you almost started to believe in plot, to expect your life would progress in a sequential order of events fitted neatly on a straight and narrow timeline. But childhood was not some point in history several miles of black line behind. Childhood was the kernel around which my adult self had been collaged. To age was not to mature but to accumulate. Achievements, expectations, experiences, disappointments—badges applied thin and too early lacquered in place, a mishmash of cheap decoupage. But under the miscellany—the adult I had made of myself—the original self would not be suppressed; she was as close and immutable and necessary as the muscle beating resolutely within my chest. And she wanted the same thing, always. From some internal wellspring transmitted a desire pure and unrelenting, masking itself behind a hundred ambitions, but driven by the same desperate desire of a little girl climbing a tree for her father, hoping, for just one moment, that he'd notice and be proud.

I ripped the photograph from Austin in half, my mother and brother and me on one side, my father on the other. I ripped his half into halves. Burying my face in my hands, I wept, mourning the years I'd wasted trying to please him. I wept in hatred for every birthday he'd missed, every Christmas pageant he'd failed to show. I hated him for not coming and then I hated him when he came. Those few appearances grew shorter and only left me strung out on hope, waiting with bated breath for the next unexpected visit, my daily life colored with suspense. No matter where I was or what I was doing, I convinced myself that somewhere he was watching and that if only I did something grand enough, he would come.

The performance anxiety that so powerfully propelled my ambition also rendered each resulting accomplishment temporarily rewarding at best. I could always do better; I could always do more. Society was no help. I wanted to be Something, but the one person I most wanted to impress was as elusive and changing as the measures of success the world threw my way. Every failure hammered through my skull in resounding unison with my father's condemnation: I was not good enough.

All my adult life I'd worked hard to forgive him for not being there for me, but I had never forgiven myself for my inability to make him stay.

The sun was up, the neighborhood waking. I wiped my face clean with the back of my sleeve, the warming air soft on my wet cheeks. A prayer welled up within me, a new kind of prayer. I was done begging God to forgive me for being too bitter, too needy, too egotistical, too tired. Repenting one day for being too much, the next for not being enough.

Now I clearly understood my real offense against heaven: the stubborn refusal to recognize that every failing I had—from the first—had been forgiven.

25

In summer Copenhagen slept. Natives reclaimed their rule. Parking spaces abounded. May melted into June, and June leisurely passed, an inner tube floating down a lazy river.

I graded ESL exams online; Wednesdays, I tutored at the campus writing center. But Zoë's survival was my chief occupation. I set her alarm, I dressed her for work, and I practically force-fed her my best efforts at vegetarian home cooking. If she wouldn't get out of bed, I'd call everyone on The Brewery phone list to find someone willing to cover her shift. And when she wept I sat with her until she was done, which seemed to offer some measure of comfort.

At first she did little more than sleep and cry and sleep again, the nights of naked grief punctuated by outbursts of irrational anger. She punched her fist in the wall after burning a plate of lasagna. She ranted for an entire hour one night about the idiocy of her father's realtor. But slowly, visibly, Zoë was becoming Zoë again. In her second week home she gained color; in the third she gained weight.

In the fourth she came to breakfast a brunette. I stared at her. The hair was shoulder length and straight with fine, fringe bangs. She wore a pink barrette on the right. The wig could have easily been mistaken for her real hair had she not been sporting a pixie cut the day before.

She poured a cup of coffee. "What?"

"Nothing."

She went to work in the wig, wearing it matter-of-factly, acting surprised when anyone cared to make an issue of it. Her wardrobe had always been inclined to drastic overhauls. She had a black phase, a lace phase, six months in which she never left the house without striped stockings. She systematically changed her jewelry and skirts. The hair, however, was a surprise to all of us.

She wore the wig for three days. By the time we'd all adjusted to her as a brunette she switched to auburn.

"How many did you keep?" I asked.

"All of them."

She was in the shower. I sat on the toilet in a face-off with the mute wig head that now presided over our bathroom sink. Today auburn, tomorrow blond. In her closet the wig heads sat in silent rows.

The boxes had arrived the week she'd flown home. I'd assumed they contained the things she hadn't been able to carry on the plane: shoes, jewelry, books—the entire collection of Zoë miscellany that had slowly migrated from our apartment to Chicago during her many trips home. She carried each box to her room and opened them in secret. "Just a few things to remember Mom by," she'd said pointedly when I asked.

I'd meant she should take a few scarves or a bottle of perfume or a memorable necklace. But the hair?

"What could I have done with them?" she asked. "They're real. Hundreds—thousands—of dollars of hair."

"They're very beautiful," I replied.

She peered around the shower curtain. Her real hair stood spiked chaotically, her scalp white and naked beneath. "You know it's not because I'm self-conscious. I don't care about my hair."

"I know, Zoë," I said. "You don't have to explain it to me."

That Zoë would hoard the artifacts of her mother's illness was surprising. That she wore them was almost too much. But I understood her enough to know this was not a stunt or a cheap grab for attention. It would, perhaps, qualify as a Statement, but that was a good sign: If Zoë already had a Statement to make, she would be all right.

Strangely, the wig days were good days. In those beautiful and horrid relics of her mother's illness she had found some mysterious source of strength. Together we perfected the art of leisure. We lounged in the living room over whole stacks of books. When we jogged, we jogged slowly. There were no deadlines to run to or prizes to win. We slept. We ate. We clung to each other and waited for our wounds to heal.

⁓

The postcard arrived in late June: *Glorified Reductions, an exhibition of the Pendleton Residency.* All the artists were participating in the final exhibition, a culmination of their six-week studio intensive. Eli's name appeared on the list of showing artists, but I was disappointed that his work had not been included on the postcard. On the back he had scrawled: *Would love to see you both. ~ELI.*

He'd been careful to invite us both, but the postcard had been addressed to me.

I clipped it to my bedroom mirror so that his note was one of the first things I saw every morning. Zoë and I hadn't talked about him. We didn't talk about Michael, either. It was safer to talk about books and films, to keep our conversations in the abstract. But when I was alone, I wondered if his feelings for me had changed. My regard for him had only grown.

I'd been to the Pendleton Residency website a dozen times. It was a sparse, functional site, providing a brief description of the program (international), the grounds (stunning), and the people (renowned). The first photo album showcased the various studios, each furnished with the finest equipment. The second contained snapshots of every group that had lived and worked in the program since the 1980s. I was insanely proud to see Eli's name listed on the roster.

Between the ostensible failure of his gallery and the fluke nature of his route to our doorstep, it had been easy to assume him a man of limited ambition. In all the nights I'd so painstakingly talked myself out of loving him, it had never occurred to me that his aspirations reached beyond firing clay pots in studio basements or that his appeal reached beyond the fawning of undergraduate art majors. He'd enjoyed Copenhagen because he made himself fit in it, because he knew when to bend to accommodate a circumstance. All the idle hours welding junk, drawing caricatures, and pulling espressos temporarily kept his latent talent at bay, but he had an energy our little town could not have restrained indefinitely.

How impossible it would be to ask him to come back.

I mentioned the exhibition to Zoë.

"It's next weekend," I said.

"It's upstate New York," she replied. "Isn't that like eight hours?"

"Nine and a half," I answered a little too quickly. I had already MapQuested the drive.

I waited for Zoë to say something. She was halfway through *The Fountainhead*. She'd been reading impossible books to stay preoccupied; she wasn't listening to me at all.

"Do you think he actually expects us to come?" I asked her anyway.

"I'm sure he was just being polite."

I might have written the note off as mere formality if not for a repeat invitation I found in my campus mailbox the following Friday. I'd gone in to clean out my desk, a ceremonial summer duty I hadn't given two seconds thought until the library mailed me fines for the five overdue books I'd left in my office.

The Humanities Building felt empty despite the business of summer school. Everyone ambled, dilatory from the heat, dazed by the shock of air-conditioning. The women had retired their pantyhose and heels for sandals. The more flamboyant professors were wearing Hawaiian-print shirts; even the most reserved undid a button or two at the neck.

In the congested mailbox I found fliers and announcements and student essays turned in too late. I threw the formidable pile on my office floor and left it there the hour it took me to tidy my side of the room. After hunting down the overdue library books, I organized my pens in matching rows and dusted the knickknacks on the windowsill. I carefully ironed out the Cheetos bag with the palm of my hand before taping it front and center on Everett's wall. He would be gone until July, parading sophomores across London for *Summer of Shakespeare*. He went every June. Every June I hated him for it.

At the now-empty desk I quickly shuffled through the pile of neglected mail. I didn't get very far. On the very top lay a copy of the same postcard Eli had sent to the apartment. I turned it over in my hands, confused. On the back he'd written a note nearly identical to the one on the previous postcard. Why send two? The possibility that he'd worried the invitation would not arrive struck me as thoughtful. Maybe even as a reason to hope.

Would be great to see you and Zoë.

After a moment's hesitation, I threw the card in the wastebasket. Nine and a half hours, I reminded myself. No woman in her right mind would go so far out of her way to attend a party without knowing the kind of welcome she would receive.

There were pay stubs to file, fliers to recycle, and halfway through the stack—unfortunately—a poem, five stanzas fit to bursting with far more openly expressed affection than I would ever wring out of a single sentence Eli had ever written me:

Untitled
by Anonymous

Love is like a pocketknife
With functions e're so varied
For cutting through the heart
For getting couples married

For boring to the core of life
With its twisting corkscrew
For dissecting the soul
To something lovers cannot eschew

My love is a knife
Buried in my heart
Rending flesh from bone
Rending me apart

As the greatest love tale tells:
Love is a happy dagger
And this, my body,
the sheath in which it fells.

Never hide how you feel
From the one whom you desire
Fly through wind and rain
Fly through heat and fire
Cross the world o'er
To tell her how you love 'er.

The poem came with a note: *For the end of the semester.* I read it
a second time. I tapped the bobblehead Garfield.

"What do you think?" I asked.

He bobbed his head.

"I agree."

Enough was enough.

I found Anonymous working in the copy room.

"Lonnie, can I talk to you a second?"

He started. "Sure. Absolutely. I was just clocking out." He rushed to clear a spot for me on the chair beside his. I sat down across the table, careful to keep a barrier between us.

"Working all summer?" I asked.

"Monday through Friday. I work at Blimpie's now, too. You should come by. I give out free chips."

I said I would have to think about it. In the ensuing pause, he took, predictably, to memorizing his sneakers.

"Since last semester started, I've been getting a lot of things in my mailbox—books and poems. I'm assuming they're from you."

"They're not mine."

"You're the only person I know whose printer ink always fades two inches from the bottom." I held up the poem, Exhibit A.

He bowed his head. His cheeks reddened, neck to ears. It was more a full-body hive than a blush. "I have to send them to a scholarship competition," he mumbled. "I thought maybe you could edit them for me."

I slid the poem across the table. "I'm not your English teacher anymore, Lonnie. And I think that—interacting—in this way is unprofessional."

He snatched the poem. The folded paper disappeared under the table with his hands. "Ms. Gallagher, you shouldn't think I meant anything. I didn't mean anything, really . . . I like you and all, but I didn't . . ." He blushed an even deeper shade of crimson.

Another professor walked in the room. Lonnie's eyes darted nervously from me to the professor and back to the floor. I'd already thought of numerous ways to discourage this childish flirtation once and for all, but in the moment the rehearsed speeches failed me. I hated to shame him more than was necessary. "It must be ninety degrees in here," I declared. "I was actually on my way downstairs for something to drink. Some company would be nice."

At the snack machines Lonnie gave the off-brand animal crackers his highest recommendation. We took our crackers and Mountain

Dews and sat beneath the overbearing oil portrait of Dr. Hoover, the building's beneficiary and (some said) ghost.

"I have a theory about you, Lonnie."

"Yeah?" He shook his hair out of his eyes. He was wearing a Ghost Busters T-shirt, stiff as the papers in the copy room and emanating a floral odor of Snuggle dryer sheets. My first kiss smelled of laundry. It was as if all the young men I'd known worked overtime to compensate for the funk of their bodies, that chemical party surging through their mind and limbs.

"You were born a romantic."

He snorted. Either he disagreed or he thought the label funny. As usual, he was not a kid whose language—verbal or physical—I could translate.

"You want a girlfriend, don't you?"

"More than anything," he said with unabashed desperation.

"Have you ever had one?"

"In the second grade."

"You don't waste any time."

"Annie Dobbins," he said.

"What was she like?"

"Super smart. She had red hair and freckles. We got married on the playground."

"That must have been interesting."

"Everybody came to see. At indoor recess we named our children. Spring and Autumn. Those were the girls. Lephen for a boy. We made that one up."

"So what happened to Annie?"

"She moved. Her dad got a new job in Michigan. But I tracked her down in high school. Now she's in Sacramento with her boyfriend." He stuffed a few animal crackers into his mouth. "She works at a Clinique cosmetics counter at the Florence mall."

Creepy stalker knowledge. Fleetingly, I imagined Lonnie in his dorm room Googling Amy Gallagher.

"Lonnie, the difficult thing about being a romantic is that there's only one person out there for you. One. Out of millions. So you shouldn't be surprised if it takes a few years to find her."

"How will I know if I find her?"

I parroted what my mom always told me, because for the first time I think I understood what she meant: "You'll know."

He took a last gulp of his soda before tossing the empty can at the wall above the recycling bin. It missed the bin and fell to the floor with a clatter.

"It's not fair. I've been single for like forever. I haven't even gotten to third base. I'm not even sure I know what the bases are." He leaned back against the wall and crossed his arms, pinched his eyes shut. "The girls in my hall don't even know I exist."

"You don't know that."

"They think I'm just some geek. Like I'm in love with Buffy or something. Don't get me wrong, she's about the most premium girl there is, but I'm not in love with her. I know she's not real."

"I've been in love with a lot of fictional men," I said. "It's easy to fall hard for people, for things, that aren't real."

"What about your guy?"

"My guy?"

"That dude with the tattoo who used to walk you to class."

It was my turn to be embarrassed. "We're not together."

"That's not what it looked like," Lonnie persisted.

"He's just a friend."

"Yeah." He closed his eyes again, leaned his head against the wall and nodded back and forth slowly. "Whatever."

For one absurd moment I was actually tempted to ask him if he thought I had a chance.

Back in my office I gave him the campus dance recital tickets one of the professors had passed off to me. I'd been holding on to them in the hopes I would have someone to go with.

"Listen, Lonnie. I want you to find a nice girl and take her to this concert, and I want you to do it for fun, okay? She doesn't have to be your soul mate to be a nice date."

He turned the envelope in his hands, studying it as if it were a complicated piece of machinery.

"What if I ask a girl and she says no?"

I genuinely hurt for him. Of all the students I'd befriended, of all the aspiring writers I'd coached, it was when looking at Lonnie—Lonnie of the Battlerstar Galactica T-shirts and the cherry berry ChapStick—that I saw myself.

"Then you smile, shrug your shoulders, and ask someone else," I replied. "And, Lonnie—no poems. Not right away. Your readership may not be ready for them just yet."

"Okay," he said, stuffing the envelope in his backpack. "I promise, Ms. Gallagher."

As soon as he left, I returned to my office and dug through the trash until I found the postcard Eli had sent. I folded it in half, slipped it in my jacket pocket.

From the office window I watched until Lonnie appeared on the sidewalk below. Maybe the next object of his love would return the interest. Maybe she would even be his age. But what can you do with a romantic, really? They're called hopeless for good reason.

⌐

"This is just like the last one; his work's not even on here," Zoë said. She handed the postcard back to me. "That's not a good sign. They always put the best stuff on the card."

She carried the dishes I'd stacked to the sink. "You know, the problem with Eli is that he waits too long and farts around and doesn't get the big projects done. It's the lack of discipline that most hurts his work."

When her criticism of his procrastination didn't cheer me up, she went on, "I've been thinking that it's a good thing you and Eli didn't work out."

"Why's that?"

"He's not the settling type."

The phrase sent bells off in my head. I heard Adam breaking up with me all over again. *"You were born settled."*

She left the room complaining about e-mails. I stayed in the kitchen and copied recipes from *Vegetarian Weekly*. I lay in my bed and tried to read. I did a Luna Lady face peel. I reorganized my closet. I put my sweaters in the boxes I used to store journals and organized the journals by date on top of the shelf where my sweaters had been. When I tried to throw one last notebook on top of an already too heavy pile, the rest fell down on my head. I hollered some unnecessary obscenity before throwing myself backward on the bed.

Zoë tapped on the door.

"Are you all right?"

"Mmm-mmm."

She peered in the closet. "What happened in there?"

I had my eyes closed. I waved my hand dismissively. "Something fell."

"You didn't hurt yourself, did you?"

I shook my head.

She lay down on the bed beside me. "I got my work schedule for next week. Did you know it's already the twenty-first? I can't believe it's been more than a year since we moved in together."

She said this with a strangely nostalgic tone. It annoyed me. I couldn't think of a single excuse she had to remember this year fondly. Because I was exhausted and because I was anxious, I said as much to her aloud.

"I don't know. It had its moments." She cracked up. "Remember when you set the fire alarm off? When Eli was first here? I think he nearly peed his pants."

I laughed in spite of myself.

"Who knows what he thought of us," she said. "Fighting over checklists, over that stupid magazine."

For no good reason we both got the giggles. Then we started to laugh, really laugh, until our sides hurt. When we'd recovered, she sidled up to me, skin sticky with sweat, and laid her head on my shoulder. When her wig brushed my skin I shuddered.

"Zoë, how long are you going to wear those things?"

"As long as I need to. They smell like her, you know."

"You could just keep her clothes," I said. "I'm sure they smell as good."

"But that would be so much less interesting."

A cool breeze rustled the curtain. Two blocks away a car rumbled by on the cobblestones. Kathryn's wind chimes jangled in that discordant way that always sounded so lonely to me.

"I'm sorry I haven't been here for you," she said.

"What are you talking about?"

"You've been thinking about Eli. I know you miss him."

I started to protest, but she stopped me.

"You'd think losing a parent would be all the hurt a body could handle. But there are still nights when I think of Michael. I miss him, too, in all his stupid ways."

I put my arm around her shoulder, forcing myself to not mind the wig and how alarmingly real it felt. "He did have a way of reducing the collective intelligence in a way that was entertaining," I agreed.

"What I said about Eli—I didn't mean for that to upset you. It's just that I don't want you to get hurt."

"It's all right, Zoë," I said. "In a weird way, you said exactly what I needed to hear."

"So can I go to bed now without worrying about you?"

The irony of her question was almost funny. If she had any idea how many sleepless nights I lay in bed waiting for her to wake from nightmares and call my name: I'd never been so worried for anyone in my life.

"You can go to bed," I reassured her.

But she was asleep before either of us found the motivation to get up.

I kissed her brow, relieved. The narrow bed was a ship in the night and sleep the safest passage to morning. I thought of Jesus in the boat with His disciples as they tried to cross the sea in a nighttime storm. Whenever ministers preached from that story, they always focused on the disciples' unbelief: If only they had truly trusted the Lord, they wouldn't have been so afraid of the waves and lightning.

What struck me, however, was that Jesus was asleep despite the violence of the storm. I was taken by the thought of a Savior who could be so utterly exhausted.

⁓

Because she was in my bed, it took me twice as long to pack. Every drawer I opened creaked too loudly. Every light was too bright. I didn't want to wake her, because I didn't want to explain.

At two in the morning, a small duffel bag in hand, I gently clicked the bedroom door shut. I studied the directions I'd printed out, memorizing the route. I set my alarm for five. I lay down on the futon fully dressed. In my head I did the math: The exhibition was from seven to ten. If I left by six, if I only took three half-hour breaks, and if there were absolutely no traffic jams, accidents, or unexpected breakdowns, I would arrive in time to get dinner and freshen up before the show.

The night dragged on. I held my eyes tightly shut, but like a child on Christmas Eve I was too excited to sleep. At the very first hint of birdsong, I threw off the blanket and reached for my shoes.

Before leaving, I stood a while in the hallway, ear pressed against my bedroom door, listening for sounds of weeping. But there was only the steady hum of the ceiling fan rhythmically stirring the air.

26

The last city (significantly smaller than the previous one) passed and it was still another hour and a half before I saw a sign for Pendleton. I nearly cried with relief. My head throbbed from ten hours of highway and a day's diet of Pepsi and Circus Peanuts. I stopped at the next gas station. In the eerie green light of the bathroom I changed out of my jeans and into the slacks I'd kept on a hanger in the back of the car; I'd hung them the way my mother taught me, mindful of the seams, fully aware that this was the kind of detail Eli never noticed. I rinsed my face, pinched my cheeks, slipped on the earrings he had given me for my birthday, then decided that would be a bit much and replaced them with inconspicuous silver hoops.

Off the exit ramp I passed an old grocery and a Wal-Mart. There was a strip of pastel-colored historical downtown. Twenty minutes past the last light, up a winding bit of country road, I arrived at the Pendleton Residency campus. It was just as the photographs depicted: a secluded, sprawling landscape boasting four closely built studio complexes, an old barn, and, upon the farthest hill, a compact, modern building of cement and glass. My destination for the

night. A shallow, decorative pool framed the perimeter of the building, reflecting its minimalist facade as flawlessly as a polished mirror.
Like a moat surrounding an impenetrable castle.

I was barely in time to catch the end of the show, but I sat in the
car five minutes gathering the courage to go inside. I actually thought
about turning around, worried that my unexpected appearance would
not come as a pleasant surprise for him. Until that moment I hadn't
even considered the horrible thought that Eli'd met someone during
the residency. I turned off the ignition. Too late now.

The gallery was as warm and inviting inside as its exterior had
been cold and intimidating. The exhibition filled two rooms joined
at center by a foyer. The tables had been spread with real linens, with
mushroom tarts and manicured fruits speared on skewers. Women
in black poured red wine into plastic cups. I walked through the
show slowly, pretending to examine each piece in turn while fur-
tively searching for napkins pinned to walls or framed lithographs
in rows. I expected to see Eli every time I turned a corner, but I
walked through each room twice without even a glimpse of his work.
My heart sank with the possibility that I had somehow misread the
card or the calendar, that in my hurry to see him and by some gross
miscalculation I had ended up at the wrong show.

A binder containing the résumés of the various artists had been
propped on a white pedestal near the dessert table. I loitered there,
reading the long list of accolades behind each name. Someone bumped
into me, and when I turned to acknowledge the man's apology, my
eyes crossed a small sign posted beside the door, all but obstructed
by the viewers crowded around the desserts. It read *Sculpture* above
an arrow pointing to the right.

I followed the sign out the back doors and into the courtyard.

I was met by a field of lights.

As my eyes adjusted to the darkness, the diffuse light gained
clarity and became not a blanket of white but row after row of glowing globes standing knee-high in the grass. Though each bubble of

blown glass varied in size, they were uniform in shape, tapering to a narrow neck. They stood on stems translucent as glass, some straight, some bent. Beneath the individual lamps, tucked in shadow and barely visible, a web of black cords like roots filled the twin patches of perfectly square lawn. A narrow sidewalk passed between.

I followed the path, feeling, foolishly, like a bride on the aisle, suffused in white and deliberating her steps amidst the hush of a summertime garden. I was so taken by the delicacy of the sculpture I did not at first notice that every other globe illuminated a phrase printed on its interior.

A strange sense of déjà vu washed over me as I read the first: *It had been taken from them.*

I walked to the next and read: *leave leaf palms open.*

And the next: *happiness like a blush to the cheeks.*

The familiarity deepened with each phrase. At first, I tried to make sentences of the neighboring fragments, but I only came up with nonsense. The words jostled in my mind nonetheless, puzzle pieces that wanted to fit into a single, cohesive thought.

I read: *muscle, puppeteer of bone,* and it struck me. My stories.

These were my phrases, bits of sentences I had cobbled together taken from their context and planted in haphazard rows like crops for some magical harvest.

When I reached the end of the garden I stooped down to examine a sign propped in the corner. It stood in a five-inch pool of light, illuminated by the smallest of the glass lights, which hung over the bit of paper like a miniature streetlight. The label listed six artists who had collaborated on the installation. Above the other artists listed, the name Eli Morretti, and above his name, the title:

Amy (Inspired)

I stared at our names printed together, as surprised by my reaction as I was astonished by the extravagance of the installation. Where I should have felt ownership over these words and some indignation at their being taken from me without my permission,

I only felt a childlike wonder. I had stepped through the looking glass into a bizarre dream world. Everywhere I turned I found my own thoughts winking back at me, full of mystery. Something I'd said, something I'd done had in a way created this. No one had ever paid me a higher compliment.

I don't know how long Eli stood watching me before he said my name.

Startled, I turned to find him walking down the aisle toward me.

"I didn't expect you to come," he said.

"I'm here."

I threw my arms out, let them fall back to my sides; I crossed them to hide the kick of nerves rioting in my stomach. Here he was in all the detail my memory and imagination combined had tried and failed to reproduce to satisfaction: the exact flecking of color in his eyes, the fringe of his beard grown thick and curly in the humidity, his skin dark and redolent from hours soaked in sun.

"What are you doing here?"

He asked without pleasure and without judgment—he almost looked worried. I didn't know how to interpret his reaction so I answered matter-of-factly, "I got your postcard. I wanted to see the show."

"Did you fly?"

"I drove."

His eyebrows shot up in surprise. "It's nine hours."

"Eleven if you drive like a grandma and pee like a racehorse."

It was as awkward as a meeting between two people who'd once felt something for each other could possibly be.

"Amy Inspired?" I asked, trying to sound playful. I quickly scanned the courtyard for another watching woman, for the date he'd brought and was now hiding.

"It's a working title," he replied, bowing his head almost bashfully, running his hand through his hair. "It was Punjab's doing, the lights—I'll have to introduce you to him—but the idea was mine. Well, yours of course. Remember what you'd said about inspiration? Like light bulbs going off? That stuck with me for some reason."

I'd never seen him self-conscious about his work before, and the work I'd seen to date had been amateur at best. Now he was awkward to the point of embarrassment.

"I'm just so shocked that you're here," he fumbled on. "I feel like I owe you an apology. I didn't think you'd come, not that that's an excuse. I should've asked you. I thought about calling you a hundred times."

"Eli," I said, "it's stunning."

He glanced up. "You think so?"

"Of course. I can't believe a person could put something like this together in only six weeks."

"It felt like a lot longer than six weeks."

"Good," I replied quickly, "because it felt like about twelve for me."

His anxiety seemed to vanish. He laughed, a nervous, hopeful laugh.

"Show me the rest of the work," I said.

We walked through and around the garden. He explained the mechanics of the sculpture, knelt with me to examine each hand-crafted lamp closely. We lay belly flat on the sidewalk to peer through the forest of wires, not caring that everyone had to step over us to walk the path.

As he continued the tour through the emptying galleries, the awkwardness between us vanished. How many times had we walked through campus this way, to class or to the coffee shop or to our apartment, talking about nothing in particular while seeming to connect on everything? As the hour went on, he became more and more talkative, but he avoided my eyes until it became apparent that the time and distance between us had mattered to him, that he'd taught himself to feel for me what he should have felt: I was a good friend, nothing more. He wanted me to know this, communicated it in the way he stood two feet from me, the way he introduced me to his friends. But I had difficulty remembering their names; I was too busy building a secret resolve.

When we'd formally met every contributing artist, when we'd exhausted every room and every topic, we took the one remaining tray of cheese and fruit and carried the picnic to the front stoop to sit and eat. Only a few people remained, idling in conversation before their cars. I sat on one end of the steps, facing the lot. He sat leaning against the wall of the building, facing me, his long legs spread lanky behind my back and folded ankle over ankle. He'd made an effort with his clothes: all black, though two very different shades between shirt and slacks, and the cuffs of his pant legs were still dirty and flecked with something white.

"I haven't asked about Zoë," he said.

"She's Zoë. She's taking things day by day."

I told him about the wig heads and the long nights. He expressed sympathy, appropriate and kind.

The gallery lights went off behind us, a warning that this night had to end.

"We've missed you," I said. Gathering all my courage, I added, "I've missed you."

I met his eyes, tried to communicate there what I didn't know how to put into words.

He set the platter we'd emptied aside, brushed his hands clean, then scooted himself over to sit right next to me.

"Eleven hours," he said. "You came eleven hours to see some art that might not have been very good and you haven't yelled at me or tried to hit me, so I'm assuming you don't hate me."

I assured him that what I felt for him was the furthest thing from hatred. I wanted to tell him how every day I'd thought of him to the point of distraction, but I interrupted myself, lost track of what I was supposed to say, and ended up asking him if he'd ever thought of me.

"See that barn up there?" He asked.

I nodded..

"It's been mostly renovated, turned into studios, critique space. A little kitchen. But there's still a loft that you have to get up to by ladder. And you can lay there on your back and look out the window at the clouds or the stars or the rain. I used to go there when I couldn't think anymore, when I got frustrated. I went to try and figure out some problem. I always ended up thinking of you."

He sat close enough that our arms touched, and at the slight brush of skin on skin I knew I had no reason to doubt.

"I would think about the first time I saw you," he said.

"At the poetry reading," I said.

"Well, then," he agreed, encouraged by the specificity of my memory. "But I saw you before you saw me—outside actually, when you were getting out of your car. You got your scarf stuck in your car door. You nearly took your own head off walking towards the building."

I laughed because I was embarrassed and because it was funny and because I was drugged with a kind of happiness I hadn't allowed myself to expect.

"Your hair was so bright," he said. "Practically orange in the sunlight. You stood out from across the entire lawn. I couldn't take my eyes off you."

He thought a moment, said carefully, "I can't go back to Copenhagen, Amy. That was always temporary."

"I know." I reached for his hand. "Who says we have to go back?"

He smiled, and in his smile I saw a hundred futures, altogether bright as our field of glowing lights.

EPILOGUE

I found an ending for my story.

Linda Pendigrass takes her box of rejections to the kitchen table. To her left is the phone book. To the right, twenty-eight envelopes and twenty-eight stamps. Into each envelope she stuffs an old rejection letter, adding a form letter of her own:

Dear Mr. Charles Andrew Plumb (Lewis Armstrong Baker, James Michael Harris, Byrone Calob Holmes, and etc.):
 We apologize, but Linda Pendigrass does not read rejections and is not accepting unsolicited criticism at this time.
 She forgives you for your gross indecorum.
 Sincerely,

       The Representatives of Linda Pendigrass
       Liberated Woman at Large

Linda Pendigrass takes the twenty-eight letters to the post office and ships them to Pittsburgh, Chicago, Boston, and so on and so forth.

Driving away from the post office, she comes to a four-way stop. Ahead, the town where she grew up, the town in which she has lived these forty-two years. To the left the Pacific, and to her right the Atlantic.

She takes her time, considering.

The End

(or: THE BEGINNING OF THE INTERESTING LIFE)

DISCUSSION QUESTIONS

1. Amy and Zoë share the same dream, the same faith, and the same bathroom—and yet they regularly irritate each other. How does their relationship evolve from that of the irksome familiarity between housemates to the intimacy of deep friendship? How can crisis serve as a catalyst for growth in otherwise casual relationships? Did their friendship remind you of any in your own life?

2. Amy is frequently forced to revise her first impressions of people; this is most evident in her relationship with Eli, who perpetually challenges her assumptions about the Christian life. Did the strong feelings between Amy and Eli in spite of their differences come as a surprise to you? How did you feel about their differences, particularly in regards to the practice of religion?

3. Eli is not the only one whose physical appearance is atypical from Amy's perception of normal: Zoë is also seen sporting a number of purposefully colorful wardrobes, from striped stockings to wigs of real human hair. What is the relationship between dress and identity for both Zoë and Eli? For Amy herself? Do you think all dress is inherently performative, even when unassuming?

4. Eli, Amy, and Zoë inhabit an adult world conspicuously devoid of children, and yet the longing for children and for childhood itself imbues the story with a poignant sense of absence. Amy sees adulthood as a cumbersome accumulation of experiences, both good and bad but above all arbitrary. She claims that her childhood self has been collaged over with "badges applied thin and too early lacquered in place." Do you relate to her angst or were you grateful to leave childhood behind? In what ways do the needs of our "inner child" compel our behaviors as adults?

5. Toward the end of the novel, Amy suspects her unrelenting ambition masks secret pain. In what ways does the fear of rejection become its own terrible motivation for Amy? How do you see it playing out as a primary source of motivation in our society? What is it about rejection that is so crippling spiritually and emotionally?

6. Amy's family played a considerable role in making her who she is, and yet Amy sees herself as vastly different from both her mother and her father. Do you think she could ever erase the influence of her background or if she should at all? How important is family in determining who people become and how they live their lives?

7. Many of the characters experience loss: the loss of youthful idealism, of significant others, even of loved ones. Despite the many crises the characters face, their sense of humor prevails. What role does humor play in the novel? In the experience of grief in your own life?

8. In his sermon on Ecclesiastes, Pastor Maddock asserts that to disregard the possibility of some kind of heaven is to in effect concede the futility of every mortal life. The belief in life beyond death, however, not only comforts the grieving but also affirms the individual. Did you agree with his interpretation of that

Scripture? Does the concept of eternity in any way influence your daily life?

9. Excerpts of Amy's own writing are included at various points in the story. Notably, these passages appear when she is grappling with an emotional conflict of her own. In what ways does she sublimate her problems in her writing? Do you think she is guilty of "borrowing from life" in the same way that she so ardently criticizes Zoë for? Have you ever done something similar for catharsis, whether intentionally or not?

10. The novel concludes with the ending of Amy's most recent short story. This is the only story we see her complete. How does the ending she chose—and the fact that she found one at all—influence your interpretation of the book overall?

ACKNOWLEDGMENTS

Thank you, Aaron, for coming across the room to dance with me at that wedding and for the adventure you've brought into my life every day since. Always, thank you, Mom, Dad, Christy, and David for making me laugh, for encouraging my flights of fancy while keeping my feet on the ground. Mark and Mary, I'm indebted to you for your advice and support through a year of transitions.

Thanks to Andy McGuire, Dave Long, Paul Higdon, and the entire team at Bethany House; without you this book would never have realized its full potential. Raela Schoenherr, you are both a wonderful editor and a "kindred spirit."

And finally, to the students who inspired me. Thank you Lindsey Bullinger and Tim Lu, for volunteering yourselves as characters (sorry to disappoint); here's to afternoons under The Arch, break-dancing and heckling tour groups. Thank you, Kathy McCarty, for macaroni and book-club/movie night; I will forever regret that I missed your victory school bus derby race. Stephanie Albers, Laura Schwietering, Corinne Dowd, Katie Gorsuch, and Samantha Brendalen, I was the one with the grading rubric, but you were the ones raising the bar for me as both an instructor and a friend. And to the many others who brought their senses of humor, enthusiasm, and iMovie skills to the classroom: thank you for making those three years interesting— and for making my life easier than Amy's.

⁘

After completing a master's in Creative Writing and working as a visiting instructor at Miami University in Ohio, BETHANY PIERCE now lives with her husband in Charlottesville, Virginia, where she is a member of the McGuffy Art Center and continues to write. Her first book, *Feeling for Bones*, was one of *Publishers Weekly's* Best Books of 2007.